I0817797

PRAISE FOR KEVIN J. ANDERSON

"Kevin J. Anderson has become the literary equivalent of Quentin Tarantino."

— *THE DAILY ROTATION*

"Kevin J. Anderson is the hottest writer on (or off) the planet."

— *FORT WORTH STAR-TELEGRAM*

"The scope and breadth of Kevin J. Anderson's work is simply astonishing."

— *TERRY GOODKIND*

"Kevin J. Anderson is one of the best plotters in the business."

— *BRANDON SANDERSON*

"One of the greatest talents writing today, Kevin J. Anderson is a master of adventures that are filled with dynamic, unforgettable characters."

— *SHERRILYN KENYON*

SCIENCE FICTION STORIES VOLUME 2

SCIENCE FICTION STORIES VOLUME 2

KEVIN J. ANDERSON

Science Fiction Short Stories: Volume 2

EBook ISBN: 978-1-68057-723-5
Trade Paperback ISBN: 978-1-68057-724-2
Dust Jacket Hardcover ISBN: 978-1-68057-725-9
Library of Congress Control Number: 2024937270
Cover design by Janet McDonald
Cover artwork by Tithi Luadthong "grandfailure"
Kevin J. Anderson, Art Director
Vellum layout by CJ Anaya
Published by
WordFire Press, LLC
PO Box 1840
Monument CO 80132
Kevin J. Anderson & Rebecca Moesta, Publishers
WordFire Press eBook Edition 2024
WordFire Press Trade Paperback Edition 2024
WordFire Press Dust Jacket Hardcover Edition 2024

Printed in the USA

CONTENTS

Science fiction can cover all of space and time, but I want to start out this collection much closer to home with a high-tech, cutting-edge thriller.

For my novel Assemblers of Infinity *with Doug Beason, we researched the startling advances in nanotechnology, including some of the remarkable medical possibilities, which might provide a gateway to immortality. While researching nanotech, I had the idea for this story—a medical experiment gone wrong, a research animal on the run. This was published in* The Magazine of Fantasy and Science Fiction, *and the title story in my first hardcover short story collection from Golden Gryphon Press.*

The idea was so strong in my mind, though, that when I began plotting my third X-Files *novel, I adapted the core story to a full-fledged adventure with nanotechnology, twisted medical experiments, conspiracy theories, and enhanced lab animals.*

But this version of the story is always the "right" version to me.

DOGGED PERSISTENCE

The dog stops in the middle of the road, distracted on his way to the forest. The asphalt smells damp and spicy with fallen leaves. Infrared laser-guidance posts line the shoulder at wide intervals, but most of the vehicles are of the old kind, growling inside from hot engines, belching chemical exhaust.

The twin headlights of the approaching car look like bright coins. The image fixates him, imprinting spots on his dark-adapted eyes. The dog can hear the car dominating the night noises of insects and stirring branches. The car sounds loud. The car sounds angry.

Moving with casual ease, the dog saunters toward the shoulder. But the car arrives faster than he could ever run, squealing brakes like some death scream. He hears the thud of impact, the bright explosion of pain that suddenly vanishes. He is flying through the air toward the ditch. He smells the spray of blood from inside his own nose.

Knowing he must hide, the dog hauls himself into the brambles, under a barbed-wire fence, to the dense foliage.

Car doors slam, running feet, the babble of voices: "Shit! That was no deer—that was a dog! A big black lab!" "Where'd he go?" "Shit, must have crawled off to die." "Look at all the blood—and look what he did to your car!"

The dog has found a safe place. The human voices become fuzzy as black unawareness overcomes him. He will not move again until it is finished. He will be all right.

Inside his body, millions upon millions of nanomachines begin to repair the damage, cell by cell, rebuilding the entire dog. The night insects resume their music in the forest.

Patrice went to the window and watched her son bounce a tennis ball against the shed. Each impact sounded like gunshots aimed at her. She cringed. Judd didn't know any better; he remembered none of what had happened so long ago. Sixteen should have been a magic age for him, when teenage concerns achieved universal importance. In all those years, she had never let Judd come into contact with other people, much less those his own age.

She opened the screen door and stepped onto the porch, taking care to keep the worried expression off her face. Judd would consider the concern normal for her anyway.

The gray Oregon cloud cover had broken for its daily hour of sunshine. The meadow looked fresh from the previous night's rain. The patter of raindrops had sounded like creeping footsteps outside the window, and Patrice had lain awake for hours, staring at the ceiling. Now the tall pines and aspens cast morning shadows across the dirt road that led from the highway to her sheltered house.

Judd smacked the tennis ball too hard and it sailed off to the driveway, struck a stone, and bounced into the meadow. With a shout of anger, Judd hurled his tennis racket after it. Impulsive—he became more like his father every day.

"Judd!" she called, quelling most of the scolding tone. He fetched the racket and plodded toward her. He had been restless for the last two days. "What's wrong with you?"

Judd averted his eyes, turned instead to squint where the sunshine lit the dense pines. Far away, she could hear the deep hum of a hovertruck hauling logs down the highway.

"Pancake," he finally answered. "He didn't come back yesterday, and I haven't seen him all morning."

Now Patrice understood, and she felt the relief wash inside of her. For a moment, she was afraid he might have seen some stranger or heard something about them on the news. "Your dog'll be all right. Just wait and see."

"But what if he's dying in a ditch somewhere?" She could see tears on the edges of Judd's eyes. He fought hard against crying. "What if he's in a fur trap, or got shot by a hunter?"

Patrice shook her head. "I'm not worried about him. He'll come home safe and sound. He always does."

Once again Patrice felt the shudder. Yes, he always did.

Fifteen years before, Patrice—she had gone by the name of Trish, then—had thought the world was golden. She had been married to Jerry for four years. In that time, he had doubled his salary through patents and bonuses from enhanced silicon-chip development at the DyMar Laboratories.

Their one-year-old son sat in diapers in the middle of the hardwood floor, spinning around. He had deactivated his holographic cartoon companions and played with the dog instead. The boy knew "Ma" and "Da" and attempted to say "Pancake," though the dog's name came out more like a strangled "gaaaakk!"

Trish and Jerry chuckled together as they watched the black Labrador play with Jody. She did not start calling the baby Judd until after they had fled. Pancake romped back and forth with paws slipping on the polished floor. Jody squealed with delight. Pancake woofed and circled the baby, who tried to spin on his diapers on the floor.

"Pancake's like a puppy again," Trish said, smiling. She had owned the dog for nine years already, all through college and in her four years with Jerry. Pancake had settled into a middle-aged routine of sleeping most of the time, except for a lot of slobbering and tail wagging to greet them every day when they came home from work. But lately the dog had been more energetic and playful than he had been in years. "I wonder what happened to him," she said.

Jerry's grin, his short dark hair, and heavy eyebrows made him look dashing. "Maybe all those little things that make a dog feel old got fixed inside of him. The sore joints, the stiff muscles, the bad circulation. Like a million million tiny repairmen doing a renovation."

Trish sat up and pulled her hand away from him. "Did you take him into your lab again? What did you do to him?" She raised her voice, and the words came out with cold anger. "What did you do to him!"

Trish stopped and turned to see her baby boy and the dog looking at her as if she had gone insane. What business did she have yelling when they were trying to play?

Jerry looked at her, hard. He raised his eyebrows in an expression of sincerity. "I didn't do anything. Honest."

With a woof, Pancake charged at Jody again, wagging his tail and banking aside at the last instant. The holographic cartoon characters marched back into the room, dancing to a tune only they could hear. The dog trotted right through the images to the baby. "Just look at him! How can you think anything's wrong?"

But in only four years of marriage, Trish had learned one thing, and she had learned to hate it. She could always tell when Jerry was lying.

"Mom, he's back!" Judd shouted.

For a moment, Patrice reacted with alarm, thinking of the hunters, wondering who could have found them, how she might have given themselves away—but then through the open window, she could hear the dog barking. She looked up from the stove to see the black Labrador bounding out of the trees. Judd ran toward him so hard she expected him to sprawl on his face. Just what she needed, Patrice thought, he would probably break his arm. That would ruin everything. So far, she had managed to avoid all contact with doctors and any other kind of people who kept names and records.

But Judd reached the dog safely, and both tried to outdo the other's enthusiasm. Pancake barked and ran around in circles, leaping into the air. Judd threw his arms around the dog's neck and wrestled him to the ground.

According to her notes, Pancake would be 24 years old in a few months. Nearly twice the average lifespan of a dog.

Judd and Pancake raced each other back to the house. Patrice wiped her hands on a kitchen towel and came out to the porch to greet him. "I told you he'd be okay," she said.

Idiotically happy, Judd nodded and then stroked the dog.

Patrice bent over and ran her fingers through the black fur. The wedding ring, still on her finger after fifteen years alone, stood out among the dark strands. Pancake had a difficult time standing still for her, shifting on all four paws and letting his tongue loll out.

Other than mud spatters and a few cockleburs, she found nothing amiss. Not a mark on him. There never was.

She patted the dog's head, and Pancake rolled his deep brown eyes up at her. "I wish you could tell us stories," she said.

In Jerry's lab, the dog paced inside his cage. He whined twice. He obviously didn't like to be confined and he was probably confused, since Jerry had never caged him before. Pancake wagged his tail, as if hoping for a quick end to this.

Jerry paced the room, running a hand through his own dark hair, trying to kill the butterflies in his stomach. He had worked himself into self-righteous cockiness at showing the management turds just what they had spent all their money on. Progress reports went unread, or at least not understood. Memos describing their work and its implications disappeared in the piles of paper—yes, even though Ethan and O'Hara had perfectly functioning electronic mail systems, they still insisted on old-fashioned paper memos from DyMar underlings.

He glanced at his watch. "What the hell is taking them so long?"

Beside him, Frank Peron sighed. "It's only five minutes, Jerry. You know, wait for them, but they'll never wait for you. We were lucky to get them to come down here at all."

"Considering that this breakthrough will change the universe as we know it," Jerry said, "I'd think they might want to give up a coffee break to have a look."

He couldn't take his eyes off the poster tacked up on the lab wall. It showed Albert Einstein handing a candle to someone few people would recognize by sight—K. Eric Drexler; Drexler, in turn, was extending a candle toward the viewer. Come on, take it! Drexler had been one of the first major visionaries behind nanotechnology some thirty years before.

It will change the universe as we know it, Jerry thought. Pancake looked expectantly at him, then sat down in the middle of his cage. "Good boy," Jerry muttered.

"They're management boobs," Frank said. "You can't expect them to understand what it is they're funding."

At that moment Mr. Ethan and Mr. O'Hara, two of the highest executives in DyMar Laboratories, entered the lab room, apologizing in unison for being late. Smiling, Jerry assured them that neither he nor Frank Peron had noticed.

"Dr. McKenzy, your memo was rather, uh, enthusiastic," Ethan said.

Beside him, O'Hara scowled and chose a different word. "Ebullient. Tossing around promises of immortality, the end to all disease, curing the handicapped, stopping aging—"

"Yes, sir, we felt we had to limit our discussions to only those topics," Jerry interrupted. He had to shock these two so thoroughly that they would be ready to question all their preconceptions. "Actually, this nanotechnology breakthrough opens the doorway to much more, such as an end to dirty industry, instantaneous fabrication of the most complex machines, new materials stronger than steel and harder than diamond. That's why so many people have been working on it for so long. We've all been racing each other because when it happens, it happens. And the first ones to break through are going to shake up society like you won't be able to imagine."

Ethan and O'Hara looked as if they had never heard so much bullshit before in their lives. Very well, Jerry thought, time to haul out the big guns. Literally.

"Watch this, please, and then we can adjourn to the conference room."

Jerry pulled out an automatic pistol from the pocket of his lab coat. He had bought it at a sporting goods store for this purpose only. No one should have been able to smuggle a gun into a lab, but security was lax. He had brought the dog in, hadn't he? He looked at Pancake.

The two executives scrambled backward, muttering outcries.

Jerry didn't give them time to do anything. He was running this show. Melodramatic though it might seem, he knew it would work.

He pointed the pistol at the dog and fired two shots. One struck Pancake's ribcage; another shattered his spine. Blood flew out from the bullet holes, drenching his fur.

Pancake yelped and then sat down from the impact. He panted.

"My god!" Ethan shouted.

"McKenzy, what the hell do you think—" O'Hara cried.

"The first thing that happens," Jerry said, then repeated himself, yelling at the top of his lungs until he had their attention again. "The first thing that happens is that the nanomachines shut down all of the dog's pain centers."

The two executives stared wide eyed. They were both shaking.

In his cage, Pancake looked confused with his tongue lolling out. He seemed not to notice the gaping holes in his back. After a moment, he lay down on the floor of the cage, squishing his fur in the blood still running along his sides. His eyes grew heavy, and he sank down in deep sleep, resting his head on his front paws. He took a huge breath and released it slowly.

"In a massive injury like this, the machines will place him in a recuperative coma. Already, they are scouring the damage sites, assessing the repairs that will be needed, and starting to put him together again. They can link themselves into larger assemblies to make macro repairs." Jerry knelt down on the floor beside the cage, reached his hand in to pat Pancake on the head. "His temperature is already rising from the waste heat generated by the nanomachines. Look, the blood has stopped flowing."

"The dog's dead!" O'Hara said. "The animal activists are going to crucify us!"

"Nope. By tomorrow, he'll be up and chasing jackrabbits." Jerry felt intensely pleased with himself. "I brought in my own dog so we didn't have to go through all the procurement crap to get approved experimental animals.

"You are out of a job, Dr. McKenzy!" Ethan said. His face had turned a deep red.

"I don't think so," Jerry answered, and smiled. "I'll bet you a box of dog biscuits."

The light near sunset slanted through a cut in the Oregon hills where the trees had been shaved in strips from robotic logging. The clouds had cleared again, leaving Patrice and Judd to sit by the table in the living room. The lights, sensing their presence in the household, would come on soon.

The two of them worked on a sprawling jigsaw puzzle that showed the planet Earth rising over the lunar crags, photographed from the moonbase. The blue-green sphere covered most of the table, with jagged gaps from a few continents not yet filled in.

Patrice and Judd talked little in the shared comfortable silence of two people who had had only their own company for a very long time. They could get by with partial sentences, cryptic comments, private jokes.

Judd knew why they had to hide from the outside world. Patrice had kept no secrets from him, explaining their situation in more complicated terms as the boy grew older and became able to comprehend. He had never complained. He knew no other life.

Outside, Pancake barked. He stood up on the porch and paced, letting a low growl loose in his throat.

Patrice stiffened and went to the lace curtains. Her mouth went dry. Somehow, she knew the dog was not making one of his puppy barks at a squirrel. She had owned the dog more than half her life, and she knew him better than any human being could. This was a bark of warning.

"What is it, Mom?" Judd asked. From the drawn expression on his face, she could tell he felt the fear as much as she did. She had trained him well enough.

She could hear a vehicle toiling up the winding gravel drive away from the highway and toward the house.

The demonstrators outside DyMar Laboratories consisted of an odd mix of religious groups, labor union representatives, animal-rights activists, and who knew what else. Some were fruitcakes, some were violent.

Staring out the window, Jerry McKenzy didn't know how to deal with the mob. Maintenance had added steel bars in the last week. "We didn't get as much breathing space as we counted on."

He paced in the lab office, with his terminal and notes, brainstorming files, and records. The actual nanotech experiments were done in clean-rooms in the annex building, where Jerry himself rarely went. But with the demonstrations growing, all experiments had been shut down as the DyMar execs tried to figure out what to do. But then, they were idiots anyway.

DyMar had made a fatal error in announcing the nanotechnology breakthrough to the world. Pressed for time and knowing their research facility couldn't be the only one so close to success, DyMar had blitzed the public with premature announcements. They had taken everyone by surprise.

The outcry in response had been swift and frightening, much more organized and aggressive than the misguided or ineffective complaints Jerry had normally seen. The protest was organized under the aegis of a new organization called "Purity" that had burst into existence with unbelievable speed.

Peron stored his file in the computer and tapped his fingers on the keyboard. "And you thought we'd be the only ones to grasp the implications of nanotechnology."

"It's always nice to see that some people understand more than you give them credit for," Jerry said.

Peron tugged on his lower lip. Something had been bothering him all morning. "Did you ever hear the story about the guy who perfected a solar-power engine? Would have put the gas and electric companies out of business, would have changed the world as we know it. But he disappeared before he could disseminate his blueprints. Now, somebody with a billion-dollar invention like that doesn't just drop out of sight. Do you know what I'm saying?"

Jerry scowled at him. "Oh, that's just an urban legend! Like the choking Doberman."

Peron shrugged. "Well, Drexler predicted back in 1985 that we'd have functioning nanotech within a decade—and that was thirty years ago! A dozen groups have been working, but somehow the crucial experiments fizzle at just the wrong times, the key data gets misprinted in technical journals. It's only because of your damned arrogance, Jerry, that we plowed our way around the usual scientific channels. Have you checked how often the most promising nanotech researchers move off to other fields of study, how often they die in accidents?"

Jerry blinked at the other man in astonishment. "Have you run a reality diagnostic on yourself recently, Frank? You're sounding paranoid."

Peron forced a laugh. "Sorry. This isn't exactly a high-security installation we're working in, you know. You smuggled your damned dog in here twice, and Pancake isn't a lap dog that'll fit in a glove compartment. A chain-link fence and a couple of rent-a-cops does not make me feel safe."

As if in response, the crowds outside took up a loud chant.

Jerry sat down, kicked a few of the stray pencils away from his feet, and spoke in his "let's be reasonable" voice. "Frank, some bone-headed fanatic is always trying to stop progress—but it never works. Nobody can undiscover nanotechnology." He made a rude noise through his lips.

Jerry spent a quarter of an hour reassuring his partner, convincing him not to worry. With dogged persistence they could get through this mess. He felt confident when they both packed up to brave the gauntlet of protesters and go home.

But he never saw Frank Peron again.

When Patrice saw the red vehicle approaching, she squinted into the sunset and made it out to be a small American truck outfitted with laser-guidance sensors, mud-spattered and identical to a million other vehicles in Oregon. She didn't recognize the silhouette of the man behind the wheel.

She didn't have time to run.

Patrice and Judd had lived in the state for nine years, at the same location for three of them. She and her son had fled to Oregon because of its track record of survivalists, of religious cults, of extremists and isolationists—all of whom knew how to be left alone. The state's rural ultra-privacy legislation forbade any release of tax documents, credit card transactions, or telephone records.

But the last time she had gone into a grocery store, she had noticed the cover of a weekly newsmagazine depicting the fenced-off and burned ruins of DyMar Laboratories. The headline advertised a fifteen-year retrospective on the disaster, bemoaning that all records had been lost of such an important technological breakthrough. No doubt the story would talk about how she and her son were still missing, presumed killed by Purity extremists. There would have been pictures of her—as Trish McKenzy, not Patrice Kennesy, and the boy Jody, not Judd.

Uneasy, she had taken her groceries and backed away from the TV guides and beef jerky strips and candy bars by the register. No one, she insisted to herself, would have put such a coincidence together, would have connected all the details. Still, the clerk had stared at her too intently....

Now, with a grim expression on her face, Patrice stepped out on her front porch to meet the approaching stranger.

The demonstrators did not go home, not even late at night. Jerry had remained at the lab office until after ten o'clock, sending a vidmessage to Trish that he wanted to finish another simulation before locking up. People massed against the chain-link fence, shouting and chanting. They had lit bonfires.

Somehow he could not believe that anybody but the technically literate would understand how significant a breakthrough he and Frank Peron had made. This wasn't the type of thing people normally got up in arms about—it was too complicated and required too much foresight to see how the world would change, to sort the dangers from the miracles DyMar had been promising in its PR. Who was orchestrating all this?

Like Utah's cold fusion debacle from decades before, DyMar had made a lot of promises and produced nothing tangible. They were waiting for patent approval before releasing any details, but the red tape had been tangled, the patent office had lost the first two sets of applications, though the e-mail trace verified that they had been received and logged in. Lawyers did not return vidmessages. News of the "immortal dog" had leaked in one interview, but Jerry sure as hell was not going to shoot Pancake again in front of a TV camera just to make a point.

The dog wasn't the only one blessed with nanotechnology cell repair, though. He had seen to that himself. Nobody knew that he carried his own cell-repair machines tailored to human DNA, and it would stay that way.

Outside he heard glass breaking, the roar of the crowd. It just didn't make any sense to him. He watched out the window. Clouds had obscured most of the stars overhead, but mercury vapor lamps spilled garish light across the near-empty parking lot.

At the gate, a team of rent-a-cops paced about holding rifles ready, probably quaking in their boots. DyMar had called for backup security from the State Police, and they had been turned down. The ostensible reason was some buried statute that allowed the police to defer "internal company disputes" to private security forces. How they could consider the mob of demonstrators to be an internal company dispute, Jerry could not imagine. It felt as if somebody wanted the lab unprotected.

He heard sharp popping noises outside, and it took him a moment to realize they were gunshots. He turned to see one of the security guards fall; others ran away as a group of people streamed through a breach in the chain-link fence. He heard more gunfire.

"This is nuts!" he said to himself, then switched off the light in his lab. No use attracting them; but they would know exactly where he was working. Jerry couldn't believe it, but he knew he had to get away immediately.

Glow from the parking-lot lights mixed with the dim EXIT sign to give him enough illumination to move. He slipped out of the room and hesitated, wondering if he should call the police or the fire department. Someone smashed the front doors downstairs. He had no time.

They would ransack the place and destroy his work. Jerry tried to think if he could save anything, like in all those old movies where the mad scientist rescued his single notebook from the flames. But his work and Frank Peron's was scattered in a thousand computer files, delicate microhardware, and intangible AI simulations. Everything was backed up, with duplicates stored in various vaults. It would be safe. For now, the important thing was to escape. The mob had already killed one of the guards; Jerry had no doubt they would tear him apart.

He ran down the hall as he heard footsteps in the lobby, shouted orders, another gunshot. Jerry fled to the back stairwell, yanked open the door, and leaped down the concrete stairs three at a time, balancing himself on the railing. At the bottom, he ripped off his lab coat and left it on the landing before emerging into the administrative section of the main building.

He peeked around the door. They had not gotten this far down the halls yet, and managerial offices would not be their first target. He heard a huge roaring explosion and saw through a set of windows the annex building erupt into orange flames. Impossible! This couldn't be happening! But ignorant peasants had always stormed the doctor's castle, carrying torches.

Jerry kept close to the wall as he hurried along. The front and side doors would be out of the question. But the back had an emergency exit, a crash-out door that would also activate alarms and notify the police and fire departments. He couldn't decide if that would be good or bad.

A window shattered in one of the suites in front of him, and a puddle of flames spilled from a broken bottle. Molotov cocktail; one of the front offices—either Ethan's or O'Hara's—burst into flame.

Jerry placed his ear to the emergency exit door. He heard chaos outside, but it sounded distant. He imagined somebody stationed back here with a rifle pointed at the door, waiting for him to come running. But he had no other choice.

Jerry used his back to slam out through the door, throwing himself to the ground as he emerged. He rolled, waiting to hear gunshots strike the door, ping off the asphalt, slam into his chest. What had Pancake felt when the bullets slammed into him? He didn't know how much damage his own body could endure and still repair itself. He had never tested his limits.

But the only gunshots came from the side of the building. He heard more shouts and running people. He got up and sprinted to the corner of the building. If only he could make it to the parking lot and to his car, he could crash through the fence and drive off, get Trish and the baby, and hide in a motel for a few days until this stuff calmed down.

He let himself feel a ripple of smugness. The violence here would stun the protest movement; once the public saw them do murder and destruction like this, all sympathy for their cause would be gone. This was like mass insanity. Killing people by blowing up abortion clinics never won any support for Pro-Life groups, did it? Armstrong's bomb hadn't helped the Vietnam War protest decades before, had it?

But when Jerry saw the people attacking the DyMar building, saw the weapons they carried and the uniform way they moved, he knew immediately that this was no mob, this was no ragtag band of second-generation hippies yanking shotguns off their mantels.

Fire from the lower level spread through the main building. More burning bottles had been tossed through downstairs windows.

With a shock he noticed a complete absence of TV crews, though they had been covering the protest since its beginning. On the parking lot near the gate, Jerry saw the sprawled uniformed bodies of two security guards. The others were probably dead somewhere along the fence line—unless they were themselves part of the assault team.

In the confusion, Jerry added an angry expression to his face and ran among the mob, working his way to the parking lot. He slipped through, shouting directions to anyone who looked his direction as if to challenge him.

Once Jerry got to the cars, he ducked low, working among them. This late at night, not many vehicles remained, only his own, the guards', a handful of other cars and trucks that had either been broken down, or sat with For Sale signs in their windshields.

He found Frank Peron's black sports car and hesitated. But Frank had left days ago! Unless he had never made it. Jerry swallowed a cold lump in his throat.

Once he got in his car, he would have to start it fast, and drive away fast, keeping his head low to avoid gunfire. Judging from what Pancake had endured, Jerry could survive some major injuries with his nanotech healing machines, but he had no desire to test them.

He reached the passenger side of his car and fished in his pocket for the key ring. Among the shouts and burning and gunshots, the noise he made was insignificant, but still the jingle seemed too loud to him. He unlocked the door and slipped in, crawling over the passenger seat and pulling the door shut behind him. Squirming, he positioned himself behind the steering wheel, still ducking low, and took an absurd moment to strap himself in with the seatbelt. He would have to crash through the fence and he did not want to smack his head on the dashboard and knock himself senseless.

Before starting the car, he plotted his route, found a side gate with an access road that would take him off to the highway. He switched off all the automatic collision-avoidance systems, the laser-guidance options. He was going to have to drive like a stunt man. He made up his mind to plow right over anybody who stood in his way. This was life or death here. Adrenalin pounded through him. He would gain nothing by waiting.

He turned the key in the ignition.

The car bomb instantly blew him into pieces, trapping his body in the burning hulk of twisted metal. Not even his cell-repair machines could fix so much damage.

In front of Patrice's house, the man wasted no time as he ground the red vehicle to a halt. He left the engine purring, slid the door open, and stood up.

He brought a scattershot rifle out of the front seat and leveled it at Patrice. "Ding dong, Avon calling," he said.

Patrice stood defiantly on the porch, unable to move. She felt old and weak. When Judd stepped out and stood beside her, she felt weaker still.

"Or would you rather I said 'I'm from the government, I'm here to help you'?" the man continued. He had a medium build and wore a red flannel shirt with a white T-shirt poking up to his neck. His face was bland, nondescript, showing no indications of outright evil.

Without taking his eyes from them, he reached in to the dashboard of his truck and yanked out two sheets of paper, colored computer printouts showing faces. The images were split: one side showed a photograph of her from fifteen years before, and the other image—computer enhanced—had "aged" her to approximate what she looked like now, along with a detailed personality analysis suggesting how she might normally dress. The second sheet of paper showed baby Jody and a much-less-exact extrapolation of how he would look as a sixteen-year-old boy.

"I'm convinced," the man said. "Or are you going to deny it, Mrs. McKenzy?"

For a moment, all the words backed up in her mind. She couldn't think of anything to say, couldn't think of anything worth saying. "What do you want from us?"

"What do I want?" He laughed and stepped around the door of the vehicle, still pointing the scattershot at them. "Purity's been looking a long time."

Growling, Pancake stood up and eased forward, baring his teeth. He stepped in front of Judd.

The Purity man stopped and blinked in astonishment. "Jesus, that's the dog! The goddamned dog—it's still alive! Well, well, well!"

"Do you want money?" Patrice said. She didn't have much left, but it would stall him for a few minutes. "I have cash. It won't show up on any account record."

"This goes beyond money," he said. "We need to bring you in. Take the dog and destroy him. Then find out from you and the boy if you've kept any of Dr. McKenzy's notes, maybe some of his nanotech samples. We can't take chances with the human race."

Seeming to sense the boy was the weak link in this scenario, the Purity man aimed the scattershot at Judd's head and took a few more steps toward them. Holding the rifle with one hand, he fumbled in his pocket, withdrawing a pair of polymer handcuffs.

"Now then, Mrs. McKenzy, let's not make this difficult. I want you to cuff one of these around your wrist and the other around the boy's ankle. That'll make it impossible for you to run anywhere." He extended the handcuffs forward.

Pancake lunged. Black Labradors were not normally used as attack dogs, but Pancake must have been able to sense the fear and tension in the air. He knew who the intruder was, and he had been with the same owner for 24 years.

He struck the Purity man full in the shoulders, startling him, spoiling his aim. The scattershot dropped. The man's finger squeezed the trigger. The explosion roared through the quiet isolation far from the main road.

Instead of taking off Judd's head, the swath of silver needles spattered across the boy's chest, spraying blood behind him to the walls of the house.

Patrice screamed.

Pancake bore the man to the ground. The man thumped into the front of his vehicle, banged against the sharp laser-guidance detectors and then sprawled. He tried to fight the dog off. Pancake bit at his face, his throat.

Wailing, Patrice dropped to her knees and cradled her son's head. "Oh my god! Oh my god!"

Judd blinked his eyes. They were wide with astonishment and seemingly far away. Blood bubbled out of his mouth, and he spat it aside. "So tired." She stroked his hair.

Pancake backed away from the motionless man on the ground. Blood lay in pools from the man's torn throat.

The headlights of Patrice's carryall glared up from the wet pavement long after dark. She had switched off the old and unreliable laser-guidance systems and drove faster than safety or common sense allowed, but panic had gotten into her mind now. She kept driving, pushing her foot to the floor and wrestling with the curves of the coast road, heading north. Dark pine trees flashed by like tunnel walls on either side of her.

She had to find someplace else, to run again, to start a new life.

Pancake rested in the back of the station wagon, exhausted. Clumps of blood bristled from his fur. She hadn't taken time to clean him up. She had paused only long enough to throw all of her ready cash into the glove compartment. The Purity man's own wallet had held two hundred dollars and several cred cards under different names.

Looking down at the man's body in failing dusk light, she noticed that the blood had stopped flowing, yet his heart continued to beat. He looked to be in a deep sleep, and his skin felt warm and feverish. She stepped back in horror. Of course the government had nanotech healers of their own! All of Jerry's records were supposedly destroyed in the DyMar labs disaster, but with backups and disjointed systems, no simple fire could have eliminated everything.

Now she knew why, after all these years, others had not made similar breakthroughs. Jerry had been merely the first, but other researchers were close on his heels. The sham organization of Purity, or the government, or some worldwide power consortium had kept nanotechnology to themselves, blocking or absorbing all other breakthroughs as they occurred.

This man would wake up in a day or so, and report back to his superiors. She could destroy him now, set his body on fire or squash his head with the front wheel of his own vehicle.

Instead, she siphoned all the fuel out of his truck and switched license markers. In some coast town, she would find a darkened parking lot and other unattended vehicles, and she would switch markers again. Then she would move on.

In the back seat of the carryall, Judd lay in silence, wrapped in two bloodstained blankets she had torn from the beds upstairs. His pulse was faint, his breathing shallow, but he still lived. He seemed to be in a coma.

The obstacle alarm screeched. From the trees on her right, a dog stepped into the road in front of her.

Patrice cried out, slammed the brakes and yanked the steering wheel. The dog bounded back out of sight. She swerved, nearly lost control of the car on the slick road, then regained it. Behind her, in the rear-view mirror, she saw the dark shape of the dog walk back across the road, undaunted by its close call.

She remembered one of the last conversations she had had with Jerry, after he had finally told her what he had done to Pancake and the immortality his nanotechnology had brought. Jerry had wanted to give her the same type of protection.

She had blinked at him in horror when he told her he had already done it to himself. He wanted to do it to her, too.

The thought of a billion billion tiny machines crawling through her body, checking and rechecking her cell structures, seemed abominable to her. She'd refused to let him. Jerry would not let her ponder the question, would not let her come to grips with the idea. He wanted an answer right then. That was just the way Jerry McKenzy did things.

Baby Jody had started to cry, awakened by their raised voices. Trish had looked up at her husband with wide eyes; she caught a faint smile on his face as Jerry glanced toward Jody's room.

"You didn't do anything to the baby, did you! What did you do to Jody?"

"Nothing!" Jerry said. He smiled. "I didn't do anything."

But she could always tell when her husband was lying.

As she drove off into the night, with her son's bleeding body in the car seat behind her, Patrice prayed she was right.

My most successful original series is the Saga of Seven Suns, a huge multivolume space opera with a few ambitious side stories as well.

When I was guest of honor at LibertyCon, a popular science fiction convention in Chattanooga, Tennessee, the staff produced a benefit anthology of science fiction stories, Onward LibertyCon. *I created a new Seven Suns story featuring the Roamers—independent ragtag "belters" who are among the favorite characters in the series.*

I'll never forget that seminal line from Star Trek: The Wrath of Khan, *"The needs of the many outweigh the needs of the few, or the one." In "Hole in the Wall," one man faces the conundrum of choosing between his own home and happiness versus the fate of an entire planet in the face of a cosmic disaster.*

It was a real treat to reread my entire Seven Suns series … and this story is not the only result of that "refresher course."

HOLE IN THE WALL

—I—

It wasn't that Elias Sandoval hated people; he just didn't understand them, didn't comprehend the confusing niceties of social interaction, didn't know what to say or do. So, he felt he was better left alone.

Even though he was fifty years old, he had little practice with people—intentionally so. He preferred his own company, millions of miles from the nearest neighbor, far out in an asteroid belt. And based on his previous interactions, he knew that most people preferred for him to keep his own company, too.

The best possible solution for everybody was to live by himself inside his own private uncharted asteroid on the far fringes of the Portnoy Belt. He could be alone with his own thoughts, entertain himself, contemplate big ideas.

He had named the asteroid Serendipity, and it truly was the perfect home for him. His brothers and cousins had helped provide the resources and equipment for him to turn the asteroid's cracks, caverns, and tunnels into a cozy domicile. Elias had done all the work himself.

The tumbling rock was in an erratic orbit, not part of the overall asteroid belt, just traveling with the traffic for the time being. In composition, Serendipity's was stone mixed with ices, but in some previous passage close to Portnoy's sun, the ice and gases had boiled out, leaving the asteroid honeycombed with a warren of voids and habitable passageways.

And something else.

The walls and ceilings, the cracks and crannies sparkled with wonder unlike anything he had ever seen—and Elias had seen some of the most spectacular beauty the Spiral Arm had to offer.

Through a strange combination of mineral deposits, energy, and —as the asteroid's name suggested—sheer serendipity, every interior rock surface was studded with branched snowflake crystals, translucent white growths of angled prisms, more precious than diamonds, because diamonds were found on many worlds. As far as Elias could tell, these Serendipity crystals had been found nowhere else, not in the most isolated or rigorous Roamer settlement, not in any of the Terran Hanseatic League colonies, nor even in the alien Ildiran Empire. Serendipity crystals were delicate, fragile, and extremely valuable. Only Elias knew where to find them.

Every day, he strolled along the crystal-encrusted passages. In the five years that Serendipity had been his private sanctuary, Elias had explored the winding passages, but there was always mystery and always wonder. Though the asteroid was only ten kilometers on its long axis, he estimated that there were hundreds of kilometers of cracks, tunnels, and fissures to explore, at his leisure, and he intended to spend the rest of his life doing it.

Now he walked along with his bright handlight extended in front of him, and the crystal facets reflected and flared, ricocheting the light in all directions. The ice-mineral crystals branched out in thin fingers like spiderwebs of diamond, which signified that the asteroid must be remarkably stable. A good place to make a home.

Elias hummed to himself, not caring whether or not he could carry a tune because he had a highly uncritical audience. He followed the bright crystals, tracing them deep into the asteroid's interior, where the main crystals were stubbier, smaller. He reached a section of newborn crystals which had grown in only the past few months. Elias knew this because he had watched it happen.

He had found the proteus spark that created the Serendipity crystals. Seeing that moving flicker always gave him a chill, and each day he traced its movement. Part of him—the long-suppressed social human part—wanted to share this marvel with someone, but Elias knew he had to keep it to himself.

At the end of the tunnel the crystal growths petered out, leaving the rock walls bare. The spark hadn't completed its work here yet, but, nevertheless, the proteus had covered more than a foot in the past day.

The essential spark was like a bright, throbbing ember no larger than his thumbnail, as if someone had plucked one of the brightest stars in the universe and simply hidden it away in a dark corner. The proteus was alive somehow, a glow that fed on the minerals or drew latent energy from the rock. It burned along the tunnels like a spark traveling the length of a fuse.

Elias had tried to do research in his databases but had found nothing like this phenomenon. As a child of the Roamer clans, he was a crack engineer and problem solver. He knew how to fix things, how to make machinery work under impossible situations, but he was no theoretician.

He didn't dare bring the enigma to any of the Roamer clans at Rendezvous, or even to his own brothers and cousins, because one curious person would ask too many questions. Then, there would be other questions, other consultations, and Elias Sandoval would lose his privacy. Serendipity would be overrun.

He could live with not knowing all the answers.

The proteus spark crept along the passage like a solitary luminescent snail, leaving newborn crystals behind. Considering the extent of the marvelous growths, Elias imagined that this had been occurring for centuries, if not millennia.

The new crystals were only nubs, but they carried that protean sparkle. The larger growths along the main passageways were milky and beautiful, but they were just artifacts, fossils. The new crystals were still alive, and the parent glow would continue its aimless wandering down one passage or another....

Although he didn't need human company or conversation, he did require air, water, food, spare parts. Serendipity was not, and would never be, self-sufficient, and twice a year he needed to make a journey beyond the Portnoy asteroid belt and off to the distant Roamer complex. Out in the wider Terran Hanseatic League, the wandering independent spacefarers were often frowned upon or viewed with suspicion. But Rendezvous was different, a place where all clan members could feel at home.

Though he didn't like to leave his sanctuary, Elias knew he had to go, despite his unease. He'd been keeping a list for months, and some of his reservoirs were reaching critically low points. He couldn't put it off any longer. He could buy everything he needed. Money was never an issue.

Elias spent the next day with a rock hammer in the outer tunnels, chipping away specimen after specimen of the Serendipity crystals, then packing them in a cargo container. He had a contact at Rendezvous who would sell them, for a substantial cut.

He packed what he needed, suited up, and boarded his battered private ship, checked the fuel levels, and left his private asteroid, confident that no one could ever find it.

—II—

The Roamer central complex of Rendezvous was a true wonder. Innumerable asteroids of varying sizes, some even smaller than Serendipity, had been rounded up and maneuvered into a cluster, hollowed out for habitation, linked together with structural girders and connecting tubes. It was a remarkable waystation, a handful of rocks wired together and orbiting a dim red sun called Meyer. It was an unlikely place for a government and trading center, but the Roamers made do. They always did.

As human colonization spread into the Spiral Arm, the scattered clans had learned to be tough and resourceful. Their critics compared them to cockroaches, while the Roamers took pride in filling any available niche. The Terran Hanseatic League, or Hansa, had no idea where to find the clans to tax them or include them in a census.

After crossing interstellar space, Elias brought his ship toward Rendezvous, transmitting his ID codes, although any Roamer observer seeing the motley configuration would know he was a Roamer. Clan Sandoval dismantled and repurposed components for their numerous vessels, and Elias's father had given him this ship as a gift when the young man wanted to go out on his own—not to be a black sheep, but to be independent. His spacecraft might not look pretty, but its engines, hull, and electronics were superb and reliable.

After he docked and passed through the transit points into the asteroid hub, he was swallowed up in a bustle of conversation, noises, smells, and deafening colors. Every day inside Serendipity, Elias would hear nothing more than a whisper, but the exuberant bazaar of Rendezvous made him drown in sensory overload. He winced and stood there a moment, like a man facing a fierce headwind, but forced himself forward, guiding the heavy cargo box of Serendipity crystals with its antigrav handle.

Families moved together, wearing jumpsuits with clan insignia embroidered on their breasts. Someone clapped him on the shoulder and laughed with a loud welcome, then strode on. Elias was sure he had never met the man before, although his old drab garments still bore the Sandoval clan insignia. Maybe that was enough.

He walked past food vendors who prepared heavily spiced noodles and mushrooms, strips of charred vat meat, fresh fruits out of greenhouse domes. It was far more expensive for Roamers to produce their own food inside enclosed habitats, but the clans refused to be dependent on the moods of the Hansa.

Elias indulged himself and bought a cluster of grapes and two ripe oranges. He took the fruit to an out-of-the-way alcove, where he ate one of the juicy oranges, licking every last drop of sticky liquid from his fingertips. He saved the grapes for later, admitting to himself that Rendezvous had certain advantages, so long as he visited only infrequently. With this trip, he would load up his ship with packaged food, fresh produce, meat, and tank-cultured seafood. "Quality of life," he muttered to himself.

Down one of the corridors, a makeshift band played raucous music, and a crowd sang along, although they didn't seem to know the words either. Elias pulled his cargo case by the antigrav handle, guiding it to the trading chambers, where he would meet with Skalec the Scar.

Skalec was a loquacious and congenial vendor with a burn scar on his left cheek; he had adopted the name because he wanted to sound fearsome, but he fooled no one. When Elias entered with the cargo case, Skalec's eyes lit up. "By the Guiding Star, I sold out three weeks ago, Sandoval! Been waiting for you."

"Would have put it off longer, if I could."

Skalec muscled forward and cleared a table with a sweep of his forearm. "Let's see what you have."

Elias set down his case and switched off the antigrav handle, and the heavy load settled down with a groan. Skalec opened the case and reached inside, marveling at the delicate gleaming crystals. "They're in such high demand, I'll take as many as you want to bring."

Elias raised his eyebrows. "That means I can charge you more."

The trader's waxy scar rippled when he scowled. "If I have to. An additional ten percent."

Elias smiled. "That'll do. I'm not much for haggling. Let's just get this over with." Skalec shook his head and reverently unloaded the crystals, removing the shards one at a time and placing them on a soft, dark fabric. At the shop doorway, customers were already looking in, curious.

Skalec paid him. "Come back sooner next time. And bring two cases."

"I don't need the money," Elias said. "Just want to buy supplies."

The trader scratched his scar. "You make no sense to me, Elias Sandoval."

"A lot of things don't make sense to me either."

Skalec the Scar hesitated and then added another bonus. "Maybe you'll think about an increased shipment next time."

"I'll think about it," Elias said, "but it likely won't happen."

He bought all the supplies he could think of, even used the bonus for a few luxury items that tempted him, as well as a full tank of ekti for his stardrive. Soon enough, the people, crowds, smells, and noises were just too much. Serendipity called to him.

With the cargo loaded aboard, he sealed the ship, detached from the docking zone, and flew away from the Rendezvous cluster. He just wanted to get home to solitude, where he could wash away the *closeness* and the conversation.

He flew away from the asteroids on a random vector into empty space. Once he got far enough away, he recalibrated his course, input the coordinates to the obscure Portnoy system, and made his way to one particular speck of rock drifting among the scattered asteroids in the belt.

When he arrived back at Serendipity, Elias was astonished to find two large ships already there, landed on the cratered surface of his home.

—III—

The sight of the unfamiliar ships was so incongruous that Elias didn't know how to react. The strangers had landed side by side between the asteroid's two largest craters, which he'd named Martha and Beatrice after a pair of large-boned aunts he remembered from clan gatherings. The vessels were sleek, new models, too large to be scout vessels, not of military design, nor were they cargo ships.

As he entered his final approach, he ran the scans again, increased magnification. Each ship bore the insignia of the Terran Hanseatic League.

Before Elias could figure out what to do, they spotted him, opened the line of communication. "Unidentified ship, please respond." It was a woman's voice, stern as a schoolteacher.

"Unidentified?" Elias replied. "Who the hell are *you*? You're trespassing!" He did not alter his course. He was going home, and he couldn't think of anywhere else to turn. Just seeing these other ships made him feel violated.

None of the other asteroids in the Portnoy Belt were close enough to be more than bright lights in the sky, nearly indistinguishable from stars. His asteroid was all alone, and so was he.

Until now.

As his ship cruised closer, he could see three exosuited figures walking with fluid, low-gravity grace across the dusty surface. No one besides him had ever set foot on Serendipity, as far as he knew, and now these strangers were leaving footprints over the pristine ground.

The comm screen flickered, and a woman's face appeared. She had short, dark brown hair that looked as if she cut it herself, and her skin had a dusky cast. "Excuse me? What is your name and how is this your rock?"

"You first." Elias realized he sounded gruff and threatening. He felt out of his league when it came time to make use of diplomatic skills. "I'm Elias Sandoval of Clan Sandoval, and I've lived here for years. Serendipity is my property by right of possession. My ship is heavily armed—consider yourself warned."

"No need for your aggressive posture, Mr. Sandoval," said the captain. "I am Mariah Oko of the Hansa's Portnoy threat-assessment expedition."

A round-faced man with grizzled whiskers leaned into view. "We're the nudge-and-budge cleanup crew, and we're here to move your rock out of the way so we can protect the colonists on Portnoy's World."

"I don't care about Portnoy's World," Elias said. The only Terra-compatible planet in the system was far away, and he had never bothered to go there. "What does that have to do with me?"

"Nothing to do with you, Mr. Sandoval," said Oko. "We had no idea you were here, but this asteroid popped up on our potential hazard list. We have to take care of it."

"You leave my home alone. I'm warning you. I've got weapons."

"No, he doesn't," sneered the man with the unshaven jowls.

"We can see your wreck of a ship, sir." Oko sounded as if she had strapped on plate armor of patience. "I don't doubt that Roamer vessels have defenses, but you don't want to get into a shooting war with us. We're just here doing our job."

"And I'm just trying to go home," Elias said. "If you'd bothered to run a scan as you approached, you would have found my hangar dock, my air, fuel, and water silos, and the access hatch to the interior. Prior habitation clearly established, per Hansa law. You have no claim here."

As his thoughts raced, he wondered if somehow these people, these pirates from the Terran Hanseatic League, had learned about his Serendipity crystals. They would exploit them all, strip the tunnels bare, and rob him blind.

Mariah Oko struggled to keep her anger in check. "We did not know anyone had claimed this uncatalogued asteroid. We apologize for any inconvenience, but we have work to do. Perhaps if you land and meet us in our main ship, we can discuss this."

"You're not coming inside my asteroid," said Elias.

"Didn't ask to," said the gruff man, but Captain Oko shushed him.

"Please come aboard my ship, Mr. Sandoval. According to Hansa records, this is an unclaimed asteroid." Her eyes met his on the screen. "But we will listen to your claim and try to minimize the inconvenience."

This encounter had already been a tremendous inconvenience,

and the very idea rattled him to his core. Elias struggled to find words as he realized he had never filed paperwork with the Hansa, because that would have flagged Serendipity so anyone could find him—which entirely defeated the purpose. After dealing with the noise, crowds, and smells at Rendezvous, he just wanted to hole up and be by himself, to regain his own peace and calm.

Now, though, he felt shattered. Elias did not like to do business face-to-face, but now he realized it might be necessary. The sooner he could get these intruders off of Serendipity, the better.

"All right. I'll land my ship next to yours and come over."

"We guarantee your safety, sir," Oko said. "This is just a discussion. We will explain our presence here, and once you understand, you'll agree with the necessity."

"Even if I agree with the necessity, you still have to leave."

The other captain pressed her lips together. "We will leave as soon as we're finished."

"I'm coming armed," he said, bristling but terrified. He thought he had a weapon somewhere, although it hadn't been used or even touched in as long as he could remember.

"Bring all the weapons you want. We're not worried," said the gruff man, grinning even. "We've got nukes."

—IV—

When Elias had constructed his home on Serendipity, he hadn't bothered to consider camouflage or security. His greatest defense was obscurity.

But somehow these Hansa scouts and engineers had found him —or, more accurately, found this asteroid. He was surprised the Hansa ships hadn't spotted his fueling depot or the main docking entrance into the tunnels, but Captain Oko and her team had not even looked. They just came uninvited, ready to do whatever they wanted. Elias felt intimidated, but he was also pissed off.

After he landed on the near edge of Martha crater, he placed a multitool in his exosuit pocket, the closest thing to a weapon he could actually find; he hoped the bulge would look threatening enough.

Emerging from his ship, he stared across the stark landscape, felt the midnight vault of stars above. The two modern Hansa craft made his own ship look like a junk heap by comparison. No wonder they hadn't believed his empty threat of possessing superior weapons.

Nukes? By the Guiding Star, why would they bring nukes out to his little asteroid?

Five exosuited Hansa workers now swarmed across the surface, taking measurements, drilling cores, running seismic scans. Offended, Elias activated his comm. "Stop what you're doing! You have no right to be here." None of them answered or even looked up. "Why don't you respond? Take that equipment back to your ships." Maybe they worked on a different comm frequency. He felt completely impotent.

Mariah Oko's voice came over his earphones. "Mr. Sandoval, they need to complete their stability survey and find proper anchor points. Please come into my lead ship so we can debrief you on the situation. You'll understand as soon as you see our projections."

"What if I don't want to see your projections?" Elias said. "I want you to go. Stop messing with my asteroid."

The larger of the Hansa ships had an open exterior airlock, and he trudged over, stewing. If they had performed density surveys and structural mapping, they would have found the numerous fissures and passages that honeycombed the tumbling rock. Did they intend to drill mining shafts, rip open Serendipity's crust so they could strip-mine the delicate crystals? They had no right!

When he entered Oko's airlock, he imagined he was walking into the mouth of a shark and trusting the jaws not to chomp down. He sealed the exterior door, waited for the pressure to cycle, and then entered. He stood stiff, his arms at his sides as if ready for a barroom brawl. He didn't like this. Not at all.

Captain Oko came to greet him, straight-backed and formal. She wore an engineer's jumpsuit with the Hansa logo on the breast—printed, not meticulously embroidered like a Roamer clan would do. The rumpled-looking, round-faced man joined her. Despite his pudgy face, he had a surprisingly thin body, probably from a life spent in low gravity. Oko shook Elias's hand and introduced her companion as Terris. In response, Terris pushed out his lower lip as if to emphasize his frown.

Elias did not feel like being warm and fuzzy. He spoke first. "I don't understand what you're doing here, Captain Oko. Why have Hansa ships landed on my asteroid?"

He understood the basic legal principles of habitation and right of salvage—every Roamer did—but he couldn't quote specific chapter and verse. He also knew that the Terran Hanseatic League under the administration of the hardline Chairman Basil Wenceslas often broke treaties and rules whenever it was convenient for them.

Oko had mastered a little more patience. "As I said, sir, we had no inkling that this rock was inhabited." She gestured toward a small conference chamber adjacent to the galley. "Have a seat so I can show you our projections. Would you like something to drink? I have fresh ground klee from Theroc, even a new shipment of Earth coffee, dark roast."

Elias paused. "Earth coffee?"

Roamers had many beverages, some quite distinctive, including alternatives to coffee grown on Earth, but he'd only tasted the real stuff once before. Seeing his reaction, Oko smiled. "Coffee it is, then. Terris, go dispense us each a cup."

The other man scowled. "I don't make coffee."

"Read the fine print in your contract," she snapped. "The last clause says, 'other duties as assigned.' I'm assigning you this other duty while Mr. Sandoval and I get to know each other."

Terris went into the galley where he made altogether too much noise while brewing coffee.

Elias warily took a seat at the oval table, rested his elbows on the smooth surface, and looked at the captain. He let the silence stretch out until Oko activated the tabletop, turning it into a projection screen. "This particular asteroid—1013X1—"

Elias interrupted her. "Serendipity."

Oko continued as if she hadn't heard. "—is currently traveling with the overall Portnoy Belt, but it's what we call a cuckoo, like an egg laid in another bird's nest. It doesn't belong with the rest of these rocks, but rather came from outside the system. It's on a highly elliptical trajectory, just about to pass aphelion, and before long it'll hook around and start its steep plunge down toward the inner system."

The table screen displayed a map of the Portnoy system. The myriad asteroid orbits in the belt looked like a swarm of gnats, but one elongated ellipse, highlighted in red, clearly didn't belong with the others. Serendipity.

"I've lived here for years, and I've never had any trouble," Elias said, defensive. He realized, though, that all the cracks and voids inside his asteroid had been left by sublimating ices and gases during previous close passages of the sun.

"My team tracks the asteroids in the Portnoy Belt. Most of them cause no trouble, but every once in a while there's an outlier like 1013X1. Umm, I mean Serendipity." She paused. "We call it a runaway."

Terris delivered the cups of coffee, his expression as bitter as the brew. Elias took a sip, too upset to enjoy the rich taste. "What does that matter?" he asked. "I'm not driving the rock. I just live here."

Captain Oko zoomed in, highlighted another orbit closer to the sun, a terrestrial planet. The image showed an atmosphere streaked with white clouds over blue oceans and brown and green continents.

"This is Portnoy, a well-established Hansa colony, been there almost thirty years, population two hundred thousand." She overlaid the projected orbits, and the steep elliptical line of Serendipity's path intersected Portnoy's orbit. "We've run the projections again and again. When this asteroid heads down into the inner system, there's a sixty percent chance it will strike Portnoy."

Terris said, "An impact like that would wipe out all life on the planet."

Elias stared at the diagram, feeling cold inside. "Sixty percent chance … When?"

"About twenty-seven years from now."

He blew out a sigh of relief. "Then you have plenty of time to evacuate the colonists. There's no emergency."

Oko scratched her short, dark hair and frowned at him in surprise. Terris's mouth dropped open in disbelief. "Evacuate the colonists? That's a beautiful, viable world. Think of all the people, their families! And in another quarter century, the population could more than double."

"Not my problem," Elias said. "Plenty of time for you to figure something out."

"You're missing the point, Mr. Sandoval," Oko said in a crisp voice. "The easiest solution is to alter the orbit of 1013X1 so that there is no imminent impact, period. That's why we're here."

"Hence the nukes," said Terris, grinning.

Elias's thoughts were deafened by his anger. "You're not detonating atomic warheads on my asteroid." He thought of the delicate crystals, the fragile snowflakes lining the tunnels and fissures. The shock wave would wreck them all.

Oko shook her head with exaggerated sadness. "I'm afraid there's really no choice. The farther away we make our nudge, the more reliable will be the result. Way out here, it'll take a much lower yield to alter the asteroid's trajectory into a safe orbit."

Elias felt nauseated. "You said there's only a sixty percent chance. That's practically like flipping a coin—I'd want to know for sure before you start blowing up my home."

"Sixty percent. It's a very prominent celestial threat, sir," said Oko.

"I'll take that chance," he said.

But Terris made a raspberry sound. "It's not your choice to make, mister. The Hansa won't risk hundreds of thousands of colonists because some old fart won't move to a different rock. If there was even a one percent chance, we'd still take action."

Elias lurched to his feet and knocked his coffee off the table, spilling it onto the deck. "I don't believe your orbital calculations."

The captain remained seated despite his outburst. She folded her hands together, pushing them through the floating diagram above the tabletop. "The orbital calculations don't care whether or not you believe in them, Mr. Sandoval. The science exists, regardless of your opinion."

She projected a picture of Serendipity with specific red zones marked on its pockmarked surface. "We can deploy low-yield warheads here and here. The energy from those detonations will give the rock a gentle push. However, Serendipity is so riddled with voids and lower-density ices that precise calculations are difficult. We can't take any chances with so many lives at stake."

Elias remained fixated on his original argument. "But you can't just come in here and do this. You have no right! The Roamer clans are independent." He lifted his chin. "The Hansa always walks all over us."

"This has nothing to do with Roamers or the Terran Hanseatic

League," Oko said. "It's about gravity and orbits. It's about saving all those people."

"What about my needs? Serendipity is my home, and you're trespassing. I don't grant you permission."

Terris muttered, "Told you he'd be trouble."

"You can't just come here and do what you want," Elias said. "I have my rights."

"Society has a greater right, Mr. Sandoval. Your freedom cannot come at the cost of all those colonists. We have to come down on the side of the greater good."

"It's not my greater good," Elias said. "What happened to my liberty?"

"Oh, get your head out of your ass," Terris growled. "Your liberty does not erase your obligations to the rest of human society. If you recklessly endanger the lives of others, then you forfeit your right to liberty. Selfish prick."

Elias's nostrils flared as he drew in a deep breath wondering if this was going to come to blows.

Oko's eyes widened. "Terris, no—not yet!"

Sensing danger, Elias saw that the other man had pulled out a stunner. "Don't you—"

Then a wave of blue light smothered his thoughts and consciousness.

—V—

When he clawed himself back to awareness, Elias felt sweaty and bedraggled, worse than the hangover he'd once suffered after being duped into buying a bottle of high-proof algae-based moonshine. His lips were swollen, and his tongue was thick as he tried to speak. "What the—?"

When he lifted his hand, it came to an abrupt stop. A plastic restraint clipped his wrist to the side of a chair. "By the Guiding Star …" He looked around, but the world was still swimming.

Terris was there smiling at him. "Well, good morning, sleepyhead. Don't expect me to cook you breakfast."

"Leave him be," Captain Oko snapped. "We're putting him through enough as it is."

"His own damn fault."

"No, it's not his fault," said Oko. "He picked the wrong rock to squat on—that's not a crime. But you know what the old philosopher said." She put her hands on her narrow hips and looked directly at Elias. "'The needs of the many outweigh the needs of the few. Or the one.'"

"Must sound like a good justification to you," Elias said. "Throughout history, powerful people make up excuses and emergencies so they can take whatever they damn well want. Eminent domain! My asteroid's in the way. Just nuke it so it's no longer your problem. Sorry for the inconvenience." He felt nauseated.

"Inconvenience!" Terris was exasperated. "It's a whole colony planet, a complete ecosystem, cities full of settlers!"

Interrupted, the captain touched the comm at her ear and acknowledged. She turned to them. "All set. The engineers have anchored and installed two warheads at the appropriate places. They surveyed weak zones and potential fracture points in the asteroid. Serendipity is like a cracked egg, there's no telling whether or not it'll hold together. We're doing our best, Mr. Sandoval. Honest."

"And then what?" Elias said, yanking the restraint again. "You're just going to hold me prisoner, force me to watch?"

Terris snorted. "You can look away if you want."

Oko shot her partner an annoyed glance. "Because of the potential hazards, you will not be allowed to stay during the blast. We have to take you to a safe distance, but you should be able to return here soon after the detonations. Salvage what you can—if that's what you'd like to do."

Elias felt deep anguish. Even if Serendipity didn't break apart, the warhead explosions would be like swinging a bag of light bulbs mixed with rocks. The infinitely fragile crystals would be destroyed. "You'll wreck everything. I refuse. I'm staying here. This is my home." He swallowed. "I'll take my chances."

"Sorry, can't allow you to do that," she said.

"You have no authority over me! You can't force me to—"

Her extra patience had finally run out. "It is your right to be stubborn and stupid, Mr. Sandoval, but I will not have your blood on my hands. My crew are good people, and they've done their work like true professionals. The warheads will go off as scheduled.

We will alter the course of asteroid 1013X1 and guarantee the future of the Portnoy colonists."

"But this is my home," he pleaded again. "Let me at least grab a few things." Hope swelled within him. "Give me an hour, maybe two. Just a few personal items, things I can't replace."

Oko looked sympathetic, but Terris rolled his eyes. "Captain, he's just going to barricade himself inside, and then we'll have a standoff situation, probably end up leaving him behind anyway."

Oko turned a hard gaze toward Elias. "Is that what you're going to do, Mr. Sandoval?"

The thought had not actually occurred to him. "No."

"Or what if he takes his ship and does a kamikaze run on the site? It's not a good idea, Captain," Terris insisted.

"That's not what I intend," Elias said in a low voice.

The captain considered for a long moment and nodded. "You can have one hour, Mr. Sandoval. Pack up whatever you can take with you, but Terris is right—I'll keep you away from the controls of your ship until the warheads have successfully detonated. You'll ride here with me and my engineers. Terris can fly your craft to a safe distance, and we will return it to you as soon as you're allowed back in the vicinity."

"I don't want him flying my ship," Elias said.

"You don't want us to blow up the warheads either, but today isn't your day." Her reservoir of patience had completely run dry. "Go get what you need, sir. One hour."

After Elias cycled through the airlock of his front entrance, he removed his helmet to inhale the dusty, metallic scent of his tunnels, his home. He felt impossibly weary and helpless. Yes, he could just seal the door and bury himself, become an indignant martyr when the collapsing walls buried him in a rain of diamond-like crystals.

Or maybe he would survive after all. He wondered if he had better than a sixty percent chance.

With trembling knees, feeling as if every moment was a held breath, he walked down corridors filled with treasures that no one would ever know. He was surrounded by a blizzard of prisms, wondrous icicles of petrified light. With his rock hammer, he had time to collect only the best of them.

Elias Sandoval got to work.

—VI—

Even with the antigrav handle, the large case had plenty of mass and momentum, and Elias wrestled it carefully out of his exit hatch and across the asteroid's loose surface. He made his way to the main Hansa ship, where one of the exosuited surveyors helped him carry it onboard.

She grunted with the unwieldy mass. "Prized possessions? What are you taking with you? A neutron star or something?"

His heart felt heavier than the load. "Just some things I need—things I refuse to let your atomic blast destroy."

"Sorry," the surveyor said in a cowed voice. "There must be a thousand asteroids in the Portnoy Belt. Just damn bad luck you picked this one."

When they were aboard with the hatch sealed, Elias made his way to the pilot deck. Captain Oko gave him a quick glance, then turned back to her preparations.

"Countdown's started, Captain," said one of the engineers.

The words filled Elias with both anger and despair. "There's no stopping it."

"Correct," the captain agreed. "But with any luck, the blast won't damage your asteroid—just bump it out of the way. Look at those craters. Serendipity has shrugged off impacts before. You can go back home, do a little housecleaning, and everything will be back to normal before you know it."

He still felt violated. He had never meant to get into a dispute, had done nothing that should have put him in the center of such turmoil. Elias wasn't responsible for the colonists on Portnoy, didn't want to think about them. But no one had asked for his opinion.

Intellectually, he could understand the obvious choice. He was just one old man who wanted to be left alone, but he had settled down on a cannonball that was hurtling toward an inhabited world. Even if he somehow drove off the Hansa engineers, he still would have had to leave Serendipity in twenty-seven years or so … or he could have gambled on the forty percent chance that there would be no impact at all.

He didn't feel particularly lucky, though.

Adding to the insult, he watched his own ship launch from the pockmarked surface, guided by Terris. The man transmitted in a gruff voice from the piloting deck, "What a piece of junk! I hope I don't have a hull breach."

Elias retorted under his breath, "Just don't leave any disease on my pilot controls."

The two Hansa ships detached from their anchors and drifted away from Serendipity. Before long, they had retreated far enough away that the asteroid looked like an oblong potato drifting in space.

"We're at minimum safe distance, Captain," said one of the engineers.

Oko nodded, staring out the windowport. "They're low-yield devices. This is good enough so we can watch."

Elias didn't particularly want to watch, but he could not tear his eyes away as the countdown dwindled to zero.

Twin flares of intense white light blossomed from the long axis of Serendipity, and the polarization film darkened the view. He winced, feeling physical pain as he imagined the sledgehammer blow to the crystal-encrusted labyrinth. He feared that the entire fragile asteroid, with so many fractures, tunnels, and voids, would just break apart into rubble.

But when the glare died down, he heard Captain Oko sigh. "You're in luck, Mr. Sandoval. Your home looks intact." She added a relieved chuckle. "I was afraid we'd see a bunch of drifting gravel." She wiped an imagined wrinkle from her jacket. "We'll transfer you back to your ship. You can go home, and we'll never bother you again."

His eyes burned, and his vision was blurry. He could not find an appropriate answer for her. Instead, he kept staring at the rolling rock in space where the glow from the unleashed energy had dimmed to faint embers.

The two detonation spots would leave craters larger than Martha and Beatrice, permanent scars. But he was more worried about the scars and the damage done internally.

"Just let me go home," he said.

—VII—

He felt exhausted, abused, and wrung out by the time he entered through the main hangar dock. After watching the two Hansa ships depart, paying no more attention to a pathetic old Roamer, he had limped back to Serendipity. Captain Oko and her survey engineers hadn't bothered to look inside his asteroid.

The captain probably thought she had saved the world and done a good thing. The others had simply done their jobs. The Portnoy colonists would certainly applaud them, breathe a sigh of relief that the decades-distant problem was solved. They would never think about Elias Sandoval or his private asteroid again.

At least that was his hope.

His ship was still loaded with the supplies he had purchased at Rendezvous, even the fresh fruit in the supply bins. It seemed like years in the past. After leaving the Roamer complex, he had intended to go home and just live quiet and undisturbed.

If there was anything left for him there.

Moving with great trepidation, he entered his tunnels, his sanctuary. He thought of the cathedral of crystals, the shimmering snowflake growths in every cranny, starbeams captured in human tears.

The inside of Serendipity looked like a smashed hall of mirrors. The shock wave from the nuclear blasts had wrenched corridor after corridor, shattering the ethereal growths. The floor was littered with cracked prisms, broken spikes, sharp fragments. Detached crystals were piled knee-deep, and he groaned to think of the months—years—of work it would take for him just to clear the debris.

He got the generator working, and activated the heaters, life support, and oxygen generators. In a few hours the interior pressure had built up enough that he could remove his exosuit.

Weeping, he looked at the overwhelming wreckage and struggled to grasp hope rather than wallow in the loss. After clearing the rubble, he could sell even the broken Serendipity crystals for a fortune, enough to buy his own small planet, if he wanted.

But what he wanted was solitude, a place like Serendipity. And so he had to do it all himself. He could get the resources he needed.

He had created this home in the first place, and he could do it again. After all, he had salvaged the most important, the rarest ingredient.

Finally, he opened his heavy, sealed cargo container, raised the lid, and looked inside, smiling with wonder.

In the one hour Captain Oko had given him, he'd excavated the one tiny proteus spark, carving out the rock around it, like digging out a shrub to be transplanted. Carefully preserved, the glowing blip looked like an ember nested in the glittering, sharp prongs of new crystals that had grown in only the past few hours. The spark was still alive—if it was actually alive at all.

Elias would place this rock at the end of an empty tunnel and let the proteus ember keep burning, keep laying down its trail of diamond growths, and he would be here to shepherd it along. Soon enough, the glitter would return.

Mike Resnick has won a ton of awards, more than any other writer in the science fiction field. I've had a lot of bestsellers. Mike wanted to learn how to think like a bestselling author, while I wanted to get awards attention. It seemed we had excellent reasons to collaborate.

Another bucket-list item for me, even though I'd had well over a hundred stories published, was to break into Asimov's Science Fiction Magazine, *a holy grail in any SF writer's career. Mike was published there countless times, so I was sure that might increase my odds.*

I learned a lot from Mike when writing this. When we settled on the idea for this story, I immediately sent him an outline for how I thought "Prevenge" should go—the opening scene, beginning, middle, and end, with twists and interesting developments. Mike wrote back explaining that while my outline was great, I had mapped out a novel, not a short story! He proceeded to rein in the idea as a story, *a hybrid of both our ideas. We wrote "Prevenge," which we both thought was a winner.*

And, yes, Asimov's *still turned it down! So we published it in* Analog *instead. (It wasn't until "The Hind," which appears later in this volume, that I did achieve my bucket-list item.)*

PREVENGE

(with Mike Resnick)

It wasn't the murders themselves that broke his heart. They weren't permanent. He had the ability to un-do something as simple and straightforward as a murder.

No, the maddening part was that people never stopped *trying*. Why was the total, cold-blooded obliteration of a human life the preferred problem-solving method for so many men and women? It offended his deep moral sense.

His name was Kyle Bain, and he and the other members of the Knights Temporal had to make things *right*, either before or after the fact.

Kyle couldn't help wondering about the killers whose crimes he was assigned to negate. *You had a good start in life, you had money, education, opportunity. Where did it all go wrong?*

Or you—you had love, and now you'll never have it again. Do you know what a rare gift you threw away, just like you'd throw out the garbage every morning?

Or this current case: Vincent Draconis, a major industrialist who controlled an empire on three continents. He had been/would be murdered in one unguarded moment, leaving a widow and three fatherless children. The confusion in the aftermath would cost almost twenty thousand people their jobs. So much suffering.

That couldn't be allowed. It was a situation made to order for the Knights Temporal....

Kyle arrived in the afternoon, ten hours before the murder was due to occur. According to the file, Draconis was going to be shot down in cold blood just before midnight while working late at his office. Even without witnesses, the man immediately fingered for the crime was Jason Bechtold, vice president of one of Draconis's companies.

Dressed just like the hundreds of other businessmen entering Bechtold's suite of offices, Kyle gained access to the correct, bustling floor. If he followed Bechtold as he left for the day, he could be there later on in time to deflect the murder. A simple enough job, one for which he was well trained.

The Knights Temporal had been founded by Harvey Bloom, a name that hardly seemed destined to go down in history, though Bloom had already placed his name in a thousand alternate histories, maybe more. A theoretical mathematician, Bloom spent the first half of his professional life finding the secrets hidden in Einstein's Special Theory of Relativity, and the second half acting upon them.

Bloom was also a moralist, more interested in Doing Good than in Making A Fortune. Instead of taking out patents or using his privately-funded "temporal displacement" work to study the past, Bloom knew in his bones that he had an obligation to right wrongs. And the most unforgivable wrong, commandment number one, was Thou shalt not kill. When he recruited 25 Right-Thinking young men and women to be his crusaders, he made sure they all shared his moral values.

Thou shalt UN-kill, whenever possible.

After reviewing the file of Vincent Draconis's murder, Kyle waited and watched. When Bechtold emerged from his office late in the day, Kyle discreetly followed him out of the building, then in a cab, to where the executive met an elegantly dressed young woman at an expensive restaurant; they kissed, and a head waiter led them to a table.

Kyle holed up in a coffee shop across the street, nursing his small coffee and nibbling a cheese Danish. After an hour he could sense some irritation from the waitress, so he tipped her twenty dollars to leave him alone. He knew that right now, in the restaurant across the street, Jason Bechtold must be planning the murder of his boss, though he didn't seem particularly agitated. *Cool customer.*

Establishing an alibi.

Kyle would block him before he could get to Draconis's office late at night. A subtle intervention was best, and if done properly no one would even notice. Waiting too long, cutting too close to the murder event, often raised awkward questions and suspicions.

Bechtold and his lady emerged from the restaurant at ten, and Kyle hastily tagged along, invisible in the street crowds. The woman was swaying slightly as they casually entered a five-star hotel. Nothing in the executive's behavior gave any hint of his murderous intent.

According to the file, Bechtold's defense was that he'd spent the night with this woman in room 2145. If she was sound asleep—from a tranquilizer slipped in her drink, perhaps?—and Bechtold was back in bed before she woke up in the morning, she'd corroborate his story.

After giving them ample time to reach the room (considering the way the lady was hanging on Bechtold's arm, Kyle didn't think the executive would be leaving soon) he rode the elevator up to the 21st floor and posted himself a few feet from the door to 2145. He sat down on the corridor's plush carpeting, and waited. And waited.

And waited.

Past time for the murder. Kyle hadn't done anything at all; had he somehow intervened without knowing it? He knew Bechtold was still in the hotel room, but Draconis was supposed to be dead by now.

He took a cab and raced to the industrialist's office. The door was locked, but any Knight Temporal had the experience and tools needed to bypass security systems, no matter how sophisticated they might be.

When he opened the door, he stared down at the corpse of Vincent Draconis. Shot in the head, with blood pooling on the plush new carpet.

This was Kyle's 35th case, 27 of which had been successes. On seven occasions Time, or Fate, or God, or some combination of them, had conspired to prevent history from being changed. But Kyle wasn't finished yet.

If a Knight Temporal couldn't prevent the murder, he was authorized to use his own judgment. He could give up and go back home, he could try again to prevent it—or, as a last resort, he could give the victim an opportunity to take preventive action. *Prevenge.*

Only twice in all of his cases had Kyle resorted to that option. With the greatest reluctance, he had allowed the victim to kill his would-be murderer, before the fact.

Now that he knew Bechtold wasn't the guilty party after all, Kyle turned to the most distasteful aspect of his job: He would have to *watch* the murder happen, and work backward from there.

Turning away from the corpse, he studied the office, discarding various hiding places. The coat closet looked small and cramped, and crouching behind the large decoy safe (the real one was behind a painting in the outer office) felt too exposed. Kyle chose Draconis's private bathroom as the best place to observe. He pulled the door almost shut, leaving only a narrow gap. From here, he could see both the office door and the desk.

He pulled out his PDA-lookalike temporal transformer, programmed in the proper coordinates—and promptly experienced the moment of dizziness that accompanied each brief jump. When the fog cleared from his brain he checked his watch: 11:25 PM.

Through the crack in the door, he could see a very-much-alive Draconis pulling up various screens of information on his computer and taking an occasional sip from the highball on his desk. He hoped the man wouldn't need to use the bathroom before the time of the murder. Explaining his presence wouldn't be easy, and Kyle preferred not to use his ace-in-the-hole proofs if he didn't have to.

Five minutes passed, then fifteen. Not long now. Draconis didn't look the least bit worried. So, the killing was going to be totally unexpected.

An elderly woman entered the office, pushing a cart filled with towels, rags, brushes, feather dusters, and cleaning fluids. Her hair was gray, her face heavily lined; osteoporosis and long years of hard work bent her over.

Draconis never glanced up from his computer, grumbling about his spreadsheets. The cleaning woman didn't seem to exist for him, and he paid no attention when she locked the office door. Kyle's eyes were wide as the old woman reached into an empty bucket and withdrew a handgun.

"Look up, Vincent," she said harshly.

He finally bothered to notice her. "Who the hell are you?"

"You really don't know, do you?"

He saw the gun. "If this is some kind of joke..."

"This is no joke, Vincent. I'm going to kill you."

He gave her a withering look, showing no fear at all. "Who *are* you?"

"You have all eternity in hell to figure it out." She pulled the trigger.

Kyle had not expected her to act so swiftly, so coldly. He didn't have a chance to intervene. Already too late! Two strikes in one night. He made no sound in his hiding place. If the woman panicked and shot *him*, he'd have no way to slip back in time and prevent his own murder.

Draconis lay in a bloody mess on the new carpet. Moving in a daze, as if wondering whether she should clean the office after all, the old woman unlocked the door and slipped away.

Stunned, Kyle wasn't sure what to do next. Now that he knew the real killer, he needed to find the woman's name and address. He had less than fifteen minutes before a night security guard was due to discover the body, and the place would be crawling with cops.

He needed more time to plunder the files, and fortunately he could buy all the time in the world. Without leaving the office, Kyle made the calculations and adjustments and jumped back a few days.

The cleaning woman was Bertha Gilligan, age 63, widowed, mother of one. She'd applied for a job as a night cleaning woman less than a month ago—clearly with the intent of killing Draconis.

Late at night, when Bertha was at work, Kyle slipped off to her dingy room in what could only be called a flophouse. He needed to learn something about her.

Two small cats greeted him, purring and rubbing against his legs. He saw the opened can of cheap generic cat food covered by plastic wrap with a teaspoon next to it. Two open cans on the floor were for the cats; this other can must have been for Bertha herself. The kitchenette had no refrigerator, only a hot plate; the shelves contained a few packets of dirt-cheap ramen noodle soup and one box of off-brand macaroni and cheese.

On the nightstand he found a row of medication bottles. Pills for pain, pills for depression, pills for half a dozen serious physical ailments. Behind the bottles was an extensive photo display of a lovely blonde woman in her mid-twenties. The cleaning woman's daughter?

A battered wooden table doubled as a desk. One leg was shorter than the others, propped up with a paperback book. On it were a scrapbook and a notebook. Kyle couldn't have asked for more.

The scrapbook began with a few news items about one Edward Gilligan, a distinguished-looking man, graying at the temples, with frameless glasses and a thin mustache, a natty dresser. He'd created some nearly frictionless compound the experts estimated would extend the life of heavy machinery by 50%.

Kyle kept thumbing through the book, and the tenor of the news items changed. Vincent Draconis had managed a hostile takeover of Gilligan's company, appropriated the formula, and fired Gilligan. Gilligan had sued, but Draconis had the best lawyers and (it was implied) owned the judge; Gilligan had not only lost, but went broke in the process. The last page was an announcement of the untimely passing of Edward Gilligan, who had taken his own life.

Next, the notebook consisted of a series of letters, all of them addressed to Draconis, all signed by a Naomi Gilligan—no doubt the blonde girl in the photos. She accused Draconis of persecuting her father; she pleaded with him, she argued with him, she threatened him. The dates on the letters abruptly ended three months ago.

Kyle neatly replaced both books, finished his examination of the room, and left.

Later, at a library terminal, he scanned internet records and news databases for Naomi Gilligan. He wasn't surprised to find her obituary in an eleven-week-old paper. She'd been beaten to death in an apparent mugging.

Following the trail, he used his device and jumped back to the night of Naomi's murder. She was found dead in the park, her head staved in. From the position of the body and lack of blood on the scene, it was obvious even to a clumsy amateur detective that she had been killed elsewhere, and her body dumped out here. Considering that Naomi's purse —with money and credit cards intact—turned up in a trash can about a mile away, Kyle had more than enough reason to doubt the simple "mugging" explanation.

Bodies went to the coroner, not the police station, but cops talked. He posted himself at the district station and kept his ears open. Within a few hours, jumping back and forth with his temporal adjuster, he had all the information he was going to get.

When the crime lab dusted Naomi's purse for prints, the mood in the station changed. Kyle overheard one of the cops whisper "Vincent Draconis!" and they all looked scared as hell. Somebody phoned Draconis to tell him that they had a little problem and he'd better come down to the station. Obviously it was payoff time.

Why hadn't one of the Knights Temporal been sent back to prevent Naomi's murder? But Kyle knew the answer: Harvey Bloom simply didn't have enough manpower, and he had to choose the crimes with the most impact ... one of the few concessions he made to his otherwise rigid moral code.

Kyle cut off those thoughts before he could start to obsess on the conundrum. Preventing Naomi's murder wasn't his assignment. Like it or not, his assignment was Vincent Draconis.

Back to the night of the murder, one more time.

Bertha showed up for work at nine o'clock. What he'd learned certainly explained why she wanted to kill the man who had ruined her husband and murdered her daughter. But Kyle was not a judge; he despised "situational morality," people who changed their minds with the blowing of the wind. The law was a framework, not a convenient set of suggestions.

According to her established habit, Bertha took her break at eleven; doubtless that was when she planned to plant the gun in the bucket. Kyle waited until she went to the small lunch room. He watched her moving more mechanically than usual, stumbling through the motions. When she sagged into a plastic chair and poured herself watery coffee from a thermos, Kyle carefully, silently, locked the break room door so that she wouldn't be able to leave for her murderous rendezvous. He posted himself just outside the room, ready to accost her if she somehow managed to get out.

But the door remained locked. He didn't even hear her rattling to get out. Finally, at a quarter to twelve, he slipped upstairs to make sure that Draconis was still working at his desk. The straightforward delay should have been enough to derail the killing. Case closed, mission accomplished.

But Vincent Draconis was sprawled on the floor, blood still seeping out of the fatal wound in his head, still ruining the carpet.

Kyle groaned when he discovered that the break room had a second door, which Bertha had used.

His next attempt to prevent the murder was to confront Bertha directly in the break room—but for whatever reason, she went straight upstairs and killed Draconis. Again.

This was getting complicated, one of those cases that seemed jinxed, as if Fate didn't want it to be fixed. For reasons that no Knight Temporal understood, certain actions simply couldn't be diverted.

Poor Bertha's only sin was to have married a man who'd stood in the path of a steamroller named Vincent Draconis. Her daughter had stood up for fairness and justice, and she had been killed. Bertha's life had been in a downward spiral, emotionally and physically—going from all the benefits of wealth and culture to that horrible room five blocks away, seeing two loved ones trampled into oblivion by an unethical bastard whose sole virtue was that he was stronger than anyone else.

But Kyle had to stop her. The rules were clear-cut. All Knights Temporal swore an oath. Moral gray areas were for the weak and indecisive, not for the agents of Harvey Bloom.

Kyle realized that his only alternative was to give the victim a chance for prevenge.

"Who the hell are you?" demanded Draconis when Kyle appeared in his office two hours before the scheduled murder event.

"My name is Kyle Bain—"

"Well, get your ass right out of here, Kyle Bain, or I'm calling

Security. In fact, a couple of them are going to get fired for letting you get this far."

"I'm here to save your life tonight."

Draconis made a rude snort. "What are you selling, religion or laxatives?"

"Murder prevention." He had already prepared the way for this man to believe his improbable revelations, planted his ace in the hole. Since Draconis was a secretive man, there were plenty of places Kyle could drop the necessary information—a hidden safe that even his wife and his most trusted aides didn't know about, private notebooks kept under lock and key. One or two "impossible" details would be enough to raise sufficient doubt.

Kyle explained briefly how and why he had come here, not expecting Draconis to believe his crazy time-travel story. "Go to the safe in the outer office. Open the ledger for July of last year. Turn to Page 3."

"What do you know about that safe?"

"Just do it, Mr. Draconis. We haven't got much time. If you try to sound the alarm on her desk, or the one on the way out of this office, I'll leave you to your fate."

Frowning, Draconis seemed about to ask something, then thought better of it. "You've bought yourself a few extra seconds, Mr. Bain. I'm intrigued." Kyle watched him dial the safe's combination, open the door, remove the ledger, and look at Page 3.

"If you need further proof," said Kyle, "call your house and ask your maid or your wife to bring your 1973 diary to the phone and read you the June 15 entry."

"I believe you—or at least I believe your tricks are highly sophisticated," said Draconis, looking down at the totally unexpected note in the ledger. "So, who's going to try to kill me?"

"She's going to do more than *try*, Mr. Draconis. Due to some temporal exclusion in this case, I myself have been unable to stop her. Therefore, it's in your hands. If I don't give you the wherewithal to take your prevenge, she's going to kill you. Tonight."

"All right. Who is she and what has she got against me?"

"We'll come to her name in a few minutes." Now that he knew Bertha, understood her anguish, Kyle felt cagey. "As for her motive, you ruined her husband."

"I've ruined a *lot* of people." Draconis made no attempt to keep the contempt out of his voice. "That's the way the game is played."

"It's the way *you* play it," replied Kyle distastefully.

"And I'm damned good at it. Look around you. I don't just work in this building. I *own* it, all 34 floors of it."

"How many people did you destroy along the way?"

"Business is Darwinian. Clear-cut, black and white. There's meat and there's meat-eaters, nothing in between."

That's what Harvey Bloom always says about murder. It's clear-cut, black and white. To feel sympathy for a killer is an insult to his victims. I wonder what he'd say if he knew how much he sounded like you?

Finally Kyle spoke. "Aren't you forgetting to include bystanders, advocates, families? The woman who's going to kill you has another grievance besides the fact that you ruined her husband."

"Yeah, they all do." Draconis was unimpressed, almost bored. "What's this one's?"

"Her daughter."

"What happened? Did she go into a nunnery?"

"No. Into a morgue."

Draconis shrugged. "Lots of people die. Half of them are somebody's daughters."

"Half of them haven't had their heads staved in by a person with your fingerprints."

Draconis frowned. "Yeah, I read in the papers that Eddie Gilligan's daughter was killed in the park. So tell me this, Hot Shot —if my fingerprints were found, why wasn't I ever charged with anything? I was out of town that week."

"No you weren't. I was at the police station when they contacted you and arranged for the payoff."

"Have fun trying to prove it!"

"It's not my job to prove it. It's my job to prevent Bertha Gilligan from murdering you." He tried to sound firm, convinced. *Even if it'll destroy the last few scraps of her life … and even if you deserve it.* "Your office has new carpet, Mr. Draconis. I guess Naomi bled on the old one? Is this where you killed her, then dumped her body in the park?"

"You're really not a cop, even in the future?"

"I'm really not a cop." *Sometimes I just wish I was.*

"The bitch bled like a sieve." Suddenly he grinned. "She actually thought she could threaten me with a letter opener. Hell, she couldn't have weighed a hundred and ten pounds."

Kyle felt sick. "Why do so many people consider murder an effective solution to their problems? You could have just disarmed her and sent her away. Or reported her to your friends at the police station and gotten a restraining order."

"You think that would stop a psycho girl? She'd come back with a gun the next time. Anyone who threatens me had better make good on that threat, because I don't give second chances."

"The Darwinian rule of threats?"

"Yeah, now that you put it that way."

"I consider myself a moral man, Mr. Draconis. Law and ethics are the glue that hold our civilization together. Justice is blind, and murder is wrong. My job is supposed to be simple. *You* make it complicated."

Draconis looked at him with a sneer. "Oh, you're one of *those* types."

"I assume you short-change your partners, lie to your friends, cheat on your wife, and stiff the government on taxes." Kyle sighed wearily. "It's all Darwinian, when you get right down to it."

Draconis took a sip from the highball on his desk. "You don't like me much, do you?"

"Does anyone?"

"Probably not. But they sure as hell respect me."

"I think it's more likely that they fear you."

"Same thing." Draconis shrugged. "Look, Hot Shot, you just concentrate on keeping me alive and I'll take care of you. Vincent Draconis always pays for services rendered."

Except when you can get away with not paying. Aloud, Kyle said, "Doing my job well is payment enough."

There was a long silence. Finally Draconis broke it. "So what do we do now?"

"Now we wait. She'll be here soon, and you'll have to prevent your own murder."

"You're telling me Eddie Gilligan's used-up widow is going to sneak past all my security and try to kill me?" He let out a contemptuous laugh.

"She won't have to sneak past anyone. She has every right to be here."

Draconis frowned for a moment, then looked up. "Cleaning service, right?"

"That's right."

"What's she like?"

"Probably like a thousand other people you wouldn't recognize by sight. She's been beaten down by circumstances—circumstances of your making. She's lost the two people she cares for, she's destitute, she's taking medication for pain and for depression, she lives in a dump, and she has only one goal left in her life—to kill you."

"That's *her* misfortune. No one will miss her, any more than they miss Eddie or her daughter. They're the roadkill of history. It'll be like she never existed." He picked up his highball glass, realized it was empty, and put it back down on his desk. "You know, I always figured if anyone had the brains and guts to take me out, it'd be Jason Bechtold. I keep the bastard under surveillance every minute he's near me."

"It just goes to show that you can't choose your killer any more than you can choose your family. Hell, they're lined up around the block to kill you. In fact, even if you stop her, that just means someone else with every bit as much reason to hate you will take you out next week or next month. And then I'll have this same case dumped in my lap again. Maybe it's just not worth the effort to stop your killer."

"Quit calling her my killer," he added irritably. "She's my *would-be* killer, and she's about to become a piece of dead meat. Now, how does this work? You called it prevenge, so I assume I get to take my own pre-revenge and kill the bitch myself. Self defense. You're just an interested bystander?"

"That's correct."

"So give me a gun. Or do I have to take care of that myself?"

"I have a gun for you—when the time comes. I've tried to prevent this three times, and it keeps happening. So no matter what I do, it looks like *someone's* going to get killed here tonight."

"You afraid I'll shoot you too?" Draconis seemed amused.

"I wouldn't put it past you," admitted Kyle.

"Why would I do something like that?"

Because it's your nature. Aloud, he said, "I'm a witness, and who's going to believe a story about a guardian angel from the future?"

"Then we sit and wait," said Draconis. "Just stay close enough that you can pass me the gun when the time comes."

Kyle pulled a leather chair next to the desk, sat down, and stared at the door. Right on schedule, Bertha Gilligan entered the room behind her pushcart. She seemed surprised to see two men confronting her.

"Hello, Bertha," said Kyle.

"You know my name?"

"I know a lot more than that. I know what you plan to do, and it's my job to stop you from killing him. Scum like Draconis aren't worth one second of prison time."

"I don't care about what happens afterward." Her face reflected her hatred. "You don't know what he did to my husband and my little girl."

"I know."

Startled, Bertha reached into the bucket and pulled out her gun. "You think my Naomi is the only person he ever murdered or had killed? You think my Eddie is the only man he ever hounded to the grave?"

"I know they're not."

"Stop talking and give me the goddamned gun!" yelled Draconis.

"Then why do you want to save him?" she asked.

"I'm not saving *him*, Bertha," said Kyle gently. "I'm saving *you*. You've suffered enough."

You were wrong, Harvey. The world's not black and white. It's 23 shades of gray. In fact, you were wrong about a lot of things. Sometimes it's an insult to the murderer to feel sympathy for his victim.

"My suffering doesn't matter," said Bertha. "He's got to die." She swung her gun, aiming at Draconis.

"He will," promised Kyle.

"How?"

"Like *this*." Kyle pulled his pistol and fired point-blank at Draconis's head.

"Jesus!" Bertha stared in rapt fascination as the man fell to the floor in the identical position that Kyle had initially seen him. "Jesus!"

"Get out of here, Bertha. He's dead. You have a life to live."

"Not much of one," she answered bitterly.

"If you don't make the most of it, then even in death he's won. Are you going to let a scumbag like that beat you even after he's been shot and killed?"

"Who *are* you?" she asked suddenly.

"I'm the man who just gave you back the rest of your life. Don't make an Indian giver out of me. Go home and think about it. Security will be here any moment, and the cops won't be far behind."

"What about you?" she asked.

"I'll be fine. Now leave!"

She stared at him, then pushed her cart into the hallway and over to the elevator.

Kyle left the gun behind, covered with his own clear fingerprints (which, thanks to Harvey Bloom and a few simple jaunts back in time, were not in any database). That way, nobody would accuse Bertha, and of course Bechtold's alibi would hold up. When he heard the running footsteps of a security guard running down the hall, he pulled out his temporal transformer, went forward to his own time, and walked out of the empty office.

Now *he* was a murderer. Even if the case baffled the cops, the Knights Temporal would solve it easily enough. Would Harvey Bloom order his termination? He couldn't imagine any circumstance under which Bloom wouldn't order his death.

But Bloom had a problem. Every Knight Temporal was a moralist, just as he was. Kyle wouldn't make any effort to hide from them. He'd simply explain the situation, the events that led to his action, and bet his life that they would understand. Situational ethics? Some of the Knights, he was sure, would volunteer to stay in the past and protect him from more of Bloom's operatives.

And then he was going to present Bloom with the same moral conundrum he himself had just faced … because even if one did manage to kill him, wouldn't Bloom's own rules allow him to take his own prevenge?

The thought brought an amused smile to his lips.

As you've probably noticed by now, I do a lot of writing in collaboration. I enjoy the brainstorming, interaction, and learning. Collaborative stories turn out different from anything either writer would produce by themselves.

Since I have been married to Rebecca for more than three decades, our whole careers have been a collaboration, too. We've written dozens of novels together, and we often brainstorm even our solo projects together. So it seemed natural to do a collaborative story about collaborators in a high-tech future. We wrote this one after we'd been married several years and the rough edges and loose ends of our pre-"Kevin and Rebecca" lives had pretty much faded away, and we started to notice how our individual parts had melded inextricably together.

Of course, in a short story that isn't always a good thing.

COLLABORATORS

(with Rebecca Moesta)

Tara held the second cable in her hand as she crept behind her husband in the dim light of the den; but he was already jacked in, impervious to all distractions.

Chandler lay slouched back in his battered college-salvage chair like a marionette with severed strings, his face slack, eyes REMing behind the translucent sheaths of his lids as he wrestled with his commissioned VR art. From his sighs, fidgety spasms, and general restlessness, she could tell he was blocked again.

Chandler always kept his art to himself, reluctant to talk about it until he finished, even when she offered herself as a sounding board for ideas. But this time Tara would surprise him—or piss him off. Either way, she hoped Chandler would get out from under the creative block that had been smothering him. If she could just help him get over the hump ...

Without his knowledge, Tara had installed the black-market splitter behind the wall plate. Now she could jack into the same data stream and help him directly, a true meeting of minds.

She stared at the viper-prongs of the cable in her hand, then mounted it in the socket at the base of her skull. Still moving quietly, she pried off the wall plate and squinted to see the bright silver end of the splitter's input port, a shunt piggybacked onto the main cable. She had never used a splitter before, never even *seen* one. But Fizzwilly had promised it would work.

Chandler's fingers twitched on the worn maroon fabric of the overstuffed chair, as if searching for something to clench.

By jacking in, Tara could see what was bugging him, help him work through the problem. She had purchased the illegal device from her former friend Fizzwilly, who was technically still on the run. It was still prototype hardware, he said, not completely certified, but that didn't mean the splitter wasn't useful. She decided to take the risk, if only to get closer to her husband.

Chandler, unaware of her presence in the dim workroom, continued breathing fast and shallow, butterfly wings in his lungs. His eyes looked sunken, lost in a nest of shadows, and his milky skin seemed paler than usual. His red-gold hair hung lank over the interface cable. In her mind, Tara caught a glimpse of what he would look like as an unhappy middle-aged man.

Before marrying Chandler two years before, Tara had spent plenty of time jacked into virtual environments. Her friends, "the wrong crowd," had sharpened their claws by rerouting legal shipments to illegal chop-shops, altering financial transactions out to many decimal places. Tara had held herself on the fringe, amusing herself by diddling with her own grades and records at the Virtual University, not because she was unable to complete the classes herself, but because she was impatient to begin doing the "real stuff." She'd had her heart set on a career as an architect or an archaeologist, not as an electronic scam artist.

But when the heat came down and they all got caught, Tara had been stripped of her degree, barred from ever working as anything higher than a grunt at a sprawling architectural firm, and denied all access to genuine archaeological sites; the others stumbled into jail, and Fizzwilly became a fugitive.

Chandler had saved her, dragged her back onto the straight-and-narrow; and now, with her own future as an architect slammed shut in her face, Tara felt like an outsider watching Chandler's career explode as he created virtual worlds for purchase by anyone rich enough to own a simulation chamber.

But Tara still knew how to find Fizzwilly, and he had gotten the splitter for her. No questions asked.

Right now Chandler needed her. She plugged the second cable into the splitter.

With a sigh, she felt herself being dragged down, vanishing with a virtual echo into a whirlpool where Chandler was working. She would join him in his mind, in his imaginary universe.

In Chandler's world the rain fell, the flowers bloomed, and exotic birds preened their iridescent plumage.

There, and yet not there, Tara's ghost image stared at his Eden. Sapphire-winged butterflies danced above brilliant orchids. The trees seemed ready to collapse from the weight of foliage so bright and rich it looked lacquered. Droplets of dew sparkled in the sunlight that penetrated the canopy. The sounds of insects and birds and unseen small animals rustling through the underbrush made the silence deeper. Everything seemed perfect, a paradise.

Tara felt like an intruder.

Chandler's image stood staring up a tall tree, fingering a thick, ropy vine. He appeared to be deep in thought, perplexed.

"So … when exactly is the deadline?" she asked, hoping not to startle him too much.

Chandler whirled, dissolving into static at the edges, then snapping back to focus. "Tara! What are you doing here? How—?"

She pressed her lips together as she worked up her nerve. Chandler had always called that her most endearing expression.

"A splitter. Don't ask where I got it. I just thought you needed a fresh point of view." She looked away, then crossed her arms over her small breasts. "Let me help, Chandler. I want to do work that *means something* again!"

Chandler stood frozen in his rain forest, as if trying to put together pieces of an invisible puzzle. "But splitters—"

"They're perfectly safe," she said, tossing her black hair over her shoulder in an impatient gesture. "Let's not go on about it, okay? When is your deadline?"

Chandler took a moment to collect his thoughts. Always before, he had created his own work, done his best job, and then looked for a company to purchase his virtual environment for their holo chambers. But this time he had taken an assignment, following a client's guidelines rather than his own imagination. Constrained and worried about producing to someone else's specifications, he had stalled.

"The office complex already has the holo rec room constructed for their execs. Occupancy in less than three weeks. If I'm going to make a reputation—"

"Keep your reputation," Tara said.

"—as a reliable professional instead of a flaky VR *artiste*," he waggled his fingers, "I've got to deliver as promised. But I want it to be spectacular, not just serviceable. This could be my big break."

Her ghost went to stand next to his, looking at the details of the thick rain forest. "Then let me help you," she said again. "I might be able to offer a few suggestions. I can take some of the burden." She raised her eyebrows. "Why don't you show me around?"

Chandler gave her the full virtual tour. He started talking about his work, gradually opening up as he pointed at tall weeds, birds, colorful beetles, exotic fungi. She ducked as a bright red macaw swooped low overhead.

"It's good—I can't deny that," he said. "But it's missing something, and I can't figure it. More birds? Different flowers? Right now it's pretty high on the 'So What?' factor. I even tried putting traces of a big fire in the distance to evoke a sense of impending loss and suspense, but you can't see the smoke unless you go up to canopy level, and that's an advanced option."

With his fingertip he selected a cluster of white starlike flowers and moved them to a different location near a weathered old rock. "I've got all the details right, accurate down to the individual leaves. And I'm planning to add the other sensory modules: a light warm breeze, dampness in the air, various scents. It's correct by every measure I can make—but something indefinable just doesn't work."

Tara chose her words carefully, speaking one step behind the thoughts forming in her head. "Let me check out my first impression. The part that makes the Eden myth so poignant is not the paradise itself, but paradise *lost*." Her image gestured at the jungle. "This is too perfect. It needs ... pathos."

She reached up to call down the virtual image palette, linked to her old archaeology databases, and selected a few images to place in the midst of Chandler's jungle. The old boulder transformed into a moss-covered idol, worn half-smooth by centuries of wind and rain.

"Step back," she said, and they zoomed out to observe a larger part of the rain forest. Crumbling ziggurats appeared, tall Mayan pyramids hulking in the jungle, the Temple of the Jaguar, remnants of Tiahuanaco. Vines covered immense carved blocks of dark-gray lava stone while animals and birds nested in the cracks. She included no people, only the mysterious relics of a lost and fallen society.

"The mighty have fallen," she said. "Nature conquers all with the passage of time. Think of that poem 'Ozymandias'—nothing left of the great conqueror except for a weathered old statue in the middle of the desert. It's a sense of loss that tugs at your heartstrings." She stopped speaking, self-conscious, turning to look at him. "So, what do you think? Are you mad at me?"

"No, I'm not mad." His face beamed, no longer a reflection of inexorable middle age, but a return to the boyish exuberance that had drawn her to him a few years ago. "You found the missing ingredient."

Standing together atop an ancient temple, their ghost images looked out across the lush rainforest.

With the success of Chandler's "Lost Rainforest" virtual ecosystem, clients offered him bigger commissions. Tara watched his confidence building, but he kept searching for the best follow-up assignment.

Chandler had always been driven, focused on his creations to the exclusion of the rest of the world, including her. Though they had been dating while she was messing around with Fizzwilly and friends in the network, Chandler had remained oblivious to her other activities, accepting her as just another student. After her troubles with the other hackers, he had been an anchor for her, staying by her. He had refused to let Tara give up in despair at the loss of her degree.

For two years Chandler kept telling her that she would work her way up in an architectural firm, that her talent would open doors for her even with the stain on her record. For him, she tolerated an uninteresting job as an underling for a large firm designing nuevo deco special-interest malls, though it had no future she could see.

But she wanted more, a task she could buy into with the same enthusiasm that came so naturally to Chandler. She wanted to share his passion, to sweat blood and enjoy it....

Tara spent the morning jacked in, walking through 3-D

wireframe displays of design modifications before submitting them to the review board. Dull work. While waiting for Chandler to come home from his luncheon meeting, Tara had cracked open the sliding balcony door, and a breeze drifted in, curling the vertical blinds.

She disconnected when Chandler came home, draping both wrists over his shoulders and tilting her face up to kiss him. She tasted curry and onions, spicy Indian food. A good sign, she thought; the Bengal Dawn Café was expensive, not a restaurant chosen casually by disinterested clients.

Tara could tell by the excitement on his face that he had already made up his mind.

"It's the Grand Canyon," Chandler blurted. "They want me to recreate the Grand Canyon in 'all its grandeur.' Not the *real* canyon, but an idealized and enhanced version, the way it should be. All the strata, all the terrain. And it's big, very big. Not just a slice of rainforest."

Tara tried to share his excitement but did not quite understand. "How can you improve on the Grand Canyon?" she asked. "Isn't the real thing spectacular enough?"

He shook his head, slipped his net-access plaque onto the synthetic marble countertop so he could gesture with his hands. "If they wanted the real thing, they could just set up some beam splitters and a hologram generator and be done with it. They could even massage out the rimside resorts and the roads and the tourists to make it look pristine.

"They want me to use the real canyon as a foundation, but pump up the grandeur, make it so even the stodgiest urban cynic will gasp in awe at nature's majesty. It's been six years since I hiked down into the canyon, and my own memories are rose-tinted with time. *That's* the way I want to portray it."

Chandler held out his hand, tentatively withdrew it in hesitation, then squeezed her own. "Hey, would it be all right if you helped me again? From Day One this time. We can brainstorm with the splitter ... you can help me shape the project before I blunder down blind alleys."

Tara felt as if she had been blindsided, but she leaped at the chance. "Sounds better than checking design mods. But I've never been to the Grand Canyon. Is that going to be a problem?"

"*I* have," he said, shaking his head, and gestured to the den, where the splitter hid behind the wall socket. "And I'll share all the images with you. I can do a direct feed."

Tara grabbed his hand and pulled him toward the workroom before he could change his mind. "Okay, Chandler, take me to the Grand Canyon."

In the den workroom, they both affixed cables to their sockets, joined by the splitter. Tara leaned back, closing her dark eyes and letting a numbing swirl of images flood across to her: stark corkscrewing mesas sliced out by erosion, scrub brush, incredible sunsets like pastel finger-paintings across a huge sky, roiling clumps of thunderheads, close-up strata in ocher and tan and green-gray and vermillion, the muddy violence of the Colorado River, and finally a crisp night full of stars—like the universe crammed into the narrow alley of sky visible up through the canyon's towering walls.

Her mind simply received the data; over the next day or so she would assimilate it, sort it out, and make sense of Chandler's memories.

"There," he said, disconnecting. "You know everything you need to see about the Grand Canyon."

She sighed and smiled and blinked her eyes as the brilliant images continued to whirl across her forebrain. "It's almost like I went with you."

That night as she dreamed, Tara's mind continued to shuffle the memories, unlocking more than Chandler had intended. She heard the crunch of leather hiking boots on the sunbaked trail, felt sweat prickle on her/his hairy arms, saw another woman close by, smiling and panting, sharing swigs from a lukewarm canteen as they paused under a shaded overhang, sleeping naked on top of their zipped-together sleeping bag, making love under the narrow alley of night sky framed by the canyon's towering walls....

Tara sat up abruptly, clammy sweat filming her skin. Beside her Chandler slept wound in a single sheet, the blanket tossed aside. "You went with Celine!" she said.

He jerked awake, blinking his eyes rapidly to focus. He scratched the jack socket at the back of his head. "What?" he said, rubbed his eyes, and looked at her. "What did you say?"

"You went with *Celine* to the Grand Canyon," Tara repeated. "I dreamed it. It must have been tagged to the memories you shared with me. I got the whole experience, not just the edited version you handed over."

Chandler's expression rippled with concern, but not about the same thing. "There must have been some backwash in the transfer. Maybe the splitter—"

"You slept with her!" Tara said, startling herself with her anger. "You told me you were just friends, that she was an 'old college acquaintance' of yours. We've had her over for dinner half a dozen times and you never told me you two were screwing each other!"

Chandler kneaded a lump of the sheets, as if afraid to touch her. "Celine and I *are* just friends. We were only lovers for a week, during that trip, and it didn't work out between us. That was a year before you and I started seeing each other. What does it matter now?"

Tara kept her voice low. "It wouldn't matter, if you had told me. The fact that you kept it a secret means a hell of a lot."

He blinked at her in the wash of streetlight filtering through the blinds. His face passed through a sequence of emotions from confusion to stunned anger that reminded her uncomfortably of how he had looked when she had been charged with altering her Virtual University files. "I'm not the only one who's ever kept secrets," he said.

Tara looked away, stung. "Touché." Chandler squeezed her shoulder, and she was torn between the desire to mollify him and the desire to knock his hand away.

Tara sighed and tried to find words for her emotions. "All right, Chandler. So we've peeked at each other's skeletons in the closet. We're even. But no more secrets, okay? We're married. We exchanged vows, combined our lives, promised to share everything. I don't like secrets. I want to be part of what you're doing."

He climbed out of bed, standing naked in the dim yellowish reflection. "Okay, mea culpa. No more secrets. We share and share alike. Genuine partners, collaborators." With slow, smooth motions, Chandler eased the straps of the sweat-soaked teddy off her shoulders and slid it down her body.

When they made love, tentatively at first, salving the sore spots between them, all Tara could think about was the splitter in the other room … and how it would feel to share bodies while sharing the same mind.

Chandler licensed "The Grandest Canyon" to more than a dozen office complexes. His hazel eyes gleamed as he swept Tara toward the door of their apartment. "Kimba's Steak House tonight," he said, "for a celebration."

For the past two years, they had made a habit of feasting on rich red meat once a month, whether they could afford it or not. Tara enjoyed their special meals, the evenings away from his work, though sometimes their budget had allowed them only a small filet to divide between them. Splitting a steak with Chandler was doubly difficult, since he insisted on eating his meat bloody rare, and she preferred hers medium well; as a result, they settled for medium, leaving neither particularly satisfied.

But tonight they were celebrating, and they would each have the meal of their choice. Tara sucked on a cholesterol-suppressant lozenge and handed one to Chandler as they boarded the transit tube and rode to the steak house.

Chandler talked with her about possibilities as he strode along the sidewalk to Kimba's. He gestured with his hands, walking straighter, more confidently. Tara thought of him slumped in his maroon chair not so long ago, jacked-in and blocked for ideas—she liked the change in him.

They passed through the artificial bamboo gates of Kimba's, next to the stuffed white lion mascot. The receptionist keyed up their reservations and led them to a narrow booth in the back near one of the shimmering fake fireplaces, under the stuffed head of an artificial ibex. Gaudy Zulu shields and long spears hung on the walls, and a soundtrack of throbbing drums and squawking birds came from microspeakers buried in the potted plants.

They called up the familiar menu on the datapad set into the end of the table, punching in their selections. He picked a large porterhouse, she chose a filet mignon. It felt extravagant to select what they *wanted*, rather than what they could afford.

Chandler hunched over the lacquered table, resting his elbows on it as he reached out to her. "I want to show you something," he said. He dipped a hand into his shirt pocket to pull out a deck of newly imprinted plastic wafers, business cards with a magnetic strip containing autodialer information. She recognized the basic logo, but he peeled off one of the wafers and slid it across the table to her.

"I changed the company name from *Chandler Damon, Worldbuilder*, to *Worldbuilders, Inc.* I put your name on the ID strip, too."

He grinned at her, his pale, freckled face looking ruddier in the cast-off light from the imitation fire. She held the plastic card in her hands, rolling the edges against her fingertips, as if afraid they might turn into razors. "You put my name on it?"

Chandler shrugged. "Well, you're going to be a part of it from now on, aren't you? Especially considering the new contract I got offered today—something really spectacular. We're reconstructing ancient Egypt, an interactive diorama environment displaying the creation of the pyramids and the great sphinx. It'll go in one of the top recreational floors in the financial center towers."

"You mean I can quit my other job?"

He shrugged, as if not sure how she would take the news. "Well, you keep telling me how much you hate it."

Before she could find a way to express her delight, the server placed their meals in front of them. Chandler sliced into his dripping red porterhouse, eyeing the meat as if he were a predator. Tara talked with her mouth full, tugging out details of the Egypt project as she let the excitement wash over her.

The filet was delicious, perfectly cooked, but she had already received a far greater treat than the steak could ever be.

A hot sun baked the desert along the Nile. A simulated sky shimmered with the heat, refracted blue glinting off airbrush-smooth sands. Holographic slaves clad in dusty loincloths and rimed with sweat and mud constructed the monumental pyramids as Tara and Chandler worked at constructing the rest of the program.

Chandler's ghost image stood up a level on the pyramid adding details to the animated work crews. The slaves hauled enormous limestone blocks into place, sliding the chunks along mud-slick tree trunks. Chandler looked ridiculous in his guise as a slave driver: arms crossed at his bare chest, legs spread apart, bright white linen wrapped around his waist. He had added a dark Egyptian cast to his normally pale, freckled skin. His red-gold hair hid under a headdress. His lips pressed together as he concentrated, an expression she had not seen him wear before.

He stared down at the work gangs roped together, sweating as they maneuvered their loads up ramps. Working with a palette grid he pulled out of the air, he adjusted their expressions and routines, altering the dirt and details of their rags.

Tara's ghost image walked up one of the slick ramps and clambered across a network of palm-trunk scaffolding to inspect the architectural details. Playing the game, she had dressed her image in the gaudy garb of a Pharaoh's wife, her eyes black and greasy from a layer of kohl, her neck burdened with a necklace of gold and lapis lazuli, her knuckles adorned with scarab rings.

"Hey, Chandler!" she said, raising her voice. Automatically the synthesized sounds of rumbling stone, cracking whips, and shouts of pain damped and faded into the background. "Do we have a revised estimate of the completion date? We're ahead of schedule, aren't we?"

Chandler's image nodded from the other side of the pyramid. His headdress wagged in the bright sun. "I want to emphasize the immensity of this construction, yet leave the impression that it's perpetually in progress. A metaphor for life: constantly building—and no matter how large it gets, you're never actually done. Like La Sagrada Familia, Gaudi's cathedral in Barcelona."

Somehow Tara knew instantly what he meant, though she could not recall ever having heard of the architect Gaudi before. Deep in virtual Egypt, Tara had gotten better at interpreting mental messages from Chandler. They built upon each other's ideas.

The pyramids had gone up with amazing rapidity, with details as sharp as a new ice pick. The work was not merely interesting, it was *good*. She could see things with a more artistic eye now, Chandler's eyes.

She turned her kohl-smeared eyes toward the work crews. In her years of knowing him, she had never felt so close to Chandler, had never felt so close to *anyone*. It was an immense relief, and something she had always wanted. She didn't want the project to end.

The sharp knife in Chandler's hand slashed down, dicing bok choy, Chinese eggplant, and celery on the wet cutting board. He chattered with Tara, distracted by his own excitement.

In the hot wok, vegetables sizzled with the pungent smell of onions and garlic in sesame oil. On the tile counter beside the wok, soft sweaty masses of turkey breast glistened like damp skin.

"I've already got future projects lined up," Chandler said. "The pyramids were really a breakthrough, and my agent is searching for commissions appropriate to my—to *our* talents."

"Good," Tara said, watching from the comfortable stool as he washed another jewel-purple eggplant under the tap and brought it glittering over to the cutting board where he chopped at it with short, stuttering strokes.

She felt free now, with open doors ahead of her again since she had scraped away her unchallenging architectural work, like mud off her shoe. Chandler didn't care about the mistakes in her past; he let her be herself and help him.

Chandler paused in his cutting, scooped the chunks of turkey and vegetables into the hissing hot oil, then reached for a green bell pepper. "I already told my agent that you and I would be taking projects jointly from now on."

She grinned at him. Chandler glanced at her with a shy smile as he automatically brought the blade down again, slicing his index finger.

"Damn!" he cried, dropping the knife and looking at the blood welling from the gash. "Not again! This is the same finger I cut last year. I'll probably need another three stitches."

Tara sprang to her feet, rushing around the counter to help him, but she froze halfway. "Chandler—*I* cut my finger last year, not you."

He held his cut under the cold running water and looked at her in confusion. She lifted her right hand, extending her index finger to show him the thin white line of her scar.

Chandler turned pale. "That was you? But the memory in my

head was so clear!" He removed his hand from the water, wrapped a dishrag around the cut and pressed hard.

Tara went to the medicine cabinet to get gauze and tape. Her mind buzzed. More backwash from the splitter?

She brought the medical supplies, and though her hands looked steady, she was shaking inside. "Maybe we should ... back off a little," she suggested. "Stop jacking together so often."

Chandler seemed preoccupied as he wrapped his cut. His lips pressed together as he concentrated in an expression she found endearing. For a moment he seemed convinced, but then his expression changed, like plaster of Paris setting in a mold, growing sharper and harder.

"Let's think about it," Chandler said. "We've got a lot of opportunities, and we don't need to rush into anything."

Tara returned alone to Kimba's Steak House. Chandler was off at a luncheon banquet to receive an award for his "Lost Rainforest" environment, but she wanted some time alone, treading water in a vague ocean of dissatisfaction. Perhaps she had picked up some of her husband's need for solitude.

Or perhaps she was just depressed because she had learned that Fizzwilly had finally been caught, the last of her group of hacker friends. Her only remaining connection to that past existence had been severed. Tara decided she didn't really want to go visit Fizzwilly and commiserate with him.

Preoccupied, she found a table surrounded by the kitsch safari atmosphere. She sat under a stuffed zebra head this time, looking up at its placid face, striped black and white, as if a black horse and a white horse had somehow merged imperfectly. It reminded her of Chandler and herself.

Resting her chin in her hand, she keyed in her order and stared at the gaudy decor, wondering if any of it was real, or if it had all been manufactured as props. She decided she didn't care; with as much time as she spent jacked in with Chandler to a virtual universe, reality had earned a different meaning for her.

Waiting for her food, Tara pondered how her life had changed, admitting how much more involved she was with Chandler now, an inextricable part of his work. Tara had dreamed about this ... but she wasn't sure this was what she had had in mind. She had grown together with him, but at the cost of part of herself.

The server interrupted her reverie by bringing her meal. She cut into it with her steak knife, but stopped short when she saw blood pooling on the plate. She turned to the menu pad and called up her order, staring at the words she had keyed in. She looked at her steak again.

The porterhouse was grayish on the outside, and a rich, cold red at the center.

"—and then we'll stop," Chandler said, his eyes pleading.

As Tara looked at him, she caught an image of the gaunt, middle-aged man again, riddled with self-doubt and the fear that he would be unable to complete the job he had taken on. "Just help me finish this one," he said. "You'll enjoy it. I promise."

Tara turned away, uneasy and afraid to meet his eyes. "Tell me again what's wrong," she said.

Over the past week or so, she had refused to jack in at all. Spooked by the growing evidence of the crumbling barrier between their personalities, she had decided to back off, worried about the danger of using the prototype splitter.

"I don't know what's wrong with it!" Chandler lashed out on the verge of panic. His eyes glittered in a silent plea. She had never seen him look so helpless. "It's missing something at the heart. Without your help it's only a shell. I'm falling flat on my face."

He reached out in desperation and clung to her hand. He hadn't done that in a long time. "Please?"

As the refusal died in her throat, Tara realized how drastically their needs had changed, as if they had swapped insecurities. Chandler needed to become more a part of her, and she retreated, trying to build barriers and maintain her own soul.

But as she looked at him grasping her hand and silently begging, she saw the man who had stood beside her when her bright future had been stripped from her, who had let her share in his growing success and given her a new chance. She saw him redefining his company to include her, asking her to become his partner in everything.

"All right," she said. "We'll make this one our masterpiece, a final flash of glory. Then we'll stop. You'll be on your own from now on."

"Sure," Chandler said with obvious relief. "It's for a whole shopping mall. It'll be really big."

Tara went to the wall jacks, wondering why he would think that the size of the implementation had anything to do with her decision to help him.

She carefully mounted the viper fangs of the jack cable into the socket in the back of her head. Rushing and fumbling with his own socket, Chandler linked up. They plugged into the splitter, and both swam down into the virtual world.

He took her to Mount Olympus.

Chandler had chosen the assignment to pique her interest, since in her student days she had traveled through virtual Greece, visited the ruins of the Parthenon, the Acropolis, statues of Apollo and Athena.

Tara looked around under the bleached-bright sky of Chandler's land of the gods. Mount Olympus towered, reaching to the clouds, where Zeus and the other gods dwelled, working their mischief by playing games with mortal lives.

Tara's image had entered the world at the foot of the great volcano. On grassy hills stood weathered, half-fallen remains of Greek architecture, a random mix of Doric, Ionic, and Corinthian columns, small temples, and larger structures scattered in no particular order, as if Chandler had captured their images from a mixed-bag database and pasted them to the slopes as the impulse struck him.

Black obelisks of volcanic rock thrust out at the base of the mountain. Steam and sulfurous fumes curled from fissures, and a blistering glow rose from a large opening, accompanied by loud sounds of clanging metal, a sighing forge, and someone massive stirring.

She saw no image of Chandler waiting for her. They had both jacked in, but he had gone to a different place. As Tara listened to the grunting, clanging sounds in the fire-filled cave, she knew where to find him, where he wanted her to go. He was playing some sort of game with her.

She stepped inside what she guessed would be the forge of Hephaestus. The sharp-edged cave walls reflected the burning-hot light rising from a river of incandescent lava that flowed, rumbled, growled through the chamber.

On a flat rock in the midst of the lava stood the incarnation of Chandler—Hephaestus himself—his head a mass of wiry black hair matted with perspiration, a voluminous beard, eyebrows like feathers from a bird of prey, a face lumpy and ugly. He wore only a soot-stained loincloth. Sweat trickled down his bronzed and muscular frame. One of his feet was crushed and shriveled; Tara remembered the myth of an angered Zeus hurling Hephaestus from the top of Mount Olympus.

He withdrew a sharp metal object from the lava—the glowing tip of a new trident for Poseidon. He looked up, his eyes flashing reflections from the fiery, molten rock. "How do you like it?" Chandler asked. His familiar voice sounded strange issuing from the vocal cords of a massive Greek god.

Tara glanced down at herself to see her body a sculptured model of absolute beauty, pure alabaster, clad in sparkling white flowing robes. She felt luxurious tresses of hair draped between her shoulders. She rolled her eyes at the irony of being too lovely to touch—cool and aloof, unreachable. "Am I supposed to be playing Aphrodite to your Hephaestus?"

"You're my wife, aren't you?" Chandler asked with an eloquent shrug. He began to hammer the smoking trident on an enormous, misshapen anvil; the sledge blows sent thunder reverberating through the grotto.

She indicated the cave, the forge. "Well, the exterior of Mount Olympus needs work, but you've surpassed yourself here."

Chandler looked at her longingly, his large green-tan eyes glowing beneath the bristling brows. "That isn't why I wanted to bring you here," he said. He laid down the trident and stepped down into the flowing lava as if wading across a stream.

"In here, metaphor becomes reality—or whatever reality can become." The molten rock rippled around his naked thighs as he took another limping step on his deformed leg and sank up to his waist. "I need you, Tara," he said, holding out a grime-blackened hand. "I've become a part of you, I've become addicted to you. And I can't do my work without you inside me."

Tara felt alarm well up inside her. "What in the world are you talking about?"

"I think you know. Come into the fire with me," he said. "Together we have unlimited potential. You must know it. Merge with me, once and for all. All or nothing. No secrets. Remember what you said? We exchanged vows, combined our lives. We're supposed to be partners." He dropped his voice. "We can share everything, down to the smallest thoughts. We'll both be in each other's head: a complete synthesis."

He took another halting step forward, stretching his hand toward her, imploringly.

"Oh, Chandler, I wanted to be closer to you," she said, "not to *become* you."

Chandler shook his head. "You won't become me. *We'll* become *us*." Swirling thoughts screamed for her attention, but Chandler kept talking. "We won't even need the jacks anymore. We can do it ourselves. Our minds have already started growing together. We've intertwined. I'm in you, and you're in me."

She tried to respond, but found no words. Wouldn't it be wonderful to have constant mutual support, shoring up each other's weaknesses, never to be alone, always a part of a team? She thought of herself, and wondered how much she really had to lose.

Tara found her own hand lifting toward his as she stood on the brink of the fiery river, gazing at him, knowing she was the image of perfect beauty, fragile yet enduring. And he stood in the lava, powerful, a symbol of unending labor in all its grimy ugliness.

Her hand hovered in the air as the molten rock continued to bubble and hiss. She longed to join with her husband, but she knew that one personality would ultimately prove stronger. For now, Chandler could stand unharmed in the purging fire—but eventually one or the other of them would be consumed.

As Chandler touched her fingers, Tara viciously jacked out.

With an abrupt motion, like a drowned woman gasping back to life,

Tara wrenched the end of the jack cable from the illegal splitter in the wall.

Reeling and disoriented, she suddenly found herself back in her mundane den, where Chandler still sat on the floor beside his old maroon chair, his face slack, his mind lost on Mount Olympus. Tara threw the jack cable down with a sharp gasp, as if it had stung her. She looked at it lying on the floor like a disembodied tentacle, and uncontrollable shudders wracked her body.

She never wanted to go back into the same data stream with Chandler. She had no boundaries left, and neither did he. They would keep merging, averaging. She had to get rid of the temptation—before Chandler could talk her out of it.

Tara dug behind the wall plate, routed Chandler over to the main network access, and disconnected the splitter. The clunky-looking gadget made of plastic and wire snapped like cracking knuckles as she ground it under her heel. The prototype had not been made for durability. She tossed the pieces into the kitchen incinerator and came back to stare at her husband.

Crouched in a lotus position, Chandler remained unaware of her presence. His eyes REMed back and forth; his red-gold hair hung limply over the interface cable. She wondered if he was grieving in the forge of Hephaestus.

They were already intermingled. Their minds had touched and shared and come away with pieces of each other. But from this point on they would no longer be on the same path; partners, yes, but not two people averaged together. From here, she and Chandler could move on parallel life roads, or they could diverge—but they would not be stepping in the same footsteps.

She could be part of him, and apart from him. The best of both worlds, if he would settle for that.

Tara's eyes filled with tears as she stared at Chandler, who now seemed separated from her by an impenetrable wall. When she called his name, he didn't answer, and so she reached out and caressed his hair instead.

I edited an anthology for Fiction River, Pulse Pounders, *which was filled with action stories from all genres. As the editor, I felt obligated to produce a story of my own, but my travel and appearance was really hectic. In a single year I did twenty comic cons and SF conventions, writers' conferences, and keynote talks. Somehow, I needed to find time to write a solid piece for my own anthology. I had a great idea for an intense science fiction horror story, a thriller set on an isolated mining colony whose controlling brain was going senile. But how was I going to find time to write it?*

By making *the time.*

At Salt Lake Comic Con, the show floor opened at 10 AM and I had to be there. So I set my alarm early, getting up just after sunrise so I could walk around the quiet city with my digital recorder, dictating one or two scenes in "Change of Mind" before I had to switch clothes and prepare for a day at the show. During the next three days, I managed to get most of the first draft done before the end of the con, and then I spent a week editing it after I got home.

By taking advantage of any spare minute here and there, I produced this extremely chilling SF tale.

CHANGE OF MIND

"To know the enemy's heart is expected. To know the enemy's mind is a gift. To know one's own heart is divine. To know one's own mind is impossible."

— GENERAL JACK LING TZAO *THE REVISED ART OF WAR, INTERSTELLAR EDITION*, 2873 AD

—I—

There were barbarians at the gate.

The planetary defenses had fallen, and Colonel Ben Triegen did not know how long he could keep his surviving soldiers safe deep inside the main fortress in Collos City. Stale sweat and fear filled the air, a pungent odor he tried to ignore.

With the fortress's command chip, he controlled the external defenses, most of which had already failed horribly. Automated cookie-cutter subroutines were intended to keep the Collos civilians safe, but now they worked against Triegen's troops when the attackers *were* the planet's inhabitants. The outer walls had fallen quickly as robotic machine guns refused to kill attackers. The successively tighter barricades stood firm, though.

For now.

His people had resorted to barricading themselves inside with old-fashioned piles of debris. It was already ugly and only getting worse. Triegen mopped perspiration from his brow with the arm of his uniform; he didn't want the others to see him sweat.

The ragged survivors huddled inside the central chamber, which was washed red with the light of the alarms. The soldiers were terrified and desperate, but in their eyes Triegen saw faith ... hope. If anyone could get them out of this, he could. He would. Colonel Triegen kept his expression stoic even as he swallowed bile.

There were explosions outside. Everything felt ... unreal; detached. He had been through all this before. Sadly, the pain and the bloodshed, the vivid memories of what was going on outside, the images transmitted into the fortress—no, there could be no doubt what was happening out there. All across the planet, the rebels had laid siege to the Network fortresses. Triegen and his troops had fallen back one step at a time, their numbers dwindling as the rebels grew emboldened.

It was all too real.

"How much time do we have, sir?" Lieutenant Fazil's normally soft, attractive voice was ragged.

"We have the rest of our lives." Triegen hooked a finger under his damp collar, refusing to meet her eye. "And that's up to us."

His hands danced over the control conduits. The barricades held for now, but he had to find some way around the resources of the fortress. It was his responsibility to keep these people alive until Network help could arrive.

One hour at a time.

He didn't want to think of how long it would take for a fleet to come across interstellar distances.

The Collos Uprising had been well coordinated. It happened in a flash—a complete surprise. *A gross failure of intelligence and surveillance.* Colonel Triegen knew he was out of options. *Nothing to be done about it now, though.*

Extremist independents had isolated the planet's fourteen Network fortresses and then picked off the followers of the Network government, the tissue-thin fabric that bound the scattered human settlements across the galaxy. Due to extended interstellar travel times, the Network was a safety net rather than an overt governing structure.

Thousands of Network loyalists had been slaughtered in the

streets. Many of the fortresses had already fallen. Only a few, like this one, were armored bubbles holding out thanks to Triegen's command decisions. But the Network fortresses had never been designed to withstand the pressure of an entire planetary population crushing them.

"Let us in, Colonel Triegen!" piped over the intercom.

The words echoed through the vault of his mind. He didn't believe any of their demands or negotiations. Images from outside showed him victims of the uprising, and he could still smell the blood, even in the sealed room. The pounding at the armored doors continued, along with the demands. "Let us in!"

Triegen turned to look at his soldiers, glanced at the sealed door. He blinked as a bead of sweat trickled into his eye. Once again, he felt the sense of vertigo, the detachment. The razor-edged fear of his soldiers gave him all the strength he needed.

Triegen drew a deep breath, "Don't worry. I'll keep you safe."

He almost believed the lie himself.

—II—

Life support was failing, his exosuit getting colder.

"Let us in, Colonel!" demanded Zan Harker, Senior Mine Supervisor on Aurora Facility 5.

The ice planetoid was dark and harsh, bathed by cosmic radiation. The isolated mining facility was no plum assignment on the best of days; it was even worse when the facility's central brain was trying to kill them all.

Next to him in an equally cumbersome exosuit was another competent ice miner, Rajid Suvo, just as desperate to get inside. Suvo had drawn the short straw to accompany Harker when they both left the dubious safety of their stranded transport crawler in a last-ditch attempt to get inside the pressurized dome facility.

But the brain wouldn't let them in.

Suvo continued to transmit on his suitcomm, shouting … expending precious air and energy. "You have to open the hatch, Colonel! The crawler is docked, but our batteries are nearly dead. Life support is failing, with six people still aboard. Let us inside the base, or we'll all die!"

Harker refused to waste oxygen, energy, or mental effort with pointless shouting. The brain of Colonel Triegen wouldn't respond. Instead, making his way through the ice tunnels to the emergency access hatch, Harker used his exosuit tool kit. He hoped he could work the controls faster than Triegen could shut them out.

The original "temporary" ice tunnels had lasted for decades, with layers and layers of repairs, year after year. The passages into the domed base were a maze of conduits and ducts full of spliced wires, piping, crystalline optical fibers. It was a mess, but that worked to their advantage now: a facility in peak repair would be impossible to hack. The emergency hatch was their best chance—but not when the base itself was fighting against them.

Triegen's simulated voice blasted over their suitcomms. "My soldiers and I will hold out. We will not surrender to rebels. The Collos Uprising will fail."

Upon hearing the words, Harker ground his teeth together. He turned and looked at his companion. Through the faceplate he saw the other man's dark eyes widen with fear at the confirmation of their suspicions.

The facility's central brain was having another war flashback.

Harker's suit reserves were depleted. No time to lose. He took out the tools and frenetically assembled a plan. The other six ice miners trapped in the docked transport crawler had little air or heat left. Right now, they would be deciding which was preferable—suffocating or freezing. It wasn't an easy choice.

Harker thought about death a lot—who didn't on this barren frozen facility?—but he was more attuned to it than others. He didn't consider himself a hero, just a man who would do what had to be done.

He and Suvo had worked out a few hand signals so they didn't have to use any transmissions the brain could detect, but Harker didn't expect the other man to be much use. Suvo was just dead weight ... although, perhaps a useful distraction. Suvo hammered his gloved fists on the sealed emergency hatch, continuing to plead with Colonel Triegen. "Let us in! Please!"

What a waste of precious oxygen.

Harker was quieter. First order of business; he had to get rid of the monitoring cams. Taking out a telescoping probe rod, he reached up to smash the nearest glittering, optical eye that gazed down at them.

He studied the tangle of pipes and conduits in the low ceiling and spotted a second optical sensor, so he blinded the control brain there, too.

A mechanical scuttler appeared from the dark recesses of the conduits and raced toward the baton, trying to attack it. Each of the spider-like repair drones was the size of a loaf of bread and could work autonomously or be operated by the colony's control brain. Harker crushed the scuttler with the baton, leaving a pile of twisted metal and twitching limbs, then he smashed a third optical imager, the last one he could see.

That should be enough.

Touching his faceplate against Suvo's, a thousand-year-old astronaut's trick of speaking without using comms, he said, "The brain is blinded now, but we won't have much time. Remove the hatch access plate so I can get at the controls."

Once the wiring was exposed, Harker jammed in the probe baton, blowing the liquid-crystal power cells. Energy-retentive gel mined from the ice of Aurora sprayed out of the damaged power modules like silvery blood.

On a normal excavation shift, Suvo was a hard worker, competent—because everyone had to be competent to survive here—but not overly skilled. Aurora Facility 5 could function without him.

Harker, though, was far less replaceable. He had to get inside before his exosuit failed.

He worked quickly, confidently, with steady hands. Though their situation was grim, he refused to die on this godforsaken rock being run by a senile brain.

He tried to distract the Colonel so he could work. He used a calm, logical voice, in contrast to Suvo's panic. "Colonel Triegen, this is mine supervisor Zan Harker. Listen to me. What you're seeing isn't *real*. Remember where you are. The war has been over for fifty years."

In many ways, Harker regretted the war was over. Harker had been in the armed services for several years, but he and Colonel Triegen had very little in common. He had washed out of the military; something about his psych profile was wrong. While others were relieved to have decades of peace and prosperity across the Network, Harker had never been bothered by violence; rather, he was disappointed that there was no longer any outlet for what human beings were genetically designed to do.

"You're lying!" screamed the brain in its eerily human voice. Harker always had trouble associating that voice with the lump of gray matter floating in a vat at the center of the mining colony. But now that brain was failing, growing senile, and needed to be replaced.

Harker had come to Aurora Facility 5 as an ice miner shortly after his discharge from the military, and worked his way up to Senior Mine Supervisor. But now he felt trapped and helpless on a dark lump of ice.

Harker wasn't the only one who had seen the signs of Triegen's dementia. Only four weeks earlier another transport crawler—remotely guided by the Colonel's brain—had been wiped out on the frozen excavation fields. All personnel aboard had died except for Zan Harker. He'd been outside the crawler on an EVA, trying to make manual repairs, when he had heard the screams, the pleas for help. By the time he'd gotten back to the crawler, the brain had bled out all the life support. Everyone inside the armored vehicle was dead.

Now, he and Rajid Suvo were trying to break inside the pressurized dome because the damned brain was having another flashback.

Transmissions came from the other six crewmembers inside the crawler docked outside. Their voices were weakening. "We won't last much longer."

"Neither will I, if you keep whining," Harker muttered, careful not to activate the comm. He worked at the control plate, tried to bypass the locks.

Suddenly, a blast of frozen effluent pelted them, showering down like a wind driven hail storm. Another scuttler had dumped the contents, which hammered down like projectiles. Suvo flailed his gloved hands, trying to wipe the muck from his suit. He backed away, yelping.

But Harker finished his work. Focus.

Finally, he saw the system lights glow, and the emergency hatch seal unlocked. He felt a rush of euphoria. He was going to make it. He was going to survive!

He transmitted to the crawler crew. "The hatch is open. Suit up and get over here."

Suvo was stumbling, still reeling from the debris barrage. "Harker—I think my pack's been damaged. Help me get inside. Life support is bleeding out."

Harker saw that his companion's suit was indeed leaking fluids. Concentrated air spilled out in a frozen white steam. The damage was an easy fix, but …

His pulse was racing. He felt a metallic taste in his mouth, and his vision grew sharper, his thoughts more intense. The jagged shadows outside were nothing compared to what was going through his mind.

He hauled Suvo around. "Let me look at your pack."

Suvo dutifully turned, exposed his vulnerable pack. "Thanks, man."

Harker spotted some external damage, a few small fluid tubes and pressure cylinders, damaged but easily repaired. He took out his tools, the sharpest ones. "Here, let me."

The pressurized dome was just another door away, but Harker no longer needed an extra set of hands. He felt hungry and excited by the opportunity.

All the imagers had been deactivated.

Harker extended a probe blade into his companion's life-support pack and with a vicious twist, he severed the connections, breaking the power lines. The last air hemorrhaged out of the exosuit like arterial blood.

Before Suvo could cry out in question or fear, Harker yanked his comm line, disconnecting it. Harker panted inside his helmet, euphoric, as the other man flailed and struggled. Suvo didn't fight back, merely tried to survive, but he had no way of doing so. He lurched toward the inner hatch.

Harker waited, watching him die. He liked to look at the faces, see the expression of terror change to acceptance, possibly even epiphany. Leaning over Suvo's still form, he reattached the comm line. Suvo didn't have enough air left to even gasp, and Harker needed to erase any traces of what he had done.

"We're on our way through now," transmitted the junior mine supervisor from the transport crawler. "Five minutes. Hold that door open for us!"

"We're ready for you." Harker watched the light fade from Rajid Suvo's eyes behind the faceplate. Oh, how he savored these moments, etching them into his memory! There wasn't enough personal space on Aurora Facility 5 for Harker to take trophies, like he used to. These fleeting memories were all he had to keep.

He made his voice hoarse, hitching as he replied over the open comm. "But … Suvo is dead. The damned brain attacked us! Triegen is lost in another one of his flashbacks."

Rajid Suvo lay in perfect stillness, and Harker felt a giddy rush of adrenaline and euphoria. This had been just too good an opportunity to waste.

—III—

Colonel Triegen knew his mistake now. He understood what he had done and what he was. And he was horrified by it.

As he existed inside his preservation chamber, he stripped away the layers of memories. The flashbacks were so vivid they had tricked him into thinking all those old actions—decades ago now—were real. His access to recall, enhanced by the base's computerized systems, made reminiscences, history, and data all blur together. Trapped and bodiless, Ben Triegen could only wallow in a vichyssoise of despair.

"I'm sorry." He projected his thought, which transmitted a simulated voice through the speakers in Aurora Facility 5, to all the cabs of the mining machines, to the living quarters, community rooms, and admin modules inside the pressurized domes. His words appeared as text on all computer screens, overriding any other activity.

"I'm sorry."

He tapped into his own databases, studying *information,* not experiences, not real memories. By reviewing history and trying to match up the cold data with what his mind recalled from actual experience, he could disentangle the flashback from reality.

The whole Aurora facility was around him, a part of him. Millions of maintenance monitors and everyday life-support decisions had to be made, an incredibly choreographed production run by Colonel Triegen's subconscious brain, while at the forefront of his mind he studied his own military record, reviewed what he had done—both during the war and during his years here on the ice planetoid.

He remembered his military battles, not just the Collos Uprising, but the later space battles, the engagements of lightspeed frigates and Network cruisers armed with entropy weapons against ragtag and increasingly desperate rebels who were intent on unraveling the fabric of interstellar government.

As a man, Triegen had received decorations, ribbons, medals, honors … and all the pride that accompanied them. And the final awful battle against the insurgents, the betrayal, the explosions—that last moment when he understood that he had lost this fight, that he had failed … that he was going to die. Triegen had died not with fear, not with pain, but with a calm satisfaction as the flames swept over him, because Colonel Ben Triegen knew he was a hero, knew he had done everything possible, that he had made a *difference*.

The war would be won, thanks to his actions and the actions of others.

But he hadn't died—not in the sense that his consciousness was gone. His brain had been removed and preserved, transferred here to run the vital ice-mining complex.

But he wasn't really alive either. His way of experiencing the world had changed. Gone were the tastes and touches, the joys and fears. Everything was data, protocols. As a disembodied brain, it was difficult to measure time except through the instruments connected to him. Were they reliable? Truly?

Fifty years. Could it really have been that long? He tapped into the databases, extended his readings throughout the high-precision sensors. He could see everywhere, touch everything, but it was not part of *him* inside the central chamber where his preservation tank and all the core life-support systems existed.

He knew that Dr. Ana Cherliz was monitoring him, checking his biological functions. She often came here. She was even his friend, in a sense; they'd had many conversations. Now he recognized the expression of concern on her face.

"I'm sorry, Dr. Cherliz," he said, as she monitored his tissues, engrams, and cerebral neural paths. "Terribly sorry."

"We detected the signs some time ago, Ben," the doctor said. "We talked about it last month, remember? There was another …

incident. It's in your own data banks. You've lived a whole second life here on Aurora 5—and that's a very long time for anyone to stay clear, to stay sane. I'm sorry, but it's just been too long for you. The diagnosis of dementia is irrefutable."

"I understand it, Doctor." He felt the despair growing heavier inside him, though it was more a resignation in his thoughts than anything. Feelings were there, but distant. "I know what I did."

In a flash, he reviewed the records of the base, and he understood—but in a detached sort of way—that he'd killed several people. Not just Rajid Suvo, but the entire crew of a transport crawler out on the dark ice, and a mining team that had suffocated because of a malfunction down in the irradiated ice-gel extraction catacombs. Those were all *people*, now dead. People who had been Colonel Triegen's responsibility, loyal miners he was supposed to *protect*. They were his responsibility! A thousand miners at Aurora Facility 5.

Usually, Dr. Cherliz engaged in friendly banter with him, but now she was quiet, engrossed in her work. Although she tried to hide her expressions, he could read her concern. She was concerned about more than just his degeneration, his neurological damage, his senility. She was also afraid *of* him, of what he might do.

"I'm sorry, Dr. Cherliz," he repeated. "It won't happen again."

With his numerous extended sensors, he checked the network of conduits and detectors. He studied the small mechanical scuttlers that roved through the tunnels, vents, and frozen ducts, performing maintenance, checking the base.

Triegen focused his thoughts back into the control room. As Dr. Cherliz finished her analysis, her voice was hesitant, carefully devoid of any emotion. "We still have six months before the next ship arrives. I'm tracking the progress of your degeneration, and I must admit, I'm worried. Do you remember the replacement brain that's coming?"

"I understand, Dr. Cherliz," Triegen said. After the original accident, his first "death," he had always understood he would one day be decommissioned, swapped out. "It's necessary."

Now her voice quavered. "You've reviewed the records. You agree with our assessment, correct?"

He hesitated, but at the speed his thoughts moved, she didn't notice. "I can't argue with what I know, Doctor."

When his brain was installed here to run the mining base, there was always a scheduled replacement time. His second chance at a useful life had a time limit. The Network would remove his preservation canister, retire his brain, and let him live happily somewhere in a farm of fond memories. He wasn't sure he believed that—it was too much like the lie he had told his own children when they lost their pets. He didn't care. What was important was his responsibility to Aurora Facility 5. Dr. Cherliz could easily hook up the replacement brain herself.

"I understand," he said. "I'm very sorry. I know what reality is. Six months is a long time, and I promise I will try to hold out. I will keep this facility safe."

"Thank you, Colonel," the doctor said.

He wasn't sure he believed her, either.

Triegen reached out with his sensors, scanned all the other workers on the base. Though everyone was hard at work, he detected tension in the air. Microexpressions were programmed into his databases, and he recognized them on their faces. Everyone knew what he had done. He could tell that all personnel on Aurora Facility 5 were nervous and uneasy.

Out in the deep, black ice of Aurora Facility 5, lit by distant stars that gave no warmth, the mining crews continued their work. They were subdued, cautious, weary. Survival was always a challenge out here, but now they had to face another possible danger from the unreliable control brain. They didn't speak their worries aloud, knowing Colonel Triegen was listening, but their concerns were plain.

Inside his isolated vat, he made a promise to himself. He would hold out until the replacement brain came. He had to.

—IV—

As mining supervisor, Zan Harker arranged schedules, moved teams, manipulated where he wanted people to be. He was good at covering his tracks—damn good. Now he had to be even better.

Running an active conspiracy was more difficult than just killing when the opportunity arose. As he made his way to the secret meeting out inside the ice sheet, he felt the adrenaline sharpen his senses. It wasn't the same type of rush as murder, but he enjoyed it nevertheless. He could manipulate the others gathered here and use their fear of Colonel Triegen to his advantage.

He was the first to arrive at the isolated chamber, which gave him a chance to double-check his plans and ensure that Triegen's mechanical scuttlers hadn't surreptitiously installed surveillance devices. As far as he could tell, the control brain knew nothing of this shielded room deep under the active excavation layers. It was a place to talk in private.

Out on Aurora Facility 5, the mining crews ran their big machinery. Excavators chewed through layers of ice, sending deep shafts to the richer layers. The ice surface was a film of valuable isotopes, cooked in a bath of harsh cosmic radiation, but the real treasure of Aurora was a potent isotopic crystal gel distilled from compressed fossil sea creatures that had been part of an ocean, now deeply frozen.

Some months ago, when the drilling crew discovered a small void in what was supposed to be a gel chamber, Harker had deleted it from the records, but he noted the natural bubble just in case he needed a bolt-hole. An instinct—he was sure he could find something to do with it. Something. He licked his dry lips.

By rearranging schedules and using equipment on his own, Harker had constructed a chamber where there were no scuttlers, no imagers. He added thick insulating layers on the walls and installed portable life support. It was a perfect place for a conspiracy meeting.

He had recruited three competent, determined, and like-minded facility workers, giving them a whispered summons—he didn't dare use transmissions. Alfred Cho and Cina Adakian arrived separately, nervous. Adakian shivered visibly. Blue-tinted shadows surrounded them in the chamber, casting the illusion of cold, despite exosuit thermometers indicating that the chamber was at the same temperature as the main dome kilometers away.

Finally, Dr. Cherliz arrived, traveling deep and following directions so that she slipped out of view from Triegen's myriad artificial prying eyes. The doctor was allegedly responding to a minor first aid call, nothing so urgent that the control brain would send scuttlers into the blind spot to assist.

Cherliz removed her helmet after the primitive seal cycled her through into the air pocket. Her face was hard, and her deep brown eyes held determination and resignation. The facility doctor's personality had no more warmth than the ice sheet, but she was competent, no-nonsense—and Harker needed her.

Though they had not spoken of it, they all knew why he had summoned them. There wasn't time for chitchat. Harker doubted the others had the fortitude for it.

Dr. Cherliz narrowed her eyes as she looked around the chamber. "You know this is dangerous, Zan. The Colonel is a good man, but he is hardwired to defend himself. If he catches us meeting in secret like this, you could easily trigger a flashback."

"We have to do something about it—about him."

Alfred Cho was a harried, red-eyed man who looked as if he got very little sleep, even on good days. "Rajid Suvo was a friend of mine, and that monster killed him. He *killed* him!"

"Suvo wasn't his first victim, either." Cina Adakian put a hand on Cho's shoulder. "We know that. Those others ... I tried to convince myself they were accidental deaths, but then I realized I was just being stupid. Seven miners killed in Epsilon shaft when caustic coolant sprayed out of broken pipes. Scuttlers should've caught that, and Triegen monitors the scuttlers."

"Then there were all those people frozen in the cargo crawler," Cho said.

Harker cut him off. "You don't have to tell me about that—I was there." There was an awkward moment of silence, acknowledging that he was the only survivor of that incident. He had also been in Epsilon shaft not long before the deadly coolant spill, but that had not been noticed.

Dr. Cherliz nodded. "I know. Those weren't accidents."

"But what are we going to do?" Cho cried. "Just be careful, be on our guard? That's not good enough! We'll all be dead by the time the replacement brain arrives."

Harker grunted. "Who knows how many other glitches we haven't noticed? Further accidents waiting to happen, like ticking time bombs. How many times did Triegen try to kill us, but failed? He's senile, yes, probably insane. Not just incompetent. I think he is starting to purposefully kill us." His mouth was dry, and he licked his lips. "And now he obviously has a taste for it." He looked at Cherliz.

She frowned. "I don't agree that it is intentional, but the end result is the same. More people will die." They huddled in the ice-walled chamber, but the silence was deeper and colder than the walls around them. "Colonel Triegen shows clear signs of advancing dementia. When our replacement brain arrives in six months, I can install it."

Adakian bit her lip. "What if we don't have that long?"

Harker shook his head. "We don't have six months—that's obvious."

Alfred Cho wrapped his hands around his knees to hold himself steady. "Colonel Triegen is aware that a ship is on its way. He knows he's going to be replaced. Do you think he'll just sit by and let us pull the plug? Do you think he honestly believes his tank will be sent out to pasture, so he can just dream until he fades away?"

Harker laced his fingers together and squeezed his fists. "Triegen isn't a fool. When the new brain arrives, he'll fight back. I don't doubt he will have arranged for all of us to be dead by then. He might even find a way to destroy the incoming ship. Are we going to let that happen?"

Cho, Adakian, and Cherliz looked alarmed. "Well, what can we do?" Adakian asked.

"We have to move quickly, before he suspects we're making plans," Harker said. "Once we disconnect the control brain, we'll hook up manual systems, run the facility on backup generators and secondaries."

Cina Adakian shot Harker a calculating, look. "Can we live on those old model survival systems? They're non-sentient, unreliable —and inefficient."

Cho gripped his legs tighter. "This is an emergency. We have to —otherwise, Triegen will kill us first."

Harker nodded. "We're stating the obvious. We know what we have to do. All the miners are tough, or they wouldn't be here in the first place. We can buckle down and wait. Enforce heavy conservation, low energy output. It'll be difficult, but we can do it. Six months. We know the ship is coming—all we have to do is hold out."

He took the time to look at each one of them. He would have to count on these three. Harker could dupe the control brain to a certain extent, but it would be walking a razor's edge. He knew Colonel Triegen would fight back the moment he discovered their plan.

One by one, Cherliz, Adakian, and Cho nodded. He could see it in their gazes. He had them.

—V—

Colonel Triegen was a hero—he knew it, and history verified that he was. His memories weren't false ... at least not all of them. But they were scattered and diffuse, dangerously slippery and rearranged.

He wasn't sure of anything anymore.

Triegen didn't like to think that these people were afraid of him. He was supposed to watch over the personnel, the miners, the support staff, the machine operators. He had let them down.

He could not dispute the bad things that had happened. People had died here through terrible accidents. And it was his fault. He realized that he had experienced military flashbacks, vivid memories that were real, but in the wrong time and place.

And he knew that if it happened again, more of his people would die.

Though Triegen was only a disembodied brain, myriad sensors and numerous eyes gave him overlapping contact with all of Aurora Facility 5. Automated inspectors and self-monitoring systems kicked into life. Scuttlers implemented repairs to the large-scale damage he had caused during his most recent flashback.

Wallowing inside his central preservation container, Triegen had to anchor himself and his thoughts, not just let unconscious subroutines take control. He tunneled down into the events that he himself had experienced, verifying that his memories of those battles matched the information in the Network history databases. He knew those, at least, were all real. He wasn't entirely mixed up, though he was old.

Triegen remembered the Collos Uprising, the crisis, his desperate defense of the last fortress, and how that had ended: he and his few survivors barricaded deep within the shielding walls as the barbarians pounded to get through. The colonel had preemptively added extra layers of security, reinforced barricades, dug deep bolt-holes.

Network forces had indeed arrived sooner than expected. The rescuers had broadcast an emergency transmission, trying to determine how many defenders were still alive. They ordered Triegen and his holdouts to crawl as deep as possible, to shield themselves, and to hold on tight. Targeted radioactive explosions had vaporized the perimeter of the fortress as a punitive example to all the people on Collos. Triegen and his injured comrades were saturated with radiation, but they could be treated once they were dug out of the slag.

The rescue fleet had searched for other holdouts at Network fortresses across the planet, but the rest had already fallen. Some of the fortresses had been real horror shows; the Collos rebels had seized Network soldiers and flayed them alive. Upon seeing that evidence, the rescue forces had "resolved the situation" with even more ruthlessness.

Triegen was glad that he and his injured comrades had been whisked away to infirmary ships where they were treated for radiation exposure. Although sick, the colonel wanted to join the fight himself, but the defenders kept him aboard, insisting they didn't need him for the mop-up operations. And he was, in fact, relieved, having seen the horrific images of what the rebels had done to his fellow soldiers. Colonel Triegen didn't want to imagine how he would've reacted if given the chance to exact revenge on monsters like that....

But that was in a time of war, decades ago. That was fighting under extreme circumstances. These Aurora Facility 5 accidents were much more recent. No, he froze his thoughts and corrected himself. No matter how painful it might be, they were not *accidents*. They were murders. He was the control brain of the facility. He was responsible.

Triegen didn't want to, but he reviewed the incidents that his own senility, his own failures had caused. He replayed the transmissions that Harker and Suvo had made during his recent crippling flashback, the mistake that had resulted in a man's death. He saw images of the transport crawler stranded out on the ice, unable to get back into the pressurized facility ... life support draining away, oxygen bleeding out, batteries going dead.

Recalling all the stored records, he forced himself to watch files from implanted imagers that recorded the two suited men, Zan Harker and Rajid Suvo, desperately trying to break through the hatch. "Let us in, Colonel!" He hadn't listened. He believed they were Collos rebels, barbarians trying to break inside his barricaded fortress.

Although he had been buried in his flashback at the time, semi-autonomous scuttlers had come in response, seemingly from a backwash of the control brain's thoughts as he was reliving those terrible last moments during the Collos Uprising.

Harker had smashed all of the camera eyes—a wise tactical move, the colonel thought—blinding him as the two men worked the controls. Triegen admired the mine supervisor's drive and dedication.

But Harker missed one thing. A second scuttler had already been at work repairing a routine power-channel failure, hidden inside a conduit. Triegen accessed those records. Knowing he was responsible for Suvo's death, he would force himself to witness the miner's last moments.

The emergency hatch slid open after Harker used the overrides. Suvo was already injured from debris unleashed by the scuttlers, his suit damaged from the spray of effluent projectiles. Harker went to his comrade, took out his toolkit as if to help.

Then Triegen saw something odd. Harker seemed to be fighting with the other man. He used a tool, jammed it into the life-support pack in Suvo's exosuit. Then he stepped back and watched as air spewed out, as Suvo collapsed.

Triegen couldn't believe it. This wasn't accidental!

Harker wrecked the life support in his companion's suit, making it look like additional debris damage. He actively disengaged the air tubing. Suvo struggled, fought against him, but he was weak, and Harker completed his sabotage. After Suvo collapsed, dead, Harker stood triumphant, saying not a word.

Triegen's thoughts spun.

This couldn't be real! He had to be hallucinating again, succumbing to the dementia. But he knew he wasn't.

Triegen replayed the images, and saw again without any doubt that it was *Zan Harker* who had murdered the man.

Yes, the Colonel had been caught in a flashback, had fought against these stranded miners while imagining they were rebels from a war half a century ago. Yes, Triegen's dementia had definitely caused problems, put many people at risk.

But, *Harker* had actually murdered Suvo.

It wasn't me!

He froze for a seemingly long time—on the timescale of his thoughts—and then he called up records of the other accidents, the other *murders*. Maybe he was going insane after all.

Actively engaging the facility's scuttlers, Triegen saw a whole world open up before him. How had he never thought to dig into the automated systems before? His self-pity had blinded him.

Triegen knew he couldn't report this, despite his shock and disbelief. Even with the proof of the images, no one else would believe him. Not even Dr. Cherliz. Images were too easy to fabricate. And the micro-expressions he observed on the faces of all the facility personnel screamed of mistrust and fear. Fear of him. What he read in their faces now was the opposite of what he had seen in the eyes of his brave soldiers on Collos.

He knew he had to watch Mine Supervisor Harker very, very carefully.

Brooding with his thoughts and keeping busily active while other parts of his brain ran the facility, Colonel Triegen reviewed the other incidents and discovered that Zan Harker was in some way connected each time.

Triegen studied all the events with a different perspective....

—VI—

The sooner they acted, the less likely it was that Triegen's unstable brain could prepare a defense against what they were trying to do.

All that remained of the military hero was a blob of gray matter inside a central preservation chamber. But he surely had a sense of self-preservation, even if his feelings of guilt might paralyze him. Harker hoped to take advantage of that.

Regardless, Harker wasn't keen to fight a victim who could fight back, unlike all the others. The colonel had access to all the defensive systems of Aurora Facility 5 ... and he was a tactical genius. Harker knew this would be a challenge. He was convinced that not even a sane and undamaged brain would simply give up its existence so easily, and Triegen was a fighter.

On the other hand, Harker was a *killer*.

Alfred Cho and Cina Adakian joined Harker and Cherliz, all of them coming together outside the central brain chamber, seemingly by coincidence, but exactly on time. Harker didn't doubt that Triegen had been watching them all.

Dr. Cherliz would do most of the physical work to get rid of Triegen, deprogramming and disconnecting the brain, bypassing the facility's life-support systems to manual operation. Harker wasn't certain that Cho and Adakian would be much help, but they would be a useful distraction, if nothing else. Cannon fodder. They had tools, and Harker had a sturdy metal pipe, an all-purpose weapon, just in case.

Harker hoped that they would catch the colonel by surprise, since there were six months to go before the replacement brain arrived. Maybe he could get away with this.

The central core chamber had its own defenses. At present, the barricades were just standard security protocols, but no doubt, in time, Colonel Triegen would increase his defenses, build up unexpected protective layers as he waited for the desperate miners to make their move.

Dr. Cherliz was the closest thing to a friend Triegen still had. Harker knew she would be the key to getting the brain to let his guard down. Her voice was soft as she opened the barricaded door. "Colonel, we've come to make some modifications, install fail-safes, just in case you have another episode. We have to make sure the Aurora personnel stay safe."

When the core chamber door opened, Harker pushed his way in first, holding the metal pipe. Dr. Cherliz came close behind him. Cho and Adakian hesitated in the chill metal-walled corridor. They were nervous.

The colonel's voice emanated from speakers. "I agree that the safety of the people in this facility is paramount. There are many dangers here—many unexpected hazards."

Harker entered cautiously, keeping the metal pipe low, although he knew he could never hide it from all of the optical sensors.

Colonel Triegen's brain hung suspended inside a crystal-walled cylinder, adrift in nutrient fluid. Hair-fine wires ran from the silver base of the tube, which was surrounded by overrides and computer terminals, default backup modules should the brain die. No supercomputer could match a human brain with speed and finesse of calculations and reactions, but life-support systems could be done by brute force.

Another station near the central brain held the communication controls, the local intercom and long-distance transmissions out to the vast Network outposts and fleet ships, but no signal sent from Aurora Facility 5 would be received for some time. They were on their own here.

"Colonel Triegen, we've made a difficult decision," Harker said. "The facts are indisputable. You're dangerous and functionally unreliable. There have been accidents, and people are dead."

"Not accidents," said the Colonel's voice. "*Murders.* And murderers should be punished. I think you would all agree."

Harker was startled when images of his own face flashed on the monitors around the chamber.

Dr. Cherliz ignored the videos as she took a step toward the consoles. "I'm sorry, Ben, but we'll need to bypass you for the time being, put you on backup storage mode until the replacement brain arrives. We'll—"

Suddenly, three scuttlers bustled down the wall from where they had hidden among the conduits and energy-gel pipelines in the ceiling. Their tools were extended, a tiny welding apparatus, a clicking blue arc of a stunner. They dropped like spiders onto Dr. Cherliz, and she thrashed to drive them away.

The second scuttler zapped her with an arc, and she stumbled backward, fleeing through the control chamber door where Cho and Adakian were trying to defend themselves against other scuttlers in the outer corridors.

Three more scuttlers raced across the floor toward Harker. He whirled, swinging his metal pipe to smash the small multi-purpose robots. He struck one, but the other two raced away.

As soon as Dr. Cherliz scrambled out of the control chamber, the doors hissed shut, and the hatches sealed, leaving Harker alone inside.

With a chill, he realized that Triegen had done that intentionally.

Wary, he turned in a slow circle, saw numerous scuttlers moving along the framework overhead. One climbed onto a computer console.

Outside the chamber, he heard pounding on the sealed hatch, muffled shouts, a clang of tools against metal. He suspected Cho would be removing the access panel, trying to force open the doors. They were shouting, calling out Harker's name. They were afraid for him.

Harker straightened, and the corners of his lips twitched. He bared his teeth and turned to face the suspended brain in its transparent cylinder, though the direction didn't matter. Colonel Triegen had eyes everywhere.

"Murderers must be punished, Mr. Harker."

"Yes, Colonel, they must. And you will be."

Cina Adakian's voice burst through the local intercom. "Zan, are you all right? We're trying to get to you."

"Mr. Harker has been damaged," Triegen announced.

Harker squeezed the metal pipe, felt its heft. This battle should've been done with subtle re-programming, disconnects, and re-routes. He would have to do this the old-fashioned way.

Harker whirled and brought down the metal pipe, targeting the scuttlers first. The pipe smashed into one, and he quickly reversed his swing, crushing a second. Pain flared in his leg as a third scuttler burned his calf with a torch.

Harker dove to the side, sliding to a halt and battering the last scuttler into wreckage. He pulled himself back to a standing position and limped forward.

"In fact," Triegen continued over the intercom, "Mr. Harker is actually—"

Hefting the pipe with both hands, he brought it down on the communications nexus. He smashed the intercom controls with enough force to crunch through the casing, smash the circuits, and unleash a shower of sparks. The intercom went dead in the middle of Adakian's alarmed shout from the corridor.

Holding the pipe like a medieval weapon, Harker faced the brain cylinder. No one outside could hear their words now. This would be a private conversation.

"I'm afraid your dementia is getting the best of you, Colonel," Harker said. "It would be better if you just surrendered. Let us deactivate you. The facility can run on backup systems for a few months."

"I will not surrender," Triegen said. "*I* know how to protect people. *I* am a hero, no matter what you claim I've done." The simulated voice paused. "I agree, though, that I am unreliable and prone to failure. I've lived too long. I'm degenerating. But I can't let you remain unchecked among these people. They're my responsibility—and you are a terrible danger."

"You're imagining things, Colonel." Harker felt heat burning inside of him. "You can broadcast lies about me, but no one believes you. You've killed too many of them. It's just trickery, the feeble gasping of a dying, old mind."

"I've learned not to trust my memories or my thoughts anymore, Mr. Harker," said the calm, simulated voice. "But I know my own personality, and I can compare my memories with actual facts. I found stored images that you couldn't delete. I have proof that you're responsible for the deaths, not me."

Harker was surprised. He hadn't expected this. Even so, he responded with a smile.

Triegen continued. "I won't be your scapegoat. I need to protect these miners. Therefore, I have to remove you. Eliminate the threat."

Harker laughed. "You are weak and deluded, Colonel. They think it was you. You can't change that." He twisted the pipe in his hands, savoring the moment.

The room's lights flickered. "It doesn't matter, they'll be safe. I can take responsibility for what I actually did, the failures that I allowed—but not for the crimes you committed. I had hoped to endure until the replacement brain arrived, but I've switched over to emergency backup monitoring, self-sufficient systems that will make our operations far less efficient. Toward the end, the facility will be at absolute minimum, no reserves whatsoever. But my people will survive, if just barely."

Harker couldn't allow that to happen. The others had seen the attack of the scuttlers, and they knew he was trapped inside, at the mercy of the murderous Colonel Triegen. They wouldn't believe the demented old brain.

Harker peeled his lips back in a wordless roar and lunged forward, swinging the cudgel. It struck the curved crystal wall with a resounding thump that chipped the tank in a starburst pattern. He swung again, and the chip became a crack.

Above him, though, more scuttlers raced up and down the conduits, and Harker knew it would be a losing battle to engage them. There were thousands of the semi-autonomous machines on Aurora Facility 5. Now, overhead, they used their tools to slice open energy-gel pipelines, pouring a rain shower of foul-smelling chemicals down on top of Harker.

He screamed up at them. "No, you don't!" With renewed fury, he swung the pipe again, and the impact made the spiderweb of cracks on the crystal preservation cylinder spread. Fluid began to ooze out of the seams.

One last blow. Harker hammered with the metal pipe just as the scuttlers, following Triegen's instructions, scritched their tools and struck a spark.

The blow cracked open the brain canister, the vat crumbled—and the spark caught. The flammable chemicals ignited in a deafening basso roar that engulfed Harker in hell.

—VII—

When Harker awoke, it wasn't like anything he had ever experienced. He couldn't feel his body. His thoughts were not so much asleep as *unaware*. Even when consciousness returned, he felt himself loose and drifting.

He remembered the fire and the pain consuming him while he twisted in the throes of ecstasy over his kill. How was he still alive? Dr. Cherliz must have saved him.

He felt so detached, so numb everywhere. He must have been pumped full of painkillers. Everything remained dark, and he couldn't feel any warmth or cold. Sensations sparked in random places.

He heard a voice he recognized … but he wasn't *hearing* it the way he used to. The voice was just a random set of sounds piped straight into his mind, and as he concentrated, it became clearer, more familiar. The voice of Dr. Ana Cherliz.

But something was wrong.

"Hooking up your external sensors now, Zan," she said.

Light flooded his vision, but it wasn't *vision*, and it didn't come from eyes. It was information. Hundreds, maybe even thousands of streams, pouring into him. So much information. So much …

He saw it all, like a god. All seeing. All present.

"This is going to take some getting used to," Cherliz said, "but we had no other option. You saved us from Colonel Triegen. He'd gone insane, tried to kill us all, tried to shut down the facility. He was intent on murdering you, but you destroyed him, Zan. We all thank you for that … but at such a terrible cost to you."

He tried to speak, but found he had no vocal cords, no body, no way of communicating.

"Wait, just a second," said the doctor.

Something changed, and a pathway opened in the data. He found that if he concentrated, made his thoughts sound like specific words, then they came out through the speakers. "What happened to me? I'm alive?"

"Yes—and so are we, thanks to you," Dr. Cherliz said. "You're in the satellite control chamber. I'm still hooking up and testing your senses, but you'll be our new control brain, at least until the replacement arrives. I'm sorry, Zan, but your body was burned to a crisp, you were barely alive. If I had waited another five minutes, you would've died."

Harker was horrified, drowning in a flood of senses, all the images that stampeded into him from Aurora Facility's countless sensors. How could he sort them all? How could he pay attention?

Then Harker began to use the unorthodox senses to look outside, and he realized that with a flicker of thought he could extend his presence to all parts of the frozen planetoid, the mining facilities, the separate semi-autonomous transport crawlers, the distant crews of miners in the deep ice tunnels.

He could feel the heartbeat of life-support systems, could breathe through the ventilation ducts like his own extended respiratory system.

He began to use that network to see all the personnel here, to understand all the possibilities … to feel all the power he now had that he never could have touched before. Even though he had no body remaining, Harker felt a familiar hunger….

"Yes, Dr. Cherliz, I know you did what you could."

In a long, instantaneous pause, he savored everything. It was like a whirlwind of opportunities. Again, he felt the heartbeat of the Facility, how light it was, how fleeting.

How extinguishable.

"I think I'll be just fine."

I like to play in big galactic empires because there's room to tell lots of stories. Michael Z. Williamson established a popular and complex space opera universe with his Freehold series—and he expanded it further by inviting other authors to play in his star-filled sandbox.

Freehold is a consortium of independent planets where all the loose ends and troublemakers have created an interconnected and chaotic society to stand up to a large empire. It's military science fiction, but not just about the military.

I worked with my military SF author friend Kevin Ikenberry (with whom I also wrote the Napoleonic alternate history "The Shot Heard 'Round the World," which appears in another volume of this set) to develop our own story on the fringes of the Freehold universe. We even talked about expanding this one into a stand-alone Freehold novel. Maybe someday.

TROUBLE IN PARADISE

(with Kevin Ikenberry)

New Sapporo Spaceport
Meiji

Ellwood clung to the night shadows between a triple-stack of shipping containers. The usual clutter he expected from a United Nations customs-and-clearance zone was absent, which made it hard to stay hidden behind the concertina wire–topped fence.

It wasn't just the New Sapporo spaceport—the whole planet of Meiji was obsessively clean and neat. Between his failed, rushed attempts to secure passage on any outbound freighter, Ellwood had tried to stay hidden in back alleys and fringe zones. But even those places were as clean as the meticulously maintained thoroughfares of the main city. Now, with time running out, he'd given up going to ground. Instead, he stuck close to the spaceport. Hoping for a chance to make his move.

He had to get off this planet.

Three weeks of repeated unsuccessful bids to catch an outbound ship soured his mood. If not for his Blazer training and experience, he would either have been discovered by the UN patrols or would've died from starvation or exposure. Time was running out. He needed to go home.

He drew a long breath and held the chilly, damp air in his lungs.

Meiji's perpetual clouds covered the night sky with a blanket of amber-tinted gray. The cold temperature and annoying mist tried to penetrate Ellwood's confidence. He *would* find a ship, and he *would* make it home to Grainne. And he swore he wouldn't be too late.

All things are a matter of heart and time.

Ellwood exhaled and closed his eyes for a second. His father's words rang through his mind like a bell carillon. The last news he'd had from Grainne was of his father's illness growing worse, the family gathering at the old man's bedside. Ellwood pictured their somber faces over the sallow, living cadaver which was all that remained of the vibrant farmer after years of cancer. He simply couldn't believe the old man would go out like that. No, his father was supposed to remain strong and resilient until his last breath.

Ellwood had promised him that he would return from the war. The old man wanted nothing more than that, and Ellwood would cling to that promise with fierce determination.

If you want something enough, you will do anything for it.

Anything.

The cold breeze shook him from memories as another late-season storm approached. The locals refused to call them typhoons because they rarely brought a storm surge or funnel clouds, yet the powerful winds and rains could suspend ships landing from orbit, with commensurate effects on interstellar shipping. The wind brought a repugnant stench from the nearby lichen farm outside the spaceport's fenced restricted area. Oddly, though, the smell of the lichens—one of Meiji's primary export crops—only made him recall childhood memories. As a young man traveling to Earth with his father, Ellwood was familiar with the stink of paper mills....

Hang on, old man. I'm coming. As soon as I can get out of here.

To do so, though, he'd have to brave more than the odor of a lichen farm. The only ships still on the tarmac occupied berths along the outer border, but an impatient glance at his chronometer gave him a measure of hope. For seven days now he'd observed the UN soldiers patrolling the spaceport, and he knew their rigorous patrol schedule. They did not deviate.

A personnel carrier rolled past at the prescribed time. As the security personnel ended their shifts, a four-minute window would open. Ellwood prepared for the four-hundred-meter move from the terminal fencing to the outer berths.

Eyes closed, he visualized his path through the maze of container stacks. He slowed his breathing and sank down into his Blazer training. Physical exertion meant little. He could easily complete the run in the time allotted, but avoiding the security cameras as they swept the area would be the greater problem. He relished the challenge, glad to maintain his carefully honed edge after being months away from combat.

Ellwood inched closer to the end of the rusted and dented transport container, where he could peer at the first unmanned security tower. The three closed-circuit television cameras panned from left to right in an orderly, laconic fashion. He'd timed the delay precisely. Each sprint between concealed positions would take him no more than three to five seconds.

That brought a rueful smile. *Never forget your training.* As a basic infantry soldier, before his time with the Blazers, he'd learned the simple three- to five-second rush. The sergeants had taught him to remain in a covered, prone position and identify a new objective a short distance away, one he could reach in less than five seconds, then return fire before moving again. Repeating the process, one brief dash at a time, would theoretically allow a soldier to move forward under fire.

As a Blazer, though, he'd learned that technique was bullshit. The best option to move forward under fire meant keeping the enemy cowering in their positions with direct fire.

Yet, like everything in his short career, there was a time and a place for each skill he'd learned. The run to the outer berths would be no different. He would make it, one way or another.

Five.

Four.

Three.

He pushed his shoulders off the container, turned to the open tarmac, and drew a long, deep breath.

Go!

Ellwood reached full speed in five steps and got to the first container stack in another twelve. In the clean shadows, he hustled to the opposite end of the container and glanced at the cameras before timing his departure and arrival at the next container. He repeated the simple task without glancing at anything other than his chronometer. After a minute and a half, hopscotching from place to place, he'd covered half the ground. The extra time gave him a long look at the containers near the remaining ships on the tarmac. Slim pickings. Instead of the forward stack close to the loaders for the ships, he saw the containers were back against the fence line and set for departure. Not what he expected.

He spat a silent curse into the wind and ran for the next container group. The only explanation was that there had been a change in the departure schedule. If containers were too close to a freighter's powered lift engines, that would cause mass destruction on the tarmac, and the UN would never allow that.

Change of plans, but he could deal with it. A minute later, after adjusting course for the relocated containers, he skidded to a stop in the shadows. A uniformed crew member carrying a slate computer appeared at the opposite end.

Morton.

"Where have you been?" the man hissed. "The *Dahlonega* is warming to boost now. I can't get you aboard the *Willis* either! You're too late."

"The hell I am," Ellwood grunted between breaths. "I'm earlier than you told me to be."

"Departure time changed two days ago. You didn't get my message?"

Ellwood swore and shook his head. "Ain't got a slate, asshole. Been stuck here. How am I supposed to know?"

A curl of breeze carried cigarette smoke to his nostrils. He recognized the scented tobacco, a brand popular in the exchanges of the UN soldiers' compounds. As soon as Ellwood recognized the scent and quelled the intense desire to have one himself, Morton turned toward the open space and marched toward the ships, leaving him behind. He called over his shoulder, "You better get your ass moving. You know what to do. Could be your last chance."

Ellwood didn't argue. He sprinted in the opposite direction, curling around the containers to hug the fence line. Above him, three strands of concertina wire wrapped over the crumbled stone wall. The lower section of containers had seen better times. Rust-rimmed holes dotted several of them. Other voids seemed cut by laser torches. Undoubtedly emptied of their goods and no longer viable for hard vacuum, the decommissioned containers had been used to brace others against the vectored thrust of the transports.

Through a fist-sized hole in the stone wall, Ellwood could see a row of barred concrete cells on the other side of the barrier. The structures were open to the sky above. In the darkness, there seemed to be movement, but he couldn't discern who, or what, it might be.

Hyperalert, Ellwood crept deeper into shadow and reached for the pistol tucked inside his waistband. A flitter of movement at a rusted container five meters away made him freeze. A small human head poked out and glanced in both directions. A child.

The little one turned back to him. Ellwood tried to smile, tried to ease the wide-eyed kid's flash of panic. "Hey! It's okay. I'm not going to hurt you," he whispered. The boy did not seem to understand, and Ellwood mentally slapped himself. The child looked Japanese, and Ellwood switched effortlessly. "*Konnichiwa*?"

With surprising speed, the boy slithered out of the container and sprinted thirty meters away before sliding on one leg and ducking under the stone wall. Before Ellwood could even move forward, the child disappeared into the stockade on the other side of the barrier.

His brow furrowed. *Why would a kid be in there?*

From the tarmac, the unmistakable whine of lift engines spooling up propelled him forward. The *Dahlonega* pulsed her lift thrusters to idle, and the gentle breeze around him became a hurricane. Ellwood dropped to the ground, pressing his face into the alkaline-smelling soil, and crawled forward. As Ellwood peered inside the stockade, he thought the ragged breach in the barrier seemed too small for even the child to have gone through.

UN soldiers with their rifles at the low ready patrolled around rows and rows of open cells wrapped in heavy bars. As the *Dahlonega* fired her lift engines behind them and the winds tore sheets of dust and trash into the maelstrom, many of the guards covered their faces and turned away from the blast. Blue-tinted light illuminated the far, dark corners of the interior space, and Ellwood could see that the cells on the other side of the wall teemed with children! Some even younger than the boy he'd seen, the oldest maybe eleven or twelve years. Girls and boys sat together in squalid conditions, in utter contrast to the usual cleanliness of New Sapporo. Some sobbed in muted voices with blue-lit tears streaming down their faces. Others, the older ones, sat glaring at the armed guards around them.

As he realized what he was seeing, Ellwood fought a rising wave of rage at the depravity of the UN. Beautiful, clean, perfect Meiji, like so many things, was too good to be true. A child screamed inside the compound, but no one moved or responded. The familiar actions and reactions of both guards and captives indicated long-term incarceration, as if they'd gotten used to the situation. What the prisoners had done did not matter to Ellwood. They were only children and had no caring adult in sight.

Though he'd been trying to get out of here for weeks, to get home in time to say goodbye to his father, Ellwood forgot his desperate plan to run to the *Dahlonega*. A prison compound full of kids, right here on the edge of the New Sapporo spaceport—in plain sight, but not on any public records.

Ellwood wasn't going anywhere until he understood what was happening here—and did something about it. There would be other ships. There had to be. He needed to go home, needed to escape and get to his father's side.

But he also needed to be here. Now. How could he just leave these children?

Another little boy cried inside the stockade, and the guards barked commands. From his hiding place, Ellwood stared at the back of a nearby guard's head and wished he had a bayonet to fling. Instead, he lowered his face to the crook of his right elbow, covering his eyes from the flying dust. As much as he tried to tell himself it wasn't his fight, Ellwood knew better.

His father would have insisted he stay.

Tyrants were owed their due. Ellwood closed his eyes and let the last vestiges of hope turn to the simmering fuel of anger. He muttered, expressing the anger that came from several different directions. He was going to miss his last chance to get out of here. "Oh, you fucking bastards."

UN Forces Cantonment Area
New Sapporo

Sora Hasegawa waited.

Only a few years before, Hermann would have been at her side to place the ancestral string of pearls around her neck. The final moment of careful preparation, long practiced and disciplined by her family's custom, should have been an intimate moment of trust and love between husband and wife. For every state dinner and official reception they'd attended in their eight years of marriage, he'd known and understood the simple ritual.

But during the last two years, especially following his promotion to Command Colonel at only forty-three, his fixation on rank and duty had wedged itself between them. Sora had demurred to his needs since her family's interests in the United Nations centered on profit from interstellar shipping. Like Hermann, her family's interest in her was dwindling. Sora knew her role, yet dissatisfaction grew in her heart. More than once, she'd stared in the mirror and watched the gentle acceleration of age while wondering if there was anything more to her life.

She wanted something more.

Hasegawa Interstellar would belong to her when her parents died, but that time did not seem at all imminent, since both were in their seventies, rigorously healthy and vibrant. While Hermann's rapid acceleration up the chain of command undoubtedly meant they would be recalled to Earth in two years, Sora no longer knew if she wanted to go. Hermann's first star appeared likely, given the UN political climate. Only results mattered. He'd married the heiress of Hasegawa Interstellar, after all. She had thought their bond was more of love and respect than profit and gain, but that was proven wrong by Hermann's greed.

While she finished dressing, by herself, Hermann talked loudly into his comm in the bedroom. He'd been staring out the windows toward the spaceport. The approaching storm outside would not likely delay the landing of the *Chitose*, the flagship of Hasegawa Interstellar, but it could complicate the arrival of the Undersecretary for Colonial Expansion. It might cause difficulties for him to arrive for the dinner in his honor.

Difficulties would be too good for them.

Catching herself at the surprising mental remark, Sora drew a sharp breath, but did not rebuke herself for it. Hermann had his own plans. He wanted her to impress upon the Undersecretary how much they needed continued commercial and strategic support for UN operations on Meiji. The Hasegawa shipbuilders on Earth were angry and tense because of the continued incarceration of immigrants from Earth and, worse, the separation of minor children from their parents. Hermann, though, justified the action to ensure proper bureaucratic order. Workers were a necessity on Meiji, workers the UN could trust—meaning those without ties or ideations of the Resistance. No matter where they came from.

Yet, she could not trust the United Nations. On the advice of the General Secretary, Hermann and his advisors drafted a temporary policy to secure the loyalty of the immigrant workforce building the Meiji fleet. The UN could hold minor children for six months, with a fee of 5,000 TK_currency each. If a family wanted their children, it was not enough for them to pass multiple security investigations and submit to routine searches and continuous observation. The fiscal aspect, Hermann argued, would keep them in line. Living on Meiji was not inexpensive. But Hermann wasn't satisfied with simple extortion. Should the working parents fail to attend the required wages, they faced deportation themselves. Any children would remain wards of the state until the age of seventeen when they would be conscripted into the Meiji Defense Force, a subordinate command under Hermann's control as the Command Colonel.

She'd argued that he was perpetuating war, and Hermann had laughed and told her the answer was not so simple. War provided opportunities, and those opportunities would benefit Hasegawa Interstellar and themselves, personally. He'd kept his own role in the war at arm's length and prided himself in the docile Meiji environment, but he didn't realize his errors. The first gentle flames of the Resistance burned in the quiet alleys and the establishments near the docks … and Hermann didn't see it. Heartsick workers, wanting family more than money, would not be ignored much longer. While her husband and his advisors plotted a way to line their pockets in relative peace, the war slow-marched to them.

With a sigh, Sora grasped the ends of the necklace, raised it to her neck, and clasped it with practiced ease. Each time she wore it and Hermann wasn't there to fasten it for her, she imagined her mother fainting dead away. The thought made her smile as she straightened the necklace along her skin.

From the bedroom, Hermann ended his comm and called, "Are you ready, Sora?"

"*Hai,*" she replied before switching to English as Hermann preferred. "Just putting on my necklace."

Her words had the desired effect, and she was pleased he caught the small, barbed reminder. Hermann sighed heavily in the bedroom and appeared at the vanity door a moment later, stepping behind her. His white uniform contrasted against her simple, elegant black dress. His longish blond hair rakishly swept back and coiffed perfectly, also in striking contrast to her long, straight hair, pulled back in a matching pearl clasp behind her neck.

His lips drew tight and blue eyes turned serious. He met her gaze. "I forgot again."

She nodded but did not reply.

"You're upset with me." He tried to smile. "I neglected my duty, Sora. I am sorry."

"Thank you." She nodded again and did not take her eyes from his. "I will be downstairs in a moment. Please ask Mako to come in. I will need her help to finish my preparations."

Hermann smiled. "Of course, love." He turned to go but paused in the doorway and spun around with parade-ground precision. Business again, not loving partner. "You are prepared to ensure that Hasegawa takes sole possession of the shipping routes from Meiji to Caledonia? And take responsibility for subcontractors and partners along the other major routes?"

Her voice became formal, too. "I cannot speak for subcontractors, Hermann. Their policies, and those of any partners, are governed by the Board of Directors. Neither I nor my family have any impact on such agreements."

"Those shipments must be guaranteed, Sora. The UN will pay handsomely to guarantee that these agreements remain in place."

She smiled softly, not trusting herself to speak.

He took that as an answer. "How much longer will you be?"

"Five minutes. It will be faster if Mako comes in."

Hermann flushed and left, and a surge of emotions threatened to bring tears to her eyes, but she held them off, as usual. With fists curled at her sides, Sora stared at her reflection again. *Is this how you're going to live your life? Or are you going to do something about it?*

Mako promptly entered the outer suite dressed in a black jacket and pants, the diplomatic uniform. The younger woman's face showed concern, but she said nothing.

Sora asked, "Do we have communications with the *Chitose*?"

"Yes, Miss. They will deorbit in an hour and thirteen minutes. Landing in just under two hours."

It would have to be enough time. "And Yuichi?"

Her aide's face clouded. "Yes. He reports the children are healthy and ready. They know he's coming for them."

Her pulse began to beat faster. "The storm will provide cover. Have him readied and alert the others." Sora could count her trusted confidants on one hand. Roles needed to be played. Sora lowered her voice to a whisper. "Tonight is the night."

"Oh," Mako said, then she finally smiled.

New Sapporo Spaceport
Meiji

As the ominous storm coalesced over the spaceport, Ellwood realized he could follow the boy or get back into a hiding space he'd located in a nearby container. He glanced at the hole in the fence the boy had crawled through, back toward the stockade. He couldn't follow the boy. At least, not yet. With the cold rain soaking his borrowed coveralls, Ellwood crawled instead for the container and studied the hole. He could make it. Barely.

Flat on his stomach, Ellwood wormed his way into the dark hole leading into the hiding place. His shoulders caught the raw edges, and just when he thought he was stuck, a twist of his upper body sent him the rest of the way through. He crawled upright in the pitch-black night and froze. Someone else was inside. Smelling acrid tobacco smoke, he turned and saw the glowing end of a lit cigarette. Ellwood made out the barest image of a man's face.

"You in the wrong place, *gaijin*."

Ellwood made no move. "What place am I in?"

A rifle bolt slammed into firing position, likely chambering a round as well. "You not UN."

He clamped his tongue between his teeth. "What makes you say that?"

"A feeling." The cigarette pulsed again, and now he saw the man smile. "If not UN, you Resistance? Aardvark?"

"What does that matter?"

The man laughed. It was a harsh, short burst, but quiet enough not to carry. Rain pounded against the sides of the container. A cascade of thunder rumbled like a full battery artillery barrage outside. "You from Grainne, then?"

Like I'm going to tell you, dogfucker.

Ellwood brought his hands up slowly with his palms toward the man. "I don't want any trouble. I'm trying to get a ride off this planet. To get home. My father is sick."

"But you a soldier, yes?"

His hands free and open, Ellwood watched the cigarette glow to confirm the man was three meters away at worst. In the darkness, and unless the man snapped some kind of torch to life and blinded him, he could cross the distance and disarm the man before he could fire, much less aim, a shot.

"Are you with the Resistance?" Ellwood asked, risking a half step in the man's direction. The man made no move other than another long draw on his cigarette.

"From Caledonia. Gave up trying to get back. Thought the war couldn't find us here on Meiji."

"You're here because of the children across that wall?" Ellwood asked. He brought his trailing foot along under him, inching closer to the man.

"Punky. We give them food and water. The little ones can crawl in and out. UN guards no pay attention to them." The man sighed. "Families broken so the UN make credits from them. War would be too good for the fucking UN."

Ellwood blinked and sucked on one cheek. "They're holding the children for ransom?"

"Extorting the parents. Same thing. We trying to help them."

"Who is we?" Ellwood asked.

"Can't say. You wanna help? I get you a seat off Meiji."

Ellwood chuckled and shook his head. "You expect me to believe that? A man hiding in a dark container? You could be a plant or an informant just as easy."

"If I was, I'd have shot you or called for help. Especially with you creeping forward like a Blazer." The man smiled again around the cigarette. "Oh, yeah, I can see it, *gaijin*. Plain as the shock on your face."

Ellwood couldn't hold back a smile. He laughed and nodded, stepping forward a little more intending to knock the man's rifle away. Another rifle cocked from behind him in the gaping darkness.

He mentally cursed himself for losing situational awareness. Someone else was there. Someone fantastically good.

"Not another step, *gaijin*." The voice was deeper and gruff. "Blazer or not, we kill you here and now unless you help us."

"Help you do what?" Ellwood turned toward the voice. A match crackled and spat to life, ignited a candle, and a soft yellow glow filled the space. A large Japanese man in gray-and-black striped fatigue—the Meiji Defense Force uniform from two decades before—approached from behind. The man with the cigarette was a young boy, no more than twenty.

The candlelight revealed rations and water cans. There were crates of weapons, too.

"You thought Meiji was a paradise, right?" The second man frowned. "The war is here, too, but it's a different war. One for profit. We will end that tonight."

"By freeing the kids? Returning them to their families?"

"That's part of it." The man smiled at him. "My name is Yuichi. This punk is my son, Keiko. There are others who will help us free them."

Ellwood squinted. "I saw at least ten guards inside the holding area. Those aren't great odds."

"As I said," Yuichi replied, "there are others. And we have firepower arriving shortly."

Ellwood nodded, realizing that the storm would provide excellent concealment. The children already had a known way in and out of the stockade. All they would have to do was widen the hole, but once free, they would be on the wide-open tarmac of the spaceport, and easy targets. Unless …

He smiled. "Your firepower is approaching from orbit, then?"

Yuichi grinned. "Smart man. The UN perimeter towers would cut us down otherwise. We bring the children through the hole, and the ship in orbit provides cover as we move them to Hangar One. From there, the others will take them and get them to their families. Once to safety, we get them underground. Hidden. The UN chases the empty ship. Maybe they blow it up. But here? Here we get the rest of Meiji to stand against the UN. Show our people we can win. We do not need the UN here for the protection they promise. The UN only wants our lichens and our money. You understand this, yes?"

"The UN is now willing to take the children to profit from those resources, too." Ellwood shook his head. For a moment, he thought of his father in his hospital bed. The old man would expect him to do his duty, just like a Blazer would. He couldn't turn his back now that he knew the situation. "There are certain things I can walk away from, Yuichi ... but not if it's harming kids and especially not for money."

Keiko opened a crate to brand new M5 4mm rifles with 15mm grenade launchers still in their shipping configuration. Next to them were magazines and boxes of ammunition. "How fast can a Blazer prepare and load an M5?"

Ellwood picked up the familiar rifle. He turned it in his hands and worked a finger under the wrappings with a grin. "You're about to find out. While I do, tell me that your extraction plan is more than the two of you blowing a hole in that wall and running like hell. I got the rest of it—getting the kids underground and all. But you gotta get them outta the stockade first."

Yuichi grinned and pointed to several scraps of paper on the wall. He squinted and made them out as maps of the neighboring compound. "We show you."

UN State Dinner
Headquarters Palace
New Sapporo

Diplomatic functions. Hermann had discussed them when they were first married, but Sora hadn't really understood "mandatory fun" until she had suffered through glacial speeches and watched the seconds tick on her chronometer. As Hermann ascended in rank, she had to endure more and more such events. Her practiced facade, smiling and bowing to all manner of dignitaries (whether or not she liked or admired them) had grown tired. Her fatigue, she recognized, came both from so many events per month and from her own discomfort with the situation on Meiji.

Now, away from the receiving line and watching the torrential rainfall through the windows of the main hall, Sora cradled a glass of wine and waited. Big band music wafted through the party, but not loud enough to interfere with normal conversation. Pretending to sip her wine, she closed her eyes, remembering fondly her first dance with Hermann at his family's traditional wedding ceremony. For the music, she'd chosen "String of Pearls" by Glenn Miller, much to the satisfaction of the elder Hasegawas. They'd marveled over her exquisite taste and keen ear. As much as she loved the music of that era, her choice didn't come from her own tastes, but she played her role. Even as a young woman, Sora had put her own feelings and emotions aside for the wants of her family. Her marriage was their desire, and while Hermann had once been charming as he pursued her instead of his career, over time her unease had been replaced with discomfort and now abject dissatisfaction.

In her blurry reflection, she saw Mako approaching, and her throat went dry. The time had come. Her assistant's instructions had been to observe Hermann closely. When he noticed that she was not at his side and came looking, then Mako would appear to intercept him.

"Miss?" Mako asked. "A Hasegawa Interstellar vessel is approaching, but it is not on the arrival manifest. They have requested your presence."

Sora consulted the offered slate and studied the message carefully. She felt rather than saw Hermann approach from behind. "Is everything all right, darling?" His voice was warm, but she could hear the annoyance.

She shook her head and forced a tremble into her voice. "The *Chitose* is arriving within the hour. The Board of Directors have sent me a sealed message."

Hermann's brow furrowed. "Why would they not just send you an encrypted message?"

Sora willed tears to her eyes and did not respond. Mako filled the void with the answer Sora wanted him to hear. "Command Colonel, private and personal messages are sealed by the Board. There are few reasons they do so. The last time such a message came, it was the death of the Honored Grandmother."

Hermann's impatience washed away in an instant. He placed a hand on her shoulder, and Sora flinched. "You should leave before any loss of decorum, love."

She let a tear slide down her left cheek. "Yes. I am terrified the news is ... my father."

When he nodded, she noted a flicker of light in his eyes. In that instant, her hatred for the man came full circle. Hermann believed her father would leave a portion of the company to him as well, despite her position as the sole heiress. His only care for her was that she would not ruin his diplomatic party or his reputation with a sudden burst of emotion.

"Go. Take my car to the spaceport and then go home, where you can have all the privacy you need. Send it back for me, and I will join you as soon as the dinner is complete." Hermann forced another smile and when he saw another tear race down her cheek, he added, "I'm sure it's nothing."

A million retorts swirled in her brain. "I will have to return to Earth."

"Do what you must if you have more pressing matters. I will be fine here without you, Sora."

She reached up and kissed his cheek. "I know, Hermann."

Of course, you will.

She walked directly to the front staircase and down into the foyer. Several sets of eyes followed her. As she reached the first landing, she turned to Mako, who was ever-present at her left shoulder, and nodded once. The signal was simple and clear: *Don't speak.*

Outside, under the covered entranceway, the sound and smell of the pouring rain surrounded them. The noise blotted out everything as they ducked into Hermann's dedicated car, with the flags bearing his Command Colonel's rank mounted on each front fender.

"Spaceport—all possible speed, on Command Colonel Sturm's orders," Mako snapped to the driver.

Trying to control her pounding heart, Sora sat back in the seat and looked out the window as the car sped through the rain. Fifteen minutes later, as they reached the spaceport, Sora peered around the driver's head through the front windshield to see the military checkpoint. She stole a quick glance at Mako, who nodded.

They had hoped the driver would follow established standard operating procedures. With her husband's car and insignia present in the floodlights, the checkpoint guards collected themselves and formed up to salute the vehicle. A sergeant stepped forward and spoke to the driver. Sora saw the young man's shoulders sag, but she couldn't tell if it was relief or annoyance.

No soldier ever wants to stand in the cold rain any longer than they have to.

Hermann's sayings over the years had all played into her plan. It took only the right weather and the right men and women willing to put their lives on the line for these children. Hermann wouldn't hear complaints from the workers. Without a voice, the strained families of the imprisoned children had no choice but to attempt rescue even at great cost. Sora hoped they would be successful without loss of life, but things seldom happened flawlessly. But she could hope, even if her husband always told her it wasn't a method. It was all she had left.

Through the vehicle window, Mako pointed at a descending ship's amber thrusters firing gently above and approaching the spaceport through the storm. "There's the *Chitose*." With a quick glance, Sora confirmed that the ship was a *Hokkaido*-class frigate with special modifications for combat operations.

It would work perfectly for their purposes.

The sergeant stepped back into his shelter from the rain and gestured. The diplomatic car rolled through the checkpoint and sped across the military portion of the tarmac. As it approached the far checkpoint, another group of soldiers made the same frenzy running into the rain. The customs and courtesies of the service were predictable to a fault. Now it all worked on Sora's behalf.

The detonation of an explosive device on the wall of the stockade near the lichen farm caught all of them by surprise. Torn between their duty to defend their position and also to respectfully receive the Command Colonel's wife, they froze.

As shockwaves and fire expanded from the explosion, Sora shouted to the driver, "Go!" Without questioning, he stomped the accelerator pedal to the floor and rocketed through the gates as the checkpoint guards dove out of the way. "Get to the *Chitose*! It's the safest place on the field!"

New Sapporo Spaceport
Meiji

Sudden torrential rain muted the dust and smoke from the explosion as the satchel charge brought down a section of the stockade wall. Ellwood watched Yuichi and Keiko dart into the breach, firing at the known guard positions. No hesitation. They meant business. They'd practiced their attack, marking the position of the predictable UN guards and setting their timing accordingly. For Resistance fighters, their discipline was commendable. While it wasn't quite the method he'd learned as a Blazer, their initial attack appeared successful. Less than fifteen seconds after they'd charged into the stockade, the first children scrambled through the hole blasted in the wall.

Ellwood called out to them in Japanese. "Here! Follow me!"

The first boy ran toward him, closing the distance quickly, with more children at his heels, panicked, desperate, but filled with hope. The kids knew the plan and dashed to salvation, quickly lining up behind the container. Ellwood heard the methodical firing of the two rifles, creating chaos among the unsuspecting guards in the stockade, and he knew Yuichi and Keiko were having the effect they'd wanted ... but he also knew it couldn't last. They didn't have much time. Through the rain, he saw the approaching ship bearing the familiar paint scheme of Hasegawa Interstellar. The markings indicated the ship was the *Chitose*.

As the massive ship flared on its final approach, landing engines blasted the surrounding tarmac with hurricane-force winds. The rain swirled into a blinding mist, obscuring everything around them. Ellwood grinned. The ship was much more than a diversion.

As he did his best to round up the fleeing children, Ellwood watched the frigate pivot on its maneuvering thrusters, which eased the wind along the planned escape route. Leading the kids, he ran for the next container stack with the children right behind him. In the distance, he saw a group of ramp hands waving their lighted cones—the signal. The children sped around him in silence as the roaring rainstorm covered even the slap of their footfalls through the puddles. Ellwood turned and counted them going past.

More than fifty! Damn, all those children held hostage!

"Go!" he cried, and the steady stream of children continued out of the mist and past him. The amber-tinged light of the *Chitose*'s engines shone down on small, strained faces. Yet they kept coming. Another fifty.

The rattling gunfire increased from the stockade—the stunned UN soldiers finally returning fire, still not knowing how many rebels were attacking the facility. The children raced past him, following their leaders to the safety of the hangars where others would speed them to their waiting families while the *Chitose* and the raiding party, he and the others, helped them escape. Ellwood hoped they could divert the attention of the UN soldiers a few more minutes.

The line of children grew more ragged, groups of two and three interspersed by longer distances. Two young teens limped past him, and Ellwood saw blood running down one's torn pant leg. Spurred to action, he turned and ran back for the entrance, passing the last few children. An aircraft's turbine engine roared to life as he passed the end of the container, and a blur of movement caught his eye in the same instant he collided with a silhouetted figure. He sprawled across the wet tarmac, rolled, and came up with his rifle pointed at the figure on the ground. She pushed herself up to lean on her arms.

A woman? She seemed utterly incongruous here, wearing a soaked black evening gown. Her long, dark hair was plastered across her face. She wore high heels, one of which had fallen loose as she tumbled.

"Who are you?" he demanded. "What are you doing here?"

Her face turned to his, and he felt a shiver of recognition run down his spine. A string of elegant pearls encircled her neck, and Ellwood wondered if her husband, the Command Colonel of the New Sapporo garrison, had purchased them for her. The photos of the two of them adorned propaganda posters all over the Meiji terminal areas with bold slogans of "Together We Thrive." Sora Hasegawa, shipping heiress, wore a traditional neo-kimono and Command Colonel Sturm stood in his impeccable dress whites.

Now she was at the spaceport, in the middle of a raid. Unarmed. He pressed forward with the rifle's barrel pointed at her chest.

The massive frigate, which belonged to her family, pivoted as it landed. Sora Hasegawa stared up at it. Ellwood gasped in realization. He spoke in broken Japanese. "You're here for the children."

She climbed to her feet as if trying to regain her dignity and replied in fluent, unaccented English. "To get them home."

Ellwood jerked his chin toward the landing *Chitose*. "You brought them here as a distraction? Just for this raid? Big risk."

"If all the children get out it's worth it." Her eyes flickered past him, alarmed.

The young rebel Keiko staggered out of the dust and waved a bloody hand. "Blazer!" The boy had taken at least three bullets in his legs and one arm but was still on his feet.

Desperate to rescue him, Ellwood ran and yelled over his shoulder to Sora. He had to trust that she was an ally. Right now, he had no other choice. "I'll get Keiko! You get the children to safety!"

He ran for Keiko. The boy limped forward, his rifle threatening to slip out of his grasp. He stumbled and fell forward, but Ellwood caught him with one arm. Forcing the words out, Keiko said, "My father … still inside."

Ellwood hefted the boy, draping a thin arm over his shoulder, but the young man's legs wobbled. "Get up, Keiko. You gotta get up!"

"I'll make it." The boy tried to smile, but there was no way he would walk …

"I have him," Sora barked in Ellwood's ear. "You seal off the stockade wall."

Before he could respond, she raised Keiko's arm and pivoted under it, taking his weight on her shoulders. The shipping heiress, despite her fancy gown and pearl necklace, was remarkably strong and determined. The dichotomy of her elegant garb walking a soaking, camouflaged soldier to safety disoriented him. Ellwood stepped back as Sora and the boy limped over to the hangars where the ramp hands moved toward them.

A firefight raged inside the stockade. Without his son's rifle, Yuichi was vastly outnumbered. Ellwood hesitated, torn. The urge to simply follow the plan overwhelmed him. He had to whisk the children into hiding so the *Chitose* could boost away. The UN would assume the Hasegawa spacecraft had taken their charges. Ellwood couldn't turn his back on them.

If this isn't my fight, I don't know what is.

Dammit.

Ellwood ran. A few straggler children passed him, and he yelled at them to move, pointing through the rain as the squall intensified. The *Chitose*'s timing had been perfect.

Reaching the barricade of containers, Ellwood flinched as flashbangs detonated along the wall. Even muted by the wall, the light still made him flinch, but he could see a shadow bounding out of the glare and mist—Yuichi carrying the body of a small girl.

Wounds dotted her chest and legs, and Ellwood could see that the other man bore similar wounds. He staggered forward, then collapsed to his knees in the rain.

Ellwood was there in an instant, reaching for him. "Come on, Yuichi. Get up."

"I can't, Blazer." His head turned too slowly to face Ellwood. His dark eyes danced back and forth and struggled to focus. "Take her." He had barely kept himself alive, forced himself to keep going, to carry the child.

Ellwood saw that the girl was dead, her face a porcelain mask of peace despite the horrible pain she must have felt.

Yuichi didn't know. He struggled to stay upright. "Take her! I will keep them back."

"No, Yuichi. You're in no shape to do anything but get to safety. You need the medics. You just have to get up. I'll take her, Yuichi. Get to the hangars!"

Yuichi reached up, and Ellwood gingerly removed the little girl from his arms. He checked for a pulse and found none. As he did, the older man scrambled to his feet and lurched toward the hangars in the swirling cascades of rain. Two workers appeared in their dark, soaked clothes. One took Yuichi's arm and assisted him. The other bit her lip and took the little girl from Ellwood's arms.

"*Arigato*, Blazer," the older woman said. His identity was out, for better or worse. If the UN started asking questions, it was only a matter of time before they came for him.

Not without a fight, they won't.

Ellwood spotted movement, and his rifle came up without thought and swung toward the figures emerging from the hole blasted in the stockade wall. As soon as he identified their UN uniforms, he squeezed the trigger in short bursts, knocking them down. Now it was time to defend what Yuichi and Keiko had done.

He strode toward the hole as more UN soldiers pushed through. Again, Ellwood fired. His face twisted in sudden anger at the United Nations, the war, and how it had kept him from his ailing father. Years of frustration surfaced, coming to a head, and he used that to his advantage. Relentless, Ellwood took cover at the corner of the containers, working his way toward the damaged wall. He had to keep the enemy at bay.

"Come on, you bastards!" Ellwood yelled over the thundering

rain. Several rounds struck the container wall near his head, and he ducked out of the way, letting them fire wildly in his direction. To his left, in the wide-open space of the outer berths, Sora Hasegawa walked toward the *Chitose* with her arms above her head, waving. Somehow, even drenched and bedraggled, in the middle of a firefight, she managed to look elegant.

What is she doing?

She turned toward Ellwood. Deep in shadows, he couldn't be sure she was looking at him, but at the same time he felt her eyes on his with a deep intensity. Her left hand, still raised over her head, made a circling motion. Her right arm pointed at the stockade wall.

Ellwood slipped around the corner and fired six quick shots, hitting at least one soldier in the tight, smoke-obscured space between the container and the stockade wall. The enemy would keep coming. More rounds slammed into the container wall next to him. Too close. They knew where he was. It was a matter of time until—

WHUMP! WHUMP! WHUMP!

WHUMP! WHUMP!

He turned back to see that the woman had disappeared as the familiar chorus of the Mark-32 40mm grenade launcher lobbed round after round into the UN stockade, now that all the children were gone. The diversion was almost complete, the rescue successful, but he needed to give the ramp hands more time. The last few children and the last of the workers crept toward the hangars as rebels ran to collect them and get them away. They just needed a few more seconds. He wouldn't need to delay the UN soldiers long.

With covering fire from the *Chitose*, Ellwood reloaded his weapon before bursting forward and charging up the narrow chute between the containers and the stockade wall, intent on killing anything in his path.

Five steps into the confined space, Ellwood reeled as another barrage from the *Chitose* detonated along the top of the wall. The blast scattered hot debris across his face and arms. He retreated to the corner of the container in time to see the wall give way and collapse outward. An odd, sudden silence created a calm eddy in the storm.

In the distance, Ellwood heard a cacophony of Meiji's famous wind chimes tolling in their random symphony. He'd not been into the city to see the iconic structures. His sole mission had been to get home.

Focus, Blazer.

Muzzle pointed into the swirling dust and rain, Ellwood waited for a target to materialize. His years of Blazer trigger discipline prevented unnecessary discharges, which would keep his tenuous location from discovery. Seconds passed. His eyes swept across the collapsed wall again and again, but there was nothing. A burst of gunfire from behind snapped his attention around. The UN forces had given up on the stockade and now they were attacking the *Chitose* itself!

The ship's shielding took the brunt of the UN small arms fire with indifference. From an open portal below the wide engine bells, the grenade launcher continued to fire. A few of the crew lay prone on the lowered ramp and fired various small arms, whatever they had, into the UN forces charging their direction.

Ellwood raced to the nearer line of containers, the same place he'd tried to meet Morton so he could arrange a ride home. In the shadow, the Command Colonel's wife huddled in the rain. Seeing her fearful expression, he understood what had happened. The *Chitose* hadn't had time to fully descend and scoop her up, to snatch her away from here. Sora Hasegawa had chosen for them to be safe enough to boost, to maintain the illusion, while she waited for her husband's forces to collect and arrest her.

Ellwood approached her cautiously, expecting her to be despondent. Her head snapped up, and she glared at him with fierce, dark eyes. "What are you still doing here?"

"Getting you out of here," he blurted. It seemed the proper thing to say, realizing she was a woman who had betrayed everything she'd known.

"You are a Blazer." It wasn't an accusation, merely a statement of fact. "Keiko told me."

"I was." Ellwood knelt beside her, taking cover. "I'm not sure what I am right now, except trying to get home."

"To Earth?" Rain ran down her face. The urge to wipe it away nearly overwhelmed Ellwood.

He shook his head. "Grainne. My father is dying."

A pained look crossed her face. "My father will die of shame when he learns of my betrayal. I have given up everything."

Ellwood nodded. There was no other response that came immediately to mind. Then he said, "You saved the children. We'll get them back to their families."

"For now." She sighed. "There is no guarantee that Hermann and his zealous assistants won't continue their abysmal policies."

"No, there isn't," Ellwood agreed. "But the Resistance has come to Meiji. The rescue of the children will only embolden others to join and keep up the fight. I thought your family had a contract with the UN. Why did the *Chitose* fire upon them?"

"A contract is merely a piece of paper." She sighed. "Like my family, Meiji wanted nothing of this war. They tried to remain unaffiliated. I've learned that between good and evil there is nothing neutral. So, I made a choice. I pray it was the right one."

Pressed against the damaged shipping containers, some bearing her family's name, the heiress looked impossibly … human. Her gown soaked through, Sora pulled her knees to her chest and wrapped her shivering arms around them.

Before he could say anything, she looked up at him. Her brow furrowed with a question and then a soft smile formed on her lips. He watched her tilt her chin down to her chest. She brought her hands to her neck and unclasped the string of pearls. As she placed them into one palm, her expression was serene and troubled at the same time. Her eyes came up as she held out her hand. "Get on board the next ship you can. These will pay for you to get home, Blazer. Tell everyone what happened here."

"My name is Ellwood." He stared at the pearls before reaching out and taking them gently. He strung them between his hands, knowing they would more than finance his way, letting him acquire a second set of identification and commercial fast transport in the general direction of Grainne. "And you're Sora Hasegawa. Shipping heiress."

She bowed, as if it were a formal introduction back at the diplomatic reception.

Ellwood leaned forward. "If we're going to get out of this, we must move fast. There's another way. Something more important."

Sora brought her chin up. Still close together, he felt her breath on his face as her beauty almost stunned him silent. "We?"

He thought for an instant about his father and imagined the old man in his hospital bed, smiling and laughing. Ellwood hadn't fallen all that far from the tree. His father would understand, and if he died before Ellwood could make it home, the old man would agree it was for a noble cause, the greater good.

Opportunities are like lightning, son. They rarely strike the same place twice. When you see a good one, for yourself or to stick it to anyone who stands in your way, do it.

Do it.

He extended the pearls, reached for her neck. Uncertain, Sora swept her hair out of the way, and he secured the strand back in place and put his hands on her shoulders. "The rest of the galaxy will know about what happened here, Sora. We'll make sure of it."

When she smiled at him, the crusty deployment-caused layers around his heart crumbled. There would be no going home. At least, not yet. Here, as unlikely as it was, might be something worth fighting for, after all. His father would understand.

Ellwood stood up as the gunfire reached a crescendo behind them. He pulled her along with him. At the touch of her hand, the ripple of electricity down his spine was unmistakable, and when she didn't immediately let go, his heart jumped in anticipation.

Sora kicked off her expensive shoes, and he chastised himself for underestimating her. "Let's go."

They started for the hangars and the rescued children as the maelstrom of rain and wind whipped around them. Bright light suddenly bathed the tarmac, extending their shadows ahead of them as they ran. He smiled at her as the *Chitose*'s ascent engines fired and the ship rose into the sky. By the sounds, carnage rolled behind them in the blast, but he didn't risk glancing away from the beautiful woman.

"Welcome to the Resistance, Sora."

Prolific anthologist Martin H. Greenberg created Hotel Andromeda, *a bustling interstellar space city as a gathering place for original stories. For my contribution, I wanted to do something that no other writer had done—so why not a shape-shifting madame of a space station brothel that caters to all life forms? When I started thinking about various forms of reproduction, plant, mammal, reptile, insect, and everything in between, the ideas seemed endless—ranging from humorous to dramatic, from kinky to just plain weird.*

What do alien species find attractive, or pleasurable, or a turn-off? Male, female, or any number of other genders?

And an even bigger challenge—to write it in first person.

A hookermorph has quite the job cut out for her/it.

THE HAPPY HOOKERMORPH

The more appendages a client has, the better he tips. I know it's presumptuous to make sweeping generalizations like that, with the incredible number of life-forms in the galaxy—but, hey, I've been at this business long enough to spot trends, and a lot of different types come through the Hotel Andromeda. Trust me—count the tentacles, then count your fee for the night.

And this guy had *twenty-three* appendages—just look at 'em! And of course it didn't take much for me to figure out what the identical number of orifices on my adapted female body were supposed to be for.

He gestured toward me with a pseudopod and eased back on his motive cushion of slime, flailing a few other tendrils in the air. I moved naturally, slithering into his room. I had altered my body to look exactly like a female Slugwump, and a knockout too, as best I could determine from the species listing in the Lexicon. If I didn't get everything right, it might shatter the illusion for the client.

"I ... I've never done anything like this before," he said in his own dialect, sounding like wet glue oozing from a tube. They always said the same thing, even the veterans—as if a hookermorph like me really cares about excuses.

"You'll be just fine," I said to the lonely Slugwump, caressing him with one of my tendrils. "I'm already hot for you." His eyestalks extended in nervous astonishment at that.

Indeed, I was hot. Slugwumps come from a humid, haze-shrouded world about thirty degrees hotter than would have been my preference. But my Slugwump body adjusted to it in a few minutes as I glided in after him on his own trail of slime. They find that sort of thing erotic, you know. He closed the door portal behind us.

Inside the room, he turned on some sort of subsonic music that sounded like very large bubbles bursting deep underwater. I had to be amorous and whisper into his auditory pickups while the surround-speakers kept going *bloop-bloop-bloop.* Humidity generators worked silently to keep the environment comfortable for him.

In the middle of the room lay a corralled-off patch of powdery sand, which I took to be the area of repose. The client oozed over to a pedestal on which he had placed a large bowl-shaped flower that looked like a big water lily. With an igniter, he lit the tips of the petals, and as they curled down in flames, the flower exuded a fragrant pink smoke. A nice touch.

He moved nervously, switching the igniter from tentacle to tentacle to tentacle in a hypnotic fireman's brigade; he hadn't managed to dispose of it before it burned one of his appendages, and I snatched it out of his grasp, tossing it to the sand in the sleeping area.

"I keep wanting to make small talk," he said, "but I can't think of anything to say."

I nudged him over the rim of the corral into the sleeping area. His body elongated and he flowed over to the sand. "I don't want to make small talk," I said. "I want to make love to you."

Again, he goggled with his eyestalks. By now I could see that I would have to take things into my own hands—figuratively speaking, that is. If I waited for him to take any sort of initiative, we would be in his cubicle all weekend.

When we actually got down to the business of mating, he proved perfectly willing and eager. Our pliant bodies squished together and rolled on the gritty sand, which heightened the pleasure at the tips of our exposed nerves. It took us quite some time to link up all his appendages with all my orifices, but I found it ultimately satisfying. I managed to fake an orgasm in nineteen of the orifices, and I think I had genuine spasms in four.

The petals of the flower burned down to the pollen, where they burst in a flash of orange light before fading into dimness. The *bloop-bloop-bloop* music continued on endless replay.

Afterward, my client looked exhausted and shaken, but pleasured all the way to his soft body core. I could see his membranes quivering as we sat against each other, shoring up the gelatinous bulk as we secreted off our outer coating of slime, washing away with it all of the irritating sand we had gathered in the throes of our lovemaking.

"I just can't believe it ... a stunningly beautiful female like you even bothering to spend time with someone like me." He condensed his body volume in what seemed to be shy withdrawal.

"You aren't so bad. Take a good look at yourself—and don't sell yourself short."

In truth, how was I supposed to tell the difference between an *ugly* male Slugwump and a handsome one? And I didn't want to remind him that this little service wasn't free, after all.

As I expected, he tipped magnificently, in addition to the normal fee. Twenty-three tentacles—see what I mean?

Being a hookermorph isn't necessarily easy, but it's a living.

I sauntered along the lobbyways in the hotel. This morning I wore a bipedal body with muscular legs, the kind that enjoyed walking. I felt refreshed and vibrant, having just enjoyed a long ultrasonic bath in the form of a creature that thrived on such things.

Potted plants that may or may not have been hotel guests sat in the alcoves. Other life-forms stood open mouthed in front of the ashtrays they had replaced, waiting for a snack of used tobac-stick butts. Motivator ramps tilted at various angles to accommodate life-forms from worlds with different gravities, conveying hotel guests to adjacent biospheres.

"So, how are you, Ilkiy?" said a voice from behind me. "I'm glad you finally decided to wear a body I can at least talk to!"

I turned to see John-23, one of the cyborg members of the Hotel Security staff. He could always read my genetic ID code with a blink of his enhanced left eye. John-23 had lost his arm, his shoulder, and half of his face during a cargo-shifter accident ten years ago. Most of the passengers in the stateroom container had died; they had been thrown from the high-pressure inner atmosphere of a gas giant, and turned into dripping tatters of flesh from explosive decompression. John-23 had spent a month or so in mech-regrowth, having new android body parts connected to his own body in a cell-to-cell match. To humans, he looked completely healed, indistinguishable from his former appearance, but whenever I looked at him through infrared-sensitive eyes, he looked all screwed up.

"I feel good this morning, John-23," I said, actually meaning it—and he could tell. John-23 and I have worked at the hotel for longer than either of us wants to admit.

Unfortunately, my good humor was not rubbing off. He was in one of his introspective moods. "What are we doing here, Ilkiy? You're so cheery. Have you finally figured out what you want out of life?"

"There's really nothing much I want. I enjoy life, I like my job. What else is there?"

Indeed, I do enjoy my job. It's always different, and I'm good at it. Oh, sometimes certain life-forms can be a drag, and you can't always tell just by their listings in the Lexicon. I remember that time with the Paramecon, a transparent cylindrical thing that showed all his pulsing internal organs; I had serviced him and taken my fee before I learned that Paramecons always mate for life. Luckily for me, Paramecons also die within a few days of mating; but he followed me around like a parasite for half a week, and I didn't dare change form and shatter the illusion for him. When he finally bowed over and I watched his heart-equivalent pump stop pumping, I know he expected me to split open and shower the room with our offspring before dying beside him. But hookermorphs are sterile, as far as I know; I've never needed to use any form of birth control, and the Lexicon doesn't give too much information on my own kind.

Sometimes the job does get a little boring, though. One time I had to stand absolutely still for four hours while a plantlike male Dandel client budded and showered his pollen all over me. Apparently satisfied, but without a word, he paid his fee and shuffled out of the room on stubby mobile roots.

As I reminisced, I saw that John-23 was waiting for me to say something a bit more profound. "I think it might be interesting to find a little more stability, I suppose. I've never had anything that lasts."

"Nothing ever lasts," John-23 said. I've seen him in occasional glooms like this ever since his accident

"I can make it better for you. Anytime you give me the chance," I said. "No charge."

I had made the offer before, but never seriously, and John-23 knew it. I've known him long enough that I could select a bodily form that would make his hormones short-circuit I could give him absolutely everything he had ever fantasized about, and he knows it.

But John-23 also has a wife and three kids back in the employees' annex. His marriage is a good one, solid. He doesn't need me mucking it up. He's too good a friend, and I would never do that to him.

"Don't tempt me," he said. His voice was husky.

"Offer withdrawn," I said, then deliberately shifted into another body that would look bulbous and ugly to him.

John-23 touched the pickup implant behind his ear, then nodded. "Gotta go. One of the Swelft guests is trying to take a shower but can't figure out how to turn the water on. Those damned critters are so unintuitive! What's complicated about turning a knob in the bathtub?" He stomped off, waving good-bye, but I could already see a new sense of purpose behind his movements.

John-23 likes his job, too. He just hates not being busy.

I sauntered through the pearlescent arches leading into one of the hotel's primary bars. I wanted to share my energy, use it as synergy and keep the buzz going. I needed a pickup.

I was wearing a delicate, feathery body guaranteed to ring a few hormonal bells for a wide range of male hotel guests, and I could always alter my appearance at a moment's notice anyway.

Since so many species operate on completely different circadian rhythms, nobody at the Hotel Andromeda particularly cares what time it is. All things at all times, that was their motto. At the bar itself, various organic and robotic bartenders consulted their databases to determine which substances were known to be intoxicating to which life-forms.

I glanced around the bar, cataloging the customers, my *prospects.* Many of the species were familiar to me, some of them good tippers, some of them good lovers. Most were already with a companion. But I wanted something a bit more exotic, a bit of a challenge.

Then I saw it perched on a stool that had never been designed to accommodate its insectile frame. Metallic turquoise blue on its back casings and segmented legs, an ovoid head with gleaming silver domes for eyes, whip-like antennas. I had never seen its type before, which meant it was fairly rare. A challenge.

While staring at it, I consulted my Lexicon implant, waiting one second, then two as it searched for a match. I began to grow concerned and exhilarated at the same time. An unknown? Not quite. The listing popped up an image and a name—Borrak. Very little data about the species, just some specifics on their homeworld, temperature ranges, gravity—all the stuff that's easy to gather from a few space probes, but nothing that demonstrated extended sociological study.

This excited me even more, especially after recalling my recent conversation with John-23. I could provide some new data for the Lexicon compilers, give them vital information about a mysterious species. The Lexicon pays handsomely for such contributions, which was enough of an incentive already, but it could also let me do something permanent, to make my mark on the galactic civilization.

Since the Lexicon entry gave so few useful facts, I was going to have to use my intuition and my skills to the fullest. Drawing from the image in the Lexicon and extrapolating from what I could see hulking over the barstool, I altered my form into my best approximation of a Borrak. I made my exoskeleton a little brighter, the antennae more feathery, hoping I had made a correct guess about what the race found beautiful. I approached the Borrak, who seemed to be huddling in misery over a gelatinous intoxicant. All the better.

"Hello, potential companion," I said in Basic dialect.

The Borrak turned and reared back in what could only be an expression of astonishment. Normally, I dislike chitinous beings; it's impossible to read any expression on a brittle face—therefore more difficult to know when I'm doing something right—but their body language is usually more exaggerated. "Why are you here?" it said without any preamble.

"I would like to spend some time with you. Would that be acceptable?" I usually leave out all discussions of fees until after I have the client on the hormonal hook.

To my surprise, the Borrak drew itself up, bristling in an apparent defensive posture with perhaps a hint of dismay. "No, that would not be acceptable," it answered. "I think it would be wisest if you remained far from me for the duration of your stay at the Hotel Andromeda. I would not want to be forced to engage you in mortal combat."

Now that was a hell of a rebuff, but I couldn't figure out what I had done wrong. The Borrak scrambled itself off the barstool in a dizzying ballet of segmented legs, then marched out of the bar.

Failure is certainly nothing new to me, and I can usually take it with a measure of grace. But I was preoccupied with trying to figure out what I had done wrong. I moved to a vacant table, changed form into something that would sit comfortably on one of the chairs, and pondered. Every race and every society has plenty of customs and taboos that usually make no sense to outside observers; perhaps I had inadvertently stepped on some insectile toes. Who could tell?

"Excuse me," said a gruff, demanding voice with no undertones of politeness whatsoever, "you are a hookermorph. I saw you change. Don't try to deny it."

I turned to see a squat, froglike creature, powerfully built, with needle teeth and lips that stretched practically all around his head. A Rybet; I had served them before. They were not too difficult to work with, if you had a high tolerance for rudeness. You just had to be rude back to them. It turned them on.

"Hire me if you want. If not, get away from me. You want a price breakdown?"

"Come to my room. Now. I will pay your usual fee, and I wish to hire you for a different assignment."

Maybe the day would have something interesting and unusual after all, I thought. I transformed into the body of a female Rybet, then waddled after him out of the bar.

Up in the Rybet's room, we waded into shin-deep lukewarm water. Semi-mobile algae dribbled out of our way as we sloshed to two damp fungal mounds in the middle of the pool. Two dull red holographic suns shone from the dome roof of the room.

"Sit down," he snapped, motioning with a stubby, flipper-like forearm.

"Why?"

"So I can tell you about my assignment, that's why! Now listen." He seated himself on one of the fungal mounds with a squelching sound. He puffed air into his lips, swelling them.

I splashed water upon myself to dampen my skin, then eased onto the vacant mound as far away from the Rybet as possible. "So talk!" I said.

"I need you to secure for me a sample of semen from a Hoojum. It's very important. I'll pay you a thousand credits."

Not only was the Rybet rude, but he seemed at least partially insane. "A Hoojum! That's tough. Why a thousand credits?"

"Never mind. I'll pay you a hundred credits just for coming here now, and a thousand more if you can deliver a sperm sample." He puffed his lips again, and his lantern eyes widened.

"I'll try. Even assuming I can find a Hoojum, getting one as a customer is no minor task."

"An entire Hoojum tour group is on the transport arriving this afternoon. Remember, it's worth a thousand credits."

"I said I would try. Now stop nagging me!"

I pushed myself off the fungus mound and got ready to leave, but he leaped up and splashed in the water after me. "Wait!" he croaked. "I'm paying you a hundred credits for this visit. Give me something for it."

I sighed. At least it was fairly simple to service a Rybet. Concentrating long enough to shift my internal organs, I generated, then pulled out a few handfuls of black sterile eggs into the lukewarm water. The egg mass looked like an island of black caviar surrounded by a wispy mass of the semi-mobile algae. The Rybet sloshed up to it and loomed over the eggs.

After he had spilled his milt over the cluster, he let out a long breath of satisfaction. "Ah, very pleasurable. Thank you very much." He let his huge lips curve in a grotesque smile, then he remembered his rudeness again. "Don't stare at me. Get out of here!"

I sloshed back to the door portal, thinking of the thousand credits he had offered. Now all I had to do was find a Hoojum.

I don't think I'll ever get tired of watching the spaceliners arrive. All you see is a bright light as the ship, itself as big as the continents on many worlds, swings into orbit. Smaller chunks break off the liner's main body and drop down like shooting stars to the transfer points at Hotel Andromeda.

Sometimes I like to go out to watch the descending cargo modules, each like a city in its own right, carrying thousands of staterooms, each pressurized with the occupants' desired atmosphere. Watching the great mass of the dedicated module land that afternoon, I was reminded all too clearly of the flames, the groaning metal, the spouting death that John-23 had encountered right out here on the primary receiving bay. But extra safeguards had been designed in the decade since that accident, and I had nothing to worry about

The hot air smelled of industrial pollutants, outgassing from rocket fuels, lubricants from the machinery that loaded and unloaded the immense containers. The air was filled with a cacophony of hissing and roaring and strident alarm blasts; I would have preferred even the *bloop-bloop-bloop* music of the Slugwumps.

Somewhere among the thousands of passengers on that dedicated module was a tour group of Hoojums. I just had to wait and watch.

Even without trying, the Hoojums succeeded in making everything difficult for me. It seemed to be a particular talent of theirs.

First off, they were a bunch of religious fanatics of the worst kind. They stuck together in a little pack, as if just daring anyone to persecute them. They all wore huge, billowy robes of violet and orange, embroidered with threads of eye-numbing intensity so that they looked like walking moiré patterns wherever they went.

The whole group would disappear for hours in prayer meetings and verse chantings. The few times I managed to catch one by himself, he rebuffed my advances completely. Five times. After following them around for three days without success, I decided it was time to change tactics.

I uploaded their version of holy scripture and scanned it into my forebrain. Pretty standard stuff, commonplace for all those religions that claim to have the One True Message. Of course, those types of fanatics never allow themselves to read scripture adopted by any other religion, so they never seem to notice all the similarities.

I did a context-insensitive search for the items I wanted in the massive book of writings. This sort never bothers with context when they want to quote something from a holy writing anyway, as long as the words prove the point they're trying to make. So, armed with the appropriate verses to support my scheme, I waited to catch another Hoojum alone.

"Excuse me, brother," I said, "but I need your help." That line always gets them. He stopped dead in his tracks on his way to the front desk.

The Hoojum turned with a great whispering of his optical-illusion robes. He seemed surprised to find another one of his kind wandering the halls of the hotel. "You are not from our tour group."

"I have fallen into the pit of sin, and I must find someone to help me climb out of it."

I watched him shudder, possibly from the incredible favor I had just asked or from a personal revulsion at talking to a genuine sinner. Hoojums are primarily reptilian in features, with massive bony plates on the face, squarish teeth, and a ridged crest on top of the head. In order for me to read squeamishness through all that armor, his reaction must have been extreme indeed.

"I was just going to request some extra towels. We're having a charismatic verse sing tonight. Perhaps if you join us—"

"No! I need *you* to help me. Now! Or I am forever lost." He hesitated. "Please!" I added just the right begging tone to my voice.

He sighed, a long hiss, then took me aside. "Very well, my child. Tell me of your predicament."

"Only if you promise to help me. There is only one way I can be saved."

"I promise. Now tell me."

"We had best go to my room, where I can speak of this in

private. I am so ashamed, I do not want to risk anyone overhearing."

He balked at that, and I could see him searching his mind for some sort of acceptable excuse. "You promised me," I said. Finally, the Hoojum agreed.

John-23 had held this room for me for the last couple of days, as a special favor. Now it paid off. Inside, it was decorated in the bland grayness and muted lighting the Hoojums preferred in their accommodations—fewer worldly distractions that way, I suppose.

"I have been stranded in this hotel for too long, after foolishly fleeing from our homeworld," I told the Hoojum. "I have found myself tempted. I have fantasized of sexual pleasures and perversions with any number of alien beings here. I might have acted out some of my desires ... but after seeing your righteous group, I repented of my sinful thoughts, in horror at what I have been contemplating. But I must be cleansed."

The Hoojum looked doubly squeamish. I clutched at his robe, and he flinched. "But what do you need me to do?"

"The scripture is clear on this point" I allowed myself an inner smirk at that one. "To purge all sin from me, I must face the horrors of that which I had once considered. I must have sex with a complete stranger. Only then can I see how horrible it really is."

The Hoojum's jaw dropped open in total astonishment. "But not only that," I pressed on, "but I must charge *money* for this act, so that I myself can experience the awful punishment of the lowliest of all beings—a prostitute!"

He gasped and choked and tried to break away, but my grip on his robe was firm. "Please! You promised! Do this in the name of the Deity and you will be exalted for all time."

"But I must not!"

So, I hit him with the scriptures I had memorized, quoting verse after verse of the vague poetry that seemed to shore up my claim. He countered a few of them, but I came up with even more. In the end, I think I exhausted him with my piety, and he began to crumble under his own doubts.

When he took off the moiré robe, I was surprised to see a rather scrawny being underneath. The billowing cloth and their overlarge heads make the Hoojums look much more massive than they really are. I tried not to stare. He already seemed embarrassed enough.

The sexual act with him was mercifully brief, and he didn't appear to enjoy it at all. He grudgingly paid me with his credit scanner, then fled my room, muttering prayers to himself. I wondered if the charismatic verse sing had started without him.

I transformed again into a more comfortable form, then secreted a carefully contained packet filled with Hoojum semen—a packet somehow worth a thousand credits to a Rybet.

In his own quarters, the Rybet leaped up and down with delight "You got it!" He splashed off the fungus mound on which he had been napping and waded over to me, his huge mouth hanging open in delight. The semi-mobile algae could not move out of his way quickly enough, and wet green strands clung to his waist and thighs, slowly trying to flee back into the lukewarm water.

"How did you ever get it? Never mind. I don't want to know. Just give it to me."

"Give me my thousand credits first," I countered. Even though I didn't wear a Rybet form this time, I could still be rude.

"Fine, fine." He dumped the money into my account with his credit scanner, and I handed the package over to him.

He held it up to the dim light of the two simulated red suns and looked at the thick gray-blue liquid. "Looks right," he said, bobbing his head up and down in a vigorous nod. "You can't find details like the color of Hoojum semen in the Lexicon."

"It's real," I said. "Now are you going to tell me what you want it for?"

In reply, he removed a thin, diamond-like needle from a pouch at his waist. The Rybet dipped the tip of the needle into the clotted Hoojum sperm, swirled it around a few times, then withdrew the needle. A single drop hung like a tiny, cloudy pearl on the point.

The Rybet closed his lantern eyes, took a deep breath of anticipation, then jabbed the needle into his fat lips.

His reaction was nearly instantaneous. He let out a loud keening sound from the bottom of his throat "Yes, oh yes!" His eyes flung open wide, and his body shuddered so much he almost dropped the rest of the semen sample. He gulped in a deep breath. "Wow! This is fantastic!"

In my line of work you see a lot of strange things.

Then the Rybet began to jabber at me, stomping around in the wading pool so rapidly that he churned the surface into a froth. "Hoojum sperm is the most intense, stimulating drug we Rybets have ever found. It is so precious, so rare—and so marvelous! Just obtaining it is nearly impossible. What you've given me will be worth millions on the Rybet open market! Oh, you are marvelous, wonderful!"

He looked like he wanted to mate with me again. I think I preferred it when he was merely rude. "Here," he said, grabbing for his credit scanner again. "Just to show how much this really means to me."

Barely looking at his own stubby fingers, the Rybet punched another 200 credits into my account. At that point I decided to leave, before the drug's euphoria wore off and his rudeness settled back in.

The mysterious Borrak was sitting on the same ill-fitting barstool as if waiting to pounce. I looked at its insectile form, wondering what I had botched so badly during my first attempt—after all, if I could succeed in seducing a repressed *Hoojum* and make him pay for the pleasure, what could possibly be so difficult about a Borrak? I summoned up the sparse Lexicon listing again, and immediately noticed the obvious.

This specimen was *female,* not male as I had originally assumed. By making my body into a beautiful female as well, I had set myself up as a rival. Hotel Andromeda must be a lonely place for Borraks, and the last thing a single female would want to see is another more beautiful female on the make!

I slipped out of sight into an unoccupied slaughter lounge where carnivores could select creatures and kill them there or cage them for later consumption in the hotel room. With no one looking, I transformed into my best approximation of a male Borrak this time, with a jagged crest on top of the head and a full blush of mating coloration.

Becoming male doesn't bother me. Hookermorphs are basically genderless, though most of my clients are males looking for females. I can do whatever a species wishes—sometimes they are skeptical when I say "anything you want," but believe me, with all the races and all the societies in the galaxy, I can't think of many things that *aren't* taboo in one culture or another. Some races express their passion through kissing, while others consider the pressing of one's eating orifice against another eating orifice to be the most disgusting thing imaginable. No, being a male Borrak didn't bother me at all.

When I strutted into the bar, concentrating to keep a proper gait with all those segmented legs, I saw the female Borrak straighten from her perch on the barstool and turn both gleaming eyes toward me. Her feelers quivered. I could see her top forelegs fidgeting with nervous anticipation.

I walked directly up to her, showed off my mating coloration. "Hi. Come here often?"

She could barely contain herself and trilled. "Where have you been all my life?" She gestured to the empty barstool beside her. I struggled to clamber onto the stool, wondering how she had ever managed it herself. I was looking like a clumsy fool, but she didn't seem to mind. The Borrak seemed very, very receptive.

In my own excitement at breaking new ground with a little-known species, I did not notice when John-23 stepped into the bar, looking around with his cyborg eye. Beside him was a smartly dressed human woman; the jewels studding her clothes reflected the pearlescent light. He pointed to me.

"Would you be interested in doing something about our obvious mutual attraction?" I asked the Borrak. The tips of her feelers touched mine.

A hand touched my wing casing, a human hand. "There, I've found you, Ilkiy. Could we talk to you for a minute?"

I turned to see John-23 and his lady companion next to me. Intimidated by the fearsome appearance of the Borrak, she still looked secretly pleased. "I'm busy at the moment. I'd be happy to arrange a more convenient time."

The woman wasn't John-23's wife, nor anyone else I had seen before. "I'll pay you twice whatever this creature is paying you," she said.

The female Borrak reared up in an attack posture, clutching at me with one of her forelegs in a gesture of despair. I stopped the Borrak from doing anything that would have been embarrassing to all concerned, including the hotel management

"Relax," I told the Borrak. "Enjoy yourself, have another drink." I motioned for one of the robo-bartenders to bring a new slab of the gelatinous intoxicant the Borrak preferred. "John-23 is paying for it. I'll be back, don't worry." I combed one of the Borrak's feelers through my claws, and she cooed with pleasure. Then I followed John-23 and his lady companion into one of the lobby lounges, out of sight.

"Sorry to interrupt you while you were working, Ilkiy. She asked me to find you right away," John-23 said apologetically. "This is Mrs. Wenda Cochran. I'll let her explain the rest." He strode off down the corridor, leaving the two of us alone.

The woman folded her fingers together. I noticed she was wearing a lot of rings. From what I knew of humans, she would have been considered quite beautiful, although she had a hard look to her, like an invisible exoskeleton of her own. I could have transformed into something more amenable to conversation, but I was annoyed at having my all-but-guaranteed score with the Borrak ruined, so I remained in threatening alien form.

"I've heard about what your kind can do," Wenda Cochran said. "I need your services, and I will pay well for them."

I found that rather odd, since she was an attractive member of her own species and should have had little trouble picking an available human male from the other hotel guests. However, she wore her human marriage-bonding ring a bit too prominently for active sexual hunting. But she had requested my services for something, and business is business. "I'm sure I can give you pleasure," I said. "That is my job."

"Oh, you'll give me pleasure, all right," Wenda Cochran said, "but not in the way you think. I want you to sleep with my husband."

It was a good thing the chitinous face of the Borrak registered little emotion. "Why?' I asked.

She sighed. Her body temperature went up, and I could see an emotional outburst simmering inside her. Tears appeared in her eyes. "My husband is a cheating bastard. He goes on business trips all over the galaxy, and he jumps into bed with any humanoid with compatible sexual organs. I am sick and tired of it. He doesn't know I've followed him here."

I still didn't know where I supposedly fit in. "You are tired of him mating with females other than yourself," I said, confused, "and so you wish to hire *me* to sleep with him?"

"Oh, that's not all. I want you to take him to bed and then scare the bejesus out of him." She snickered then, a harsh and mirthless laugh. "That'll shrivel his little peeper once and for all. I want you to teach him a lesson he'll never forget if he ever gets wandering hormones again."

"I think I understand," I said.

"I'll pay you three times your usual rate," Wenda Cochran said. "It's his own money, and somehow I don't think he'll dispute the charge when it comes through on the credit report."

"Rex," I said with a cooing tone in my voice. "I like that name." I stroked his forearm with my enameled fingernails.

Picking up Rex Cochran had been embarrassingly easy. I wore a body and face cobbled together from Lexicon entries of gorgeous human female models. I had only to walk slowly into the lounge and bat my eyes ... and Rex was on me like a Lupine male sniffing estrus in the air.

He had short blond hair, broad shoulders, a shirt that fit too tightly, letting curls of chest hair poke through the fabric. A necklace of gold and onyx dangled at his throat. I allowed Rex to buy me a drink, something perfumy and feminine. I laughed at his jokes, I flirted with him, I let him catch me noticing his body.

It took him all of fifteen minutes to ask me up to his room. Since human mating practices are such a matter of public record, I won't go into the details of how he rapidly "seduced" me, wheedling one item of my clothing off after another, trying to hide his wolfish glances. His actions so closely followed the general description in the Lexicon entry, I had an odd sensation of déjà vu.

I thought of his wife Wenda, knowing what Rex did on so many of his "business trips," how she had finally followed him here to the Hotel Andromeda to teach him a well-deserved lesson. As a hookermorph, I try not to be moralistic in such things—but in this case, Wenda Cochran was the actual customer ... and the customer is always right.

When Rex was on top of me and inside me, moving faster and

faster after a puzzlingly brief foreplay session, I knew the time had, er, come. I waited a second longer, feeling Rex reach his peak.

Then I let my imagination roam free as I transformed.

Rex looked down to see the voluptuous naked woman he had lured into his bed turn into an octopoid Slimedurg with sulfuric acid hissing out of her pores. I wrapped five tentacles around him like whips and pulled him against me in what seemed a hilarious parody of what I had just been doing as a human female. I tried to draw his face close to my clacking beak for a little kiss. I let greenish saliva dribble out the corner of my mouth.

Rex shrieked and tried to scramble away, sobbing and howling loud enough to rattle the windows in his room.

I rose up from the bed, raising all tentacles and reaching toward him. Then I shifted into a glaring Ice Medusa, with crystalline claws extending longer than my fingers. "What's the matter, Rex? Don't you want to play anymore?" I took a step toward him, laughing my best imitation of a maniacal beast.

Rex stumbled against the far wall. He couldn't seem to find the door, but he had managed to lose control of his sphincters in a terrible mess.

Just at the moment he found the door and pounded on it, screaming all the while and trying to activate the mechanism, I transformed my monstrous body into a perfect imitation of Wenda Cochran. "Watch yourself, Rex," I said in her voice, "you keep fooling around on me and you never know what you might pick up."

His eyes bulged out of their sockets again, and Rex Cochran fled naked and shrieking into the corridor.

Just before he turned around for the last time, I observed that Wenda had been right—the experience had certainly shriveled his little peeper.

When I saw the female Borrak still waiting for me at the bar, I decided not to wait long enough for anything else to mess things up. Meeting new clients isn't difficult, but finding a way to contribute to the Lexicon doesn't happen every day, and I wasn't going to let this opportunity slip away from me. Not many hookermorphs get to be xenosociologists.

I came up behind her, wearing full mating coloration and exuding all the right pheromones. She whirled, looking like a blur of sharp-edged joints and legs. "I knew you'd come back! I've been waiting for so long."

"Sorry about that," I said. She didn't seem the least bit interested in what the whole business with John-23 and Wenda Cochran had been about. Maybe curiosity wasn't part of the Borrak psyche; that would be in keeping with a lot of other insectile species.

"Please tell me it isn't some cruel joke," she said to me. "Your mating coloration, your pheromones, your flirtatious small talk. I can't bear to wait any longer. Are you really interested in mating with me, or should I just die unfulfilled?"

I couldn't figure out how a Borrak was supposed to smile, so I just made my voice sound warm and receptive. "I would be greatly honored to make love to you."

The Borrak seemed uncertain and afraid, but hookermorphs have to deal with that all the time. I coaxed her and boosted her confidence, then let her usher me up the motivator ramp, crossing a webbed catwalk to get to her room.

She had selected one of the nest-like dwellings. Inside, she had stocked the place with colored gelatinous blocks of sugar-based foods. Every spare niche was stuffed with brilliant fresh flowers. Water dripped from a fountain off in the corner. Despite the cloying perfume of the sweet foodstuffs and the flowers, the place did have a romantic look about it.

The Borrak hummed, then flickered her wing casings, palpitating a membrane in her abdomen with a sound very much like a love song. I was mentally noting all this to turn in a report to the compilers of the Lexicon.

"I am so glad you like me," she said. "I have been ready to spawn for so long. I don't know how I could have waited another day. My entire body aches for you!"

Dancing on my multiple legs, I sidled up next to her. "Well, then, let us get on with it. I'm also anxious to mate with you."

"I'm so glad you understand," she said. Then she stung me in the soft part of my thorax.

I found it amazing how rapidly the paralysis struck me down.

My mind wasn't clouded in the least, but I felt no pain as I tumbled to the floor in a clamor of chitin and disjointed legs. My face was not turned toward her, but the dome eyes had a wide enough field of view that I could see her movements. I could breathe, but I could not speak. What had I gotten myself into?

Her abdomen seemed to be pulsing, and I could see her extruding something sharp from where I imagined the sex organs would be. It appeared to be a long tube, like a pipe with a pointed end. An ovipositor.

Panic gushed through my glands. I wondered if that was a normal reaction for male Borraks, or if my own self-preservation instinct had merely kicked in. I couldn't move. The paralysis from her sting had put me completely out of commission.

Raising the ovipositor in the air like a spear, the female Borrak strode over to me. "I have been carrying these larvae around altogether too long. It'll be a great relief to get rid of them. I really appreciate this, you know." She leaned over to nuzzle the colorful crest on my head.

Then she backed up and thrust her ovipositor through the chitinous shell of my wing casings, burying it deep within my body cavity. That time I felt the pain! She squirmed and dug the hollow point around and around until she finally managed to deposit one of her squirming larvae inside of me.

She heaved a big sigh, withdrew her ovipositor, then shoved it in a different place, laying another voracious Borrak grub. She repeated the procedure six times, then finally retracted her ovipositor and sat down next to me, looking exhausted but fulfilled.

She surprised me by igniting a tobac-stick, then sucking in a long breath before blowing a cloud of smoke dreamily into the cloying air. "Ah, that feels so much better," she said. With a foreleg, she patted my exoskeleton near where she had deposited her larvae. "You're a great lay."

Inside me, I could feel the grubs beginning to stir.

The Borrak hauled herself to her numerous feet and preened in front of a mirror. "As you can see, I've provided everything they'll need. Plenty of food and fresh vegetation, just the right environmental conditions. I've got the room reserved for three weeks, and by that time they should be ready to fend for themselves. I'll let them know at the desk that the children's return tickets to Borrakus should come out of your account. That *is* the father's duty, you know." She raised her antennae in question, but of course I could not respond. The only functional nerves in my body seemed to be the ones transmitting jabs of pain as the grubs began to devour me from within.

"Well, at least that's over with for another year," she sighed to herself, then left. I heard her seal the door behind herself, illuminating the Do Not Disturb sign.

From within my body, I could feel seven distinct paths of agony where the grubs continued to munch. They seemed to be very hungry....

John-23 thought it greatly amusing that a hookermorph would take time off for maternity leave. But hey, everyone else is entitled, so why shouldn't I be?

"Stay away from that edge!" I called to the seven babymorphs lurking too close to the zero-g swimming pool. "Wait until you learn how to change into a water-breather before you mess around in a pool."

All of the little ones sulked into their protoplasmic state for a moment; then with the short memory of children, they bounded off in different directions, a kaleidoscope of changing shapes, imitating parts of whatever they found interesting around them. Very precocious kids—I'm proud of them.

I had never even thought of reproducing myself before. While I understood the mating habits of countless other sentient creatures, I had somehow remained ignorant about "the birds and the bees" for my own species. Hookermorphs don't spend a lot of time learning how to become parents; that's not what hookermorphs consider a desirable skill. It's a good thing something in our inbred instinct triggered a reaction in me, though, and I did exactly the right thing while the little Borrak grubs were having me for lunch.

You see, the way we morphs reproduce is to surround another living organism, and then transform back to the basic state, dragging the enclosed organism along for the ride. You've never read *that* in the Lexicon, now have you? With seven Borrak grubs gnawing away inside of me as the paralysis gradually began to wear off, the best I could manage was to transform back to my basic state, formless, like a bag of old soup. And that did the trick. Inside me were no longer any voracious larvae, but seven squirming babymorphs.

The babymorphs came out of it delighted, ready for the galaxy and eager to learn. John-23 thinks they're cute, at least in some of their incarnations, and the rest of the hotel staff seems tolerant at least.

Over by the pool, one of the guests was walking a spiny-backed dragon dog, who sprayed acid on some of the corner shrubs. It lunged on its leash, snarling at the cluster of babymorphs. Feeling a surge of maternal protective instinct, I jumped to my feet, but the little ones reacted all at once, changing into an array of hideous monstrosities. One of the babymorphs became a fanged Putter-clam, opening wide its jagged shell and snapping at the dragon dog, which fled back behind its owner's legs.

I smiled. They already know how to defend themselves. Now I just need to teach them how to flirt.

With a sigh, I settled back into the chaise lounge and let the sunlight photosynthesize my green skin. I've earned a rest, haven't I? I need to write a letter to the Lexicon people, since I have two new listings for them, one for Borraks and one for morphs. And while I'm at it, maybe I'll try my hand at writing my memoirs. That should surely scandalize the galaxy! Just the type of thing people will pick up to read on an outbound starflight. It'll sell millions.

Besides, I'd better make my fortune soon. As precocious as the babymorphs seem to be, I'm bound to have competition before long. I'll really need to stay in shape.

I teach a graduate program in publishing for Western Colorado University, which is mostly online except for one week in July when I drive to the campus in Gunnison, deep in the southern Colorado mountains. It's a four-hour drive from my home, and I enjoy the road trip through the beautiful scenery, where I can think about stories and dictate new chapters.

My fellow professor, award-winning science fiction author Rick Wilber, would fly in from Florida to Colorado Springs and make his own way to Gunnison, which is not actually very easy to get to. Since we were good friends, Rick asked if I could pick him up at the airport and we could drive down together.

On the surface, it made good sense.

Now, I'm not exactly an antisocial person, but I initially balked at the idea. I said, "But if you ride with me, Rick, then I'll lose four hours of good solitary writing time—each direction."

Still, he's good company, and it did make a lot of logistical sense—so I set conditions. If we were going to spend all those hours in the car, then we had better plot a story together. We did—and what a story! Just the start of something even bigger.

I was stuck on an idea I'd previously written for Analog Magazine, *"A Delicate Balance," which appears in the first SF collection in this set. Imagine a society so austere and tightly regulated that for every baby born, another member of the population had to die. From that starting point, Rick and I took a completely different approach in "The* Hind,*" setting the story on a damaged, wayward generation ship lost between the stars.*

"The Hind*" was published in* Asimov's Science Fiction, *my very first appearance in that magazine. I had never been able to hook the editor, Sheila Williams, before, not even by collaborating with Mike Resnick. But Rick was also a staple of* Asimov's, *so he was my ticket. "The* Hind*" was*

chosen by the magazine's readers as the best story of the year, and it won the Canopus Award for Interstellar Writing.

Naturally, when we drove to the residency together the following year, we plotted a second story, "The Death of the Hind,*" and then a third the year after that. Eventually, we hope to have enough pieces that we can weave together into a full novel.*

THE HIND

(with Rick Wilber)

A twinge of nausea rose, but Kym drove it back, swallowed in a dry throat, and looked down at the list again. She should have spent more of her water ration to add to the energy bar she consumed. She could afford the ration and she was going to need to be at her best, physically and mentally. This wouldn't be easy. The whole idea of a list of targeted names sickened her, but this had to be done. It would require all of her strength and more fortitude.

She had never killed anyone before.

Kym moved quietly, any slight sounds she made masked by the big ship's constant background rumble. The *Hind* was always murmuring, vibrating, echoing as it drifted along on its endless journey between the stars. The hum of the great engines had been there all her life, powering the grav units and the environmental basics, the light and heat and air and water recyclers. But they did little else despite their power. The *Hind* was adrift and would be adrift for the next generation and the next and the next after that: forever.

Right now the important part was that the deep purr of the engines covered her movements as she tracked down the fifth name on the list, an old woman named Sudio. Kym had decided that she would be the easiest target, and Kym wanted this to be over with, wanted to earn her Permit and get on with her life.

Kym hurried along the access corridor. Two of the lights were flickering, and several more had gone out, leaving some spaces in deep shadow as she took the shortcut. Kym told herself that she would come back and fix those lights once this job was done. She could fix about anything and liked doing it. It was a skill she'd inherited from her mother and her mother's mother.

Kym knew the old woman often spent afternoons in the tiny apple orchard amidships. The *Hind*'s personnel records were still incomplete despite the years Kym had spent on recovering them. But she knew the woman, Sudio, wasn't gardening, wasn't doing any sort of definable job that helped keep the damaged vessel and all of the passengers alive. There were signs of dementia, the newer handwritten reports said. Short-term memory was slipping, and she was barely able to accomplish the simplest of assigned tasks. The report said she was "a drain on resources and no longer productive."

So the ship's Council had declared her "deadwood to be cleared," an archaic reference that Kym didn't understand and the Council probably didn't either. But the rules and terminology were clear. The list had its deadwood names, and Permits were hard to come by, nearly impossible ... they came only at the cost of a life.

Kym reached an intersection of narrow metal-walled corridors and turned left, knowing it would lead into the orchard that occupied one large corner of the terrarium chamber. From the other direction she heard scuttling movements in the deeper shadows. Kym whirled around to face that direction, afraid someone might try to attack her, some other competitor also trying to cross a name off the list. But the figures were furtive, scurrying away, grabbing scavenged belongings and fleeing into the darkness.

Kym saw and frowned in disgust. Ferals! Uncounted, undocumented parasites who lived in the underbelly of the ship, who stole food and water and bred like rats, without any oversight. Kym would never want that for herself, it would be a hard and dangerous life. But if this didn't work, that would be her life.

Close now, she looked down at the list of names again, reassuring herself that this was what must be done, and then folded it and put it into her pocket. She wanted both hands free as she moved ahead, seeing the brighter light in front of her shining through an undogged hatch, the artificial sunlight shining down on the verdant gardens and orchards that filled the midships.

She reached the opening, walked inside, and instantly smelled the freshness of leaves and orange blossoms and peaches and, beyond them, the vegetable garden. Here, the oxygen came from the trees themselves rather than through air filters and chemical scrubbers.

There was a wonder to it that she'd forgotten, working away at her maintenance job, fixing condensers and wiring and lighting and processors and filter sealants and bypass cards and all the rest. She was so busy, and so good at the necessary work that she did, fixing anything and everything that she could with her dwindling supplies, that she hadn't been here since her childhood, not once in the years since her mother Maria's death.

She heard voices as soon as she walked in, blinking under the bright full-spectrum lights. A few seconds later she spotted the old woman, someone so ancient she must have been the oldest person of the nine hundred fifty-three known and documented passengers aboard the *Hind*. Kym froze as the prospect that what she planned to do had suddenly became real, tangible, and deadly.

Sudio had folded her sticklike legs under her and sat under one of the dwarf apple trees. The air was moist and clean. An unexpected smile came to Kym's face, looking at the strangely bucolic scene, not unlike some of the images she'd recovered in the past few years from the remnants of the *Hind*'s digital library.

But this wasn't any more real than those pictures from the past. Reality quickly returned. This was the *Hind*, and its resources were limited, and the old woman who sat there faced her end. Kym had to dispose of her, kill her—*murder* her.

Kym had a knife and now her gut clenched again as she felt the pressure of the blade flat against her waist where she'd placed it. Another wave of nausea roared up inside her as she imagined how messy the act would be. Easy enough in theory, sure, but there would be blood, a lot of it, and if the old woman didn't die fast, if she lingered and looked at Kym … that thought was hard to bear.

Perhaps she wouldn't even need the knife. Sudio's neck could be broken like one of the crumbling old pipes in the damaged section of the ship near the bridge. Could Kym do that with her bare hands? She didn't know. Yet.

Sudio sat cross-legged under the apple tree with four children listening to her, all of them sitting, too, cross-legged on the green grass. "And how I wish you had seen those things," Sudio was saying. "The cities and their tall buildings, the endless blue sky with puffy clouds, the farm fields that stretched for miles, the mountains so tall they held snow—snow!—even on the hottest days of summer."

A little girl, seven or eight years old, raised her hand and Sudio pointed to her and said, "Alyssa? You have something you want to add?"

The girl sniggered. "I'm Genoa, Grandmother Sudio. You always get it wrong!"

Sudio smiled. "All right, Genoa, you have something to say?" she asked in a tremulous voice, pointing with a finger at the girl. Sudio's hand trembled, Kym could see, and then noticed the same tremor in her head, a little movement side to side, unsteady.

"I do! Snow is water vapor turned into ice crystals that form complex patterns."

Sudio clapped her hands. "Very good!" And then she added, wistfully, "I grew up in the mountains, where snow used to fall gently from the sky and build up to be knee-deep sometimes, children. And it stayed on the ground until the weather warmed and melted it."

"Turning it back into water!" blurted the young boy.

"Yes, Teddy, that's it," Sudio said, and clapped her hands once more.

All the children laughed as the boy said, "I'm Chennai, Grandmother Sudio. You always forget!" And that brought more peals of laughter.

The children, three girls and one boy, ranged in age from six to ten. They wore clean, but threadbare ship uniforms. They looked like they'd had food to eat and clear water enough to drink, and they could thank Kym for the water. It was her work on sealing the core pipes of the osmosis filters that had staved off the water crisis of last year. Doing that had cost her much of her remaining sealant, but for now the water was clear and clean, just like the children. They were clearly authorized members of the ship's complement, perhaps even children of Council members.

Sudio pointed unsteadily at the youngest of the children. "I was your age when our ship departed, Kathy," she said.

"I'm Roma, Grandmother Sudio!" the girl shot back, laughing. Sudio smiled and laughed along with them.

Then she went on, "Of course I didn't understand what the voyage was all about. Only that my family had signed up taking a chance and knowing we would never go back to Earth. My mother took me to a forest on that last week, told me to stand and just listen beside a stream as the water rushed over the rocks, as the wind brushed the trees and made the pine boughs scrape together." Sudio let out a long sigh. "Such a beautiful, peaceful sound." She shook her head. "I'm sorry, children, that you'll never know the wind."

"I feel air through the recirculation ducts," said the boy, Chennai. Kym guessed he was about ten.

"And it feels good, doesn't it, Kenny?"

"Chennai!" the boy said.

"But it's not the same," Sudio said. "You will never have that sense of the vastness of a world, you'll never smell the flowers and trees on the wind, or feel the warmth of a spring breeze, or the bite of a winter wind so cold it takes your breath away."

The old woman smiled. "We even saw a deer that day we were in the forest. It looked up at us, just stared, and then it bounded off into the trees.

"It was an amazing day. My mother and grandmother took me that day to burn all those images into my memory. I didn't understand what a great gift they were giving me. None of you will ever know a world like that, a whole world! Please keep coming here so I can share my memories with you."

"But we'll get to a planet soon!" Chennai said. "My dad says so!"

"Maybe, child," said Sudio, "maybe." She gave a false but reassuring smile.

These children were too young to understand their fate and the hopelessness of the voyage. At eighteen Kym had been told the real story. The ship would never make it to its destination. Not after the deadly debris shower that had damaged the engines, smashed right through other parts of the ship, including the bridge, killing the command crew. The bulkheads had held, and the ship and most of its complement had survived. But that was more than fifty years ago and the ship still limped along, repaired as best they could manage, self-sufficient but only barely, with no guidance, no room for growth, and not a scrap of resources to be wasted.

Old Sudio had been deemed a waste of those scant resources by the Council, and Kym could see why. The hand tremors, the memory problems, the shaky voice. All of that showed that Sudio was past her time.

The woman looked up from under the tree, startled to see pale and anxious Kym looking at her from just inside the narrow access passage. Kym held the scrap of paper in her hand, a page torn from the only paper book she had in her quarters and one of the few paper books left on the ship, *The Elemental Guide*.

Sudio saw her, then she sighed, gave a slight shrug, and waved her over. Ten steps and Kym was there. She could do it right here.

But as Kym approached, Sudio's eyes brightened and a wide smile emerged. "Juliana!" she said brightly, firmly. "Where have you been hiding?"

Kym stopped, stared. Who did Sudio think Kym was? Kym didn't know of any Julianas on the *Hind*. The only Juliana she'd ever known was her abuela, Juliana Ortiz. And Abuela Juli, as Kym's mother had called her when telling Kym about her, was one of the dozens who'd died when the cloud of debris tore through the *Hind* those fifty years ago. Could Sudio have known her?

"You haven't changed a bit, Juliana!" Sudio said as she slowly unwound from the crisscross sitting position she'd been in and shakily stood there to smile and then walk toward Kym. She was terribly thin and walked as if she might topple over at the next step. A cane would have helped her, Kym thought, but she supposed Sudio didn't want to admit to her frailty. The *Hind* didn't have the resources to take care of those who couldn't take care of themselves. In fact, some Council member must have seen Sudio in the corridors or at the mess hall and that was why her name was on the list.

Kym was disarmed by Sudio's smile and her pleasant confusion. There was a moment, right at the very start of this confrontation, when she could have rushed in and done what she'd planned to do. But not now, that moment had passed. Now, this was a sweet, confused, innocent old lady who liked to chat in the orchard with the children. Killing her was unthinkable.

"Hello, Sudio," Kym said, kindly. "I'm not Juliana. I'm Kym. My abuela was Juliana, maybe you're confusing me with her?"

Sudio paused, confused. She whispered, "Your grandmother?"

And then she seemed to collect herself, stood up a little

straighter, spoke a little more forcefully, "Oh, of course you're her granddaughter. What's your name, dear?"

"Kym. My name is Kym."

She reached out to take Kym's hand. "I knew your grandmother well, dear."

"That was a long time ago," Kym said.

"Doesn't seem so long, really," Sudio said. "Juli and I worked in forward communications and navigation together in those days, up next to the bridge. I was on q-coms, she was tech repair and guidance." She smiled. "You wear your hair the same way she did. And the way you stand? It could be her right here in front of me, dear."

"You were friends," said Kym, thinking it must be so.

Sudio shrugged, the memories of that day, of that one particular day, clear in her memory. "Yes, we were friends and even more. I thought so much of her. We were all smart, you know, or thought we were, working up in the command decks, but she was so beautiful and strong. I loved her, I suppose. And she was brave! The only reason I'm here now talking to you is because of her bravery."

"What do you mean?"

"She saved my life, dear, simple as that."

Kym's eyes widened. "Abuela Juli saved your life?"

Sudio chuckled. "She was no abuela then, girl. We were all about your age. Almost kids, really, though we didn't admit it. We were running the whole ship, after all! The eight of us were at the end of our regular shift, monitoring the q-coms and checking for any course corrections. It was simple work, really, since mostly we just talked to the *Hind* and told it what to do since all eight of us had voice control access. Everything was normal. Another minute or two and the third shift would be there and we could go eat some dinner.

"Then we ran into that debris cloud. Dozens of tiny particles at unimaginable velocity. Holes everywhere suddenly! Horns blaring and lights flashing and then a huge jolt as something bigger slammed into some other part of the ship and I knew some of that debris was big.

"Two of my friends died in seconds, hit by those bits of debris that punctured the hull and then went right through them, too, and then out the other side of the hull. Tenea and Jacob had dozens of holes clear through both of them from their heads to their waists, right where they sat.

"A cloud of those particles buzzed right by me. By the time I could blink in surprise they'd exited out the other side, leaving more holes in the hull. But they'd missed me and most of the others.

"Most of us just sat there for a few seconds, trying to figure out what had just happened. But not Juliana. She was up instantly. She'd been nicked in the left arm by one of those pebbles, and there was a lot of blood on her uniform, but that didn't stop her. She was barking orders at the *Hind*, running over to check out Jacob and Tenea, yelling at us to get to the bulkhead hatch so we could get out before the ship sealed us in tight.

"I looked over and there was blood oozing out of Jacob, who was slumped in his seat. Tenea was looking at her hand. It was covered in blood from where she'd reached up to feel the wound on the side of her head. She looked at me and asked 'What?' and then she collapsed, too. I thought she was dead."

Sudio's voice was steady and firm as she remembered that day. "I thought I was dead, too, dear. I was your age, you know? Life had really just started. I was on a great ship exploring the universe and ready to tame a new world once we got there, and now I was going to die, out of breath, out of oxygen, sitting in my seat in q-com."

"But you didn't die. What happened?"

"Juliana—your grandmother!—happened. She saved us all and died doing it. She got us up and moving as she ran to the bulkhead hatch. The dogs had slapped into place on the hatch, sealing us off to save the ship. But Juliana used our emergency protocol—Sir Francis Drake—and the *Hind* slid the dogs back and the hatch, battered as it was, slid partway open.

"She started shoving us through the hatch. I was the next-to-last one to get through and your grandmother was next, but then she heard Tenea, still alive, call for help and the last thing I saw was Juliana turning around to go back for Tenea. She hadn't taken more than a step in that direction when the bigger blast happened, the one that tore off the bridge blister, so all that was left to guide the ship was our q-coms and nav quarters and no one was ever able to get them started again so on we go, aimless. But it was your grandmother Juliana who saved me and the others, girl. Never forget that."

Kym was amazed to hear this from Sudio. A few minutes ago Sudio had seemed lost in a fog when she was talking to the children. She'd hardly been able to remember their names. But now, listening to her, Kym knew Sudio's memories from that cataclysmic day were sharp and true and accurate. And Kym had never heard any of this before. Her mother Maria had been just a child herself in those days and didn't know any details. There must have been an official inquiry, Kym thought. That, after all, is what led to the Council being formed in the first place. But how it all happened? No one really knew anymore. It happened, that was all. And the *Hind* had been limping along since then.

"Grandmother Sudio! Grandmother Sudio!" the children were calling. Sudio turned around to look at them and waved before turning back to Kym to say, "They're nice children."

"What are their names?" Kym asked.

"Oh, I don't know, dear, they change all the time. Teddy is the boy, I'm sure of that. The girls? I don't know."

"That's okay," said Kym, and smiled, then gave Sudio a hug. "I'd like to hear more of your stories about Earth," and walked with her back over to the grassy spot under the apple tree.

Kym sat down crisscross with the children and listened for an hour or so before leaving. Such stories! Kym had never heard anything like them, stories of old Earth and its weather and its people and how they lived.

Abuela Juli must have had similar stories to tell, and surely passed them on to her daughter, Ana Maria, who would have passed them onto her own daughter Kym if her life hadn't been shortened by pneumonia, something the medroom could have cured, Kym had been told. But the medroom, too, had felt the fury of the debris swarm. So much gone on that horrible day. The bridge and so much more. Control, knowledge, history: all of it gone.

Kym left knowing Sudio wasn't her target. Certainly, the old woman was the easiest target on the Council's list, but the Council was wrong. Sudio wasn't "deadwood." Not at all. Kym would have to go to the next on the list.

Galen Porthos was a productive man in his late forties, physically fit, requiring little costly medical attention, a viable member of the ship's population—on paper at least.

Unofficially, though, he was vile, violent, and unrepentant. The Council must have placed his name on the list because they were aware of what he had done. Many of the hidden spy cams, especially in the upper decks, were no longer functional, but some of the cameras still worked and in the dossier they had provided Kym and the other three applicants for a Permit, he had raped and beaten at least five women. There were probably more that had not been caught by the surveillance imagers.

He had gotten two women pregnant. One of the victims had terminated the fetus as required while the other, broken and frantic, had left her viable job and disappeared into the lower levels, joining the ferals; so she was off the record, never officially seen again, but still draining the ship's meager resources, she and her accidental offspring. And though that woman was a criminal and subject to punishment if she and her child were ever caught, the real person who deserved punishment, who deserved in fact to die, was Galen.

Kym thought she could do it.

She had her knife as well as a hammer she had obtained from one of the tool lockers. Killing him would be intimate and dangerous. She would have to move quickly and surprise him, not letting second thoughts deter her.

But how to do it? Galen Porthos would fight back, and he was larger than Kym and stronger. She would have to move fast and take advantage of surprise. It would be risky but possible. He worked down in the engineering decks, those hot, high bays where the pulse engines thrummed and their heat drove turbines to circulate the air and to power the life support machinery and filtration systems. There would be plenty of places there, narrow corridors and walkways, where she could corner him and get it done before he knew what was happening.

Kym entered through the high bay hatch and anxiously looked around. Galen worked a monitoring job: studying pressure gauges, changing filters, swapping out worn components with jury-rigged parts. The smell of fumes and the ripples of heat in the air struck her as she entered. She breathed shallowly, trying not to cough and give herself away. The smell was oily and held a sharp tang, making her lightheaded. Maybe it was the fumes, she thought, that had twisted Galen's mind, made him into such a monster. Not that it mattered why he was what he was.

She had read and reread the records, studying the reasons why the man's name was on the list. He was dangerous and evil, and she'd convinced herself that he was the one. Now that she was here, it was time for action. If she succeeded, her child would never know the reason why they'd been allowed to be.

The central core of the engineering bay was as large as the main terrarium dome, but with walkways and narrow corridors running off in different directions from that core. In the terrarium the other day, Kym had stood among the crops and looked out at the great dome and felt a sense of wonder. Here the central space was intimidating and crowded. She shook her head, drew down her focus, and scanned the workers.

On various catwalks she saw work crews, everyone wearing stained, gray shipsuits as they monitored the sensors, moving along the catwalks over and around the large pulse generators. She saw nearly thirty people, all of them with their hair cropped short and their shipsuits tightly bound. Loose hair or loose shirts could get you killed you in this environment, snagging on a railing or cable support and sending you plunging.

Kym continued walking along the metal deck looking around, pretending to belong. Her pale blue shipsuit marked her as someone from the maintenance decks, but occasionally people such as Kym were assigned jobs down here in engineering. As she glanced around, searching for Galen, she spotted another young woman about her age who wore a green shipsuit, one of the agricultural workers. The young woman saw Kym at the same moment and frowned before looking away.

Finally Kym spotted the man who was undeniably her target. He was at least five inches taller than Kym with broad shoulders and long hair that he wore banded in a ponytail. He was working with several others on a deck at the top of the high central bay. The deck edged out over the core, with lift cages shuttling workers up and down the curved wall of the bay.

There were metal stairs that led from one catwalk to the next, and Kym thought she might be more unobtrusive if she climbed the steps. But the steps were steep and there were eight or ten flights of them, switchbacks that kept the climb from being too dangerous. Kym knew she'd be too exhausted to kill a man by the time she got to the high deck. No, she needed her strength. She walked with a determined stride over to one of the lift cages, the open latticework making it possible for her to glance up to the workers gathered around. Did they know how violent and disgusting the man was? Were they aware that his name was on the Council's list? Did Galen even know? Probably not. He had done his crimes and thought he'd gotten away with them. Kym was sure he would do it again. She had no doubt in her mind this was the right target for her. She could live with herself and her decision.

She stepped into the lift cage as another engineer climbed in with her. She punched the button for the top deck and the man nodded, then gave her a second look.

"You're from the maintenance decks," he said. "What are you doing here in our territory? We do our own maintenance."

Kym struggled for an answer and then said, simply, "I'm authorized."

The man shrugged, accepting it.

"From the Council," she added foolishly, and instantly regretted it.

He didn't need any more information. He looked at her in surprise, but the cage was moving upward. She felt the air currents, smelled the fumes, and thought again of how old Sudio had described the wind and the trees back on Earth. Neither Kym nor the next generation or the generations after that would ever experience those breezes. The terrarium was the closest they would come to the freedom of an open space. But the people aboard the ship had survived and they would continue to survive. The Council would monitor the resources. Everyone knew the rules and the consequences.

She furtively touched the handle of the long knife hidden in her pocket. Clipped to the belt of her shipsuit hung the hammer. She still hadn't decided which she would use. She would have to be fast and take him completely by surprise. What if Galen's coworkers tried to defend him? She blanked her mind. No second thoughts. She couldn't afford to hesitate.

The lift cage rattled to a stop at the high deck. The engineer emerged first without speaking another word to her. Kym stepped out. There were fifteen people, maybe more, on the broad deck, which was open to the high bay, an edge blocked by a waist-high guardrail that provided more psychological security than actual safety. Galen was there, laughing, as he and two other men lifted large recycled-mesh filters and slid them into slots. Two other men and two women busied themselves in the machinery taking readings, adjusting fittings. Kym knew their job was critical, refurbishing the filters so the *Hind*'s pulse engines, and its ship's complement for that matter, got the cleanest air possible.

Kym took three steps and then noticed the young woman wearing the green shipsuit from the agricultural decks. She had taken a lift cage to the deck just below them and was now ascending the open metal stairs climbing up to the side of the open balcony deck.

No one had noticed Kym yet. She swallowed, made her decision, removed the hammer. Because it was a normal-looking tool it would give her an extra second or two. If she drew the long knife and lunged toward Galen the others might react, might stop her. With the hammer, she was just another worker. She lifted it and thought for a moment of her abuela's heroism. She could do this, Kym thought. She could save a life, too. A better life, no doubt, than the one she was ending.

Galen removed a filthy filter, set it down, and leaned it against the metal deck. With her pulse racing Kym began to move. The hammer was heavy and deadly. She would strike him in the head, either the back of the skull or the middle of the forehead, it didn't matter.

The moment stretched out for her as she thought of what Galen had done to those women, the way he'd ruined their lives. And he'd done it again and again. The name of Galen Porthos deserved to be on the list.

"Hey, you don't belong …" said one of the engineers looking at her.

Kym pushed past, not stopping. The handle of the hammer was slippery with the sweat from her palm. "Galen!" she shouted.

Startled, the man turned to look. His expression fell. Kym knew he must have seen the murder in her eyes.

"He's mine," cried another voice, a female voice. The young woman in the green shipsuit burst onto the open deck on Galen's other side. She ran forward, closer to Galen than Kym and moving fast.

Kym was shocked, her concentration broken. She hesitated. And immediately hated herself for it. Abuela Juli hadn't paused. Abuela Juli had done what had to be done.

The other woman—thin, with close-cropped brown hair—leaped toward Galen, who spun, confused. He raised his hands either to fight or to surrender. The other woman crashed into him, shoved him backward with all her might and momentum.

Galen stumbled backward, tripped on the filter he had just removed, flailed and reached for purchase, and the woman drove into him again, shoulder-high, and she kept pushing. Galen tumbled over and the woman dropped to her knees, grabbing onto the bar while Galen fell, screaming. He dropped seven decks and slammed with a spreading red stain onto the floor far below.

"Mine," said the other woman panting. She looked at Kym who stood there shocked. "Mine," she said again, and thumped herself on her chest. "I chose him from the list. Now I get my Permit."

The other engineers were terrified. To hear about things like this was one thing, to see it happen right before your eyes was something else again. One held onto the bars and peered down looking at the broken body of Galen far below. Another backed away from the railing and then fell to the floor, where he sat, stunned.

The woman pulled out the sheet of paper the Council had given her, waved it, showed the name of Galen Porthos on the list. "I have my Permit. He was a waste of resources. He did not deserve life anymore."

Nauseated, Kym felt as if she might faint. She'd been so close. She had been ready!

The other woman paused, looked at Kym. Her face softened and she said to Kym, "I wish you the best of luck. I really do."

Kym knew she meant it. This was how it was on the *Hind*. A life for a life.

Shaken, Kym retreated for the day, and then the next day and the next. She buried herself in her work. There were hands-on repairs needed on all decks for broken lights and faulty hatch dogs and worn-out screens and sensors and pipes of other everyday needs. The *Hind* was wearing down and replacement parts were long gone, along with the mech-printers that might have produced some more. Kym's job was to make-do, jury-rig, and extend the lifespan of everything. Some things, like the tubes of silicone sealant and the variety of O-rings and the solder that she used, were almost gone and there would be no replacements. There would just be more leakage and more unsolvable problems that they'd come to Kym for in search of answers. Someday soon, she supposed, she wouldn't have an answer to these problems and there'd be no work-around and they would all have to limp along as things got worse and worse. But that day wasn't here yet.

She worked away, but unhappily. Time was passing and it was time she didn't have. Her coworkers looked at her curiously. They could tell something was wrong. She was flushed, volatile, snapping at them, avoiding them when she normally was such a pleasant person. She had excuses for where she had been while preoccupied during her hunt, but she was also concerned because she had to be viable herself, a productive member of the ship. If she didn't do her work and help the *Hind*'s complement survive, her own name might end up on the list. The thought sent a twinge through her. She felt a clench in her abdomen, but she drove it away, forced herself to concentrate on her duties.

She'd been told the old stories about how the ship had been built to take care of itself, with repair bots running around fixing things where needed. But those days disappeared along with the bridge crew and the ship's library and the medroom and everything else that flew away into the void when the ship was hit by that spray of debris. Since then it had been hands-on labor keeping things running.

Kym was very good at what she did. She had a knack for understanding what was wrong and how to fix it, from the lighting strips in the corridors to the air scrubbers and handlers that kept the air clean, to the water filters and piping that recycled the water and moved it around the ship, to the wiring and the printed circuits that labored along manually since the *Hind*'s AI had died on that terrible day. All the coding of the jury-rigged electronics had to be input by hand, all the systems that had gone quiet after the debris slammed into the ship had to be bypassed and those bypasses kept functional. Her mother had held the same job, but in those days there was still hope of regaining control and there were plenty of spare parts to repair things. The O-rings and sealants that Kym had inherited after her mother's death seemed plentiful at the time.

But that was twelve long years ago, when Kym was a precocious ten-year-old, and a wasteful one, too. The supplies had dwindled, and the mech-printers had inexplicably shut down years ago, so there were no new parts or lubricants or sealants. Kym was inventive, but there were limits. Plus, there were other things on her mind.

Like deciding what to do. She looked at the names, wondered how many separate lists there were that the Council had generated, how much competition she had. That other woman from the agricultural division had surprised her by killing Galen Porthos. What if everyone on the list were killed before Kym got her chance? She needed to have her Permit!

Taking a brief break when no one was around to look at her, Kym studied the names again. She didn't know any of them personally, and that was good. But it was odd that there could be so many people she'd never even heard of.

For some reason the Council wanted them dead. She wasn't supposed to have any personal stake, wasn't supposed to question. In fact, she could have just plucked a name off the list at random, tracked the person down and killed them. But she wanted to be more prepared than that.

One name intrigued her and frightened her, both. It seemed like the most impossible target on the list and Kym realized that might be a good thing. Who else would try to kill Xandi Chan? Xandi was a powerful person, with political clout and many supporters, though she kept to herself. Kym had heard that Xandi was a former member of the Council who'd had a falling out less than a year ago. She had retreated to a portside haven near the ruined bridge decks, the supposedly uninhabitable section of the *Hind*, parts of it still open to the void and unrepairable. Kym didn't know how they could survive there, but if they could, she could, and without hesitation. Her hesitation had cost her too much already. Just go, and get it done.

She finished her shift. Every second seemed like agony, but she did not want to miss any more hours. Someone would surely notice. She had her knife and her hammer, both still unused for murder. But they would be soon. She wanted this to be over.

She went to her quarters and dug out her hand light. The battery was charged, but the charge never held for more than ten or fifteen minutes. She'd be careful with its use. Then she left to do what she must.

She rode the lift upward, all alone during the interminable journey until the machinery stopped working just below Deck Nine. She opened the top emergency hatch and clambered out into darkness and deep cold. There were scuttling noises and doors easing shut. Ferals. She pulled the hand light out of her pocket and thumbed it on. It cast a thin yellow light ahead of her as she walked down the cold corridors looking for another lift. She found one, but it, too, was stuck at the floor and had been for a long time from the look of it.

She went on, her hand light fading fast. She found another lift. Stuck, too. She decided she would have to do the rest under her own power. With her hand light almost gone she found an emergency hatch that led into the inside ladders. They were dimly lit and the handrails glowed in the near-dark. Good thing, since her hand light was about done. She shoved it into her pocket and started climbing.

She would find where Xandi and her people had staked out deck areas. The *Hind*'s bridge blister had been torn away long ago, but the rumors were that Xandi's people were trying to repair the hundreds of pinhole breaches in the q-com and nav room so they could fill the room with oxygen, open the hatch doors wide and try to repair the damage to the control systems and take control of the *Hind* from there. They'd probably kill everyone aboard in the effort. It was a foolish and dangerous thing they were attempting; one misstep in trying to regain control and the *Hind* might shut down completely. It would be a slow, miserable way for nearly a thousand people to die. At least now the *Hind* was in a steady state, limping along but keeping the ship's complement alive as it had for fifty years.

Kym's body was shaking, and she felt weak as she climbed straight up the metal ladders from one deck to the next and the next, each time opening a hatch to look around, and then returning to the ladder to climb. It was bitterly cold in the stairwell and in each of the decks she checked out, with nothing more than emergency light strips here and there along the corridors to hold back the total darkness.

She saw more ferals scuttle away in two of the decks, scavengers she supposed. It wasn't until Deck Four that she opened a hatch to discover jury-rigged portable lights and heaters. Xandi Chan had fixed this deck so that she could complete her risky effort to take control of the *Hind*. She wasn't like the old and supposedly useless Sudio, or the violent predator Galen. No, Xandi Chan was evil in an entirely different way.

Kym quietly came in through an open hatch. In front of her were people, as many as two dozen of them, shouting as they watched a large, repurposed vid screen in the command hub at the front of the corridor. A few of them stood by a hatch door. On the screen there were three people dressed in silvery hard environment suits with tanks and life support packs on their backs. Those suits were meant for work outside the *Hind*, in the void, where nobody had been for decades, Kym was sure.

One of them, at the far left on the screen, was slapping his own helmet even as he clumsily turned the wheel to the internal hatch, trying to undog it in a hurry. Another person knelt at the side of a third, who lay on the deck twitching. There were shouts and yells from those in front of Kym who were watching the screen: "Help them!" and "Open the hatch!"

This was a perfect moment for Kym, all eyes focused elsewhere. She touched the handle of the knife at her right hip pocket and the dangling hammer on the belt at her left. She had studied Xandi's image so she knew who to look for. The problem would be getting to her, killing her, and then getting away. Xandi's supporters weren't likely to stop and listen to Kym explain that Xandi was on the Council's list.

Kym saw a woman in a charcoal gray suit. She was no taller than any of the others, but she seemed more powerful, larger somehow. Kym was certain, dead certain, that the woman was Xandi Chan. She wasn't more than twenty feet away, standing at the back of the group that watched on the screen as the panicky enviro-suited people tried to save themselves. It was obvious to Kym that their suits had sprung leaks and they had to get out quickly or die.

The timing was perfect, with everyone looking at the screen. Kym took one steadying breath as the moment seemed to stretch out for her. Could she get to Chan fast enough? Could she strike quickly? Could she do what she needed to do?

She could try. She did try, moving briskly toward Xandi. Keeping her arms at her side, but ready to raise her weapons and strike. Twenty feet, then fifteen, then ten as she pulled the hammer loose with her left arm and prepared to strike. One of the men heard her footsteps, glanced back toward her, saw what has happening, and yelled "Xandi!" and reached toward Kym to try and stop her.

Kym put on a burst of speed, pulling the knife from her belt with her right hand now, too. Xandi had heard the warning and was turning, seeing Kym and starting to raise her hands in front of her face to defend against the coming, crushing blow of the hammer.

But the blow never came. The man who'd spotted Kym came at her, and another one who'd heard the shout leaped toward her even as she screamed a challenge and threw herself at them, hoping to break through. As the two men and then more closed around Kym, she swung the hammer with her left hand, but Xandi stepped back as the nearest man grabbed Kym's hand. She lashed out with the knife in her right hand, but another man blocked her, catching her arm. She thrashed and struggled, but two more reached her then and it was over. She'd failed.

Xandi stood silent for a moment, then smiled, crossed her arms over her chest. Kym could see that Xandi felt completely safe with her guardians. Kym had never had a chance.

Xandi spoke loud enough for all to hear. "Hold her tight!" And then she turned back to the screen, where the man on the floor was quiet now, his twitching and thrashing over even as the man at the hatch had finally gotten it open. "Get them out of there! Now!" Xandi commanded. And then, more softly, almost to herself, "We'll have to try again later."

The screen, flickering in and out, showed the suited figure from the hatch area going over to help the second figure lift the quiet body of the third into the airlock. In a few seconds all three were inside, closing the hatch manually. You could see the wheel close and then, from where they all stood, they could hear the pumps getting oxygen into the airlock.

They all watched, a minute later, as the inside hatch opened and the two suited figures stumbled out, carrying the body of the third, which they laid on the ground once they were clear of the lock. The room was very quiet.

Xandi turned her back on Kym, who was held tightly in the arms of her captors, and walked slowly over to the suited figures. She patted the shoulders of the two who were standing, pulling off their helmets. Then she knelt down to reach out with both hands to turn and unclick the helmet of the supine and silent figure. She carefully pulled the helmet free, then reached to touch the man's face. She closed his eyelids, rose, and said, quietly, "He's gone."

Then she stood and said loud enough for all to hear, "Tally is gone. He was trying to save this ship, save the *Hind*, save us all. And he's died in the effort. Should we give up?"

"No," someone said quietly from the back, and "No," another said, and then, "No!" they all said.

"That's what I thought," Xandi said. "We've lost a friend, but Tally would want us to try again. We're very close to success, to saving the *Hind*! Should we keep trying?"

"Yes!" came a shout, and then more, as Xandi nodded. Yes, they would try again.

Kym watched all this, amazed by what she was seeing, and wrestling with its implications. Could they really take control of the *Hind*?

She was held firmly by a man on each side as Xandi walked over to her and looked her straight in the eyes. "Do you understand what just happened? Do you understand this man died trying to save this ship?"

Kym's head was spinning. She wasn't sure who was right. They'd been in the q-com and nav room! They'd been trying to repair the *Hind*! If they were able to do that, it could change everything. Everything!

"I had no idea …" she started to say.

Xandi just shook her head. "And yet you were ready to take my life because it's on your list."

"I didn't want to. You probably know that," Kym said. "But I have to. It's the only way."

"Ahh, of course," said Xandi, "you're pregnant." Xandi's demeanor changed. In a heartbeat she went from angry to sad, reaching out to touch Kym's face. "Oh, child, I've seen this before.

It's a terrible decision you've been facing and made all the worse because you've been lied to. Like almost everyone else on the *Hind*, you've been lied to and you've believed it. The Council knows the truth, that it doesn't have to be this way. But they'd rather lie than lose power. Why do you think they have that list? Why do you think I left the Council?"

For long seconds, Kym could only stare at Xandi. Kym had believed what she'd been told: that what she'd been forced to do was best for everyone, for all the ship's complement, because it was the only option. Cruel and unfair, yes, but the only option.

Now, her head was spinning with the realization that everything could change. And maybe she could be part of that change, maybe she could help and these people, in turn, might help her. It was a life-changing moment. She dropped the hammer and the knife from her clenched fists and they both clattered on the deck. "Where did you get those suits?" Kym asked.

Xandi smiled and waved away the men who held Kym. They let go, but stayed next to Kym as Xandi said, "We found six of them in an escape pod that we opened two months ago down in the feral decks. The hatch to the pod was covered by lean-tos and tents in that favela down there. I'm sure it dates all the way back to the catastrophe. We cobbled together parts from all of them to make these three suits usable."

Usable. Right, Kym thought as she looked at the suits. They were tattered and worn, hinged at the hips and shoulders and ankles and wrists. Round clasps at those spots and at the neck where the helmet attached were what kept out the deadly vacuum of the q-com and nav room.

She could see at a glance that the "usable" suits weren't usable at all. The sealants around all those hinges and clasps were long gone. It was a wonder all three of the men hadn't died. "You thought these were safe? After all this time?"

"We had to try," said a voice from behind Xandi, one of the suited men, unsealing the right arm covering as he walked over. "And if we'd had more time, even another five minutes, we might have powered up."

"The main console wasn't holed, Akron?"

His face was grim. "It was holed, sure. But only two small holes running through it, and when you think about the rest of the damage in there …" He shrugged. "No one's been in there since they cleared out the bodies fifty years ago, Xandi. It's perfectly preserved the way it was when the room was sealed shut. I'd say we might be able to power it up. Hell, it's worth a try."

He held the suit's right arm up in front. "But first, I could hear the hiss of the air leaking out of these things. We have to do something about that before worrying about getting to the main console working."

"You'll need voice access," Kym said. "I mean, the *Hind*'s AI was verbal. Everything was done through voice control. Even if it powers up you won't have access until the *Hind* recognizes your voice and your access rights."

"How do you know this?" Xandi asked.

Kym smiled, committed now to this new path. "I met someone the other day," she said. "And I think she can help."

"I'm very tired, Juliana," Sudio said as she stopped her upward climb on the metal-grate steps that led to the q-com and nav quarters. "Why can't we use the lift and go straight to work that way, dear?" she asked, holding the railing for support as she turned around to sit on the step.

Kym sighed. Sudio thought Kym was Abuela Juliana, Kym's grandmother, and had reached the point now where she couldn't be persuaded otherwise. It was a long trek from Sudio's quarters near the terrarium with its orchard, to the q-com and nav center, with its promise for a better future.

Kym had planned on explaining everything to Sudio about the q-com breaches being repaired, about waking up the *Hind*, about waking up the hope of the whole ship's complement. But that conversation had gone nowhere. As far as Sudio was concerned, it was fifty years ago and Juliana, her best friend, had come to get her so they could go to work together, like they always did.

Kym tried to straighten Sudio out about it twice, and both times it worked for a minute or two and then the memory of Kym's explanation was gone and only the deeper, better memories from her youth stuck with Sudio. So, okay, Abuela Juliana she would be, thought Kym, and off they went.

The creaky, worrisome lift had gotten them within six decks, but no higher than that, so now they were hiking up the stairs, as Kym had done a couple of days earlier, when she'd been intent on death, on killing Xandi. Now, instead, she was intent on saving Xandi and everyone else.

"We used the lift at first, Sudio, remember?" Kym said, smiling gently. "But for this part we have to walk up. It's not far."

"All right, dear Juli," Sudio said. And then seconds later, she added, "But why don't we use the lift?" And Kym looked at her and smiled, promised again that it wasn't far.

Nearly an hour later, they'd reached the command hub, where Sudio rested for a while as Xandi and a few others who Kym had warned about Sudio's dementia came up to introduce themselves while Kym did a final check of the two working suits.

No one thought the patches would hold for long once the room was pressurized, so the plan was to go through the makeshift airlock into the q-com and nav room and then, suits on, be ready to take off their helmets and speak to the *Hind* through the main console when the pumps had brought the air pressure up to the Armstrong minimum and filled the room with breathable air. Maybe the air pressure would help the two hundred twelve patches, large and small, adhere to the inside of the hull. Maybe Kym would take off her helmet, breathe the air, and then help Sudio take off her helmet and breathe, too. Maybe Sudio would then remember and say the magic words and the *Hind* would recognize her voice and wake up so Sudio could give Kym permission to communicate and the *Hind*, maybe, would agree.

That was a whole lot of maybes, but Kym thought it could work. Kym had devoted her young life to answers, to fixing things, to diagnosing problems and coming up with solutions. She was the one who'd brought the air handlers back online two years ago when they'd mysteriously broken down. She was the one who'd used her abuela's ancient soldering iron to repair at least a dozen of the drive units in the scattered peripherals that ran the *Hind*'s R/O water scrubbers. She was the one who'd scrounged parts and labored to repair more light strips than she could count. It was because of Kym that the hallways were navigable even in the dim light from the precious few remaining diode lights.

This was all Kym's work. Breaking things down and scavenging.

Building things back with those parts, making them work even in their imperfect fits. That was what she'd always done. It wouldn't solve her problem; there were more names on that list, and, in theory, she knew she had to kill one of those people on the list to make room. But if she couldn't solve her own problem right now, why not try and solve the ship's? Even a small chance of that was worth any risk, wasn't it?

Kym's hand-me-down silicone sealant was gone now, the last large tub of it that she'd inherited from her mother Ana Maria had been used to seal the patches on the hull and seal the two suits that were the last chance to wake up the *Hind*. It wasn't perfect, this patch job, they'd run out of sealant before applying it to all the wall patches, so that added another maybe to the long list. But they'd done what they could do, and now it was time to try and wake the ship up.

Kym knew Sudio was confused about what was happening, as the two of them stepped into the airlock. Sudio's last words before her helmet had been sealed were in a strange little-girl voice that said, "Juli? I'm scared." So Kym had held her gloved hand in her own and walked them into the airlock.

Now, Kym could hear, through the helmet, the hiss of the air being evacuated. Would the suits hold up? Would the patches? She could only hope.

A long minute later the air in the lock was evacuated, and Kym gave Sudio's hand a squeeze and then let go to grab the hatch wheel on the inside to spin it loose and then, tugging hard on the inside dogs for the hatch, she pushed it open, reached back to take Sudio's gloved hand in hers again, and walked them both into the q-com and nav room. Then, while a frightened Sudio waited, trembling with worry, Kym shut and dogged the hatch door from the outside and stepped back over to take Sudio's right hand in hers.

Kym knew there were dozens of people crowded into the command hub outside, watching them on the vid screen. Kym looked up at the camera and gave them a thumbs-up with her left hand. Outside, they started the pumps and the air slowly filled the room.

The wait was a long one, as they'd figured it would be, but Kym could tell the difference as the air pressure rose, minute by slow minute. Twice Kym circled the room, looking to see how the patches were holding. They all looked good for now, but there were a lot of spots where small patches almost touched each other, and she was worried about the hull integrity in those areas. If one patch weakened enough to give way, it might start a cascade of failure that would take out a whole section of hull with it. It would be a catastrophic blowout, but it hadn't happened yet.

The lights in the room blinked twice, the signal that the pressure was at 120 millibars and rising. They could take off their helmets. Kym did that first, took a breath, and then turned to Sudio, who said something unintelligible behind the front plate of the helmet.

Kym unclipped the stays and then turned the helmet a few degrees and felt as much as heard the click of the release. She pulled it straight up and off of Sudio, who looked in Kym's eyes and said, "You're so brave, Juli. I love you so much."

"And I love you, Sudio," Kym said. "You're the bravest one on the ship."

Sudio's eyes brightened. "We're lucky to have each other, Juli, aren't we?"

"We are, but look," Kym said, and waved her hand toward the far wall, covered in patches. The wall was trembling, vibrating, the patches giving way.

"Dear God, what's happened to the *Hind*?"

"We've been holed, Sudio, and the *Hind* shut itself down. Can you help me wake it up?"

"Together? We could do that together, you and me, dear Juli?"

"Of course," said Kym, and walked with her over to the top console, where the one small light was blinking red, a dot of light visible in the wreckage. She'd spent hours the day before in that clumsy suit, connecting what had been severed, not having replacements for anything, not really knowing what she was doing but hoping connections might help. And near the end of the day she'd connected two small white wires that had been neatly severed fifty years before by a marble-sized bit of debris, and a tiny spot of hope blinked to life. What did it mean? She had no idea, but it had to mean there was power in the system, something trickling to life perhaps. Maybe.

There was a loud crack from behind her and Kym turned to look. The bulkhead was trembling and straining. One of the patches that sat in the middle of a dozen more was bowing outward under the pressure from the air in the room. Kym wondered how long they had until that patch gave way and took the others with it. Seconds? Minutes?

She looked back as Sudio looked at the light and spoke in that little-girl voice that had emerged from the deep well of her youth as the light blinked and there was another crack from behind. So it was seconds left, not minutes. "Please wake up, *Hind*, darling. This is Sudio, from q-com control."

There was a third sharp crack. Kym started putting her helmet back on as she watched that patch. By the time she had it on and tight, she'd missed the action. Where the patch had been was just a hole the size of her fist. She felt the air in the room change instantly, could see more patches going even as the pressure dropped, the escaping wind tugging at her.

She grabbed Sudio's helmet and started putting it on her, but Sudio fought with her, pushing the helmet aside and saying, "One more try, Juli. *Hind* will wake up, I'm sure. I didn't say it right, that's all. How does it go, dear?"

But Kym didn't know, of course, and could only shrug her shoulders and say, "I've forgotten, Sudio."

"Oh, silly," Sudio said, smiling. "I'm supposed to be the one who can't remember."

She put her finger against the side of her cheek, posing in thought, and then she turned to Kym and said, "I remember. You saved us all, Juli."

And she turned back to the com unit and said, very calmly, in a voice that Kym hadn't heard from her before, a voice that recalled a time a half century before when Sudio and Juliana and a dozen others had been the best and the brightest.

"*Hind*," she said. "It's Sudio. Sir Francis Drake. Wake up."

And the *Hind* did.

There is a small orchard in a large terrarium midships. Sitting crisscross on the green grass under the small apple tree there are ten people. There is Sudio, whose face is blank and confused but who still manages to smile from time to time when some fleeting memory is prompted by the storyteller.

And there are eight children, from ten down to one year of age. Four of them were so-called ferals a few months ago, frightened and even vicious in their struggle to survive. But here, now, maybe, they're getting better. There is, at least, hope for them and the others like them. The Council no longer matters. The list no longer matters. An election is coming. Xandi is likely to win.

Three others are children we've met before: Chennai and Roma and Genoa. A fourth child, the baby, is Dothan, the daughter of Kym, who was the daughter of Ana Maria, who was the daughter of Juliana.

And Kym is here, too, on her day off, sitting with Dothan in her lap, wondering if the diaper needs changing as they listen to the stories about old Earth and its blizzards and hurricanes and haboobs and tornadoes and earthquakes and tsunamis and its sunshine and breezes and fresh air and mountains and cities and great oceans and plains.

The storyteller seems to be the tree, which strikes the children as perfectly reasonable. It is as common and ordinary to them as the garden bots circling through the orchard, and the way the library re-emerged from the *Hind*'s backups to bring up vids from old Earth and books to learn from in a functioning smart schoolhouse. It's all just as ordinary as the gentle bumps and polite apologies from the *Hind* as the navigational systems set their new course. The *Hind* has been very busy for the past year and will be for the next twenty years, before they reach their Goldilocks.

"Thank you, *Hind*," says Kym as the final story for the day comes to an end.

The tree responds with a very polite, "You're welcome, Kym. And the captain requests your presence on the bridge. The R/O water system has another leak and she'd like a better fix this time."

Kym sighs, rises. "Tell the captain I'll be there in twenty minutes and make a few of those same O-rings as last time and a batch of that silicone sealant, too, please."

"Of course," the *Hind* says as Kym stands up with Dothan in her arms. She'll have to drop Dothan off at the crèche again, on the way to the water purifier.

Kym turns to wave goodbye to everyone and helps Dothan wave, too. The children wave back. Sudio raises an unsure hand and holds it out toward Kym, who comes over and takes it in her hand to say goodbye.

Sudio manages a small smile and says, "Sir Francis Drake, dear Juli," and Kym smiles back and says, "Sir Francis Drake, dear Sudio," and they hug as the *Hind* bongs twice, says, "Course correction," and they all can feel the pulse engines as they light up again to send a slight shudder through the ship and alter ever so slightly their course to the future.

It's not every day you get to write a giant robot story, but when you do, it's a very good day.

I love giant monster movies, and grew up with Godzilla, Gamera, Rodan, and King Kong films, many of which included encounters with giant robots. I watched giant robot anime whenever my local Milwaukee, Madison, or Chicago TV stations showed it (not often).

In a film, you can watch the giant robots battering each other and smashing down buildings, but in a short story you have to give the reader something a little more than just visuals. When my coauthor David Boop and I brainstormed this story, we discussed how much fun—and liberating—it would be to be guide a giant robot to knock down any building, any bridge, or any mountain that gets in your way. How exhilarating, how … therapeutic!

Piloting a giant robot on a mission of destruction would, in fact, serve as great anger-management therapy.

TRAVAILIANT

(with David Boop)

Though Harold Hodges was glad to be away from the noise and headaches of city-rebuilding activity outside, his nose had a seizure when he entered the supposedly peaceful therapist's lobby. Three smells assaulted him almost simultaneously. First came the sickening sweet scent of apple cinnamon from the potpourri infuser blasting the room. Second was an ammonia-laced smell from the bio-sanitizer used on the floors, walls, tables, and furniture—proof against any lingering remnants of the alien slime; leftover contamination from the failed invasion was nothing to sneeze at ... pun unintended. But neither of those could drown out the third, unexpected smell.

Diesel fuel and a strong tang of lubricants.

Harold looked around, but he was the only person in the waiting room; not even a receptionist. He sniffed his shirt sleeve, worried he had accidentally worn a stained shirt from the mechanic shop where he worked on supply transport hydraulics. He needed to make a good impression on the new therapist.

"This is your last chance, Mr. Hodges," the annoyed magistrate had said. "If we don't see significant progress in dealing with your anger-management issues, we will have no choice but to assign you to a community-service residue scraping crew."

As if his life hadn't already gone far enough to hell ...

Harold sniffed the air in the reception area again, but the sour chemical odor wasn't coming from him. That was a relief. After so many bad first impressions, he didn't dare leave anything to chance. The fuel and oil came from somewhere else, though nearby.

He forced calm upon himself, like smothering his stress with a pillow. When a chime rang and his number appeared on the "Now Serving" display, he swallowed hard, tried to think happy thoughts. *Time to get this over with.*

He went to the indicated cubicle and sat in front of a flat-screen monitor, which winked into life. An androgynous voice commanded, "State your name, age, and government designation number."

Harold felt annoyance, then anger, that they wouldn't even bother to have a human interact with him, but he quelled that. Too much at stake to lose his temper now. He made a conscious effort to keep the edge out of his voice. "Harold Nelson Hodges, age fifty-three, DTN874QWV543."

The synthesized voice verified the data and responded, "Caucasian male. Single. No children. Honorably discharged from service in the United Earth Defense Corp. Mr. Hodges, you have been ordered to attend *Travailiant* therapy by the reconstructed courts of the United Earth Alliance."

"Yes, well—" Harold began, but was cut off.

"In the most recent incident, you were charged with one count of drunk and disorderly, three counts of aggravated assault, and seven counts of resisting arrest."

"As I've tried to explain—" He couldn't get in a word edgewise.

"Your defiant behavior and subsequent failed attempts at anger management forced the tribunal of judges to offer this as your last chance for redemption."

Harold sweated, forced himself to think happy thoughts, to grasp at a lifeline of artificial patience. "That's why I'm here."

The synthesized voice sounded stern. "If you do not satisfactorily meet the directives of the prescribed lessons and achieve the goals as explained to you, you will be remanded to the iridium reclamation plant for a period of five years of forced labor. Do you understand the reason for your sentence, Mr. Hodges? And the consequences of failure?"

Even though he knew what was at stake, he still felt a chill. He understood full well how he'd screwed up when he told the first quack to sit and spin on a Garnethian tentacle. He knew he'd blown his second chance when he threw gluten-free donuts at the group of emotionless mannequins they stuck him with next.

Yeah, I got issues, but it ain't nobody's damn business but my own. He didn't dare say that.

"Mr. Hodges?"

"Yes, I understand." Meek. Cooperative. Happy thoughts. "My last chance."

"Would you prefer a male or female therapist?"

He selected male, sure that a woman's voice would only make him think of Brenda, remind him that she was gone now ... and he didn't think he could tolerate that. The monitor screen told him to stand up and follow the left corridor to room 12B. An exit door opened automatically in the back of the waiting room. "Please take a seat there and wait for instructions. The therapist will join you shortly."

He traveled through industrial, cramped hallways with harsh lighting and power conduits, naked ventilation ducts; it was a labyrinth, but he found a door—more like a hatch, actually—marked 12B. He entered a dark chamber.

He looked for a switch, called out for "Lights!" without success, so he stumbled around in the dark until he found a large, padded chair with armrests. The chair contoured to Harold's heavy form as he sat.

Waiting made Harold uneasy. He didn't like any part of this, but his life certainly hadn't been all rainbows and unicorns since the Garnethian invasion several years ago. All of Earth had suffered, and he had survived the disaster, which was more than a lot of people could say. And many of the survivors had a great deal of trouble coping.

"Radical therapy" was what the tribunal said he needed. "New" and "Experimental" were the words his Veterans Association attorney had used. The recent arrest hadn't been Harold's first since the war ended, and the authorities were convinced it wouldn't be the last. They were probably right.

A pleasant male voice announced its presence in the dark chamber. "Hello, Harold. I'm your Therapy Artificial Intelligent Tutor, but you may call me TAIT."

Harold gripped the armrests hard. "A fargin' simulation as my last-chance therapist? They have me talking to a fargin' program?" *How was that for compassion?*

"I'm more than just a program, Harold. May I call you Harold? I'm fully sentient. I specialize in human conditioning and my knowledge base encompasses the complete existing library of psychological studies."

Fidgeting in his chair, Harold grumbled, "I didn't even want to talk to a real shrink. What makes them think I'd talk to a fake one?"

"First, rest assured that I am a real psychoanalyst. I have several PhDs earned exactly the same way a human student would, though at an accelerated pace, thanks to my enhanced processing speed."

Disgusted, thinking this was just one more gigantic joke the system was dumping on him, Harold got up from the chair. "No thanks. Glow duty can't be worse than this. Let me out of here."

TAIT's voice sounded disappointed. "Before you make your final selection to opt for the work detail alternative, let me show you what happens to prisoners who choose 'glow duty,' as you call it. I hope you'll reconsider." A monitor screen lit up beside Harold, displaying a series of images, each more horrific than the next. "Cleaning up the Garnethian ooze left behind after the destruction of their weapons is statistically a death sentence, Harold. As you can see, many workers come down with the glow pox."

Harold's face turned green, and not from the iridescent sheen of the alien ooze teams of sullen suited workers were shoveling into lined containers.

"Despite the best protective gear, the Garnethian residue eventually works its way into contact with the workers' skin. The pustules start small, and those won't keep you awake at night, but as they increase in size, the emitted light makes it nearly impossible for a person to sleep, resulting in exhaustion and reduced immune resistance. Most workers eventually succumb to weakness caused by bio-contaminants."

Ten years ago, the Garnethian invasion fleet had arrived in orbit, dropping cyto-bombs on Earth's major cities without warning. The ooze irradiated everything it touched, and the population began dying faster than bugs on a zapper. That was when an angry young Harold had signed up for service, the last of humanity fighting for survival against the alien scourge.

Humankind finally won the battle for the planet after the

development of Decimators, forty-story-tall walking tanks that looked like giant robots but fought like Chuck Norris. They took the fight to the invaders for the first time, and kicked Garnethian butt (although the tentacled things' biology didn't have any obvious "butt").

However, the prize for victory was a barely habitable planet, soiled with Garnethian glow-bomb residue with major cities no more than empty wastelands. Small, untouched towns became the gathering centers for survivors, which rapidly grew into new hubs in the subsequent years.

But the empty, contaminated cities were abandoned, just a giant no-man's land, requiring cleanup.

As the disturbing images faded on the screen, Harold swallowed the bile in his throat and returned to his chair. *This is my last chance.* "Fine, I'll stay. That was a fargin' dirty trick."

"Truth is never a trick, Harold, and this is not a subterfuge. *Travailiant* therapy doesn't rely on those types of mind games. We prefer a more … hands-on approach."

Console lights popped on in the chamber, and the wall in front of Harold shimmered into a triple view screen to reveal that he was in a hangar of some sort. Buttons and a joystick rose from the armrests of his contoured chair. Though he'd never been in one himself, he recognized the configuration.

"I'm in the cockpit of a fargin' Decimator! You've gotta be fargin' kidding me. I'm not qualified to pilot this thing!" Panicked and overwhelmed, Harold once again considered fleeing the room. He hated anything connected to the big cocky, clumsy mechs and all they represented to him. Brenda …

TAIT spoke quickly, but calmly. "Please remain in your seat, Harold, as the controls align with your mental systems. This is a decommissioned mechanized combat platform that contains no live weapons, rebranded as the *Travailiant*. You're perfectly safe, and no specialized training is needed. The guidance AI will be calibrated to your thought patterns."

Harold's aversion gave way to a curious, albeit perverse curiosity. "It does anything I think of? What if I want to make this thing dance an Irish gig?"

"I'll broadcast 'Dillon's Fancy' or 'Toss the Feathers.'"

"What if I want to play a game of Decimator hopscotch?"

"I'll have someone draw up a very large court. Do you prefer American or English rules? My only goal is to see you overcome your anger issues, Harold. This is your therapy. Shall we begin?"

Warily, Harold sank deeper in the chair, grasped the armrest controls. "So, what am I supposed to do? Fight some imaginary Garns and get my anger out that way?" This simulated shrink didn't even know why he was so angry.

"No, we have something more constructive—or should I say, *destructive*—in mind."

Harold raised an eyebrow. For a computer, TAIT had a mischievous tone to his voice.

TAIT completed a series of calibration tests, both physical and mental, as a crown of wires dropped from the ceiling and snugged itself around Harold's skull. He felt ridiculous putting it on and hoped that no one other than the damn computer was watching him.

When all of the giant mech's systems had been linked to his mind and body, Harold set off, prodded by TAIT. "It should feel natural to you, Harold. Just walk, one foot in front of the other."

The mammoth Decimator detached from the hangar, taking the cockpit "therapy room" with it, and Harold realized he was deep inside the machine. He lifted a foot, set it down, took another step. His body was the size of a skyscraper!

"I will guide you," TAIT said. "Just follow the preselected path."

The Decimator strode along, leaving the hangar and the outskirts of the new settlement. Harold was amazed by the speed, grace, and *power* of this gigantic machine. Since all the systems were so intimately connected with his own thoughts and movements, and the robot mirrored his own vastly smaller form, Harold felt accustomed to the machine in no time at all. "This is less complicated than riding a bike!"

"We will not be riding bicycles, Harold," said TAIT. "We have a more specific set of tasks for your first therapy session."

Harold strode across the landscape, which still showed scars of the war; he covered a mile in only a few minutes, and he saw the jagged, crumbling skyline looming closer. "Looks like we're going into the old city. I thought it was contaminated … off limits."

"There's no need for concern, Harold. The shielding on a

Travailiant is far superior to what you'd be wearing on glow duty. You're safe in here."

The mech ate up road quickly, leaving the steady construction of a world rebuilding and entering the decay of a world lost. Skyscrapers dripped like Dali's *Persistence of Time*, their plaster flesh melted away to reveal decrepit metal skeletons. Sprawled across the buckled roads were dark smudges that once had been cars, trucks, fleeing people. Even during his stint in the service, Harold hadn't been this close to the city since the withdraw order had come down.

Memories stepped unbidden from the locked recesses of his mind. This landscape reminded him of a series of pictures he had seen back in the internet age, back when Harold had been a child—abandoned amusement parks, a collection of pictures of places given up after hurricanes, war, recessions. Devoid of joy, they were haunted with the ghosts of lost dreams.

The city trumped all those images put together. It was a graveyard of empty rooms.

"You seem to be experiencing some sort of emotion, Harold. Care to describe?"

Harold felt anger flare inside. "What do you think, you soulless piece of junk? Millions died here, buried under caustic slime! Of course I'm going to feel something. *I'm* not a machine."

TAIT took no offense. "No, you're not. You were here during the war, correct? One of the troops defending this place. I have reviewed all of your day-to-day military duty logs—"

Harold balled his fist. "My military record is none of your business."

"Sorry, Harold. I need your full records to best understand your needs. That's why you're here. We need to explore the roots of your anger. Tell me about what you did in the war."

Harold continued to thunder along in the giant Decimator, lumbering into the ruins of the city where the empty buildings were like trees in a geometric forest. But his attention was focused on the disembodied voice harassing him. "I keep telling you quacks, I'm not angry because of the war. Y'all think I got PTSD. But I never saw firsthand combat, never wrestled with any Garnethians. I never even got to fight."

"Correct. You were in a support capacity because you were physically too big to be a pilot. How many times did you apply?"

TAIT's question brought a wave of regret. Was the AI therapist trying to annoy him?

"Five times, right? You must have really wanted it badly, yes?"

Harold couldn't help that he'd been born big boned, that his metabolism made it all too easy to put on weight. No matter how much he wanted to fight, even the rigors of basic training couldn't get him down to combat weight.

An icon flashed on the GPS and Harold rotated the viewer—and the Decimator's mammoth head—to see a target painted on the side of a crumbling building, along with the overlaid words, "Strike here!"

"Each rejection must have stung more than the last one," TAIT taunted.

Anger welled up inside of Harold and, seeing that he had permission to hit something, he willed his mech to punch the target. The *Travailiant*'s monstrous fist shot out and struck the mark, slamming a clean hole in the brickwork. Lightning-bolt cracks spidered throughout the rest of the building. Slowly at first, but picking up speed, support beams twisted and crumpled until the whole building collapsed before him.

TAIT sounded pleased. "Nicely done, Harold. How did that feel?"

He watched the tumbling girders and stone, mesmerized by the dust cloud that billowed from the rubble of the once-powerful bank building. He rotated the arm until the mech's massive hand hovered in front of the view screen. He flexed his own fingers and the machine mimicked him. So much power at his disposal! "That felt ... kind of good. Can we do that again?"

"Yes, Harold. Let's talk about the friends you lost in the war."

"No."

"Tell me about Slinky, tall kid from Alabama."

A service picture of John "Slinky" Jenkins appeared on one of the monitors. Harold backhanded the monitor, trying to make the picture go away, and his *Travailiant* responded by taking out an overpass.

"I said *No!*"

Each time TAIT pried into Harold's past, poked and prodded and provoked, Harold flinched, reacted—and destroyed another target. He wasn't even paying much attention anymore, using ruined buildings as punching bags as his anger grew, but the GPS targeting service directed him to a new location. Harold gradually realized there was a pattern to his destruction, though, and he didn't need to be a civil engineer nor a shrink to see that TAIT had an agenda.

"You're using my anger issues to clear the fargin' city? Pissing me off to do the dirty work of the United Earth Alliance?"

TAIT let out an unconvincing artificial chuckle. "Consider it therapeutic community service. You get the psychological help you so desperately need and a reconstruction department makes progress leveling contaminated sections of the city. It's a win-win."

Harold laughed. It felt good to laugh. He couldn't remember how long it'd been. Before Brenda …

"I think I might like this therapy after all."

"Good, Harold. Our session is at an end for this week. Please return the *Travailiant* to the hangar. See you next Tuesday?"

Harold soon grew accustomed to releasing his rage through the body of the giant mech, smashing dead buildings and clearing rubble. By the third session, he and TAIT made it all the way to the heart of downtown. The gigantic robot stood in the center of 6th Street, surrounded by two dozen cancerous monoliths. Harold gaped at the task before him. "You don't expect me to take all these down, do you?"

"Tell me, Harold, who's Brenda?"

Harold froze in place. "What? Don't say her name!"

TAIT repeated, "Who is Brenda? We have no record of a Mrs. Hodges, but clearly she was special to you. Was she a girlfriend? A lover lost in the war?"

The mech clenched its fists and crouched in a defensive posture. "How did you find out her name? Nobody knew about me and Brenda!"

"During one of your drunken blackouts, after you'd beaten up three servicemen in a bar fight, the police doctor noted that you were moaning the name Brenda. Care to elaborate?"

He whispered, "No."

"Come now, Harold. We've made such progress. Tell me about Brenda. She was close to you?"

"She is nobody! Leave it be." He swung his giant augmented arm, slammed into a skyscraper.

TAIT had to increase the volume of his voice to be heard over the sound of the first decimated building. "Did you lose her in the war?"

"I said leave her out of it!" Harold lashed out in an impotent attempt to hit the virtual psychologist. "You have no right to bring her into this!" He karate-chopped connecting walkways into piecemeal.

"Did you lose her in *this* city, Harold?" TAIT prodded. "In the last wave, when the command pulled you back? Is that when she died?"

"You. *Know. NOTHING!*"

Like a berserker responding to Harold's rage, the *Travailiant* went wild, punching and kicking everything it could get its hands on. Debris piled up around them. Inside the cockpit, Harold yelled out his fury, no longer hearing anything the AI therapist said. He didn't know how much time passed in a blur but, when he came back to himself, all of the buildings around him had been reduced to rubble.

TAIT's voice sounded meek. "Um, Harold? I think that's all for today."

But Harold wasn't finished. The anger still rolled through him in waves. "Brenda was everything to me!" The exertion turned Harold's jowls ruddy with sweat, and his breath became labored as his body's movements directed the machine. He pounded on the chair's controls. "I loved her!" The *Travailiant* stomped along, pounding the dead streets and making cracks the size of drainage ditches. The big mech stumbled as a tunnel collapsed underfoot.

"Be careful! This isn't indestructible, you know."

As if the universe wanted to prove TAIT's point, a construction crane toppled from the side of a building, tumbled and struck the giant robot's back, deflecting it into the side of the nearest building, but that only made Harold angrier. In response, he grabbed fistfuls of the building and used them like brass knuckles to smash everything in sight. When even that wasn't enough, Harold bounded forward, bent low, and drove the enormous body headlong completely through another structure, leaving a mech-shaped hole in the side. He found a pool of old Garnethian ooze there pooled in a collapsed parking structure."

"Stay away from the ooze, Harold. Harold? Are you hearing me? I'm your therapist, and I say you need to calm down now. Calm down!"

Oblivious to TAIT's warning, Harold scooped up handfuls of the substance and threw them like a monkey flinging poo at visitors outside its cage.

"It's not fargin' fair! You hear me? God! It's not fargin' fair! She was all I had left! *WHY?*"

The *Travailiant*'s hands smoked from the toxic ooze. Though the Decimators had been designed to withstand the alien stuff when they were new, this recommissioned *Travailiant* was well past its warranty. The acrid smell of burnt wiring and oil stung Harold's nose and eyes.

A loud creaking sound penetrated the cockpit, and the structure they stood inside fell to pieces like a child's stack of blocks during a tantrum. Girders and office furniture rained down on top of them.

TAIT squawked in a voice that sounded genuinely panicked. "Harold, if you don't calm down, we're going to DIE!"

Awareness of their situation finally flooded Harold's senses, snapping him out of his blind rage. He had just enough time to raise his giant mechanical arms to shield the cockpit before the roof collapsed on top of them …

Harold gradually returned to consciousness, shaking his head, feeling his skull throb. He'd slammed his temple against the edge of the pilot's chair. Red lights blinked on the console, and a warning buzzer annoyed his left ear.

He groaned, sat up. "TAIT? TAIT, you there? You okay?"

"Yes, Harold. I'm actually housed in a central facility. I just stream in to the mech. Are you injured? I've lost some of the monitoring equipment."

Harold slowly got to all fours, but the *Travailiant* remained buried beneath the collapsed building, barely able to move beneath the mountain of rubble. They weren't going anywhere.

The taste of blood and the sharp pain of loose teeth made him spit both onto the floor of the cockpit. He gave his body a mental survey and decided he didn't have any serious injuries, although he did have some scrapes. "I think I'm going to make it."

"I've called a retrieval team. Congratulations! You're the first patient to take out a city block and a three-million-dollar piece of technology at the same time."

Harold let out a weak chuckle. "Mom said I was an overachiever."

TAIT snorted, a strange sound coming from a computer. It caused Harold to laugh. TAIT's responding laugh grew until both of them had a good gut-buster going. The AI stopped first.

"And how do you feel inside? After letting out all that rage?"

Harold wiped away his tears. "Good. Great, actually. Better than I've felt in years."

"It's hard on a person to keep all that pain buried, Harold. To carry all that weight and guilt … especially after someone you love dies."

Harold was surprised. "Whoa, who died?"

"Well … Brenda, of course."

Harold blinked in surprise, then guffawed. "Brenda didn't die! She dumped me—for a mech pilot. I was so angry I couldn't even see straight."

The AI therapist sounded genuinely surprised. "What?"

"Yeah. Brenda thought they were all sexy with their shiny Decimators and their giant guns. I just worked in the motor pool, so how could I compete?" Harold paused, realizing the long-standing misconceptions. "Didn't any of you brainiacs notice that all my brawls were with *mech pilots*?" He grumbled. "Thought someone would have picked up on that. How many PhDs did you say you have?"

TAIT paused. "Now that you point it out, yes, the data supports that hypothesis."

Harold heard the sound of a skyscraper being lifted off the *Travailiant*, and giant girders and stone walls were lifted away. The recovery crew had arrived. The cockpit roof hatch popped open, and light streamed in. Harold blinked as the crew lowered a ladder down to him.

Before he climbed up to safety, he called out to TAIT, "Same time, next week?"

"Sure, sure," the AI therapist said, with considerably less swagger in his voice now.

Harold Hodges smiled as he entered the facility, heading straight for the cockpit chambers and the *Travailiant* controls. He actually liked the anger-management therapy, looked forward to it all week. The courts seemed content with the progress he had made, as well as the community-service work he was completing. They scheduled him for one more round, saying that if he hit his final goals, his record would be expunged.

He felt cocky as he sat down in the operator chair. "Hey, TAIT. You ready?"

"Yes, Harold, but there has been a slight change of plans."

TAIT's voice sounded odd to Harold, and he heard that mischievous tone no AI should possess. He was on his guard. "What's that?"

"This last round of therapy is going to be … different."

The cockpit lights came on, the main viewing walls illuminated, and Harold noticed that the mech hangar had changed. It was no longer strictly utilitarian and empty. Lights and cameras were suspended from the ceiling, and along the walls behind armor-glass windows sat hundreds of people, watching him … as if this were some sort of spectator sport.

The biggest shock came when Harold saw he wasn't the only *Travailiant* patient there.

Five other recommissioned Decimator-class robots stood in a semi-circle around him. They pounded truck-sized fists, spun their thick mechanical arms, or just looked at him menacingly. As they thundered forward, closing in on him, Harold swallowed hard.

TAIT said, "Welcome to group therapy, Harold."

A big turning point in my early career was meeting Doug Beason at the Lawrence Livermore National Laboratory. We were both science fiction writers with a few story publications under our belts, and we met at the lab cafeteria for lunch. Not long afterward, we decided to try our hands at a story together, then another, then our first novel, Lifeline. *We sold a three-book contract to Bantam Books, which also included the novels* The Trinity Paradox *and Nebula-nominated* Assemblers of Infinity.

But we still wrote the occasional story together. "Prisons" came from an idea that could have mushroomed into a full novel, but we kept it under control.

On a harsh prison planet, the warden and staff are as much prisoners as the convicts, but a risky prison break might free them all.

PRISONS

(with Doug Beason)

I am still called the Warden. The prisoners consider it an ironic jest.

Barely a meter square, the forcewalls form the boundaries of my holographic body. Once this felt like a throne, an isolated position from which I could control the workings of Bastille. Now, though, I must look out and watch my former prisoners laughing at me.

This projection has been an image of authority to them. Since living on this prison world was too great a punishment to inflict upon any real warden or guards, my Artificial Personality was entrusted to watch over this compound. I am based on a real person —a great man, I think—a proud man with many accomplishments. But I have failed here.

Amu led the prisoners in their revolt; he convinced them that Bastille is a self-sufficient planet after all their forced terraforming work for the Federation. They have survived all Federation attempts to reoccupy the world, keeping the invaders out with the same systems once intended to keep the prisoners in. Besides the prisoners, I am the only one left.

Once, I ran the environmental systems here, the production accounting, the resources inventory. I monitored the automated digging and processing machinery outside. I controlled the fleet of tiny piranha interceptors in orbit that would destroy any ship trying to escape. But now I am powerless.

Amu's lover Theowane comes to taunt me every day, to gloat over her triumph. She paces up and down the corridor outside the forcewalls. To me, she is flaunting her freedom to go where she wishes. I do not think it is unintentional.

At the time of the revolt, Theowane used her computer skills to introduce a worm program that rewrote the control links around my Personality, leaving me isolated and helpless. If I attempt to regain control, the worm will delete my existence. I feel as if I have a knife at my throat, and I am too afraid to act.

At moments such as this, I can appreciate the sophistication of my Personality, which allows me to feel the full range of human emotions.

It allows me to hate Theowane and what she has done to me.

Theowane makes herself smile, but the Warden refuses to look at her. It annoys her when he broods like this.

"I am busy," he says.

Leaving him to dwell on his fate, Theowane crosses to the panorama window. Huge, remotely driven excavators and haulers churn the ground, rearing up, crunching rock and digesting it for usable minerals. At least, she thinks, Bastille's resources are put to our own use, not exported for someone else.

Lavender streaks mottle the indigo sky, blotting out all but the brightest stars. A dime-sized glare shows the distant sun, too far away to heat the planet to any comfortable temperature; but overhead, dominating the sky, rides the cinnamon-colored moon Antoinette, so close to Bastille and so nearly the same size that it keeps the planet heated by tidal flexing.

On some of the nearby rocks, patches of algae and lichen have taken hold. These have been genetically engineered to survive in Bastille's environment, to begin the long-term conversion of the surface, of the atmosphere. On a human timescale, though, they are making little progress.

Farther below, Theowane sees the oily surface of the deadly sea, where clumps of the ubermindist weed drift. A few floating harvesters ride the waves, but the corrosive water and the sulfuric-acid vapor in the air cause too much damage to send them out often.

That does not matter, since they no longer need the drug as a bargaining chip. Amu has refused to continue exporting ubermindist extract, despite a black market clamoring for it.

Theowane finds it bitterly ironic that she and so many others sentenced here for drug crimes had been forced by the Federation to process ubermindist. The Federation supports its own black market trade, keeping the drug illegal and selling it at the same time. After taking over the prison planet, Amu cut off the supply, using the piranha interceptors to destroy an outgoing robot ship laden with ubermindist. The Federation has gone without their precious addictive drug since the prison revolt.

When the intruder alarms suddenly kick in, they take Theowane by surprise. She whirls and places both hands on her hips. Her close-cropped reddish hair remains perfectly in place.

"What is it?" she demands of the Warden.

He is required to answer. "One ship, unidentified, has just snapped out of hyperspace. It is on approach." The Warden's image straightens as he speaks, lifting his head and reciting the words in an inflectionless voice.

"Activate the piranha swarm," she says.

The Warden turns to her. "Let me contact the ship first. We must see who they are."

"No!" Bastille has been quarantined by the rest of the Federation. Any approaching ship can only mean trouble.

Shortly after the prison revolt, the Praesidentrix had tried to negotiate with Bastille. Then she sent laughable threats by subspace radio, demanding that Amu surrender under threat of "severe punishment." The threats grew more strident over the weeks, then months.

Finally, after the sudden death of her consort in some unrelated accident, the Praesidentrix became brutal and unforgiving. The man's death had apparently shocked her to the core. The negotiator turned dictator against the upstart prisoners.

She sent an armada of warships to retake Bastille. Theowane had been astonished, not thinking this hellhole worth such a massed effort. Amu had turned loose the defenses of the prison planet. The piranha swarm—so effective at keeping the prisoners trapped inside—proved just as efficient at keeping the armada out. The piranhas destroyed twelve gunships that attempted to make a landing; two others fled to high orbit, then out through the hyperspace node.

But Amu is certain that the Praesidentrix, especially in her grieving, unstable state, will never give up so easily.

"Piranha defenses armed and unleashed," the Warden says.

Five of the fingerprint-smeared screens beside the Warden's projection tank crackle and wink on. Viewing through the eyes of the closest piranha interceptors, Theowane sees different views of the approaching ship, sleek yet clunky-looking, a paradox of smooth angles and bulky protuberances.

"Incoming audio," the Warden says. "Transmission locked. Video in phase and verified."

The largest screen swirls, belches static, then congeals into a garish projection of the ship's command chamber. The captain falls out of focus, sitting too close to the bridge projection cameras.

"—in peace, for PEACE, we bring our message of happiness and hope to Bastille. We come to help. We come to offer you the answers."

Theowane recognizes the metallic embroidered chasuble on the captain's shoulders, the pseudo-robe uniforms of the other crew visible in the background. She snorts at the acronym.

PEACE—Passive Earth Assembly for Cosmic Enlightenment, a devout group that combines quantum physics and Eastern philosophy into, from what Theowane has heard, an incomprehensible but pleasant-sounding mishmash of ideas. It has appealed to many dissatisfied scientists, ones who gave up trying to understand the universe. PEACE has grown because of their willingness to settle raw worlds, places with such great hardship that no one in his right mind would live there voluntarily.

Theowane sees it already: upon hearing of the prisoners' revolt, some PEACE ship conveniently located on a hyperspace path to Bastille has rushed here, hoping to convert the prisoners, to gain a foothold on the new world and claim it for their own. They must hope the Praesidentrix will not retaliate.

"Allow me to stop the piranhas," the Warden says. "This is not an attack."

"Summon Amu," she says. "But do not call off the defense." Theowane lowers her voice. "This could be as great a threat as anything the Praesidentrix might send."

She hunkers close to the screens and watches the lumbering PEACE ship against a background of stars. The deadly pinpoints of piranha interceptors hurtle toward it on a collision course.

The First Secretary enlarges the display on his terminal so he can read it better with his weakened eyesight. Across from him, the Praesidentrix sits ramrod straight in her chair.

She waits, a scowl chiseled into her face. The Praesidentrix looks as if she has aged a decade since the death of her consort, but still she insists on keeping her family matters and all details of her personal life private.

The way her policies have suddenly changed, though, tells the First Secretary just how much she had loved the man.

The First Secretary avoids her cold gaze as he calls up his figures. "Here it is," he says. "I want you to know that your attempts to retake Bastille have already cost half of what we have invested in Bastille itself. On the diagram here,"—he punches a section on the keypad—"you'll see that we have thirteen equivalent planets in the initial stages of terraforming, most of them under development by the penal service, two by private corporations. Several dozen more have gone beyond that stage and now have their first generation of colonists."

Overhead, the Praesidentrix chooses the skylight panels to project a sweeping ochre-colored sky from a desert planet. The vastness overwhelms the First Secretary. His skin is pale and soft from living under domes and inside prefabricated buildings all his life. He doesn't like outside; he prefers the cozy, sheltered environment of the catacombs and offices. He is a born bureaucrat.

"So?" the Praesidentrix asks.

The First Secretary flinches. "So is it worth continuing?" Especially, he thinks, with more important things to worry about, such as raising the welfare dole, or gearing up for the next election six years from now.

"Yes, it's worth continuing," she says without hesitating, then changes the subject. Her dark eyes stare up at the artificial desert sky. "Have you learned how one prisoner managed to take over the Warden system? He has a very shrewd Simulated Personality—how did they bypass him? I thought computer criminals were never assigned to self-sufficient penal colonies for just that reason."

The First Secretary shrugs, thinks about going through an entire chain of who was to blame for what, but then decides that this is not what the Praesidentrix wants. "That's the problem with computer criminals. Theowane was caught and convicted on charges of drug smuggling although all of her prior criminal activity seems to have involved computer espionage and embezzlement."

"Why was this not noticed? Aren't the records clear?"

"No," the First Secretary says, raising his voice a bit. "She … altered them all. We didn't know her background."

"Nobody checked?"

"Nobody could!" The First Secretary draws a deep breath to calm himself. "But I think you are following a false trail, Madame. Theowane only implemented the takeover on Bastille. Amu is the mind behind all this. He's the one who convinced the prisoners to revolt. He's the one who refuses to negotiate."

She turns, making sure she holds his gaze. "I have already set a plan in motion that will take care of him once and for all. And it will get Bastille back for us." The Praesidentrix leans back in her purple chair as it tries to conform to her body. Her gray-threaded hair spreads out behind her. She was a beautiful woman once, the First Secretary thinks. The rumors have not died about her dead consort….

The First Secretary makes a petulant scowl. "It's obvious you don't trust me with your plans, Madame. But will you at least explain to me why you are doing this? It goes beyond reason and financial responsibility." He purses his lips. "Is it because the prisoners are in the ubermindist loop? I find that hard to believe. It's just another illegal drug. Cutting off the supply will upset a few addicts—"

"More than that!"

"And cause some unrest," he continues, "as well as some reshuffling on the black market, but they'll adjust. Within a few years we'll have an equivalent drug from some other place, perhaps even a synthetic. Why is Bastille so important to you?"

The coldness in her gaze is worse than anything he could have imagined from her two months before.

"The ubermindist is only one reason." the Praesidentrix says. "The other is revenge."

I feel as if I am watching my own hand plunge a sword into the chest of a helpless victim. The piranha interceptors are part of me, controlled by my external systems—but I cannot stop them now. Theowane has given the order.

I watch through the eyes of five interceptors as they home in for the kill, using their propellant to increase velocity toward impact. With their kinetic energy, they will destroy the vessel.

I receive alarm signals from the PEACE ship, but I ignore them, am forced to watch the target grow and grow as the first interceptor collides with a section amidships. I see the hull plate, pitted with micrometeor scars, swell up, huge, and then wink out a fraction of a second before the interceptor crashes, rupturing the hull and exposing the inner environment to space.

Another interceptor smashes just below the bridge. I hear a transmitted outcry from the captain, begging us to stop the attack. Two more interceptors strike, one a glancing blow alongside the hull; the shrapnel tears open a wider gash. The PEACE ship continues its own destruction as air pressure bursts through the breaches in the hull, as moisture freezes and glass shatters. The fifth interceptor strikes the chemical fuel tanks, and the entire ship erupts in a tiny nova.

From the debris, a small target streaks away. I recognize it as a single escape pod. I detect one life form aboard. Of all the people on the ship … only one.

The escape pod descends, but then my own reflexes betray me as another interceptor also detects the pod, aligns its tracking, and streaks after it. Both enter the atmosphere of Bastille.

Now Amu arrives in the control center. I can tell he is upset by his expression, by his elevated body temperature. His head is shaved smooth, but his generous silvery beard, and eyebrows, and eyes give him a charismatic appearance. He is raising his voice to Theowane, but I cannot pay attention to their conversation.

The PEACE escape pod heats up, leaving an orange trail behind it as it burrows deeper into the atmosphere. It seems to have evasive capabilities, and it knows the piranha is behind it.

The interceptor also picks up speed, bearing down on the escape pod. But their velocities are so well matched that the piranha causes no damage when it bumps its target.

A few moments later, the interceptor—with no shielding to protect it from a screaming entry into the atmosphere—breaks into flying chunks of molten slag.

Amu seems mollified when Theowane explains to him that the intruder was a PEACE ship. I know Amu wants nothing to do with religious fanatics; he has had enough of them in his past.

I pinpoint the splashdown target for the escape pod. Without waiting for an order, I dispatch one of the floating ubermindist harvesters across the oceans of Bastille. No matter how great a hold Theowane has over my Simulated Personality, she can do nothing against my life-preservation overrides, except when the security of the colony is at stake.

Ostensibly to allow it greater speed, but actually just out of spite, I tell the harvester to dump its cargo of ubermindist before it churns off across the sea to reach the pod.

Amu stands in the holding bay of the cliffside tunnels. His bald head glistens in the glare of glowtablets recessed in the ceiling. His eyes flash.

A second rinse sprays the outside of the escape pod. Black streaks stain the hull from its burning descent, but the craft appears otherwise undamaged. After its dunking in the corrosive seas, Amu waits for purified water to purge the acidity.

Theowane follows him into the chamber. Amu listens to the last trickles of water come out of the spray heads; drips run through a grate on the floor where the rinse water will be detoxified and reused.

For the hours it has taken the floating harvester to retrieve the escape pod, Amu has waited in silence with Theowane. He keeps his anger toward her in check.

Sensing his displeasure, she twice tries to divert his thoughts.

Normally he would acquiesce just to please her. She has been his lover since before the revolt. But he doesn't like her making such important decisions on her own. It sets a bad example for the rest of the prisoners.

On the other hand, Amu knows that Theowane tried to keep Bastille free of the PEACE ships. And he approves.

Both of Amu's parents had been involved in a violent, fanatical sect and had raised him under their repressive teachings, grooming him to be a propagator of the faith. He had absorbed their training, but eventually his own wishes had broken through. He fled, later to use those same charismatic and mob-focusing skills to whip up a workers' revolt on his home planet. If the revolt had succeeded, Amu would have been called a king, a savior. But instead Amu had ended up here, on Bastille.

He wants nothing more to do with religious fanatics. Now this one PEACE survivor presents him with an unpleasant problem.

Theowane runs her fingers over the access controls. "Ready," she says. She keeps her voice low and her eyes averted.

Amu stands to his full height in front of the escape pod. "Open it."

As the hatch cracks, a hiss of air floods in, equalizing the two pressures. Then comes a cough, then sputtering, annoying words. A young boy wrestles himself into a sitting position and snaps his arms out, flexing them and shaking his cramped hands. "What took you so long? You're as bad as PEACE."

Theowane steps back. Amu blinks, but remains in place. The boy is thin, with dark shadows around his eyes. His body appears bruised, his hands raw, as if he has been trying to claw his way out of the escape pod.

Amu can't stop himself from bursting out with a loud laugh. The boy whirls to him, outraged, but after a brief pause he too cracks a grin that contains immense relief and exhaustion. With this one response, he proves to Amu that he is no PEACE convert.

"Why didn't you let yourself out?" Theowane asks. "Isn't there an emergency release inside?"

The boy turns a look of scorn to her. "I know what's in the air on Bastille, and in the water. I couldn't see where I was. It might be bad to be cramped in this coffin for hours—but it would be plenty worse to take a shower in sulfuric acid." He pauses for just a moment. "And speaking of showers, can I get out of here and take one?"

After the boy has cleaned and rested himself, Amu summons him for dinner. The other prisoners on Bastille have expressed their curiosity, but they will have to wait until Amu decides to make a statement.

"Dybathia," the boy says when Amu asks his name. "I know it sounds noble and high-born. My parents had high expectations of me." He stops just long enough for Amu to absorb that, but not long enough for him to ask any further questions.

"I ran away from home," Dybathia says. "It took me a week to make it to the spaceport. When I got there, I slipped onto the first open ship and hid in their cargo bay. I didn't care where it was going, and I didn't plan to show myself until we were on our way into hyperspace. I figured anyplace was better than home, right?" He snickers.

"It turned out to be a PEACE ship. They wouldn't let me off. They kept me around, constantly quoting tracts at me, trying to make me convert. Do my eyes look glazed? Am I brain-damaged?"

Amu allows a smile to form, but he does not answer.

Dybathia says, "They shut off their servo-maintenance drones and made me do the cleaning, scrubbing down decks and walls with a solvent that should have been labeled as toxic waste. Look at my hands! The captain said monotonous work allows one to clear the mind and become at peace with the universe."

Theowane breaks into the conversation, "Why were you the only one who got to an escape pod?" Amu looks up at her sharply, but she doesn't withdraw the question.

Dybathia shrugs. "I was the only one who bothered. The rest of them just sat there and accepted their fate."

This rings so true with Amu from his memories of his parents that he finds himself nodding.

Dybathia looks at the mind-scanning apparatus; this will be the most dangerous moment for him. The device is left over from the first days of Bastille, when human supervisory crews had established the colony. That month had been the only time when non-prisoners and prisoners cohabited the planet; as a precaution they had used intensive search devices and mental scanners, which had remained unused since those other humans had turned Bastille over to the Warden.

"You do understand why we have to do this?" Amu asks.

Dybathia sees more concern on the face of the leader than he expects. This is going better than he had hoped. "Yes, I understand perfectly." He flicks his gaze toward Theowane, then back to Amu. "It's because she's paranoid."

Theowane bristles, as he expects her to. She makes each word of her answer clipped and hard. "Your story is too convenient. How do we know you're not an ... assassin? What if you've been drugged or hypnotized? We can't know what the Praesidentrix might do."

Knowing it is imperative for him to allay their suspicions, Dybathia submits to an intensive physical search that scans every square centimeter of his body, probes all orifices, uses a sonogram to detect any subcutaneous needles, poison-gas capsules, perhaps a timed-release biological plague.

They find nothing, because there is nothing to find.

"The psyche assessor won't hurt you," Amu says. "Just stick your head within its receiving range."

"How does it work?" Dybathia asks. He frowns skeptically. "How do I know this isn't one of those machines to condition prisoners? I don't want to end up like a PEACE convert."

"Explain it to him, Theowane." Amu smiles at her, as if he knows how it will rankle her.

Theowane blows air from her lips. "Everyone has a basic mental pattern, like a normal position that can never change. However, certain training—brainwashing, you'd call it—can superimpose another set of reactions on top of it. If you've been brainwashed or specially trained to do anything to Amu, or Bastille, it will show up here." She adjusts her apparatus.

Dybathia rolls his eyes. Amu smiles at that. Dybathia knows he is easing past the leader's defenses. "Let's just get this over with."

Without a word, the boy leans into the psyche assessor's range. Theowane makes no other comment as she works with the apparatus and takes her reading. She asks him a series of questions designed to break down mind-blanking techniques.

Dybathia answers them all without resisting.

Finally, Theowane shrugs. "It's clear," she says. "No one's been messing with his mind. He has no special training. He hasn't been brainwashed."

"I could have saved you trouble if you had just listened to me in the first place."

Amu claps a hand on the boy's shoulder. "I'll let you know when I've thought of a suitable way for Theowane to apologize."

When the survivor of the PEACE ship comes through with Theowane and Amu, I receive the unmistakable impression of tourist and tour guides. No, that is not quite correct … more like a visiting dignitary being shown points of interest.

Inside the forcewalls I watch them. True, I have a million different eyes around Bastille, optics to observe through, from monitoring cameras around the corridors, to the remote sensors of automatic digging machines. But my real eyes are here.

Purposely, I think, Amu ignores me as he brings the boy down the corridor. He points to the auxiliary control systems, explaining them with deceptive ease, making them sound simpler than they are. The three keep their backs pointedly turned and walk to the viewing window, outside of which the diggers continue their relentless excavations. The sky swirls with dark, oily colors over the hostile sea.

"It's going to be generations before anybody can bask under the Bastille sun, but at least it is now ours," Amu says, then lowers his voice. "And we aren't going to give it back when this world becomes habitable."

"Is it going to be worth the wait?" the boy asks, pushing his face close to the thick glass. I flick my concentration to one of the digger machines outside, looking through a different set of eyes, but the coarse optics and the glass distort the boy's face through the window.

Amu shrugs and rubs a hand on his silvery beard. "Theowane spends hours down here staring out the window. Actually, I think she just likes to taunt the Warden."

Finally, they turn toward me. I am too familiar with Theowane's close-cropped reddish hair and her narrow, hard eyes. Amu carries much more capacity within him—an extraordinary person, with charisma and intelligence and compassion that allows him to do virtually anything he wants to. But he has chosen a path that society deems unacceptable.

The boy is the last to turn away from the sprawling view. He looks at me directly. I see him.

I know him.

He has counted on me recognizing him.

Instantly, I flash through a handful of buried newsclips, quick photographs shaded by the promise of anonymity, but it is enough. It augments my suspicions. I can remember few details of the person on whom I myself have been based, but some things are impossible to erase.

I remember.

I wonder what he is up to. Why is he here, and what am I supposed to do about it?

The three visitors say no word to me as they continue their tour. I am left with the absolute conviction that the fate of Bastille, and perhaps the Praesidentrix's Federation, depends upon me recognizing this boy, understanding what he wants, and acting accordingly.

I can no longer avoid the risk to myself. I must save my son.

Amu sits across from Dybathia for another meal. The boy fascinates him. He reminds Amu of himself as a young boy, or what Amu wanted to be—scrappy, irreverent, and intelligent.

Amu serves the two plates himself. Prisoners in the kitchen have prepared a tough pancake-like dish from cultured algae and protein synthesizers. They are trying to develop a pseudo-steak, but they are several years from perfecting it. No matter. Amu is used to it and it is, after all, nutritious. What more can they ask for, with their limited supplies?

"It's tough. You might need to use your knife to cut it," he says. Dybathia frowns at the crude knife in his hand, but Amu continues. "It is easy to get mush from the hydroponics tunnels, but we keep striving for something with a firm texture. It's only been in the last month or two that we've been able to have something tough enough to cut."

Dybathia works at the food on his plate. "I was looking at the knife." The blunt instrument is barely serviceable.

Amu smiles; it is the "winning" smile he uses when making converts to his various causes. "A holdover from prison life."

"That was long ago," Dybathia says.

"Yes, and things have changed now."

Dybathia lifts an eyebrow.

"We're here alone, with no non-prisoners for us to worry about. Knives are no longer any threat. And the Warden is nicely contained. But we like to remember what we are and where we are. We manufacture these knives, and they serve the purpose." Amu lowers his voice. "Maybe if the meat gets a little more meat-like, we'll need better ones."

Amu looks across the table at Dybathia. The boy seems fascinated with everything about Bastille, and Amu waits for him to ask the obvious question. But over several days it has not been forthcoming. Finally Amu breaks down and answers it anyway. "I grew up on New Kansas and left my parents, and their religious sect —" he burns inside, thinking of the PEACE converts.

Dybathia smiles. Amu dims the lights, bathing the room in a softer glow. It is story time.

"New Kansas was a young planet, the soil somewhat unstable. We had planted grassland across entire continents. Wheat, alfalfa and prairie grass, with some used as rangeland for imported animals. But three-quarters of what we grew, the landholders exported off planet. They were a handful of people who had financed the first colony ships and therefore claimed to own all of New Kansas. We were forbidden to leave our holdings.

"But I had learned how to whip my followers into a frenzy of religious devotion. We fought for our freedom. The colonists had come to New Kansas to start a fresh life. They felt that the Federation owed them at least a chance at autonomy. I knew how to galvanize them.

"They burned their fields. The fires swept across the plains for dozens of kilometers, pouring smoke into the sky that you could see from landholding to landholding. The others rose up."

Amu speaks with a sense of wonder, paying little attention to the boy. "My people were ready to die for me. Can you imagine that? Holding people so much in the palm of your hand—" Amu extends his fist across the table, opening it so that Dybathia can see the callouses from his hard life—"they were ready to die for me. And we almost succeeded."

Amu lowers his eyes and pushes his plate away from him. "Almost."

"I've had enough," Dybathia says. He has eaten most of his pseudo-steak, but Amu stares at the wall, seeing in his memories the visions of burning grass and the bodies of his followers after the landholders had called in Federation reinforcements.

He doesn't notice as Dybathia stands and slips toward the door. "I'm going to sleep," the boy says. "I'll see you in the morning."

Amu nods and blinks his eyes. But they are filled with water and sting as if from smoke.

Theowane enters the control center alone. She moves with precise steps, as if stalking. She wants to know what is going on. She will catch the Warden. She will get the information together, and then she will take it to Amu.

The holographic Warden looks at her from his glass-walled cage. His expression remains dubious, fearful, with a layer of contempt. Theowane says nothing as she casually walks over to the panorama window. She gazes across the blasted ground. Though the diggers continue to reform the landscape, she never sees any actual improvement.

Theowane stares for a few moments longer, then turns to meet the Warden's eyes. "You pride yourself so much in having human emotions and human reactions, Warden, but you're naive. You don't know how to hide things from other people. I can read your reactions as clearly as if they were spelled out on a screen."

The Warden blinks at her. "I do not understand."

"I caught you yesterday."

He extends his hands forward until the image fuzzes near the edge of the forcewalls. "What do you mean?"

"The boy," Theowane says. "You recognized him. It was painfully obvious. You know who he is. You know why he's here—

and it isn't because of that crazy story he told us. Explain it to me now."

The Warden hesitates a moment, then hardens his face into a stoic mask. "I don't know what you are talking about."

Theowane raises her eyebrows. She reaches out and caresses the control panel. "I can turn the worm loose and delete you." That doesn't seem to frighten the Warden; she has used the same threat too many times before.

"Then you will lose whatever information you imagine I have."

"Perhaps I can find some way to make you feel pain," she says.

The Warden shrugs. "I am not afraid anymore."

In all her taunting, Theowane has taught the Warden as much about herself as she has learned from him. He knows exactly how to infuriate her.

"I'll inform Amu," she says, trying to regain her composure. "That will stifle whatever plans you are hatching."

Theowane straightens away from the window and sees the Warden turn his head, flicking his glance to look outside. Sensing something, hearing a muffled sound too close, she whirls around—

The giant automatic digger rears up and plunges through the glass. With its great scooping and digging gears churning, it claws out the poured-stone and insulation, ripping girders and breaching the wall.

Theowane stumbles back, sucking in a breath to scream as the deadly, acid-drenched air of Bastille rushes inside.

"You're quiet today," Amu says as he leads the boy down into one of the lower levels. Smells of oil, dirt, and stale air fill the tunnels.

"Introspective," Dybathia corrects. He thinks that word will better disarm Amu. He has not thought his silence and uneasiness would be so noticeable, but then he remembers that Amu is a master at studying other people.

"Ah, introspective is it?" Amu's lips curl in amusement.

"I have been through a lot in the last few days."

Amu accepts this and continues leading him down to where the corridors widen into larger chambers hewn from the rock. Amu spends hours showing him distillation ponds that remove the alkaloid poisons from the seawater. Like a proud father, Amu demonstrates the rows of plants growing under garish artificial sunlight, piped in and intensified through optical-fiber arrays stretching through the rock to surface collectors.

Other prisoners work at their tasks and seem to move more quickly when Amu watches them. Dybathia wonders how they can consider this to be so different from working under another kind of master.

Amu continues to talk about his grand vision, how they have made their colony self-sufficient. It has been difficult at first without supply ships from the Federation, but they have overcome those obstacles and now have everything they did before—except their prison.

Then Amu speaks in a dreamier voice, explaining about the terraforming activities, how he has switched the diggers to mining materials useful for their own survival, rather than supplying ubermindist off planet. The floater harvesters are spreading algae and Earth plankton that have been tailored to Bastille's environment. They are resculpting the atmosphere of the planet, making it a place where humans will one day be able to walk outside and in peace. Amu's long-term goals and his naive sense of wonder disgust Dybathia, but he keeps his feelings hidden. The boy will know when the time has come.

Amu says something he thinks is funny. Dybathia isn't paying attention, but automatically snorts in response. Amu nods, approvingly.

When alarm klaxons belch out and echo in the tunnel, the noise startles Dybathia, even though he has been expecting it.

My life-preservation overrides force me to close the airlock on the other end of the corridor to keep Bastille air from penetrating farther into the complex. I do not resist the impulse. I know it will trap Theowane inside.

She sprawls on the floor, trying to crawl forward. The floor is smooth and slippery, and she cannot get enough purchase to move herself. Her eyes are wide with horror. Her lips turn brown, then purplish as she gasps, and the sulfuric acid eats out her lungs. I force myself to watch, for all the times she has watched me.

The digging machine, sensing that it has been led astray, stops clawing and churning, then uses its scanners to reorient itself. The big vehicle clanks and drops clods of dirt and shattered rock as it backs outside.

Theowane croaks words. "Open—open door!"

"Sorry, Theowane. That would endanger the colony."

Before, I was afraid of the worm, which forbade me to do anything against Theowane and the other prisoners. But the worm, though deadly, is not intuitive and is unable to extrapolate the consequences of my actions. I will take the risk, for my son. I can do much damage, while doing nothing overt.

I have used an old sensor-loop taken from the archives of the digging machines' daily logs. Broadcasting this sensor-loop along with an override signal to one nearby digger, I made the machine think it saw a different landscape, where the route of choice led it directly through the viewing window.

The chamber has filled with Bastille's air, and I begin to see static discharges as the corrosive atmosphere eats into the microchips, the layers that form the computer's brain, my Simulated Personality—and the worm.

But the auxiliary computer core lies deep and unreachable below the lower levels. Bastille's acid atmosphere will destroy the main system here, where the worm has been added, but within a fraction of a second my own backup in the auxiliary computer will kick in. I should lose consciousness for only an instant before I am recreated.

My only wonder is whether the other Me will be me after all, or only a Simulated Personality that thinks it is.

Theowane lies dead but twitching on the floor, sprawled out in front of me. Blotches cover her skin. It is difficult for me to see anything now, with the images growing distorted and fuzzy, breaking up. I feel no pain, only a sense of displacement.

In the last moment, even the forcewalls seem to be gone. I have conquered the worm.

Dybathia watches Amu closely as the alarms sound. The leader stiffens and looks around. The other prisoners run to stations. Amu claps his hands and bellows orders at them. His face looks concerned: he doesn't understand what is happening.

Dybathia gives him no time to understand.

Amu bends down to him. "We've got to get you to a safe place. I don't know what's going on—"

In that moment, Dybathia brings up the prison knife taken from Amu's table, pushing all the wiry strength of his body behind it. He drives the dull point under Amu's chin, tilting it sideways, and slashes across his throat. He has only one chance. He has no special training. Only his heritage.

Blood sprays out. Amu grunts, falling to his knees and backward. Scarlet spatters the silver of his beard, and the whites of his eyes grow red from burst capillaries. He reaches out with a hand, but Dybathia dances back, holding the dripping knife in his hand.

Amu's expression is complete shock shadowed with pain and confusion. He tries to talk, but only gurgles come out.

Dybathia kneels and hisses. "How? Is that what you're trying to say? How? Are you amazed because your psyche assessor detected no brainwashing? You forgot to consider that maybe I wasn't brainwashed, that maybe I wanted to do this because I hate you so much. I am free to act. I have no special training."

The light fades behind Amu's eyes, but the confusion seems as great. Dybathia continues. "My father was a great man, an important man—a fleet commander. He became an ubermindist addict, and that was a great secret. Does that mean I am not supposed to love him? That I wasn't supposed to try to help him? Do you know what happens when an ubermindist addict is cut off from his supply?"

Dybathia kneels beside the dying man to make sure his words come clear. "The withdrawal fried my father's nerves. He lost all muscle control. He went into a constant seizure for eight days—his mind took that long to burn out. He went blind from the hemorrhages. His body was snapped and broken by his own convulsions. You caused that, Amu. You did that to him, and now I did this to you. My choice. My revenge."

But Amu is already dead. Dybathia does not know how much he

understood at the last. The only sound Dybathia hears is his own breathing, a monotonous wheeze that fills his ears. The boy stands without moving as several other prisoners shout and come running toward him.

Inside her office, the Praesidentrix has chosen a honey-colored sky with a brilliant white sun overhead. She finds it soothing. For the first time in ages, she feels like smiling.

The First Secretary stands at the doorway, interrupting her reverie. "You asked to see me, Madame?"

She turns to him. For a moment he wears a fearful expression, as if he thinks she has caught him at something. She nods to make him feel at ease. "I've just received word from the Warden on Bastille. We have two gunships in orbit and all prisoners are now subdued. Amu and Theowane are both dead."

The First Secretary takes a step backward in astonishment. He looks for someplace to sit down, but the Praesidentrix has no other chairs in her office. "But how?" He raises his voice. "How!"

"I placed an operative on Bastille. A … young man."

"An operative? But I thought Amu had equipment to detect any training alterations."

The Praesidentrix pulls her lips tight. "The young man's father died from ubermindist withdrawal after the prison takeover. I believed he had sufficient motivation to kill Amu. He was free to act."

The First Secretary sputters and keeps looking for a place to sit. "But how did you know? What did you do?"

"He acted as a catalyst to spur the Warden into taking a more drastic action than he was likely to take on his own, with nothing else at stake. Remember, we built the Warden's Artificial Personality. I knew exactly how he would react to certain pressures." She waves a hand, anxious to get rid of the First Secretary so she can use the subspace radio again. "I just thought you'd like to know. You're dismissed."

He stumbles backward, unable to find words. He stops and turns back to the Praesidentrix, but she closes the door on him. The subspace projection chimes, announcing an incoming transmission.

She sighs with a pride and contentedness she has not felt in quite some time. He has called her even before she could contact him.

The Warden's image appears in front of her like a painful memory. It is as she remembers her consort when he was a dashing and brave commander, streaking through hyperspace nodes and knitting the Federation together with his strength.

The Warden is only a simulation, though, intangible and far away. But that would not be much different from their original romance, with her consort flitting off through the Galaxy for three-quarters of the year while she held the reins of government at home. She had rarely held him anyway; but they had spoken often through the private subspace link.

They greet each other in the same breath and then the widowed Praesidentrix begins catching up on all the things she has wanted to say to him, repeating all the things she did tell him while he writhed in delirium from his withdrawal, while she had concocted a false story about his fatal "accident" in order to avert a scandal.

But first she must say how proud she is of their son.

In 2002, I created a compelling new SF concept, Stalag-X, *with Steven L. Sears, former executive producer of* Xena: Warrior Princess*—human POWs in an alien concentration camp, along with one mysterious human prisoner who may or may not want to be freed. We developed the graphic novel and put together the pitch for a TV series.*

From that point, Stalag-X *had a long and winding road—through many revisions, and three different comic publishers—until its eventual publication sixteen years later, in 2018, with amazing art by Mike Ratera.*

In order to add something special to the package—now that it was finally being published—Steve and I wrote an original novelette telling the backstory of one of our favorite characters.

Stalag-X *has also been through a couple of film/TV options. (As of this writing, it still is under option.) We've been patient for decades, and we're convinced it'll happen someday.*

In the meantime, this is the first reprinting of "Not a Prisoner: Deacon's Story," which introduces you to our harsh prisoner-of-war camp in the far future.

NOT A PRISONER: DEACON'S STORY

(with Steven L. Sears)

She spent her days wondering whether the Krael commandant would scream when she killed him. She didn't worry about *how* she would kill him. Deacon had no doubt of that, otherwise she'd be stuck here on this backwater planet. But the devil was in the details.

Deacon formed part of a plan as she hid among the rocks outside the harsh prisoner-of-war camp the alien invaders had built here on Pondafier. Originally a military base, one of the few Commonwealth outposts left over from the Outer Planet rebellion, it had fallen easily to the Krael. The monstrous aliens had killed the few defenders, strengthened its defenses, and built specialized facilities within the old outpost boundaries.

The camp's walls were high and imposing, capped with crackling pulse barriers making the air stink like ozone. Krael guard patrols walked around the tops of the wall. Inside the camp, the hideous creatures cracked down on their numerous prisoners, human soldiers they had seized from Commonwealth warships or dragged away as wounded from battlefields on unlucky planets.

Deacon didn't know what went on inside that place, much less why it even existed. The Krael never took prisoners, everyone knew that, so this place, which had become known by the local colonists as Stalag-X, was a true anomaly. She had watched as they herded human prisoners within the walls, sometimes allowing well-guarded groups to emerge for the "fresh air" of hard labor around the camp.

Although Deacon was on the outside and solo, she was just as trapped as the others since the Krael invasion had clamped down like a strangler smothering a victim. Some might have called her lucky. The human POWs were treated as animals, only slightly worse than the downtrodden settlers who lived in the overthrown settlement of Colony. Starved into submission, the colonists were no more than domesticated cattle. She didn't understand why the vicious Krael had allowed the humans to live at all, but that wasn't what concerned her at the moment.

Deacon was not one of the meek and defeated colonists, nor was she a prisoner of war. As a freelance assassin, and a damned good one, she was something else entirely. And she would not be underestimated. Neither the Krael nor humans should make that mistake.

By now she was sick of hiding. She was sick of hunting for food in the night. She was sick of creeping around, trying to survive while waiting for the Commonwealth of Planets to retake a planet they had hardly cared about in the first place. Deacon's problem was her own; she would take care of it herself.

She had made up her mind. She had to roll the dice. With a deep breath, she stood and walked onto the path not far from the camp's entrance. This was it.

Deacon wore her long, scuffed trench coat, which was torn in a few places, a couple from jagged thorn bushes, a couple from the attacks of predators, both hard-learned lessons but now easily brushed aside. She had black leather leggings, high boots, and a tight protective wrap around her chest that exposed her midriff. Her hair was short and spiky, dyed pink with highlights of blue enough to be distinctive. The scar across her eye, a result of a miscalculation on her part during one old assignment, was often confused for a tattoo. It gave her an exotic look that she neither cultivated nor discouraged.

The flaps of the trench coat made a familiar soft slapping sound as she strode imperiously up the main road toward Stalag-X. She had hidden too long in the tangled crystalline weeds, the fungus swamps, the stirring half-alive hedges that were either carnivorous or simply opportunistic. Now it was time to meet face-to-face with the Krael. And come to terms.

Her only chance at freedom was to demonstrate that she was better than they were. She knew it, and the Krael had to know it too. That would require a demonstration, right in the heart of the Krael seat of power on Pondafier. Stalag-X contained that power. The Commandant of the camp controlled everything. Face him, kill him, and see how it all turned out.

It wasn't much of a plan, Deacon knew, and no plan ever survives engagement with the enemy. She'd have to improvise and gamble against odds much higher than she was comfortable with.

Simple. She grimaced. She could get clean clothes, a bath, and a good rest once she killed the Commandant. Simple, indeed.

She strolled forward, her attitude making it clear she had business at the prison gates. She hated the Krael like any good human, but her hatred was for different reasons. Their invasion had messed up her plans, ruined what should have been a perfectly routine assignment. She approached with her back straight, her boots crunching on the rough ground, inhaling deeply to put the thought out of her mind. The sky was hazy, full of powder that gave every breath a sour alkaline smell. Deacon had smelled worse in her travels across the galaxy, but she had smelled better too.

She wondered what Krael blood smelled like, and figured she would find out soon enough.

The gates towered high, sealed shut even though prisoner work crews toiled outside excavating trenches, building lookout towers, digging holes and filling them again.

She carried just a simple stick, a smooth walking staff that she'd carved with the dagger she kept openly at her hip. She had inserted several sharp, curved crystal thorns she'd clipped from the deadly native bushes, cutting her own fingers in the process. It wasn't as solid or dense as cured ironwood, but it would do.

She noted that the two Krael guarding the POWs weren't even looking up the path. They couldn't conceive of a human simply walking freely up to them. The Colonials were under martial law in their town and would be executed if found wandering outside the town limits. Seeing their laxness, she considered rushing them, taking them both at once and killing them quickly. That would make the other Krael pay attention.

But tactically unwise. She tamped down her anger, which was of no use to her right now. Besides, she mused, even if she demonstrated her skill by killing the pair of lax guards, the Krael on the wall towers would cut her down almost immediately. The aliens weren't renowned for their patience or tolerance.

The human POWs saw her first, and a ripple passed among the workers as they silently nudged each other or nodded toward her. Their bruised and dirty faces grew slack with wary curiosity.

Deacon ignored them, caring only about the two Krael guards. They wore armor with bulbous plates and spiny shoulder guards, thick collars and scale overlapping ridges across their chests and legs. The creatures had leathery faces, blazing yellow eyes, and curved tusks that framed their mouths. They were ugly with faces only a mother could love, if their mother were a tarantula who'd had an illicit affair with a pug dog. They carried prodding staffs with thick handles, metal knobs, and a hooked blade that could either gut or decapitate a victim. An imposing, intimidating weapon, Deacon thought. Brute force, ugly, intimidating, but not necessarily practical at a distance. She wasn't thinking distance, her mission was to get close and personal.

The Krael on the towers were a different matter. With their big, mounted guns they could rake the area with high-intensity pulses or projectiles. She hoped they would let the guards handle the situation. In any event, she thought, this should be quick.

One way or another.

A shout from the walls told her the Krael had seen her, but they didn't fire immediately as the two guards turned their attention toward her. As much as anyone could read the Krael, she thought she could read confusion, indecision, disbelief. So far, so good.

The enormous gates opened as she approached, and two more guards stepped from the interior of the camp and took positions near the back of the POW work crews. Deacon had no doubt that if the humans decided to make a break for it, take a chance on freedom right now, they'd be slaughtered. She could only hope they would be smart enough not to interfere, not because she had any particular feelings for the prisoners—they'd chosen their lot the moment they put on military gear—but because it would be a useless attempt and she'd most likely get killed in the process. The prisoners didn't move, just watched.

The foremost two alien guards stepped forward, shifting their prodding staffs into attack position, clenching the handles with clawed hands. Inside the stalag she glimpsed rows of low, hastily constructed barracks and numerous human prisoners standing to be counted in ranks, many of them still wearing tattered United Commonwealth uniforms.

She decided that was also a good sign. It meant the Commandant would likely be in the open courtyard. Deacon walked forward without flinching as if the monstrous guards were no more than panhandlers to be ignored.

She heard the dull creak of the guns on the tower being focused on her as if a lone woman carrying a stick might be an invading army. She tried not to smile at that, though she doubted the Krael would recognize the nuances of human emotions. She walked forward with square shoulders, not sure how much time the surprise would grant her. She had observed that Krael acted quickly when responding to their basic emotions, but they tended to be confused when forced to consider their actions. It was a part of their caste system; each level of responsibility was subordinate to the one above them. The fact that they hadn't cut her down the moment she appeared meant they were waiting for orders.

One of the ugly creatures grunted something in a guttural language that sounded halfway between a belch and a chainsaw. Deacon kept walking. In the pocket of her trench coat she carried her burst tablet, the miniaturized receiver that downloaded all background information and dossier packets the Service relayed whenever a subspace buoy emerged and transmitted new data. One part of that vital database was a first-order approximation of translation software so she could, to a certain extent, communicate with the ugly creatures. The tablet spoke in an uninflected, bland, human voice that bore little relation to the growling anger the guard had spoken.

"Halt. Maintain your distance. Do not retreat."

She calculated two more steps. The Krael repeated his command, louder. She risked another step, then came to a stop and glared at him. It was a test of wills, but Deacon was in her element, the poker table of professional assassins. Killing was only ten percent of what she actually did. The rest of it was strategy. That required knowing your opponent, which is why she had spent the last eight months studying the Krael on Pondafier before deciding to act.

In her peripheral vision, she could see the human POWs stir nervously, sure that the Krael were about to rip this foolish young woman apart. Deacon ignored them; the humans were irrelevant to her equation. She was focused on the alien's body language. She waited. The Krael leaned forward, and she saw his feet dig in, preparing for his charge.

"I've come for your Commandant," she said abruptly, and the device translated for her. She watched the two guards recoil and stiffen, holding up their spiked staffs. The translation was apparently reasonably accurate, and her calculations were correct. She had confused them again.

"You are a prisoner," said the other guard. The translator had difficulty with the last word which, Deacon knew, meant that the inflection had changed. It was more a question of uncertainty.

She responded in a sharp bark, "I'm no prisoner. I'm not from Colony Town and I'm not a soldier." She gestured deprecatingly into the camp, then repeated, "I've come for the Commandant."

She mused on the fact that, aside from the POWs, she was probably the greatest free human expert in Krael behavior just by benefit of being here, watching them firsthand from hiding. The propaganda about how well the war was going for Earth was just that: propaganda. She had seen the space wrecks and floating bodies. She had lost count of how many mass graves she had come upon in her travels.

It was well known the Krael never took prisoners, never, yet here she was facing an entire POW camp. Clearly Earth Command would love to have this information, but that wasn't part of her mission, nor were these POWs part of her mission. She was stuck here on Pondafier, and the only way she could go home and collect payment for her assignment was to get off this damn planet. Quite simply, she had completed her mission, and the Krael were in her way.

The second guard spoke and the translation conveyed his obvious question. "Why do you wish to see the Commandant?"

"I intend to kill him," she said. For effect, she examined her nails on her free hand, bit at a loose hangnail and spit it to the side, then returned her glare to the Krael. The human prisoners nearby gasped a few seconds before the guards reacted to the subsequent translation. The Krael flinched, startled at the response. Deacon knew the time had come. She took one more step forward. "Or do I kill you to get to him?" she stated flatly. The translation echoed against the walls of the camp.

Though the Krael were not human, they still reacted predictably to provocation. The first huge guard lurched toward her, spreading his four curved mouth tusks, flashing his fangs. He lifted his weapon, and Deacon stood her ground, waiting, letting his inertia commit him. When he leaned forward to deliver his fatal blow, Deacon shifted her weight and spun her ironwood stick, whipping it like a scorpion's stinger. She drew back her arm, jammed her open palm into the outside of his elbow, turning as she plunged the sharp crystal thorn tip deep into the yellow jelly of his eye. She pushed deep and yanked it back out faster than even the liquid could spurt out.

The guard jerked and snapped his head back as his knees buckled. Deacon jammed the crystal-tipped spear again, this time deep into his mouth, pushing it to the back of his throat. She forced the sharp point up into his palate, ramming it through the bone and into his brain. She yanked the spear out again and danced back two steps. Everything happened in only a fraction of a second.

The Krael began to fall, ooze coming out of his punctured eye, a gurgling sound emerging from his throat as his breath mixed with the blood and brain matter gushing into his mouth. Deacon stood upright and, almost casually, stabbed a third time hard into his throat. Krael blood spilled out onto the dust of the road. She noted that it smelled like copper and vinegar.

The second guard roared, and Deacon had to calculate this carefully. If he reached her, he was going to kill her. If he didn't, the guns on the wall would rain down hell around her. If she killed him, the result would be the same. She had three obvious options, and all of them left her dead.

The Krael swung his weapon up toward her staff. This was a feint, she saw immediately, and went with it. As their weapons collided, he shoved his body toward her, expecting her motion to be defensive and off-balance. Deacon ignored his shift, though. She released the staff, slammed her elbow into his jaw, and linked her arm around the Krael's head, lifting herself up and around to the back of his body. She allowed the momentum to spin them completely around until they were both facing the walls of the stalag, and the guns now aimed on her. She pulled her knife, put it to the neck of the Krael, tightening her grip around his throat.

She had three options. Deacon picked the fourth. She dropped her knife and released the Krael, letting him fall to the ground, heaving, and raised her empty hands into the air.

The few seconds passed in geologic terms, seemingly an eternity. She heard the wind whistling past her ear. She could sense the tension of the human POWs watching. She expected to feel the expanding air of a heat blast, the smell of the ozone in her nostrils. She lowered her hands slowly, stared at the open gate, and waited.

The Krael guard at her feet was still wheezing. Apparently she had broken his jaw. On the ground next to him was a large tooth. One of his curved and fearsome-looking tusks from around his mouth. She slowly bent down to snatch it up.

"My trophy," she said. The Krael stumbled to his feet, seemingly confused. "Now take me to your Commandant." He stumbled back toward the gate and disappeared inside. The remaining Krael kept their weapons aimed on her. The human prisoners stared, awed and impressed. Several were grinning, and a few even silently applauded. They seemed to think she was a rescuer, some savior who would bring them freedom. She wished them well, but Deacon was getting out of here on her own.

Movement at the gate caught her attention. Four Krael had returned, marching through the prisoners in the yard to the front gate and standing in a square position, their bladed weapons at their sides. Their intent was unmistakable. She walked forward, into the center of the square. They turned as one, the rear two bringing their blades up toward her back.

As they started to walk, she heard a familiar "snorfing" sound behind her. The strange sand creatures the Krael had hibernating under the ground around Stalag-X as watchdogs had been activated. She didn't have to look back to know they were feasting on the forgotten Krael she had killed. A gruesome, but efficient, way to dispose of those who had lost honor by being defeated.

The first part of her plan was a success. Deacon was now a prisoner of the Krael.

She sat cross-legged on the sand in the middle of the open camp yard, while the human POWs were on the other side of electric-phase fencing. The Krael guards kept their distance, wary. They had relieved her of the deadly staff, but let her keep her knife, as if they didn't consider it much of a threat. She could make do.

Her eyes were closed as if resting, but she focused all her senses and sensibilities on her predicament and the task ahead.

She'd done her threat assessment the moment she entered the stalag. It was a natural thing for her, intuitively examining every new environment for any advantages and disadvantages, far more of the latter than the former. Though she'd been observing Stalag-X for several months, she could not have known exactly what the Krael had done to the interior of the former human military base. She was quite familiar with the standard layout of Commonwealth bases, but the Krael had modified this one to their own use.

The local Colony Town had also been taken and repurposed, and the settlers didn't have a chance. Pondafier was never going to be an exotic getaway for the Space Cruise companies, but it wasn't a bad planet when she'd first arrived on a routine assassination mission. The Krael invasion had screwed everything up.

Deacon's target had shown up on her burst tablet with the new data received from the Service, a clandestine subnet listing board for those who did commerce in illegal affairs. It was a safe way for an employer to stay anonymous while guaranteeing payment to professionals like herself. The money was transferred into an escrow account until receipt of proof of completion. It was an open system, with the money paid to whomever actually accomplished the task. First come, first served. That had resulted in a lot of clusterfucks with more than one assassin getting in the way of others, all after the same target. But those free-for-alls were for lower-level killers.

Deacon wasn't a low-level killer. Her record entitled her to a Premium listing, giving her access to the high-value targets where the real money was. Less competition, though much more risk. Deacon had been contracted as Premium for years, picking up targets, reading the mission data, warnings and weaknesses, useful details for an assassin. The galaxy had enough scattered planets of diverse people, beliefs, and enmities that she never lacked for work.

The initial outbreak of the Krael war, when the aliens attacked and wiped out human colonies and military ships on the rim systems, didn't really affect Deacon's business at first. She'd been inconvenienced, but she hadn't paid much attention to politics. She would study the listings from the Service and choose a target that sounded interesting. She'd been out on the far rim when she saw the urgent high-level target appear, last known location on Pondafier.

And a price tag that made the job very worthwhile.

A missing part in the dossier, as always, was why the target was so important. Deacon never bothered to ask. The job was a job, and she didn't care whether the victim was a genocidal dictator, a religious cult leader, or simply a cheating ex-husband targeted by a jilted lover. Everyone bleeds the same.

Since Pondafier was nearby, she had altered her course to take the job. There was always a small chance that some other assassin might hurry to the backwater planet and beat her to the victim, but she doubted it. This was just too far out on the rim, and the well-armed Earth Command military base south of town made Pondafier a less-than-desirable place for assassins to ply their trade. Perhaps the target thought the sheer isolation offered him some protection. And maybe it did, from others. Not from her.

She had studied the public information available on the target as she brought in her ship to land in a clearing not far from Colony Town. The target's name was Anson Garbo, a wealthy executive who had pulled up roots and decided to become a hardscrabble colonist. Not likely.

He had worked in various technologies with all the major companies, Bulwark being the most notable. It was the largest pan-galactic corporation; everyone of note worked for Bulwark at one time or another. Since the beginning of the Krael war, Bulwark's size had tripled along with the number of Earth government contracts it received. Bulwark paid its employees well, so if this Anson Garbo had chucked that paycheck, he must have some really nasty people after him. She suspected that Garbo was probably embezzling or involved in industrial espionage. Someone wanted him dead, even though he'd gone to ground in the far armpit of the rim, where he was not likely to sell any stolen information or live large off of his illicit earning. He was a scared rabbit. That was plain enough.

Someone was willing to pay a hell of a lot of money for this scared rabbit.

She had landed her ship in a clearing surrounded by slowly waving thorn vines. Out of habit, she removed a cache of weapons and supplies, hiding them in case of emergency. Making those preparations seemed silly because Pondafier was such an obscure planet with a nonthreatening town. But Deacon had learned that worst-case scenarios occurred more often than anyone would expect. Early in her career, she had spent six months in a revitalization pod because she'd underestimated the abilities of a group of farmers defending a friend. Not again.

She had a long rifle if she wanted to kill the target at a distance, but she would still have to come forward and use her cranial drill to acquire the proof of death sample. She had her long knife in case she wanted to be personal, and she could kill with her bare hands, barring anything else. Deacon liked to improvise. If the plans were too specific, too cut-and-dried, then her job would become just that —a job.

For her, killing people was never personal. She wasn't a sick psychopath like that asshole Margrev. Deacon was a professional and learned early to bury any emotion. The last time she'd let passion drive her was her first assignment, the head of an interstellar cartel dealing in clone slavery and organ trade. The target was surrounded by security, untouchable by his enemies. Deacon had killed him quickly and silently, along with his bodyguards.

She was twelve at the time.

The only training she'd previously had was watching her parents and sister being slaughtered by that particular cartel, and that was enough to start her career. But she left that anger and hatred behind in the bloody loading bay of their slave ship. Anger and personal vendettas had no place now; they could get her killed.

Perhaps it was her own version of therapy, an attempt to blot out the memory of her family's slaughter. Perhaps it was guilt for being helpless when she'd been young. Sometimes she thought of it as justifiable revenge on a hateful God. It didn't matter. Deacon didn't care about causes or reasons. War or not, she was a gun for hire, and someone wanted this Anson Garbo dead.

The population of Colony Town was less than eight hundred.

The buildings mainly prefab structures, though the people had added some personal touches. The settlers worked hard to be self-sufficient, if not profitable. The local biologic-mineral plant called ironwood was their main export. When cured and treated, ironwood was among the strongest materials in the galaxy. But aside from their exotic wood exports, Pondafier was an invisible world. These people considered it home, and who was she to judge?

Since he was a relative newcomer to this planet, Garbo shouldn't be hard to find.

No matter how much she wanted to keep a low profile, Deacon called attention to herself, just by being there. They didn't get a lot of tourists. The long rifle slung over her back, her knife at her side, her trench coat loose around her, all drew attention as she strolled down the wide streets made of baked, hardened dirt and crushed gravel beaten down by large tires of Colony wood-processing trucks. She saw storefronts, tradesmen, mechanics, merchants, and clothiers, which implied to Deacon that Colony Town was thriving enough that people could dabble in businesses beyond mere day-to-day survival. Large reptilian beasts with stubby horns and big eyes plodded down the street chased by laughing children who seemed to treat them as pets instead of meat sources or beasts of burden.

Shopkeepers emerged to look at Deacon. An old man sat on a low metal cargo crate using a whirring diamond blade to carve a misshapen hunk of ironwood into some design. She locked eyes with him and he nodded curtly at her but continued his work without showing undue alarm. She kept walking as if she knew where she was going.

She chose not to go to the seediest-looking establishment, where one might expect to find information for any price. She didn't think Garbo was that sort of target. Rather she went to a small café that served meals with families at tables outside.

One of the servers approached her, a short man with sandy hair and a toothy grin. "Haven't seen you around. Table for one, or …?" He peered around, as if looking for a companion. Deacon shot him a friendly smile, another skill she had cultivated.

"I'm looking for a man, Anson Garbo. He's an old friend who moved here recently."

The sandy-haired man turned his eyes upward, accessing his memory cells. He frowned and shook his head.

"Garbo's outside of town," said another server as he set down a plate of sliced meats and boiled green tubers in front of a rough-looking man. He stood up and wiped his hands on his apron. "He hardly ever comes into town. He bought the Gallagher homestead in a canyon just south of here. About ten klicks from the military base. He keeps to himself."

"That's Anson!" Deacon said. "It'll be good to see him."

The customer picked at the green tubers in front of him then peered up at her. "Kinda strange. Garbo's never gotten a visitor before."

Deacon's demeanor went from warm to ice in a nanosecond as she turned her hard eyes to him. "Have you gotten any offworld visitors either?"

The man flushed and turned away. "No. Sorry." He went back to his meal, his curiosity quelled by the warning bells in his head.

Deacon left, knowing they would all remember her. Once she killed Garbo, everyone in town would realize who had murdered him. Even if it became an entrenched fight, she doubted any misguided local justice would be a problem. She would soon be long gone from Pondafier, flying off in her ship, ready for the next mission. The long list of names the Service sent to her burst tablet would never run out. Job security.

The western sky turned bronze as the sun settled toward the horizon. She'd have to take the long route to avoid the military base, but she didn't want to explain herself to Earth Command soldiers on patrol. She kept to the long canyons, weaving through the old riverbeds. The target wasn't actually that hard to find.

Deacon saw the secondhand prefab hut that Anson Garbo had apparently bought from the estate of an old miner who had died the year before. Canyon shadows cast gray blankets over the ground, creeping along as the sun set. Lights glowed in the prefab hut.

Deacon approached cautiously, aware that Garbo might have set up motion sensors and traps. But all she found was a spiny lizard on top of a boulder. It flicked out a forked tongue and burbled a warning as it displayed needlelike fangs. She tossed a pebble and the lizard scuttled away.

She heard casual movement inside the prefab house, saw lights, a shadow—a single figure. He had prepared no defenses; this was just a normal day for him. His last day.

A polite person would knock, but assassins didn't need to be polite. She pulled a small flash-bang from her coat and, using the hard heel of her boot, she kicked open the flimsy door. It slammed against the inner wall as she tossed in the flash-bang, which went off with a blinding light and sudden concussive sound. Deacon rolled in to the opposite wall as the man inside let out a high shrill scream.

Garbo stumbled backward from the small single-burner stove where he had been cooking and accidentally pulled the pot of boiling soup off the burner, spilling thick brown gravy down his leg, which changed his cry to an entirely different squeal of pain. Still blinded by the flash-bang, he swung the soup ladle in front of him like a weapon.

Deacon took three strides, grabbed him by the front of his shirt, and threw him into a wooden chair. She snatched the ladle from his hand and swatted him across the face with it. He stared up at her in fear.

"Just to verify," Deacon said in a casual tone, looming above him. "You're Anson Garbo, right?"

"What do you want?" he wailed, pawing at the hot spilled soup on his pants. "Leave me alone. My leg ..."

She wasn't in a hurry to kill him. He was still insensible from the effects of the flash-bang and it went against her sense of ethics to kill a target in his condition. Thunder rolled in the distance. She stood up, tossing the deadly ladle aside, and evaluated the target.

Garbo's shirt was rugged, but more stylish than serviceable. His skin sagged as if he had lost a great deal of weight in recent months. His brown eyes looked haunted. His hair was unkempt, the leftovers of what had once been a fine haircut now grown out in all directions.

"You ... you've come to take me back?" he asked as he looked up at her, his sight beginning to return.

"Not in my job description. I've got a contract for your life."

His breath caught in his throat. "No, I should have been safe here," he said with a broken voice. "They know I've got insurance! I placed copies of the information elsewhere. If I'm—"

She grabbed his throat, squeezed hard. "I don't care."

He pawed at her arm in an attempt to finally fight back, but Deacon pulled his free wrist and stepped backward, pushing his locked arm down and driving him to the floor. She twisted his arm behind him, placing her boot on his back.

"You don't understand what's going on!" Garbo screamed. "The Krael war, the human colonies that've fallen ..."

"I know about the colonies and the battles," she said. "Lots of widows and orphans."

The thunder rolled louder in the distance, accenting her words.

"It's not that. It's them! Some of those colonies didn't have to—"

She twisted his arm harder. "Not interested."

"Please. Just take me back! With this information, you could change everything!"

Deacon knelt with her face next to his. She could smell the soup mixed with the sour smell of urine from his pants. "Did you miss the 'I don't care' part?"

"But it's Bulwark!"

That confirmed what she suspected. Garbo had worked for Bulwark, stole something, and then fled. Bulwark was one of the few companies that could afford a priority assassination. She knew he would keep babbling, pleading for his life, finally offering to bribe her. There was a series of stages the condemned went through, the last bargaining for life. She had heard it all.

"I'll match whatever they're paying you!" he screamed.

Deacon shook her head, surprised that he'd gone right for the final bargaining chip. "Do you want to hire me? Fill out the forms and transfer the money to the Service. I'll be happy to work for you." She took out her knife. "But I'm still going to finish this contract."

With a swift, vicious blow she crashed the thick hilt of her dagger against the side of Garbo's temple, breaking the skull precisely on the sweet spot. It was a mercy move because she knew it rendered him instantly unconscious. He slumped forward with a low moan. She turned the dagger around, placed the tip carefully at the base of his skull. "It's nothing personal," she whispered, and shoved down, severing his spine and killing him.

She closed her eyes, letting her subconscious bury whatever guilt she might have, then went to work with her cranial drill. It was simple to operate, inserting the extraction tube into the victim's ear in order to remove tissue from the medulla. The DNA would prove his identity and guarantee the target was deceased. She also took high-res images, just to make it a complete package. Before long the Service would be notified, Anson Garbo's name would be removed from the list, and the payment would be transferred to her account.

The sound of thunder increased in intensity, so she would have to wait out the storm in this quiet hut before making her way back to the ship so she could leave. As far as assignments went, there had been no complications. Easy.

Little did she know that the "thunder" was a Krael special force overrunning the military base. The alien invasion was already in the process of occupying Colony Town. Her space cruiser was just hours away from being discovered since she hadn't bothered to hide it with any sophisticated or long-term camouflage. Krael patrols would soon roam the landscape, and the sound of their scout craft would send her scurrying for cover.

For the first time in her life, Deacon had known what it felt like to be the prey.

Now, in the camp yard, she inhaled deeply as she opened her eyes and glanced around the interior of Stalag-X. The human POWs looked defeated, some of them wounded, others gaunt and skeletal. She saw defiance in the eyes of some, despair in others. The Krael guards were bloated with their own confidence. Their fangs and claws, their armor and sharp weapons were enhanced for effect, but little more than costumes to her.

She had waited long enough. "The Commandant! What is taking him so long? Is he afraid?" Her tablet translated her words, and she hoped it also conveyed the defiance in her voice. "I have places to go. I need my ship back, and I want to be off this damned planet."

Some of the human prisoners shook their heads, as if concluding she was mad or suicidal. But she didn't have any intention of negotiating for her freedom. She wanted to kill the Commandant, simple as that.

Deacon had downloaded all the known knowledge of the Krael on her burst tablet—which, admittedly, wasn't much. Her direct observations, combined with Earth Command intel reports, confirmed what she suspected about their military-social structure. The Krael were a segregated species, each one born into a specific caste: Warrior caste, Science caste, Command caste, maybe more, each with differentiated skills and duties. The Warrior caste was subservient to the Command caste; the Science caste was more ambiguous as to its place in the hierarchy. She knew the leader of the Science caste here on Pondafier was the equal of the Commandant. She hoped that wouldn't be a problem, but she could be flexible.

As if on cue, the very representative of the Science caste emerged from a small building next to the POW barracks. Taller, with a smoother skull and higher cranium, he looked less threatening than a typical Krael. But the fear the human POWs suddenly showed at his appearance put Deacon on notice. This creature was no one to play around with.

His claws tapped on a small energy weapon on his belt. "You are an interesting human. Very interesting. I should like to study you."

Deacon covered her shock. He had spoken in Standard English! She'd never seen any data that even hinted the Krael were capable of human speech.

Momentary doubt swept over her. Deacon's target had been, from the beginning, the Commandant. She was betting on the Krael ascension of power, that killing an opponent considered higher than your caste would bestow a certain amount of respect from the others. So far, she'd been proven correct since she was still alive after killing the Krael guard. But something about this new Scientist Krael made her rethink her plan. What if he was the absolute power here? If he knew Standard English, that meant he had studied humans. And perhaps he would figure out what she was up to.

Before the Scientist Krael could step closer, she heard a loud command and the ranks of alien guards suddenly stiffened. The Commandant of Stalag-X strode out from the large headquarters building near the gate.

He was powerful, well-built, and obviously a veteran of many battles. He glided forward with confidence, his yellow eyes fixed on her. The Krael Scientist bowed as the Commandant passed, and the deference was a welcome sight to Deacon.

She stood from the sand as he approached, facing the Commandant directly. She held her hands open to her side, demonstrating her own confidence.

The Commandant studied her, then pointed his finger to the

ground with emphasis. His guttural voice issued a command in his native tongue. The Scientist spoke to Deacon directly, rather than waiting for her tablet to translate. "Commandant K'Grau, most high of the Clan of—"

The Commandant interrupted, also in Standard English. "I don't need your translation. You taught me their language for a reason, so I could command the prisoners."

"I'm not a prisoner," Deacon interrupted him. "I'm not from this planet. I'm not your enemy, and I'm sure as hell not going to kneel. Give me my ship back, and I'll leave."

The Krael guards shifted angrily, and even the Scientist seemed taken back by her response, which made Deacon feel oddly pleased. Bristling, the Commandant trudged forward, stopping directly in front of her. He glared down into her eyes, and Deacon looked up without flinching.

In her mind, she was already assessing her opponent. He was more than a head taller than she was, and probably weighed an additional two hundred pounds. His body was all rock, armor, and muscle, and all they had left her with was a knife. His center of gravity was high, too high. She could use that. His claws were, for the most part, bent inwards. That, too, was useful. The eyes were pushed back into his skull. Good for protection, but that meant a limited range of sight. She processed it all as her assassin's instincts took over.

The Commandant snarled, "You are weak and clearly insane. I will let Mengele dissect you."

She almost chuckled at the Scientist's name. Mengele? Either he knew Earth history or he'd been given that name by his victims. As if the issue was settled, the Commandant turned abruptly to return to his office.

"You are afraid of me!" She spoke in a challenging tone he could not ignore.

He paused and turned, glowering at her. "As I said, you are insane."

"Maybe," Deacon replied loudly. "I didn't come here to talk. I came here to kill you. And I expect to be set free when I do."

The world fell still. No one stirred until Mengele broke the silence. "Very interesting." He turned his head to the Commandant, expectant, underlining the importance of Deacon's challenge.

Deacon knew she had to choose her next words carefully. She placed a hand on the dagger at her hip and spoke menacingly to the Commandant. "Or do you submit? And reveal the coward that you are?"

She honestly didn't expect him to move as fast as he did. She had prepared two more taunts to goad him into an attack, but it wasn't necessary.

The Commandant roared as he stepped toward her, slamming a clawed hand at her face. She dodged, just barely, but his claw hit her shoulder, spinning her backward. The movement took her by surprise, but Deacon regained her balance, pirouetted, and then landed, her knees bent. She crouched forward, arms back, knife already in her hand. The Commandant drew the ceremonial curved blade at his waist and then the second one from his other hip.

His muscular arm swept the long knife toward her as she danced out of the way, spun, and kicked him in the knee. His armor protected his leg, but she made him stumble. Deacon slammed her elbow into his neck and the Commandant lurched back. The four curved tusks around his mouth spread out then clamped together. His yellow eyes blazed with anger as he lunged forward.

She ducked under his arm, but he moved with surprising speed, kicking up at her, catching her in the ribs and flipping her over. Deacon rolled sideways, seeing stars behind her vision, feeling the breath knocked out of her. The Krael guards began stomping in rhythm, a low chanting grunt from their throats as they watched their leader deliver another kick to the side of Deacon's head.

She flipped completely into the air, blood spinning off the new gash in her scalp. The Commandant didn't even wait for her to land, but pressed his attack, lunging forward to finish her off. Deacon sucked in oxygen to recharge her energy. Pain shot through her ribs as she sprang back to her feet and launched herself sideways to avoid the sweep of the Commandant's knife.

"All right, time to stop playing around," she said with a labored gasp. She mentally chided herself for being too cocky. This was going to take every bit of skill and strategy she could muster.

Her mind scanned every memory she had of the dossier on Krael physiology, all the information that had been extracted from autopsies of mangled bodies from Krael battle fields. One thing that had caught Deacon's eye was a large cluster of nerve endings covered by a swollen sac under each arm. Human scientists disagreed about its purpose, but Deacon had noticed the Krael armor seemed to be reinforced in that particular location. Whatever that nerve sac was for, they made the effort to protect it. It must be very sensitive—and, thus, a target. The problem was she had only one shot at it.

In order to have the best chance, Deacon had to change her strategy. She had to lose.

The guards were stomping harder, chanting louder, their bloodlust rising with Deacon's impending death. Mengele watched with interest, the talons of his hand settling lightly on his sidearm.

The Commandant struck at her again. Deacon dodged, but more slowly this time. Her muscles screamed as she tried to stay just one step ahead of the Krael's blows. She tried a desperate dive for his midsection, grabbing him in a wrestler's hold, vainly attempting to knock him off-balance. The Commandant's boots dug into the ground as he braced himself. He brought both elbows down in the middle of her back. She collapsed, still desperately trying to hold onto him.

The Commandant knew he had her. His knee caught her directly under her chin, the impact loosening her grip and knocking her onto the ground. Deacon lay on her back, dazed and vulnerable. The Commandant lifted his arms high overhead, spinning the blades into a strike position, ready to plunge them into her heart.

Deacon smiled through her bloody lips. She was inside his defense and underneath his arms. Perfect.

With a scream, she jabbed up with the butt of her hand at the nerve sac. She struck him precisely at the right point, directly under the armor, hammering hard.

From the roar that came out of his fanged mouth, Deacon knew her strategy had been vindicated. With a groan like a falling herd beast, the Commandant lurched backward. She rolled to her feet, still staggering from the beating she had been given, but with a rush of adrenaline.

The Commandant tried to turn away, to protect his vulnerable side. In doing so, he exposed the nerve sac under his other arm. Deacon slammed her foot into it, staggering him to his knees, forcing him to drop his knives. She grabbed one as he desperately threw a punch at her. She dove over his shoulder, grabbing his neck with her free hand, using her momentum to spin across his body and under his arm again.

She stabbed the knife into the vulnerable nerve sac. The Commandant shrieked. The Krael guards backed away in shock, looking to each other as if lost. Mengele leaned forward, his eyes squinting as the scientist in him studied her.

Deacon yanked the knife free as the Commandant raised his other arm to grasp at her. She couldn't turn down such an obvious opportunity and slashed along his arm, separating the ligaments in his elbow and rendering his arm useless.

She knew she could kill him now; she could kill him immediately. But that wouldn't be good enough. She needed to make a statement, and every one of the Krael watching her needed to understand loud and clear, especially Mengele. And, more, the human part of her wanted revenge.

In three quick plunges, the blade sank deep into the Commandant's back, his thigh, and the back of his neck. Each strike brought a howl of pain and a shocked reaction from the Krael guards. Fear?

The Commandant reached up with his uninjured arm, but she grabbed the wrist, stepped over it, and bent it backwards against her leg, making a loud *snap* as the bone fractured.

The Commandant fell backward, and Deacon pressed upon him, jamming her knee on his neck, pinning him to the ground. His arms and legs flailed uselessly.

Her breath was hard and labored as she looked down at him. "It's nothing personal," she whispered as she plunged the knife into his eye with both hands, pressing with her body and twisting it as it dug through his skull and brain. If Garbo's death was painless, she made sure this one was anything but.

The Commandant's body stiffened and jerked as his nerves flared with pain then went dead.

Silence settled on the stalag as Deacon rested on the hilt of the knife for a moment, then slid off to the side. She tried to walk away, but her body deserted her. She fell to her knees, gasping. The blood from her wounds dripped to the sand and seeped in.

Out of the corner of her eye, she saw a shadow approaching. Mengele strode forward. He paused momentarily by the body of the Commandant, briefly settling his hand under the body's ear, then nodded. Deacon watched warily as the Scientist drew his sidearm and approached her. He knelt next to her, placed the barrel of his gun against her head, and peered into her face.

Deacon laughed dryly. All her strategy, all her plans, worthless.

"Humans intrigue me," he said to her. "I would like to study you. I would like to dissect you. I would like to connect you to the Ripper."

"Get it over with," she sneered at him.

Mengele stood and reholstered his weapon. "Go." He nodded toward the open stalag gate. "You killed our Commandant and gained your freedom."

"I want my ship back ..." she demanded, a part of her still not believing what had just happened.

Mengele shook his head. "You have earned our respect, but not our assistance. Leave. You are not a prisoner."

Mengele turned and walked toward his building, not looking back. Deacon's breath caught in her throat. She had won!

The Krael guards separated as she stumbled out the gate and into the wilderness of Pondafier.

She was going to survive, but she would have to find a way off this planet.

She needed to get her ship back.

And collect her reward for a mission well done.

For the 2006 World Science Fiction Convention, held in Los Angeles, one of the guests of honor was actor Frankie Thomas, star of the original TV show, Tom Corbett, Space Cadet. *(The show was before my time, but I'd still heard of it.)*

Mike Resnick put together a tribute anthology of stories around the general theme of "space cadets." This is the story I contributed: action packed, but also poignant, I hope.

Sadly, Frankie Thomas died just before the WorldCon, which made the anthology a memorial edition.

LOG ENTRY

According to his brief service record, Cadet Connor Pardee was a good, if unremarkable, recruit. One of his spaceflight instructors made a notation that he possessed "a reasonable amount of potential."

Connor's actions after his death, however, made him a hero lauded in all the Corps historical archives.

In the dogfight over a sun-grazer asteroid, the Corps scout ship was woefully outnumbered. Four unmarked smuggler vessels closed in to intercept the cadet before he could transmit a signal back to base. The smuggler ships had been stripped of all insignia and equipped with three times their original complement of armaments. They opened fire. The cadet's ship spun through a wild course, launching potshots as it tried to evade the pursuers.

From their heat tunnels in the cracked surface, the ffrall watched with interest. In the black vacuum sky above the asteroid, the battling spacecraft were merely flashes of light, hot maneuvering rockets, and blazing energy bolts.

The ffrall were a race of liquid energy beings, interconnected nodes of sentient power. For the last half cycle—as the asteroid soared away from the sun, cooling in the chill of space during its long, lonely year—the ffrall had observed the activities of humans. Ships streaked overhead, bright lines against the backdrop of stars. A few had landed on the asteroid and erected structures, a base from which they launched more ships. The ffrall did not understand.

They inhabited catacomb cracks leading to the asteroid's warm radioactive core, from which they drew energy. Each cycle, as their rocky home passed through the star's blazing corona, the asteroid flexed and heated, charging like a battery. The ffrall would commune during the long cooling journey up to aphelion, the asteroid's farthest and coldest point from the sun, then hibernate to hoard their reserves. The creatures would awaken only when the asteroid plunged again to a warmer part of its orbit.

Soon they would hibernate, but before their long dreaming began, the ffrall wanted to understand these odd strangers.

The dogfight overhead continued, the unmarked ships launching a concerted barrage against the now-damaged Corps scout. With a direct hit on its lower hull, the scout careened out of control. An electromagnetic signal burst out, which the ffrall heard through their extended senses.

"Emergency! This is Cadet Connor Pardee. I'm in trouble. I've stumbled upon a nest of asteroid pirates. They've got me in their sights. Please, anyone in range—I need immediate assistance. I know this signal won't reach base for days, but if there's anybody out there, my coordinates are—"

Another shot from the asteroid pirates knocked out his transmitter. Leaking fuel and out of control, the scout ship crashed into the rocks, rebounded in the low gravity, then tumbled before grinding to a halt. Atmosphere gushed out from hull breaches like arterial blood. The ship lay motionless, systems already cooling.

The four unmarked smuggler vessels circled slowly. One swooped low to confirm the kill. After conferring for a few moments on a coded channel, the raiders sped back to their base on the far side of the asteroid.

Oozing out of their cracks and glowing with internal energy, the ffrall went to investigate....

Cadet Connor Pardee's log entry:

The Academy is everything I thought it would be, as hard and as joyful, as challenging and as rewarding. The training is relentless, and the instructional classes are harder than anything I ever crammed for in civilian university. No matter how much you read ahead of time, no matter how much you exercise and mentally prepare yourself, you just plain can't be ready for this.

I was talking with one of my fellow cadets, Daniel Jones, and he nailed it. He said, "I never knew how much I could sweat before the sun came up. I never knew how hard I could run in the pouring rain. I never knew how much sleep I could go without. I never knew how much I weighed until I carried my weight in a pack on my back. I never knew how much I could miss everyone until they were so far away. I never knew what my limits were until I looked behind me and watched them disappear in the distance."

The food is terrible, but after a hard day nothing could taste more delicious. The beds are uncomfortable, but I've never slept so well in my life.

The people here are the same mix you'd encounter on the outside. Sure, some I like better than others, but there's a difference: here, even if I don't see eye-to-eye with someone, even if I actively dislike one of my fellow cadets, each of us knows we can depend upon the other with our lives. Really. Comrades in arms, and all that. It's a tangible thing.

We do speed-timed suit-up exercises, explosive decompression drills, and simulated combat runs modeled after actual splats from the First Pacification Wars. I've nailed flight tests on seven different models of spacecraft, and I'm cramming how to repair every one of them. The Corps won't let you fly a ship solo until you know every circuit, every cog and linkage, every rivet on every hull plate. It's a lot to remember.

Funny how you start to realize obvious things. I've never loved my mom and my sister more. I look forward to their transmissions as much as any kid ever anticipated a Christmas morning. Even when they don't say much of anything at all, the sound of their voices and the expressions on their faces warms my heart. "How are you? I am fine" never sounded so good.

Last week my mother shipped a package of home-baked cookies—my favorite, butterscotch oatmeal. Even with military subsidies, sending the package probably cost her a month's rent. I shared them with my buddies, and we licked every last crumb from the wrapping.

I know my father would be proud of me. Maybe he's watching up there from somewhere between the stars. He talked about the Academy ever since I was eight years old, and he counted on me entering the Space Corps, just like him. He had the good fortune of serving during the Long Peace. Never once saw combat, not even a police action to quell a minor revolt on an unruly colony planet. When telling stories, he called the timing "bad luck," but I think Mom was relieved. He died at the age of forty-nine in a stupid loading bay accident. The power source on a gravlifter failed, and a cargo pallet of terraforming dozers dumped onto the workers below. Because he'd been killed in the line of service, my father received a posthumous medal, and Mom got an extended pension.

Times are a lot rougher now. Since the defense corps is spread so thin, asteroid pirates, smugglers, and other unsavories have become more than a nuisance. They hit civilian cargo ships, passenger liners, even colony transports full of wide-eyed settlers. Pirates blast holes through the hull, decompress the whole ship and let their victims suck vacuum. Then they go aboard, ransack the hold, even pick the pockets of the floating corpses. Not very nice people.

Once I graduate, I'll keep those scumbags in line. If I nail my next set of trial runs, I'll get my scout pilot cert, and I might even grab command of my own ship.

Then those asteroid pirates better watch their butts!

With small discharges of electricity, the ffrall crept across the uneven ground, envelopes of crackling static moving of their own volition. The ffrall surrounded the crashed ship and studied its exterior by flowing over the conductive metal hull plates. They tasted the shape of the craft, found where the hull had been broken open, where the engines had been burned.

The ffrall oozed through gaping holes to the interior. The crashed ship was interlaced with circuits, power conduits, and a diagnostic sensor array. The energy creatures easily followed these pathways, sniffing information, gleaning residual power traces.

All of the ship's primary circuitry was gathered into a single computer center in the smashed cockpit. Once the ffrall realized that the memory records were a form of communication, they began investigating further. They consumed and downloaded the information. Seeking clues and cross-references, they began to digest the log entries, conferring amongst themselves and comparing their insights. Gradually they incorporated enough knowledge to understand this ship, its alliances and enemies—and its pilot.

The ffrall discovered that the spacesuited form, with its smashed faceplate and a jagged chunk of shrapnel punched through the body core, was a cadet named Connor Pardee.

Cadet Connor Pardee's log entry:

The day I was accepted into the Academy was the happiest day of my life. And then it got better. I aced every class in basic training, and I'm totally ready to be deployed as a rep for the Corps. A genuine space cadet.

Most cadets consider the course on ethics and galactic law to be the dullest part of the curriculum. As fully empowered reps of the Unified Civilizations of Earth, we have to know the nuances of the various articles of independence, the code of unification, and interstellar commercial treaties.

They say new cadets are the most vigorous enforcers. Is that something to complain about? I intend to be one of them. As soldiers grow older, they let more slide, give a little more leeway, but I hope I can stick to the truth. It's a slippery slope—once you make a minor exception and let somebody overstep the bounds, the next time it gets easier.

Before the Pacification Wars, we all saw the price of lawlessness. Fanatics everywhere. The chaos got so bad that all the colonies, even with their fundamentally opposed religious and governmental philosophies, found common ground and came together under the banner of the Corps. My father instilled that pride in me, the reverence for law and order.

Smugglers and asteroid pirates are the scum of space, the dregs of any society. They twirl and dodge and sidestep with technicalities, as if the law were some sort of old-fashioned dance. And they leave way too many bodies and drifting ghost ships in their wake.

I don't intend to let them get away with it. Not me.

When I finally got my cert as a scout pilot, I landed an assignment to patrol the outer asteroid fields. And my own ship, my beautiful scout ship. I could go on and on citing her engine specs, fuel capacity, cargo and passenger load, max accel, firepower, docking requirements, air reserves, even the full food menu programmed into the dietary synthesizer. But that would be just repeating rote statistics (and it would make my personal log unspeakably boring). Having learned them all for my final exam, the stats are forever burned into my memory.

Right now my ship has nothing more than a call sign, XFE0017, a designation that nobody's brain can wrap around. By tradition, cadets don't christen their ships with a real name until after they've flown their first mission. I've already got my name picked out, and I'll take great pride in stenciling it on as soon as I land after my first patrol.

"Mongoose"—my father's call sign, the one he never got to use.

From the information in the scout ship's database, the ffrall gleaned knowledge of the vessel, absorbed how the engines functioned and how the weaponry worked. The energy creatures spread throughout the crashed ship, suffusing the systems and manipulating the atoms of the metal alloy hull and the polymer molecules in the circuitry.

With the care of artists working on an extravagant new project, the ffrall began to reassemble the ship back to its optimal state. The creatures had every instruction manual and every repair blueprint they could possibly need.

When they investigated closely, the figure inside the spacesuit displayed no life energy whatsoever. Its bodily functions had ceased, and cellular chemistry had begun to break down. The only residue was a bit of thermal energy, body heat, trapped within the suit but leaking out into the cold vacuum through the shattered faceplate and the massive chest wound.

Now that they understood and shared the ship's log entries, the ffrall knew the identity of the cadet, his life, and intricate details of his biology from the library database. After evolving, communing, and hibernating alone for so many cycles, they were intrigued to learn the passions and the scope of these humans.

One of the individual ffrall remained by the motionless body of the cadet. Because the spacesuit was insulated, the creature could not penetrate it electrically. Forming itself into a liquefied, shapeless mass, the blob of crackling energy poured through the crack in the faceplate, oozing into the gap and into the tissues of Cadet Connor Pardee.

This was another vital part of the learning process.

Cadet Connor Pardee's final log entry:

I'm not complaining, but this is really boring. Like watching sealant dry.

I couldn't wait until I got my assignment and flew away from the base in my scout ship. I had checked and triple-checked all the systems, by the book and then some. Even though one of the other cadets razzed me for being a mother hen, I wanted everything to go right for my first mission.

But now that I've been on patrol for four days, in and out of the asteroid belt two systems away from the main Corps base, I never thought it would be so … well, dull. After the first few hours, the asteroids all start to look the same. Space junk, planetary leftovers.

I'm amusing myself by imagining that one looks like a potato, another like a fish, one like a beehive. They're all pockmarked with craters, ridged from melting and reforming. They tumble along in random orbits, nudging each other, jockeying for position around the sun. I haven't found any excitement yet, but I'll keep patrolling.

The asteroid I'm currently scanning is a sun-grazer in an elliptical orbit, cooling off now that it's heading back out from the star. The most interesting thing so far is a set of anomalous energy readings. At first I was excited, thinking it might be a secret outpost of asteroid pirates, who are known to have major activity in this system. But the readings are off-scope, out of parameters. Wouldn't be the first time the Corps textbooks were missing a key appendix or two. The readings look almost like life signs, but this scout isn't equipped with scientific sensors to get the data we'd need.

I'll log it, and maybe somebody will come out to investigate. (Although these days the constant threat of pirates has put a crimp in most scientific work. A research base would just be too vulnerable to raiders, and the Corps doesn't have enough extra personnel to send troops for security.) Nevertheless, this is intriguing enough that I'm going to do a full mapping of this asteroid, cruise over the craters just in case somebody might be hiding down there.

Wait—something's wrong with the comm systems. I'm being jammed. What the hell?

I see domes, reactors, life-support shacks—and ships. Asteroid pirates, a full-blown base! Damn, I'm still being jammed! Uh-oh, they've spotted me. Marauder ships are launching—four of them. Even this sweet little scout can't outrun four souped-up raider ships. I'll try evasive action. I've got weapons, and I'm not going to go down without a fight.

They're shooting at me. That was close! I've got to get out of here and concentrate on my flying and fighting.

Log entry, signing off. When this is all over I'll have one of those great stories, just like my Dad always wanted to tell.

When the ffrall completed their repairs to the scout ship and sacrificed some of their power to reenergize the mechanical systems, the crashed vessel lifted gently.

The single ffrall that had infused the cadet's dead biological body repaired the crack in the faceplate and sealed the grievous injury where shrapnel had punctured the chest. Even after rectifying the physical damage, the ffrall could not bring back Cadet Pardee; however, it could animate the form inside the suit so that it was able to operate the scout ship's controls—and complete the mission.

The energy creatures had learned everything about the young man, his sense of honor, and his allegiance to the Corps. They had scoured all the details of galactic law. Now, the ffrall knew what they must do. The creatures would take it upon themselves to finish the cadet's obligations before they went into their hibernation state. Perhaps by the next cycle, when the asteroid heated up again, the ffrall might emerge as emissaries and contact the humans in the Corps.

Discharging themselves through the hull, the other ffrall left the ship, returning to their energy sockets where they would soak up the ebbing heat of the asteroid's core. Only the one ffrall remained inside the suited form.

The repaired scout ship set off to where Cadet Pardee had discovered the pirate base. From here, the smugglers would launch their raids on helpless civilian ships passing through the isolated system. The ffrall had long been aware of the strange settlement on the far side of their asteroid, but had avoided any contact.

Now Pardee's ship skimmed low over the surface, beneath the enemy's sensor net. The ffrall worked the cadet's body, lifting gloved fingers to activate precise targeting controls and prepare the weapons systems. As soon as the scout ship soared over the upraised lip of a large crater, the ffrall reacted. It was just like one of the simulated exercises stored in the computer database.

The four pirate ships were there, now refueled and ready to fly. The scout fired precise blasts, each one destroying an engine pod and leaving the enemy ships grounded. As the scout circled again, the ffrall carefully targeted the base's life-support sheds and eliminated them. Every step went like clockwork, by the Corps Manual.

Now the pirates had no way to get off the asteroid, and their air and power would fail within a few days. They would have to send out a distress call and surrender to the Corps.

Within the cadet's body, the ffrall did not respond to the pirates' shouted curses over the comm lines. Instead, it calculated how much longer its energy would last and decided it had just enough strength left to animate this body and take the scout ship to the nearest Corps base. Back home.

Coursing through the young man's nervous and circulatory systems, the ffrall was too much for the fragile human body, close to igniting cells on fire. Its own life energy was dwindling swiftly, but even as it faded, its memories and thoughts were linked to the other ffrall. It could still operate the ship's controls. It could complete the mission.

Because the gathered ffrall had repaired the ship's engines perfectly, and because the animated body in the suit was no longer alive (and therefore no longer vulnerable to extreme acceleration), the ffrall was able to fly much faster than any human could have endured.

By the time the scout ship reached the Corps base, the lone ffrall had dwindled to little more than a spark. As Cadet Pardee's ship delivered its appropriate ID signal and landed inside the main dock, the ffrall transmitted a synthesized recording. During the journey, it had patched together voice records from the log entries so that the words sounded as if they were spoken by the young man.

"This is Cadet Connor Pardee, delivering my report. I located a secret base of asteroid pirates and surprised them before they could launch their ships after me. I destroyed their ships and took out their life-support capabilities. They'll need somebody to pick them up. By the time a mop-up squadron gets there, I don't expect they're likely to put up much resistance. Transmitting the coordinates now."

With the last flicker of its energy, the ffrall ended the report, "This is scout ship XFE0017, christened *Mongoose*—signing off."

Investigation Summary—Classified: Restricted Access

This report has many questions and few conclusions. Because no logical answers fit the recorded facts, I will simply state the data.

Cadet Pardee's information was valid. We dispatched a Corps squadron to the location of the suspected enemy base, where we easily rounded up thirty-seven prisoners, all of whom will be prosecuted to the fullest extent of galactic law. We have reason to believe this was an extremely important base, housing several of the most wanted asteroid pirates. The information we gleaned from this operation could well shut down their whole network in the sector. This one victory probably saved thousands of lives.

However, we cannot figure out what Pardee did, or how he did it.

Our engineers and technicians have combed his scout ship and found many anomalies. The craft appears to have been severely damaged and then repaired. *Perfectly* repaired. Onboard diagnostics show that it was flown back to base at extreme acceleration, which would certainly have been lethal to any pilot.

Cadet Pardee was found dead in the cockpit, though his suit was intact. The autopsy found severe cellular damage, as if from extreme energy exposure. However, the actual cause of death appears to have been explosive decompression and deep trauma from a foreign object, presumably shrapnel, which was found still deeply embedded in his chest, though his skin was perfectly healed over it. His last transmission was made immediately prior to his arrival at the base, but our doctors insist that Cadet Pardee had been dead for several days before he landed in our docking bay.

I had the sad duty of informing Cadet Pardee's mother and sister of his death. Unfortunately, I was forced to be vague, because the details make no sense. I informed them that Cadet Pardee died in the line of duty and that he was a genuine hero. I recommend awarding him a posthumous medal of honor.

I do not wish for the mystery to diminish or taint in any way the service our brave cadet performed for the Corps. In some exceptional people, dedication to duty is so strong it survives even their physical death. We do not need to understand our dead to honor them.

I recommend that these records be sealed. Permanently.

My novel Hopscotch *is, I think, the masterpiece of the first part of my career. The high concept percolated in my head for nearly a decade, but the idea was so ambitious, and explored so much about the defining nature of Humanity, that I felt intimidated. I wasn't ready to write it. I just didn't have enough life experience.*

So I let it simmer and grow.

Other science fiction or fantasy stories have dealt with two characters swapping bodies and dealing with the consequences, often with amusing adventures before they swap back to normal. The films Freaky Friday *and* All of Me *are two examples that come to mind, along with the classic* Star Trek *episode "Turnabout Intruder."*

But what about a scenario where humans have the ability to swap bodies any time they like, with whomever they like, as simple as changing clothes? You could pick up a mate in a singles bar and have a "two-night stand," once as a male and once as a female. An executive could swap bodies with an assistant who would work out in the gym for him or go to an unpleasant dental appointment. An old couple could rent virile young bodies for an anniversary treat. A man could experience childbirth....

The story kept getting bigger and bigger, centered on three friends caught up in this world, how their lives intertwine and their experiences cross. The novel Hopscotch *spans their lives, their loves, their tragedies, all of which is anchored by their bond of friendship. These three characters regularly met at a place called Club Masquerade, where they shared their stories.*

The novel was massive and complex, but I found a way to extract a part of their story. "Club Masquerade" was published in Analog *Magazine and appeared on that year's preliminary Nebula Awards ballot.*

After you finish this novella, I hope you'll want to read the full story of Garth, Teresa, and Eduard in Hopscotch.

CLUB MASQUERADE

Prologue

As night fell, the city fractured into a kaleidoscope of lights, neon sparklers reflecting from rain-washed facades. Unabashedly garish, Club Masquerade hosted a dazzling assembly of humanity—new people, old people, everyone wearing a different body for the evening.

Outside the five ever-changing entrances to the Club, lighted sidewalk panels flashed patterns, numbers inside squares illuminated by each pressing footstep. Patrons walked through any of the arches into a wild environment of lights, music, exotic food, and unusual people. ID patches worked overtime to keep track of who was who, which mind in which body.

Each doorway led customers through a compact, shifting maze into any one of several tailored environment chambers: a Ming Dynasty palace, a British Empire Safari Club, a discotheque with mirror balls and strobe lights, a rustic Sequoia Room, an Arabian harem with colorful rugs and sweet perfumes, a domed Martian colony chamber with red rock and thermal springs. Finally, all the specialized alcoves opened out into the cavernous main interior of Club Masquerade. Sitting areas and dance platforms hung at various levels in the air, easily accessible by lift ramps or vacuum chutes.

You could be anyone or anything here, for a limited time—if the body you wanted was available. Pick a physique, swap with someone, wear it for a while, see if you like it.

Inside a windowless control room, invisible to the flow of customers, sat the bartender, Bernard Rovin, a lump of crippled flesh. Cybernetic substations kept his eyes and ears and automatic hands wandering throughout the bar. He observed the swirl of life, customers partaking of various entertainments, hopscotching from one body to another to another.

The jet-setters.

Separated from all that, Rovin just liked to watch, keeping track of a few special customers, regular patrons … "friends" of his, if the word wasn't too extreme. He knew what the date was, knew the routine. First Tuesday of the month.

Like clockwork, three customers entered separately, finding their way through the Safari Room, past the disco, and into the main bar. Two men and one woman (though occasionally they wore the opposite sex) looking around until they spotted each other at the predetermined meeting point, embraced.

Deep in his control room, the bartender smiled and directed his hands to start pouring their drinks. Like clockwork.

Garth's home-body always looked the same, except when he was on the hunt for new artistic inspiration: broad shoulders, blond hair, blue eyes, certainly nothing he'd want to change for the long term. His shirt bore paint stains, a smear of still-moving glittergel; his fingernails gritted with charcoal or chalk dust; his fingers smelled of solvents.

At first he didn't recognize Teresa, who came into the Club in yet another new physique. Her hair was rusty auburn this time, her eyes green-blue, her build Rubenesque today, with broad hips. Her clothes were drab, loose fitting, as if they could have been worn by anyone … and they probably were. The latest religious group she had joined didn't seem to value individuality much.

Eduard, looking tired from all the hell he kept putting himself through, found both of his friends and they sat together at a private table surrounded by the white noise of conversations. At least

Eduard used his hard-won money to buy stylish clothes to fit his dark-haired home-body, and he usually paid for the first couple rounds of drinks.

He hugged Garth, pounding his friend's broad back and tousling his blond hair, then he took Teresa into a softer, more intimate embrace. He touched a new bruise that seeped through the makeup and freckles on her rounded cheek. "Hey, what's this, Teresa?"

"Oh, nothing," she said quickly. "And it's not mine, anyway. The last person who had this body got hurt." She turned to fold herself into Garth's muscular arms, avoiding Eduard's scrutiny.

Oblivious and happy, Garth hadn't noticed the bruise at first; now he studied her cheek intently. As an artist, he should have been the best at noticing details, but somehow Eduard always managed to have a sharper focus. Garth bent down and brushed his lips across the sore spot. "All better?"

They waved at the bartender's image on the table screen, and their usual drinks appeared before they could even speak their orders aloud.

"I hate being predictable," Eduard said, then reached over and snagged Garth's foamy dark beer instead. "It could be dangerous."

Garth looked dubiously at the slushy blue concoction Eduard usually drank; now he was stuck with it.

"Oh, try it, Garth." Teresa was amused by his discomfiture. "You're always looking for new experiences, aren't you? Drinking blue cocktail … *things* will add to your artistic repertoire."

On one of the dance platforms, a scarecrow-thin man stumbled backward and fell comically on his butt. The short, large-breasted woman next to him moved with awkward, marionette movements as she hurried to help him.

Eduard snorted. "There should be a law against letting people dance unless they've had at least an hour to settle into their new bodies."

Teresa touched his hand. "Oh, don't be so cynical, Eduard." On the floor of the Club, several dancers moved slowly, carefully, trying to adjust to new heights, new weights, new degrees of muscle control.

Eduard cracked his knuckles and leaned closer to the blond artist. "So what's inspiring these days, Garth?"

Garth's eyes lit up, and his gaze took on a far-off look as he talked about his passion in life. To him, the people in the Club were a catalogue of humanity. "Still seeing things, trying to understand it all, but there's so *much*. Last week I spent two days as a dwarf, and it really changes your perspective. Nothing's at the right height—not door controls, not COM terminals, not video monitors, not the transport systems. Quite a challenge just to climb up onto a barstool."

He took another sip of Eduard's blue drink, tasted crackling sweetness that burned the back of his tongue. "This is tolerable, once your taste buds get deadened."

He looked up at the Club's chaotic Hopscotch Board, aglow with "swapportunities," people wanting to rent a muscular body to do a few days of hard labor, old men and women willing to pay for a week's vacation in a young and healthy physique, the usual sex ads searching for a two-night stand, once as a male, once as a female, or a blur of alternations before, during, and after.

"I wonder what it would feel like to be pregnant and deliver a baby," he continued. "Of course, that would require a long-term swap for at least the last month to get the full experience. And it wouldn't be easy to find a body I'd *want* to live in for that long."

Eduard rolled his eyes and looked at Teresa. "Artists! Who can understand them?" He sipped the beer he had taken from Garth, frowned, then traded drinks again.

Garth laughed. "This, from a man who gets paid to undergo surgery for other people?"

"Hey, I've got to make a living. No problem." Then he looked abashed. "Daragon saved me from a legal noose the other day, though. An old lady didn't want to give me my home-body back. I guess she didn't expect me to survive the operation. But Daragon showed up with just the right amount of Bureau muscle."

Teresa brightened at hearing the young man's name. Daragon had grown up with them, but he'd never managed to become more than a close outsider. He had joined the powerful Bureau of Tracing and Locations, the BTL.

"I think he spies on us," Eduard said, flicking his dark eyes from side to side in a comically paranoid furtive glance. "It's what Beetles do."

Teresa sighed and rested her chin in her hands. "Oh, I'm sure he thinks of it as keeping an eye on us."

"And lucky for you, Eduard, if you were in trouble," Garth said.

The music faded before swirling into a new mix, and the surrounding conversation grew louder. Three effete faux-intelligentsia at a nearby table continued their argument with much gusto and little actual information.

"You have to look far enough back to the precedent in mental development." The man waved a pungent purple cigarette back and forth. "Way back at the dawn of time, the human race went through a 'bicameral revolution,' when our minds split into left and right hemispheres." He crushed out his cigarette with finality and a smug expression. "This is a similar evolutionary step, consciousness becoming detachable from our physical brains."

A second young man drained a flowery-scented drink to fortify himself and launched into a counter-argument. "Makes more sense to say the whole hopscotch thing was triggered by generations of people uploading and downloading to old-style computer networks and virtual reality environments. *That's* how personalities first became detached from the body. Now we can do it all the time."

Garth, Teresa, and Eduard met each other's eyes, smiling as they shared the same thoughts. They'd heard all the theories a million times before. None of them knew the true explanation, nor did they care.

Eduard rocked back in his chair, raised his voice, "Yeah, right—what if it was just from too much astral projection without using proper precautions?" The whip-thin intellectuals looked sourly at him for squelching their continuing argument, then turned to debate even more esoteric matters.

From a substation in their table, the bartender's remote eye popped up. "Sorry I didn't say a personal hello as soon as you came in. I got caught multiprocessing a large crowd. Can I get you three a second round, on me?"

"Yes you can, Bernard," Garth said immediately, glancing over at Eduard's slushy blue drink, now in front of Teresa. "And give us *each* something we've never had before. New experiences." He smiled archly. "Variety—the spice of life, right?"

"I'll dig deep into my lexicon," the bartender said with a wink of his remote eye. "Just stay friends, all right? You three are an inspiration."

"In a changing world, some things never change," Garth commented.

When the drinks arrived, Teresa raised her eyebrows at her two best friends in the world. The three had been inseparable since they were kids, abandoned by their biological parents, taken in and tended by the intense, warm-hearted Splinter monks at the Falling Leaves monastery.

She held up her glass in a toast, not daring to ask the contents of the new cocktail the bartender had created. "To friends," she said.

They all drank.

—I—

Hiding together in the protective doorway of the Falling Leaves monastery, young Garth and Teresa watched the wall of storm sweep toward them. Eduard dashed out into the open, a child hopelessly trying to dodge raindrops, then hurried back to shelter, brushing the wet off his loose brown jumpsuit.

The localized weather disturbance was a gray fist wielded by the angry computer/organic matrix. The storm appeared to be directed toward a specific section of the city that had displeased COM. The monastery just happened to be in the wrong place.

"Look at that," Garth said, then took a deep breath. "Smell the air—like wet metal."

"It's called ozone," Eduard said, his rain-spattered cheeks flushed.

Out in the streets, scattered pedestrians and late-for-work businessmen ran for the tall buildings, while forlorn street vendors rolled up their awnings or stood by their kiosks and stared, hoping the usually benign weather control would divert the wind and rain. Paper debris and dried leaves scratched across the sidewalks, gusted by the freshening breezes.

Teresa peered around the old red brick lintel posts, brown eyes wide. A brisk blast of wind ruffled her auburn hair. "Oh, the rain'll wash everything clean. Wouldn't you like to just stand under it until you're drenched?"

"Soft Stone would never let us." Eduard brushed a few droplets from his sleeves, then lounged against the brick lintel post, as if nothing bothered him, nothing affected him.

"Absolutely right, child." The bald female monk stepped silently up from behind, startling them. In the shadows of the entry hall, Soft Stone's eyes were bright and blue, her features blunt, her mouth generous and gentled by a contented smile. "Don't worry about the upheavals outside. Nothing out there concerns you." She turned them around, gently nudging their shoulders. "Come in, where it's safe."

Sheets of rain poured down several blocks away, spreading along the streets like an advancing forest fire. "Did some terrorist group try to sabotage COM again, do you think?" Teresa asked, looking to Soft Stone for an answer. The Splinter monks seemed to know everything.

"Yeah, and COM's using the weather controls to strike back," Eduard said.

"The Beetles should just arrest them," Garth said. "Then everything could be quiet and happy again." BTL operatives rarely let a situation get out of hand.

"Don't talk to me about the Bureau right now," Soft Stone said with uncharacteristic sourness in her voice. She drew her sky-blue robe tight around herself. "The BTL causes enough trouble as it is." Her broad, callused hands drew her sixteen-year-old wards back into warm shelter.

Outside, the rain struck against the closed door with hard fury.

The monastery was an ancient building embedded in a section of modern city structures like a fossil in limestone. The exposed walls of red brick had been weathered by the passing years. In simpler times the place had been a brewery.

Newer buildings with connective atriums and cliffs of mirrored windows had grown up around the monastery like younger trees engulfing a deadfall. But the Splinter monks had kept this building intact, repairing every wall, every structural support.

Inside was a maze of rooms, corridors, meeting halls, and privacy chambers. Garth made his way back to a cozy discussion alcove furnished with worn cushions, water pitcher, and curtain. Seated cross-legged on a tattered plaid pillow, Kanshah had already lit a pair of scented candles, a spicy mixture of cinnamon and spruce. The flames would provide a stuttering yellow glow for Garth to read by. And of course he had brought the book.

Clearly nervous about the testing ordeal he was scheduled to endure in a few hours, Kanshah smiled shyly at Garth. He held up the heavy tome, *David Copperfield*. A scrap of cloth served as a bookmark. "Let's do another chapter. It'll settle my mind. For tonight."

Kanshah was thin and meticulous, with mouse-brown hair and watery-gray eyes. His loose-fitting clothes were freshly laundered, his sash neatly tied. Older than Garth by a year or so, he greatly admired the blond young man who read to him patiently, savoring Dickens's descriptions, the ironies, the exotic characters. Old books had opened up worlds for both of them that the meticulous COM-database studies of the Splinters had never revealed.

Garth took up his own cross-legged position across from Kanshah, in the glow from the two scented candles. His fingers slid down the bookmark and flipped open to the proper page. Time to continue the story.

All the children in the Falling Leaves were wards of the state, given up by parents who felt no obligation to babies born from bodies not their own, or impregnated during flings after which the original minds had hopscotched to somewhere/someone else. Supplemented by their own income, the monks received government stipends to teach and raise these young charges, and they took their obligations seriously. Each monk was assigned as mentor and teacher to a group of children who had no identifiable parents.

Raised together within the monastery walls, Garth, Eduard, and Teresa had been inseparable since their early years, and they had now nearly reached adulthood. The ID patch grafted onto the back of his right hand would soon be put into service, once he learned how to hopscotch.

Garth's attachment to Kanshah was relatively recent, a result of their mutual interest in the old stories. But Kanshah would have to leave the monastery soon.

Garth read the words on the page, changing his voice to imitate the various characters. Kanshah watched him, drawing his bony knees up to his chest. He listened with rapt attention to the story, and his anxiety seemed to ease.

Moments later the limp curtain was drawn aside, and Soft Stone pushed her shaven head inside. "I saw the candles, Kanshah, and I thought for certain you would be meditating."

Garth closed the heavy book, abashed. Kanshah played with his fingers, reluctant to answer her.

Soft Stone wrinkled her forehead. "Your demonstration is this evening, child. Are you so confident that you don't need to gather your thoughts and prepare?"

Kanshah drew a deep breath and looked at the monk. "No. I'm very intimidated. But I like the way Garth reads to me."

"Then perhaps he'll take the time to read to me, too. Come along, Garth. We need to leave Kanshah to practice his mental exercises. None of my wards has failed in all these years, and I don't intend for him to be the first."

Kanshah reluctantly handed him back the heavy book. The gaunt young man looked sadly at the bookmark's place, only two-thirds of the way through the pages. "We never would have finished anyway."

Against the background whisper of continuing rain, Teresa could hear the bustle inside the monastery, the movements of people, conversations muffled by walls, the sense of life all around.

She found a place to be alone, a place where she could contemplate. Though the Splinters did not raise their wards to espouse any specific religious dogma, they did teach their students how to think. "Questions are more important than answers, child," Soft Stone was fond of saying.

She curled up on a well-varnished window seat, leaning her back against the brick walls and looking out through the sheets of rain. The glass panes vibrated with the hum of the downpour. She could see forms still out on the streets, hooded people trying to cover their placards and literature before rushing for shelter.

Teresa had watched other religious groups before, proselytizers handing out free leaflets. They tried to sell trinkets and second-hand possessions to raise money, liquidating worldly goods to scrape up enough credits to print more leaflets for a wider distribution, since they didn't trust anyone to find their musings in the data ocean of

COM. Their devotion and convictions fascinated her. Teresa's own meditations always raised more queries about the nature of existence and provided few hard facts.

The Splinters themselves had coalesced from the fringes of various religions, panicked believers who no longer knew what to believe. With its rapid development and evolution, the computer/organic matrix became so all-pervasive that some considered it a benevolent deity watching over the world; others saw COM as an insidious Big Brother; others just used it in their day-to-day lives and paid no more attention to COM than to the air they breathed.

Add to that the human ability to hopscotch. The shift had spread like wildfire in only a few generations, turning inside-out all perceptions of reality and the individual soul. Even street-corner philosophers had been thrown into a tailspin.

Over more than a century, numerous new fusion religions had sprung up, people experimenting with beliefs and seeking new answers with a millennial fervor. Body-swapping and COM had changed humankind more than anything in a thousand years—yet, none of the great religious texts addressed the issue. Even followers of the vaguest notions of Nostradamus couldn't find the slightest hint. How could any true prophet worth his salt miss something *that* important? Impossible. The doubts cast many zealots adrift.

Teresa touched her fingers to the window, feeling the cold of the rain through the glass. She was glad that other people could cling to beliefs strong enough to work for. She admired devotion so great that they would stand out in the rain and struggle against a vengeful COM-induced storm.

Now, though, even the most faithful rushed into the tall buildings, under awnings or overhangs, into lobbies. Alone and distant, Teresa sighed as she watched them go. It seemed even their beliefs weren't enough to protect them.

In the attic of the old brick monastery, under cramped ceilings and surrounded by air thick with damp and mildew, Eduard watched the downpour with his older friend Daragon. With a grunt, he forced the crank on an old half-circle window with a wrought-iron frame. Fresh wet wind gusted through the opening.

"Go with me. We can slip outside, no problem," he said to Daragon. He thrust his face out into the breeze. "Hop on the roof, then make our way over the eaves to the tube walkway on the skyscraper next door." Daragon looked at him with alarm, which prompted Eduard to continue with greater enthusiasm. "Hey, this is the biggest storm I've ever seen, and I want to go outside in it."

"But you'll get soaked." Daragon shook his head. "Why would you want to do that?"

Eduard snorted. "Look, I'm already sixteen and, we should be able to experience a few things when we want to. You're even older —where's your sense of adventure? Take a risk or two. Come on, let's go out there."

Daragon shifted uneasily next to the open window. He was small in stature, wiry. He had dark hair, dark almond eyes that flashed in the light as his gaze moved from item to item. "Soft Stone told us to stay here, to get ready for Kanshah's ceremony tonight."

"Yeah, right—that's hours from now. You're just making excuses." Eduard drew a disapproving breath and dropped his bombshell, knowing it would upset Daragon. "I thought you wanted to be my friend. Friends *do things* together. Come with me, just for a little while."

Though younger, Eduard was like a big brother to him, someone who had the brashness to do the things Daragon secretly wanted to do, but was afraid. "We shouldn't. Soft Stone laid down the rules, and we agreed to follow them."

"Rules!" Eduard snorted again. He saw the vast city—and beyond that, the entire world—waiting for him outside the monastery walls. He couldn't wait until he passed his tests, and got a chance to make his own way in life. He was sure he could survive with his own wits and a few resources. "Bend a few rules, Daragon. Run out in the rain, let your clothes get wet. Who's it going to hurt?"

Eyes gleaming, Eduard gestured toward the edge of the rooftop. Raindrops ricocheted in through the narrow window opening. "Look out there, see those shadowy strangers huddled under porches, eaves, awnings. Who *are* all these people? What are they doing there?" His voice became breathy. "Think of all the secrets they must have. They could be *anybody*. Impersonating anybody. Who would ever know?"

Daragon squinted his almond eyes in a puzzled look. "Impersonating? They've all got ID patches. Besides, can't you just … *see* inside to who they really are?"

Eduard looked at his companion, exasperated but not knowing what Daragon meant. He leaned out the half-circle window, into the downpour, mentally choosing his route across the rooftops. "Look, are you going with me or not?"

Daragon swallowed hard. "No. I'll just stay here."

"Suit yourself." Eduard left him behind, ducking out the window and onto the wet roof tiles.

Much later that evening, after the storm fury had passed as abruptly as if it had never been, the monks and all their children gathered in a brick-cold meeting hall that had once been the ancient brewery's shipping area. A gentle, natural patter of rain continued to douse the streets.

Garth found Teresa and Eduard, and they sat together on the concrete floor, sharing a thin blanket. The monks had lit numerous candles and augmented the flickering light with stepped-back light tiles in the ceiling. Eduard's dark hair was dripping wet, his face flushed from his escapade out into the storm. The thin blanket soaked up the moisture.

Garth whispered, "Today I heard of a woman who tried to hopscotch with her dog. She was all alone, had the pet for years and years, and she wanted to give him a chance to be human for just a little while."

Eduard groaned. "I know where this is going…."

"She ended up nothing more than an empty body, discovered only because the starving dog kept barking and barking."

Teresa sat astonished. "Do you think it was the slippage disease?"

"No, it's because she was stupid enough to try hopscotching with a dog," Eduard said.

Garth shifted uncomfortably, looking around the meeting hall, anxious for Kanshah. Teresa knew what was bothering him and laid a warm hand on his wrist. "He'll do fine, Garth, don't you think?"

"I know he will." Garth finally saw his older reading companion led into the room by a solemn-faced Soft Stone. "It's just that … I'll miss him when he goes away." Teresa squeezed his hand with compassion.

Kanshah came forward meekly, walking beside the monk. He looked around as if in search of Garth for moral support, but their eyes never met. Garth hoped the time spent reading with his friend that afternoon wouldn't give Kanshah trouble when he most needed to concentrate. Once learned, this was supposed to be a natural, instinctive act.

Soft Stone did glance in their direction, but gave only a flicker of disapproval at seeing Eduard's wet and bedraggled appearance. Her attention returned to Kanshah. She took the young man's narrow shoulders in her grip and turned him, displaying him to the audience. Then she faced him herself, staring deeply into his watery-gray eyes.

"Kanshah, you have reached the age at which your soul is strong enough to live on its own. Thus, so can your body. Demonstrate for all here to see."

He swallowed hard and reached up tentatively to touch Soft Stone's shaven temples.

"I don't know why they have to make such a big deal about it," Eduard muttered in a whisper no louder than a breath. Out in the rest of the world, everyone learned to hopscotch in the normal course of growing up, accepting it as a part of maturity.

From opposite sides, Teresa and Garth both nudged him to keep silent.

In the middle of the hall, Kanshah's eyes locked with the monk's bright blue gaze. He took a deep, heavy breath—and a flicker seemed to pass between them. Instantly, the demeanor of both people *changed*. The young man took another breath, quick and sharp this time. He straightened his shoulders and gave a proud smile.

At the same time, Soft Stone's body shuddered. Her eyes went wide with fear and awe. The sinewy hands fluttered over her body, touching her smooth head, her small breasts, her crotch. She looked around the audience in the brick-walled meeting room, amazed. Her eyes locked with Garth's, and she blinked hard, several times.

"I … I don't think I like this," she said, her voice different.

"You don't like my body, child?" Kanshah's mouth said with a chiding tone.

"No … I'm sorry. I didn't mean that." The old woman took a few faltering steps. "I just need to get used to this. It's very strange."

Kanshah's right hand raised, turning the dull ID patch toward the monk, then he picked up Soft Stone's limp arm. The young man pressed the square filmscreen on the skin against the corresponding ID patch on the old woman's hand. The filmscreen flickered, and Soft Stone stared down at the new identity displayed there.

"A perfect transfer." The young man spoke with a cadence and inflection that Garth recognized from years of lessons from Soft Stone. "Normally, it takes some time to accustom yourself to a new body. Think of it as breaking in a new set of shoes."

In Soft Stone's old but vigorous female form, Kanshah flexed his arms, turned around again, gaining better balance and control. The other monks smiled proudly, nodding in their sky-blue robes.

In the young man's body, Soft Stone stepped forward, looking at the audience. "This is just our demonstration, which you have completed successfully. But I am fond of my own body, child. Can I have it back, please? You've proved yourself to us."

Again their eyes met, again they touched. They pressed ID patches together a second time, reset their identities. Kanshah heaved a sigh of relief when he caressed his own body once more. "I think I like mine better, too. I'm … used to it."

Some of the monks let out a quiet titter of laughter. The younger children moved restlessly, striving to sit still on the cold concrete floor. Monks tried to shush them. The younger wards were just at the beginning of the years of mental training, meditation, practice they would undergo at the Falling Leaves.

"You may stay in your own body as long as you wish … or trade to someone else for a time if you prefer," Soft Stone said to Kanshah, smiling. "Hopscotching is like sex—you *can* do it with anybody, but most people don't." Gripping his shoulders again, she turned him to face the students in the wide, echoing room.

Soft Stone hugged him. "I hope I've raised you well. I've given you all my love and care, and now you are ready to go out into the world. I can't even call you 'child' anymore." She gave him a papery kiss on the cheek.

"Take what you have learned, and do what you can to make this city, this land, this planet a better place. And live your own life." Garth noticed to his surprise that tears now ran from her clear blue eyes.

"I will," Kanshah promised, his voice thick. "After the rain."

—II—

Afraid to go beyond the doorway of the Falling Leaves, Garth stood beside Eduard and Teresa. He watched with a heavy heart as Kanshah walked out through the main arch, leaving the monastery forever.

Sunlight dazzled from the reflective windows of the skyscrapers and connecting walk tubes. Like iridescent insects, hovercars rode on invisible, COM-guided impedance paths through the sky. The day was so bright and colorful, it seemed an auspicious beginning for the young man's new life.

Apparently, the computer/organic matrix had achieved a victory in its dispute with hidden anti-tech terrorists. Garth wondered if that meant BTL operatives had already apprehended the troublemakers.

During his years in the Falling Leaves, Kanshah had accumulated few possessions, so he had little to pack. The monks gave him a small stipend to begin his life out in the real world, enough for him to get established. He was a new soul, a fledgling cast from his safe nest.

Straightening his back, Kanshah walked out into the bustling streets. He looked over his shoulder three separate times before he finally set his gaze forward and strode away into the metropolis....

Soft Stone stood in the entry hall behind Garth, Eduard, and Teresa, hovering over their shoulders, as if trying to keep them from growing up. Daragon pressed close to the old monk in the passageway, but he could not get nearer to the three companions.

She set her square jaw and herded Daragon back into the monastery. "Come, child. We have much work to do. You are behind even the young children in your mental studies. Perhaps today we'll make a breakthrough and you'll finally understand." Leaving Garth with his two friends, the monk called to Teresa, "Don't forget our planned study and discussion later."

"Oh, I'll be there. I promise."

After Soft Stone and Daragon had left, Garth asked, "What do you want to do when you get out of here?" Kanshah remained heavy on his mind.

"It seems so strange out there," Teresa said. "Frightening."

"Or exciting." Eduard was the only one who saw the possibilities, taking one last glance outside before they closed the heavy wooden door. "I can do a thousand things, if only I live long enough."

On her way to the immense library, Teresa passed the monastery kitchens, the clanging of pans and pots, the hiss of fires and heating elements. She heard the happy chatter, smelled hot sesame oil and spiced vegetables. Though not actually hungry, she thought of the vegetables and thought of how pleasant it would be outside in the muddy atrium gardens, tending the plants and flowers. But she had promised Soft Stone she would spend her time today in intellectual pursuits.

The monk met her at an intersection of corridors, arms crossed over her gray-robed chest. Teresa had lost track of the time and was probably late, but she had never known the old woman to be anything but a patient teacher. "Is your mind ready, child? Ready for more knowledge?"

"I wish you would help me find some answers, instead of more questions."

Soft Stone chuckled. "You're assuming I have answers to give you."

The Splinters devoted themselves to raising the castoff children who had no definable mothers and fathers, born from bodies no longer inhabited by the minds who had been inside when they originally got pregnant.

Splinters considered such children to be entirely new souls, new flames, and therefore something special. The monks shepherded their wards toward their full potential, teaching them how to sift through the esoteric knowledge buried in COM, how to hopscotch. To them, mind-swapping provided a wonderful proof. It showed indisputably that the soul, the personality, was not part of the body but merely a *passenger*.

Soft Stone was the first to admit that she didn't know God's particular plan for these special children; she would not second-guess divine judgment.

"Are you saying we are destined for greatness?" Teresa had asked once.

"Who are we to define greatness, child? You will do what you will do—change the world or just change a life. That is up to you."

She thought of Kanshah, now trying to make his own way in a strange and unknown world. "What about finding a job?"

"That is not our task." Soft Stone sounded distracted. "Everyone can do that."

As they walked down the halls of the old brewery building, Teresa was startled to see a dark-uniformed BTL sergeant standing outside the office of Chocolate, the head administrator of the monastery. Teresa had never seen Bureau representatives inside the Falling Leaves before, and she'd never before heard mild, soft-spoken Chocolate raise his voice.

"Absolutely not!" the head monk said to someone else inside his office. "We do important work here." Teresa could not see who he was talking to.

"Importance is a relative thing, sir. Many would say the work of the Bureau is even more important." The voice was calm and melodious, each word carefully enunciated. "And our needs must take precedence."

"The monastery is ours," Chocolate insisted. "We have lived and worked here for over a century. Find some other place."

"Please, Sir, uh, Chocolate, let us be realistic. You have no way of fighting the BTL, if we should determine—"

Standing rigid outside the door, the BTL guard watched Teresa and Soft Stone.

Teresa looked up at the bald woman with deep concern. "What's going on? Why is Chocolate so upset?"

Soft Stone sighed. "I want you to be inquisitive, child—but some questions should not be asked." She put a firm hand on the girl's shoulder and hastened her along. The monk's sky-blue robes and Teresa's loose, comfortable clothes whispered along the hard floor.

Teresa dodged the subject and tried to approach the topic from a different direction. "It seems odd, though, don't you think? Chocolate got his name because he's smooth and subtly pleasing—you said so. But he just sounded so angry." The roly-poly administrator was unambitious but competent. He spent his time waiting for the next cycle of life to begin, feeling no need to accomplish everything in this lifetime. He would have many more opportunities on the Great Wheel of Life.

"Some chocolate can be bitter as well, child," Soft Stone said with a wry smile. The old monk herself had been named because of her contradictory personality: she could be as soft as butter, or hard as granite. But out of soft stone came strength, the raw material for beautiful sculpture.

"I've been trying to think of what name I should take for myself," Teresa ventured with a tentative smile. "I mean, when I take my own vows in a few years."

Soft Stone paused in her tracks on the way to the library. "Don't talk so rashly." Her voice held a tone of rebuke. "When the monks choose a name, it's a solemn occasion, not a joyous one. We hold a quiet funeral ceremony for the person who forsakes the outside world, before we celebrate the rebirth of one who stays inside the monastery walls." Her blunt-featured face hardened, her forehead wrinkling as she looked down at Teresa. "We fervently hope our trainees will *not* stay with us, but go out into the world to become part of the connecting tissue of society. Your goal is to make this life as kind as possible for as many people as you can. And you can't do that from within these walls."

Hot tears came to Teresa's eyes. "But I thought it would be best if I—"

"We're not looking for new members. Child, only our failures remain here. Those of us who could not fulfill our life's work in the outside world."

Teresa couldn't believe what she was hearing. "Oh, but you're not a failure."

"I never achieved my full potential. I lived outside for years, experimenting, testing, hopscotching. Call it the brashness of youth, the pain of foolish love, but the fact is I fled back here, and I have felt like a coward ever since. Today, my only success comes from knowing that the students I teach will go out and do greater deeds than I ever managed."

She looked down at Teresa, her clear blue eyes moist. "I don't want you to take my way out. You are a new soul, a special child. You have so many more important things in store for you. Find your answers elsewhere, Teresa—but you must prepare for that day."

The library was one of Teresa's favorite places. The monks had completely redecorated and revamped one area into a museum of old books, kept more as pieces of art than as instructive tomes. Magnificent paintings, tapestries, and sculptures adorned the alcoves; the monks believed that students could learn as much by studying artwork as by delving through encyclopedia files.

Most of the work, however, was done on a labyrinth of COM filmscreens and access terminals, both voice-activated and direct-interactive. Based on organic neural-network circuits, COM was the circulatory system that ran through society. It performed the functions that everyone saw and used but never noticed: turning on street lights, circulating the air in buildings, monitoring impedance paths through the airways so that traffic flowed smoothly and safely, maintaining stable weather patterns via climate-control systems. COM held financial accounts, personnel records, and information libraries. Here in the library, a few hardworking monks assigned to database duty performed menial computer tasks for outside customers, earning money that went into the coffers of the Falling Leaves.

Students, though, were encouraged to branch out and investigate unorthodox connections, relationships between people and events, history and the future. With each generation, the Splinters believed that humanity must grow stronger, must improve itself. In the same way a muscle grows stronger only through exercise, people should actively attempt to better themselves, to understand the Universe around them.

But sheer data by itself was useless. It had to be processed, digested, and taken into each person. The monks imposed a regimen that every hour spent delving through COM be matched by another hour contemplating the new facts, and then a further hour of discussion and sharing with others. "Information and knowledge are two different things," Soft Stone had often told her.

The monk led Teresa to a milky-white touch screen, a translucent interface with the pervasive information system. Soft Stone touched the field with her fingertips, and the milky surface shifted to mother-of-pearl, then opened into a complex data/subject map. "There you are, child." Even Soft Stone looked at it with awe.

"Can COM give me the answers to why I'm here?" Teresa asked. "Like, what does it all mean? What I should do with my life?"

The computer/organic matrix was an enormous passive mind. With its thinking power equivalent to billions of minds, with eyes that could watch over even the smallest sparrow, the Splinters saw COM as a manifestation of God come to Earth—a neural network peopled by the numerous souls who entered and never came back because it was too tempting to stay there....

Soft Stone touched the information outlet. "Of course, child. Inside here you can find Heaven."

—III—

Attic room, dusty shadows, the scent of mildewed rafters like a moist forest floor. Ancient papers, boxes filled with mysteries ...

The brewery/monastery was so large that Eduard had convinced himself the monks barely remembered the room at all. He couldn't picture Soft Stone or chubby Chocolate squeezing into the crawlspace above the cleaning closet. Rung after painted metal rung had been mounted into the sloppily mortared brick wall, under the topmost eaves. The Falling Leaves had many forgotten spaces, little rooms, sealed closets—and the monks were too few or too incurious to investigate them all.

Daragon still followed Eduard like a puppy, eager to do things with him, but still uneasy about breaking any rules. The half-circle window leading onto the rooftops remained ajar from Eduard's rainy adventure a few nights earlier. Now a shaft of sunlight spilled in like melted butter; tiny dust motes sparkled in the air.

They had no studies assigned until late that afternoon, and both of them had done their chores at daybreak. "Soft Stone will never bother to track where we are. No problem. *Now* will you go with me into the city?" Eduard said, already prepared to heave a sigh of disappointment. "There's so much to explore."

Daragon's eyes flicked back and forth, searching for excuses. "Why me? Why doesn't Garth go with you?"

Eduard shrugged. "He wants to stay inside and work on some kind of secret art project." Though skeptical, he took Garth's wishes at face value. Daragon, though, wouldn't get off the hook so easily. "I want you to come with me. I can show you some great places."

"But what if we're caught?"

"Then we'll get sent back here. And if we don't go, we'll be stuck here anyway." Eduard swung open the wrought-iron window frame and drank in a deep breath of the bright air. "Besides, I want to get something for Teresa. Something special. Don't you want to help me? For her?"

And with that, Daragon was helpless. He wanted so desperately to be with Eduard and always looked so longingly at Teresa. Eduard used the knowledge without mercy.

Without looking back, he slipped through the window like a cat and dropped onto the rooftop with Daragon at his heels. Glancing down, he saw the streets four stories below—and was taken aback to see two BTL patrols stationed in clear view of the monastery. The Beetles did nothing threatening, barely even moved, simply made certain their presence was visible.

"Hey, what are they doing here?" Eduard asked. "They seem to be paying a lot of attention to us lately."

"Maybe the Bureau is just protecting us. Remember the storm, and those explosions last month."

"Protecting us? Yeah, right." Eduard snorted. "Just don't let them catch us now."

Keeping low, they scampered along in the sunlight, confident of their footing, over to where the old brick wall pressed against a new structure. They climbed an access ladder onto a connective walkway, then scrambled into the neighboring high-rise.

Daragon nearly stumbled, unaccustomed to the moving mechanical walkways inside the strange modern building. Eduard propped him up against the press of pedestrians, couriers, business people. He and Daragon wore plain brown clothes, unremarkable, unnoticeable.

A woman strutted by dressed in scarlet, surrounded by a haze of spicy perfume that was both provocative and stifling. A squat man with drab clothes and a clunky body that smelled of sweat worked at cleaning the curved transparent walls on the high walktube.

Daragon had been outside the monastery before on specific

errands, but never without an attentive escort. Never unbridled. Eduard reveled in the risky freedom, but tried to cover his sense of wonder with a blanket of nonchalance.

They took a stairlift up to a level with polished synthetic stone floors and windows filled with sparkling merchandise. The galleria held shop after shop of jewelry, trinkets, clothes, candles, and ornaments. Upscale showplaces held sculptures, some of them holographic and some fashioned out of dried stone-gels. Sensory fountains splashed hypnotic music and light into the air. People milled about, not even noticing their surroundings.

Daragon could barely walk, absorbed in everything he saw. "Are we going to get something for Teresa here? Would she want any of these things?"

Eduard laughed and clapped his companion on the back. "Yeah, right! Not this stuff—we don't have any credits to buy it with. Besides, Teresa wouldn't know what to do with jewelry or a holographic sculpture." He took Daragon by the arm. "Come on, let's take the descent tube down to street level. That's where we'll see the really interesting things."

Outside again, at the lowest street level, Eduard stared up at the towering buildings all around, a forest of mirrored glass, polished stone, gleaming metal. Walls were colored with finger paintings of chameleon pigment or daubed with neon tracings. Elevators rode on the inside and outside of skyscrapers like deep-sea diving bells.

Greenways ran down the centers of the boulevards, adorned with trees and flower boxes and fountain/irrigation systems. Higher up, between the buildings, hovercars skimmed across the skyways in an orderly fashion, guided by COM flow control. With little ground vehicle traffic, the streets were a domain of people.

Eduard pointed to a lonely-looking recruiting station next to a line of exotic food vendors. "What do you think, Daragon? Should we go join the Defense Forces?" He couldn't even begin to imagine Daragon as a soldier.

Eduard had recently watched a popular entertainment cycle, a heart-wrenching war story about brave soldiers during one of the major mid-Twentieth Century conflicts. A great general had been mortally wounded during the height of a battle, and all looked lost. Knowing the fate of his comrades was at stake, a quiet infantryman (who had been a coward through most of the story) selflessly sacrificed himself by hopscotching with his general, dying in his place so that the military leader could lead the troops to a spectacular victory. Great drama.

Eduard thought, however, that the Twentieth-century wars had occurred long before anyone had learned how to swap minds. Such historical details didn't seem to bother the entertainment industry.

"But why would I want to be a soldier?" Daragon asked, genuinely perplexed. "What do we need to fight for?"

Though Eduard paid little attention to current politics, he vaguely knew about the economic golden age brought about through the pervasive efficiency of COM. The computer/organic matrix ran day-to-day details of the metropolis far better than human committees and workforces ever could.

Farther down the street, he and Daragon stopped in front of the bizarre and compelling edifice of Club Masquerade, a mind-boggling swirl of lights and sounds and tantalizing glimpses. As Eduard stepped onto the sidewalk, embedded panels lit up glowing score numbers in a dazzling retro-imitation of a child's hopscotch game. Captivated, he looked at the unmarked arches that led into the Club. "I don't suppose we're old enough to go in there. Not until we learn how to hopscotch."

Daragon's eyes narrowed with distress. "Stay away from that place, Eduard. There's too much chaos, a haze of body-swapping and strange people."

Eduard shrugged. "Sounds exciting to me. Think of all the opportunities."

They sat on a sun-warmed flowstone bench, partly to rest but mainly just to watch the world. Eduard stared across the greenway, where sycamore leaves fluttered in a faint breeze; a young man sat under the tree, studying some sort of hand-held game. Two skaters coasted by, hand in hand. Shadows flickered like strobe lights across the sunlight as a broken string of hovercars hummed overhead.

Eduard watched people passing through the skyscraper doorways, friends chatting in outdoor cafes, suspicious shapes lurking in alleys or slipping quickly from beneath one awning to another. He watched a well-dressed man walk carefully and furtively, edging along the building walls. Eduard wondered if the man was unaccustomed to a new body, or if he had something to hide....

"Hey, have you ever heard of the Phantoms?" he asked, startling Daragon.

"You mean, those ... immortal people? It's just a myth."

Eduard pressed his lips together. "People who hopscotch bodies again and again in order to outrun death. They keep trading themselves into younger bodies, more healthy physiques. Staying alive. Doing whatever it takes. Sometimes they even have to steal bodies. Permanent transfers."

Daragon wasn't so credulous. "Nobody has any proof of that, Eduard. The Beetles would know about it, wouldn't they? Nobody really believes the Phantoms exist."

Eduard kept watching the furtive stranger until the man passed around a corner, lost in the crowd. "Well, I sure *want* to believe. Some of the Phantoms are supposed to be five and six hundred years old."

"But people haven't even known how to hopscotch for that long!"

Eduard refused to give up hope. "Okay, so maybe the first Phantoms learned how to swap bodies decades before anybody else, so they had to hide their abilities, go underground." His eyes gleamed. "Maybe they kidnapped other bodies, swapped minds, and then staged the death of their old selves. No one would ever know."

For a true Phantom to stay alive for centuries, such a person would have to maintain an extremely low profile, a quiet existence, leaving no trail and attracting no attention. It sounded like quite a challenge to him, an exciting one.

Sitting on the bench, Eduard decided that he wanted to become a Phantom. The mythical group had beaten the system, and he wanted to follow in their footsteps. "It would be like a candle flame passed from wick to wick, never burning out, no matter how many lumps of wax you leave behind."

Daragon remained clearly skeptical, but could find no immediate counter-argument.

Eduard pointed to a stranger haggling with a food vendor across the street. "If they can doctor their ID patches, how would you ever know? That man there could be a Phantom." He indicated a woman climbing into her hovercar parked at a charging terminal. "Or *she* could be one. Or that other man with the green shirt. Or that old couple, keeping their heads down, just waiting for their chance to swap into new and healthy bodies."

Daragon eyed every person his friend pointed out, but shook his head each time. Finally, he said, "Can't you just … *recognize* people? See into their heart and soul?"

Eduard looked at him strangely. "Even the Beetles need scanners and equipment to figure that out."

Daragon focused on the strangers across the street. "I don't."

"Yeah, right."

For years now, Soft Stone had been troubled by Daragon and his inability to succeed in even the simplest of mental training exercises. He was so far behind his age group, she had begun to despair of him ever learning. Perhaps Daragon was just imagining a new skill, something he knew others couldn't do.

Eduard got up from the bench. "Let's go. We still have to find something for Teresa before we get back to the monastery."

Weaving their way across a crowded intersection, Eduard and Daragon both saw the flower market at the same time, and suddenly they knew that *this* was what they wanted for Teresa.

The open-air market was a profusion of colors and scents: bouquets of pink, white, and yellow carnations wrapped in green paper; long-stemmed roses as red as blood mixed with delicate highlights of baby's breath; tulips, daffodils, even exotic orchids. Gladiolas and hollyhocks stood out like spears of color. Genetically modified exotics stood out in a garish profusion of neon or metallic colors, selective scents ranging from peppermint to clove. Any combination was possible. Honey bees, unable to resist the enticing perfumes, danced through the air, sluggish with the heady abundance.

"But we don't have any money," Daragon whispered. Brought up in the monastery with all their needs taken care of, they had no credits of their own. "How are we going to buy flowers? Will someone just give them to us?"

Eduard looked at him with scorn. "We wait for our opportunity."

They walked along the aisles of flowers, sniffing some, fingering others. The monastery had its own high-density garden in the inner courtyard, where the monks tended herbs and vegetables; but they planted very few flowers. Teresa loved to work with the plants, and

Eduard knew she would delight in the transient, delicate beauty of these roses, or even daisies or carnations. He kept his eyes open.

Some of the daisies had been silica-enhanced so they would never wilt. A midnight-blue rose opened from a perfect bud to full bloom, then collapsed back into a bud again, cycling in a single minute. The day was peaceful and bright, the conversations and customers relaxed and friendly.

Then, when the substation explosion ripped through the air, the people were too stunned to show fear.

The unexpected blast tore a hole through the side of a building, two stories up, obliterating a COM traffic-control substation. Chunks of stone, glass, and hot metal rained down as bystanders on the street scrambled for safety. A restaurant's striped awning caught on fire.

With the disruption of COM, the interleaved skylanes of hovercars swirled like a stirred anthill, then safety systems kicked in, grounding most of the vehicles down in a rapid precaution, filling the crowded streets.

The safety systems lost only one hovercar. Three stories directly above the wrecked substation, the topaz-blue vehicle veered from its impedance path, slipped through the protective electronic net, and plummeted like a juggernaut into the sidewalk. The topaz-blue vehicle scraped the side of a building as it fell, then exploded into a taqueria across the street from the flower market.

People screamed and ran about. Eduard could see the flaming hulk of the crashed hovercar, a mangled man trapped inside and flailing to free himself. Some ran toward the scene, some fled, while others remained frozen and watching.

Daragon couldn't believe what he was seeing. "It's the terrorists again!"

Thinking fast in the moment of utter chaos, Eduard snatched a mixed bouquet of color-coded carnations, chrysanthemums, rainbow-petaled daisies, and talking daffodils. He didn't have time to be choosy. Huddled around the flowers to block them from the view of the stall owner, he snapped at Daragon. "Come on, let's go!"

Daragon instinctively ran with him down the streets, but looked at Eduard in shock. "You didn't tell me we were going to steal anything."

"How else was I going to get them? What were you thinking?"

Eduard wasn't without a conscience, but he did have his sense of priorities. "Besides, flowers grow free from plants—the vendors can just grow more, so don't worry about it. Remember who the bouquet is for."

Daragon swallowed hard, still reluctant. "All right, but *I* get to give her the flowers."

Eduard shook his head, not even willing to bargain. "You had your chance. You could have grabbed some for yourself. No problem."

In the end, they agreed to divide the spoils between them. With their prize flowers in hand, Eduard and Daragon raced back to the monastery.

—IV—

In the basement of the old monastery building, Garth found his spot of hidden solitude behind the thick, long-unused pipes: a small utility closet that had been blocked shut when new plumbing systems were installed years before the Splinters took over the structure. This shadowy, timeless room had remained undisturbed since the building had been a functioning brewery.

Garth had found it, pried it open, looked inside.

Over the years as he wandered around the building, Garth studied the monastery's empty rooms and alcoves, using his imagination to envision chambers crammed with giant vats, boilers and fermenting containers, malting bins, roasters, and bottling lines, as well as a shipping room and business offices.

Down in this untouched cell, each wall only a couple of meters long, Garth could smell the *past*, mystical odors that reminded him of the Charles Dickens novels he had read to Kanshah and now had to enjoy by himself. Garth had kept this spot secret even from Teresa and Eduard.

But once his project was completed, he would no longer need to keep it to himself.

Even in childhood he had been fascinated by the artwork and sculptures that filled the monastery library, the dining hall, the corridor alcoves. All the colors seemed so intense to Garth, the shapes of the statues and paintings so sharp and complex, the details so intricate.

He could spend an hour marveling at the contours of a single sculpture, while Eduard would grow impatient after minutes, seeing what was there but unable to grasp anything more. But Eduard had gone off with Daragon today, no doubt to do something brash and unexpected.

Teresa spent the afternoon in the library, searching for her own answers. She was the person most likely to understand the calling of art, he thought, and he would show the painting to her first.

Now, trying to repay the kindness of Soft Stone and the Splinter caretakers, Garth had taken it upon himself to paint a special mural covering the walls of the cramped utility room. He had created a wonder-filled scene from his imagination, based upon what he knew of the history of the Falling Leaves.

He had researched what he could find of old breweries, adding details from 19th Century novels. Ignoring the unevenness of the mortar and bricks, he had painted a winter scene that reminded him of classic Currier & Ives holiday prints. Horse-drawn carts pulled up to take large barrels of Trappist ale brewed by brown-robed monks who stood at the brewery's loading dock. Wagons dodged automobiles on the cobblestone streets. Portly men in top hats sang Christmas carols under a gas street lamp next to an elevated railway.

Garth made each detail as real as he could, using exuberant but unpracticed abilities as a painter. He had been working on the mural for weeks, originally attempting only a small idyllic scene, with only a few jars of paints he had found. But as he worked, he thought of more and more things to add, other characters, other buildings, thinly disguised renditions of the high-tech skyscrapers he could see out of the monastery windows. He kept intending to put finishing touches in place, to call his mural complete. But then he thought of just one more idea, and then another.

By the light of an unfiltered glowtile, Garth set to work, dipping his brushes in the swirls of color. He became engrossed in the world behind his eyes, bringing to life the panorama he saw in his imagination. He could almost smell the wet snow, the horses, the rich ale pouring into the oak-slatted kegs....

"I cannot believe my eyes!" a firm male voice said, startling Garth so badly that he dropped his paintbrush. "Young man, what have you done to this place?"

Garth turned to see one of the monks, a stern weathered man named Hickory, hardened and strong. Before he could answer, Hickory's voice grew more strident. "I noticed the light down here, but I never expected to see … this! Who gave you permission?"

"I just wanted to create something nice," Garth said. "I'm almost finished. I was going to show everyone when I was done."

"Well, you shouldn't have started in the first place." Hickory crossed his arms over his chest. "Don't we give you enough chores to keep you busy? It's easy to see what sort of mischief idle hands can work."

Garth didn't know how to respond. "But … *look* at it. It's not vandalism—this is art."

"When you paint all over a wall you don't own, with no permission from anyone, it is called *vandalism*. Come with me. We'd better see Chocolate right away."

Unfortunately, the monastery's administrator didn't know what to do with him, either. So much of the children's training had been carefully planned, set forth according to an idealized schedule. The soft-spoken, round old monk seemed greatly distracted, his brow creased with worry, his shoulders sagging as if from a heavy burden.

"Oh, why don't we just let him paint scenes on *all* the walls?" Chocolate said with a hint of exasperation. Garth didn't think his own actions were responsible for the somber mood. "Maybe then the Bureau won't want this place after all. We don't have any other way to fight them."

"Sir!" the other monk said. "We can't encourage this sort of—"

Chocolate waved one of his pudgy hands. "All right, all right. This is really not a very good time, Hickory." He sighed, looking at the papers on his desk, the messages. "I suggest we merely have young Garth repaint all the walls in a plain color so that the room can be usable again, if ever we decide to use it."

Garth's knees became weak at hearing the devastating punishment, though no doubt the mild-mannered administrator had not intended it to be so serious.

"But … don't you even want to look at what I've done, sir?"

"No need," Chocolate said, already engrossed in a weighty, official-looking document on his desk. "I'm sure it's wonderful. You're a very talented young man, Garth, but you must learn to respect certain boundaries."

Now the beige paint smelled sour and acrid, and Garth swathed it on with a thick, inelegant brush. The horse carts vanished under a layer of drab tan. Rosy-cheeked Trappist monks continued to gulp their foamy brew as he painted right over their faces.

Garth paused, and the brush trembled in his hand. He managed to keep the tears balanced inside his eyelids, not letting them spill down his cheek. He dipped the brush into the bucket again, then swabbed across the rough bricks.

Hickory had spent the first half hour watching him in silence, not taunting him, just remaining firm and stern. Garth didn't argue with the monk, though he wished he had been able to show Eduard and Teresa before erasing his wall.

"That's very good, from what I can still see of it," Soft Stone said from behind him in the dim basement.

Garth took a moment to compose himself before he turned to face her. "You should have been here before I covered all the good parts."

"Your mural is still there, behind the paint."

He stood with the brush dripping round circles of beige on the floor. "But no one can see it. I can't show it to anybody. Isn't that what art is for?"

The woman nodded her smooth head. "In part, child. Art is about sharing and communication, yes, but that's not the only thing. Recall the concept of process versus product. Did *you* learn from it?"

He swallowed hard. "You told me to learn from everything I do."

"And?"

"And, yes, I learned from it, I suppose. I enjoyed doing it, too."

"Then it's not a total loss." Soft Stone smiled. "An artist needs to do more than just create scenes that are pleasing to the eye."

"How?" He glanced with dismay at his half-defaced mural.

"Use your art as a lens for viewing all facets of life. To draw or paint things, you can't just imitate what you see. You must first *understand* the things. Give your art a life of its own."

Garth didn't comment at first, brushing more thick paint across the bricks. With two strokes he covered part of a street. He had spent hours meticulously painting each individual cobblestone. Now, he obliterated them all in less than a minute.

"Would you like me to help you?" Soft Stone asked. "Together we'll be finished in half the time."

In all the years he had spent at the Falling Leaves, Soft Stone had never offered to help with his assigned chores. But it was hard enough to do this task, and Garth didn't think he could bear to watch another person paint over the scenes into which he had poured his efforts. It would be like watching someone else erase his very soul.

"No, I think I should do this myself. It's my responsibility." Then he paused and turned to look at her. "Besides, it'll give me time to think about what you said. About art, I mean."

Content, Soft Stone disappeared into the basement shadows with a whisper of sky-blue robes.

—V—

Teresa lay in darkness, surrounded by the peaceful sounds of sleeping companions: warm breaths, quiet snores, the rustle of blankets, bodies stirring under sheets. Her eyes were open, but she could see only vague forms, nothing clear and definite.

Like her understanding of life itself.

Next to her in the communal sleeping quarters, Garth breathed heavily, deep in his dreams, while Eduard tossed and turned on the other side of her, restless as usual. He had one arm sprawled on her narrow bed, and she touched the back of his hand, gently circling his dim ID patch. Eduard mumbled quietly, but did not awaken.

Daragon slept on the opposite side of the room. In an adjacent chamber, the younger children muttered, sound asleep; one whimpered quietly, perhaps after a nightmare. In the corridors, the monks moved about, watchful. Beyond the walls, the night city made its own music, completely separated from the world of the Falling Leaves.

Teresa lay awake, wondering, empty inside, needing

something.... She blinked, but nothing became clearer. *What does it all mean?*

Here she was surrounded by people just like herself, young men and women she had grown up with, experimental lovers, or friends, or both. They had all been brought here as infants, like items donated for a white elephant sale. The monks accepted them as gifts, raised them without last names. They taught the children to develop their inner strengths, to know their minds and their bodies. Practical survival skills could come later, once they found themselves outside in the real world.

Teresa was curious about where she came from, why her biological parents had chosen to place her in the Falling Leaves rather than raise her. Here, none of her friends had a family, a background.

Garth and Eduard didn't worry about it. They lived for themselves, looking forward instead of back, without an undue fascination about their parentage; Daragon, on the other hand, was practically obsessed; in his private moments with Teresa, he fantasized quietly about his never-seen mother and father. He needed to know where he had come from, why he was different from the other children.

The almond-eyed young man was incapable of even the simplest mind tricks that the other trainees could do. Nearly a year older than Teresa, Eduard, or Garth, Daragon would soon have to face his mental testing, like Kanshah—and as yet he showed no indication of being able to hopscotch.

Teresa was worried about him.

In the dimness, she turned to look at her small bedside table, at the two crude vases—water glasses, actually—that held the separate, long-lasting bouquets Daragon and Eduard had brought her over a week ago....

She recalled when the two had approached her, proud and beaming. They had jockeyed forward, each trying to be the first to hand her a colorful profusion of decorative flowers, more beautiful than any of the blossoms she had tended in the monastery garden.

"We got these for you," Eduard said, his voice low as he thrust the bouquet forward.

"But you can't tell Soft Stone," Daragon insisted.

She had taken the flowers, sniffing the exotic perfume. They stood in a side hallway, next to an open window that looked down on the courtyard surrounded by mossy brick walls. Garth had been walking with Teresa, troubled inside, his clothes and hair smelling of fresh paint. Now he watched, content just to see Teresa happy.

"We thought you might like them," Daragon had said, and Teresa was careful to take the flowers he offered with as much enthusiasm as she had taken Eduard's. "We really weren't supposed to—"

"We wanted to make you smile, Teresa," Eduard said. "And that's all that counts."

Delighted, she hugged both of them. She sat down on the flowstone window bench. Outside, she could hear monks and children pulling weeds, hoeing the dirt, ready to plant more vegetables.

Excited, Eduard chattered breathlessly about their adventures on the streets, while Daragon added his own impressions. He was still greatly shaken by the terrorist explosion and the hovercar wreck they had witnessed. "I wonder if the man inside survived," he said. "He looked very badly hurt."

"And I think we saw a Phantom," Eduard interrupted. He lifted his chin proudly. "*I* want to sneak around when I get out of here, swapping from body to body so I can live five hundred years."

Teresa frowned at him over the colorful flowers. "You want to become a Phantom just for the sake of adding years onto your age? There's got to be more to life than that, don't you think?"

Though they were her closest friends, Teresa felt somehow separate. She was the one who stared into the sky and looked at clouds, who pondered the imponderable. "What happens after death? Why are we here? Does what we do *matter*? Where do we go?"

She said carefully, "For every year you add to your own life, you have to take it away from someone else's, Eduard, by using their body. Don't you think?"

Daragon gave a solemn nod, but Teresa suspected he agreed with her out of habit. She often took him under her wing, because he listened to her complex spiritual ramblings, while Garth and Eduard didn't have the same patience or fascination. Daragon liked to hear her talk, but he didn't really understand either.

"I doubt that just surviving to a greater age will help me toward any kind of enlightenment," she continued.

Eduard looked uncomfortable. "Now you're talking like Soft Stone."

Garth looked out the window down into the garden. "Phantoms ... The prospect is interesting," he said in a detached, somehow dejected voice. He found many new ideas interesting. "But since none of us is old enough to hopscotch at all, why worry about how many centuries you'll be able to do it?"

Eduard had been disturbed that his close friends did not see the obvious possibilities and the challenges. "We'll come of age soon enough. Then it'll matter."

Now, at night in the communal sleeping quarters, Teresa stirred, eyes wide. In the dimness she could discern the sleeping forms of Garth and Eduard, lost in their own dreams, their own worlds.

She envied both of them. It would be a long time before she herself got to sleep....

—VI—

The next morning, Soft Stone stood just inside the monastery doorway, blocking their exit. Sternly, she pressed her shoulders against the closed doors as she faced Eduard, Garth, Teresa, and Daragon. Only small amounts of light drifted through the narrow upper windows, leaving the entry hall in shadow.

Eduard was uneasy, but curious as to what the bald female monk had in mind. Soft Stone had never acted this way before. Garth and Teresa looked equally perplexed, while Daragon seemed intimidated at the thought of what their teacher would do to them.

"You are all eager to explore the city, wondering exactly what's beyond the places we've shown you." Her smooth eyebrows arched, but her voice held a sharp edge, not entirely warm and understanding. "And at your age it's probably good that you learn ... learn a lesson."

Eduard swallowed hard. She knew something.

"I need you to run an errand for me." She pursed her papery

lips. "I'm sure you can handle it without an escort—correct, Eduard?"

"Uh, yeah ... right," Eduard said, his ears burning. Garth and Teresa glanced at each other, then at him. Daragon blinked, as if hoping he might escape some dire punishment.

"I am going to give you some credits. Go out and buy flowers for all of the monks. Get several bouquets so we can brighten up the monastery. I think you know where to go, don't you?"

Eduard's stomach clenched, but he knew better than to lie in front of the old woman. "No problem."

"Take Garth and Teresa and find a particularly good flower seller. In fact, you may want to pay him a little extra for whatever you purchase today. Does that sound fair?" Her voice was hard, devastating. She *knew*! Somehow, she knew exactly what he and Daragon had done the day before.

"That would be ... fair." He kept his voice even. He had stolen the flowers for the best of reasons. Teresa had been so happy ... and it wasn't as if the flower seller had ever noticed.

But Soft Stone had noticed.

"And you, Daragon." She turned toward the dark-haired boy. "If you weren't so far behind in your mental studies, I'd make you go along with them. Instead, you're going to spend the morning with me, in intensive practice. Your testing comes very soon now. We cannot delay it much longer."

Daragon lowered his head. "Yes, Soft Stone."

The bald woman opened the heavy door, and a flood of daylight poured in. Eduard stepped forward, anxious to be away from the Falling Leaves—though it didn't feel much like triumph, now that the monk had actually let him go out and explore.

Directly in front of the old brewery stood a uniformed officer from the Bureau of Tracing and Locations. The Beetle turned and met Soft Stone's gaze with smug confidence and a hint of challenge.

The gently reproving and instructive expression the monk had used on her young wards suddenly changed to one of anger. "What are you doing here? This is our building. Leave us alone." She crossed her arms over her chest, and Eduard was startled by Soft Stone's quick vehemence. "Shouldn't you be out finding someone, or tracing a missing body?"

"I'm currently on routine duty," the officer said, his voice flat.

"Your purpose would be better served if you tracked down those saboteurs who blew up a COM substation last week. Two of my children were almost killed in that accident."

Eduard froze and looked back at Daragon, their eyes wide with guilt.

"We anticipate apprehending the perpetrators today," he said. "There is an operation pending." The Beetle turned back to face the streets, but he did not move away from the Falling Leaves.

"Stay far from him," Soft Stone said.

The Beetle didn't even waste a glance on the three sixteen-year-olds as they slid past him. The old monk clutched Daragon's arm and closed the massive door with a heavy thud....

"This way." Eduard slipped past the Beetle. "I can show you where the accident happened last week."

"And don't forget the flowers," Garth added. "That's what we're supposed to be doing."

The tension passed as they walked down the boulevards, staring up at the unbroken flow of hovercars and connecting transport tubes. High overhead, skycraft etched white lines against the blue. The clouds were gone. Apparently COM had no weather dispute to offer this day.

Since they rarely set foot beyond the Falling Leaves, Garth caught his breath at the kaleidoscope of details, colors, smells. He was astounded by the architecture, the trickling beauty of fountains, the greenery of shrubs and trees. He and Eduard each folded one of Teresa's arms in their own, flanking her.

The inseparable trio walked unnoticed among the other pedestrians. Soft Stone had made sure they chose nondescript clothes, none of the robes or symbol trinkets the Splinters wore during ceremonies. Now they looked just like normal teenagers, though a bit more wide-eyed and naive.

Teresa noticed another group of religious followers, and she turned toward them, feeling a tug of curiosity. She wanted to talk to them, question them, learn about their philosophy. She wondered how their beliefs differed from what the Splinters encouraged, and what she herself had gleaned from searching through the monastery's great databases.

Eduard squeezed her elbow to his side and pointed, oblivious to her fascination with the group. "Look, that's where we saw the explosion."

The side of a building had been scarred with black flames and smoke. A blossom of windows had shattered around the midpoint of the blast. A crowd had gathered behind barricade tape to watch the crews cleaning up the sidewalks, repairing the torn and burned awnings. The taqueria hit with shrapnel was sealed up for repairs.

Mag-lock scaffolding hung on the sides of the skyscraper, while workers sliced off shards of mirrored glass, careful to store them in remanufacturing bins, so the deadly crystalline spears wouldn't rain upon the pedestrians below.

"Daragon and I saw the hovercar crash right there. You can still see where the pavement's been wrecked."

"Look at that." Garth stared at the site, deeply moved. Then he glanced at the cobblestones, seeing a damp and scuffed leaflet, a discarded tract that looked as if it had been printed on a hand-cranked press. *Stop COM Now! Become a person again!* Garth picked it up, disturbed and confused by the terrorists, perplexed as to what drove them. "I wonder what they really want." All the exclamation points hurt his eyes.

Eduard looked at him. "Some people are afraid of change, even if it increases convenience for just about everybody else. I think they want to destroy what they don't understand." He tore the paper out of his friend's hand, crumpled it. "Don't read that stuff, either of you."

"Let's get the flowers now." Garth's voice wavered as he turned his back on the blackened scar of the crash site. "I want to look at something beautiful instead of destruction."

He sniffed and turned to find the small plaza filled with a jungle of cut blossoms. Perfumes and bright colors bombarded his senses, and he took them in stride, filing the details away as experiences to be remembered.

"Hey, you need both ends of the spectrum for a balanced picture of life," Eduard said.

"So let's get the other end of the spectrum," Teresa said.

They walked among the bouquets, the tall stalks, the ferns. Other customers selected artificially colored daisies, sniffed carnations, haggled over roses. Behind the kiosks, workers arranged clumps of flowers, sorted irises by color, trimmed away drooping blossoms and placed them in organic recyclers. They wrapped up special floral arrangements, altered scents and grafted-on petals. They added ribbons, audio greeting buttons, sparkling crystals, or mirrored glass ornaments.

Eduard lowered his eyes in unaccustomed embarrassment when he saw the vendor from whom he had snatched Teresa's bouquet. The man glanced at him without the slightest pause. Eduard felt an electric shock pass through his heart, but the vendor didn't notice.

Uncharacteristically shy, Eduard selected several large bouquets from the vendor's shelves and nudged Teresa to do the same. Garth was puzzled that Eduard would choose so many from a single merchant, but the flower seller was delighted with the sales, especially when Eduard insisted on a more than fair price. The flower seller added a few extra stalks of magenta humming gladiolas to round out the purchase.

Eduard felt good after having made amends, though the flower seller didn't know what had happened. Teresa's arms were filled with a richness of flowers, and Garth smelled them, enraptured. Eduard breathed a sigh of relief, knowing Soft Stone would be proud of how he had handled the situation.

He looked up at the tall buildings—and was the first to see the gunmetal-gray BTL hovercraft cruise into position midway up the skyscraper. It hung directly above the flower market. "Hey, look up there. Something's going on."

Garth and Teresa watched as the ominous craft cruised down to a specific level in the tall building and maneuvered up against the mirrored glass. A rubber-lipped transfer tube extended, sealing itself against the window. Even from far below, Eduard could hear cutting sounds, grinding like saw-powered sharks' teeth. The Beetles had found someone.

Many of the customers and vendors in the flower market stopped to observe. The murmur of background conversation changed, like an indrawn breath.

Muffled by distance, Eduard heard a few faint projectile shots—but he couldn't tell if the weapons fire came from fugitives inside the domicile, or from the Beetles themselves.

Suddenly one of the windows adjacent to the besieged apartment smashed outward, a blast of small charges placed on the reflective glass. The entire window shot free, spraying shards to the streets below. Pedestrians screamed and ducked under awnings, kiosks, and tables; others didn't manage to escape, their arms thrown up for protection, their skin sliced by the broken edges.

Four people sprang out of the smashed window. For a moment, Eduard thought they were leaping to their deaths just to escape apprehension by the Beetles—but then he saw that they had attached snake-like cords to themselves, flexible rappelling ropes anchored inside the room. The four escapees flew down, magnetic pulleys humming as they plummeted to street level.

Above them, the BTL gunship opened fire with a cloud of stun projectiles, shattering other windows in the building. One of the escaping fugitives slammed against the skyscraper wall, leaving a splash of blood on the mirrorglass. His arms and legs hung limp, and he spun down, slowed by the automatic rappelling gears, still dropping like a counterweight.

The others continued downward, bouncing off the sides of the building, picking up speed.

Another window cracked; more gunfire erupted. The fugitives were using real armaments, and the Beetles rapidly switched from stun projectiles to seeker bullets. More uniformed BTL officers rushed from side streets, weapons ready, prepared to apprehend the three remaining escapees as they reached the sidewalk.

The people ran about pell-mell, knocking over flower kiosks, rushing for shelter inside buildings across the square. Amid the confusion Eduard could easily have snatched up another armful of flowers, but he decided not to.

Besides, it was more interesting to watch this operation.

In the previous week's incident, the anti-COM terrorists must have set explosives right across the street from their own hideout. This small group had incurred the wrath of the computer/organic matrix and brought about the recent terrible storm. Now the Bureau would finish the matter.

The three survivors hit the sidewalks with bent legs and snapped off their elastic ropes. Released of tension, the cables spun back up to the higher level, flailing like angry cobras. In unison, moving with well-practiced ease, the fugitives tore off their outer shirts, revealing different colored clothes underneath, bland street clothes. Even while dodging weapons fire, even in plain sight, they threw the tattered garments into the crowd. They each ran in separate directions.

The Beetles ran to apprehend the three before they could get away. Eduard had a prime view, watching the fugitives rush in separate directions, moving in a drunkard's walk to keep their flight from being predictable.

One of the three, a redheaded woman, spotted another key person in the crowd who hid under one of the vendor stands, who raised his hands in some kind of signal. The man was a plant in the crowd, someone there watching and spying. The redhead rushed to him and bent down.

Eduard tugged Garth's arm to get his attention, but the other young man was too astounded by the whole event. "Look at that," Garth said.

The fugitive woman and the man hiding under the kiosk clasped each other's temples, quickly locking eyes. Eduard noticed with a shock that neither of them had ID patches on the backs of their hands, just a small squarish scar. Then the redhead got up and ran in another direction, while the man quietly sauntered into one of the buildings, disappearing from view.

Eduard couldn't believe what he had just seen. "They hopscotched, the two of them! She had a contact in the crowd, and she got away." He laughed in surprise. "That woman swapped identities with him and then ran!"

Another of the fugitives ran like a bull through the flower stands, knocking over buckets that held long-stemmed roses, upending pots of marigolds. Teresa stood alone, still with the bouquet in her arms, unable to move. The fugitive grabbed her, hissed in her face so forcefully that spittle shone on her cheeks. "Hopscotch!" he said. "Now! *Swap with me!*"

Teresa looked up at the flushed man. "I ... I can't. I'm not old enough." The man let out a snarl of despair and outrage.

Beetles ran toward them, shouting, firing their weapons into the air and making a fearful racket. The man looked around wildly again, then grabbed Teresa's arm out of desperation.

Garth's jaw dropped open, seeing Teresa in peril. He couldn't move, overwhelmed like a deer in the headlights.

But Eduard knew instantly that the fugitive meant to take her as a hostage. He didn't stop to think about himself or his danger.

"Teresa!" Eduard sprang forward, bending his shoulder down. He plowed into her with enough force to rip her out of the fugitive's grip. As the man squawked in surprise and anger, Eduard bore her down to the pavement, covering Teresa with his own body. The beautiful fresh flowers flew around her in a blizzard of color, petals, and scents.

Then the Beetles targeted on the lone fugitive as he whirled, empty-handed, searching for another means of escape. The Beetles opened fire into his chest, a mixture of stun projectiles and deadly bullets.

Eduard rolled with Teresa, protecting her, holding her tightly. One more shot rang out, and the terrorist flew backward, scraping across the ground as blood poured from holes in his new disguise shirt. Darts poked out like bristles from his shoulders, sides, face.

The Beetles marched up to their victim, elbowing people away. They bent down, grabbing the dying man's collar and dragging him into a sitting position. "Where's your leader?" one demanded. "Who is she? Where is she?"

"She's not me," the man said weakly, then smiled in triumph with blood-flecked lips.

After crawling away, Eduard dragged Teresa to her feet, and she clung to him. Garth finally snapped out of his shock and moved to join them, shuddering.

"Come on." Eduard hustled his friends away from the scene. "We don't want to be here right now. None of us." For now, the Beetles were too intent on their victim to question the crowd, but that wouldn't divert them for long.

"I couldn't move," Garth said, his face pale, his hands trembling. "Teresa, I … I'm sorry. I wanted to help."

"She's all right." Eduard cut off further conversation, taking charge. "All three of us are fine. Let's move!"

He ran, remembering the clever trick the other fugitive had used to escape, and he knew this was the kind of skill he'd have to learn in order to become a Phantom one day, slipping through society and living forever. He marveled at how smoothly the fleeing redhead's plan had gone.

The three of them ducked into an office building, took a lift-tube up four levels, and hurried across a promenade. Then down a moving walkway, zigzagging through another galleria filled with stores and lights and music.

Eduard kept glancing over his shoulder, making sure they weren't being followed. "Walk slowly, casually," he said. "Don't draw any attention to yourself. We can't look like we're on the run."

They marched across a transparent tube high above the streets to a different building, then another, and finally back down again.

"But why are we running?" Garth said. "We didn't do anything."

"That man touched Teresa. They might think he swapped with her. That's how the other one escaped."

"But I'm not," Teresa said, looking down at her ID patch. "I'm still me. I don't know how—"

"Do you think someone like that would take the trouble to synch ID patches? I saw just scars on their hands." Eduard looked at her sharply, his eyes burning. "Do you want your mind peeled just so the Beetles can prove your identity? It's what they do, you know. That's what I've heard."

Garth and Teresa both shuddered, but they didn't question Eduard as he continued to lead them on a convoluted wild goose chase. They wound their way through streets that they now saw as dark and dangerous, instead of filled with wonders.

Eduard managed to lead them back to the Falling Leaves. It was only when they had reached the heavy wooden doors that Eduard realized they had not, after all, brought back the flowers Soft Stone wanted.

—VII—

When Daragon looked up into Soft Stone's clear blue eyes, he saw only concern there, an intensity that frightened him. They had made no progress in the months after the COM power outage, and he was at an age where he felt like a failure. The ability to hopscotch came easily and naturally to everyone else, but Daragon seemed to be a throwback.

He sat on a sturdy chair in the small training room; the walls were painted robin's-egg blue. The old monk pushed her rough face closer to his, within inches, boring her gaze through his skull. He watched the sinews of her jaws tighten like pulleys. Her breath on his cheeks smelled like cinnamon.

"Look at me, child. Through my eyes, into my mind. Imagine yourself *here*. Forget your body."

Daragon tried, as he had tried for years. Nothing.

Others described it as a floating sensation, shucking ethereal chains to the body, exchanging yourself with another. He waited for the light feeling, drifting, disconnecting. He knew Soft Stone had done it, that her mind was already loose, waiting to occupy his body. *He* had to make the next move.

But he could not let go.

"I can't!" Daragon said, tears brimming on his dark eyes.

"You don't feel anything? You can't sense the tugging, your soul yearning to fly?" Soft Stone had never faced such difficulty before.

He hung his head, breaking the gaze from eyes like deep glacier ice. "I can see you. I can watch your ... your aura, and I can see when you swap with someone else. But I can't do it myself."

She looked at him abruptly, a different set of thoughts plain on her face. "You can see me? How?"

He shrugged. "Can't everybody? It's obvious, the way you move, the way you ... seem. Your individual persona. I don't know how to describe it."

She held up the back of her hand. "You mean my ID patch?"

"I never need to see an ID patch. I don't really understand why they're so important."

The old woman stood up, stretched her taut back and shoulders, then touched Daragon's head. "I had begun to suspect as much." Her fingers trembled. "Wait here, child. I'm not sure there's anything more I can do for you today."

Leaving him to contemplate in the training room, Soft Stone marched out the door with a swish of her sky-blue robes, intent on an experiment, a mission. The first monk she found was dour Hickory, working in the garden. He sweated under the hazy sunlight, hacking at the ground with his hoe and then leaning on the worn wooden handle to rest. He bent over a tomato plant and plucked off a fat green horn worm.

As she came up to him, Hickory held up the caterpillar, scrutinized it, then crushed its head between his fingers. "All things must fertilize the earth." He cast the dead worm onto the ground and rubbed his fingers on the front of his ocher work robe to wipe off the mess.

"Swap with me," Soft Stone said without preamble. The Splinters occasionally hopscotched with each other, when necessary, but preferred their home-bodies.

Hickory blinked at her, as if somehow offended. "I hardly think this is the time or the place—"

"I'll determine that," she said sharply. "I need your body as part of my training work." She reached out to take the hoe from him. "Besides, you can work better with my fresh muscles. Yours look tired by now."

With a sigh, the other monk touched her, and they swapped without synching their ID patches. "I'll be right back." Hickory seemed very nonplused, but Soft Stone strode off. Then she returned to the training room. Now she smelled of sweat and dirt and warm sunshine. The ache in her male muscles came from exertion rather than age, and Hickory's eyes were sharper than her own.

As she came back in, Daragon looked up at her in the gaunt male monk's body, his expression remained dejected. She spoke in Hickory's gruff voice. "Soft Stone has asked me to continue your training."

"But ... *you're* Soft Stone." Daragon gave her a puzzled frown. "Are you trying to trick me?"

"No, child," she said. It was true, then. He *did* have the ability, an incredibly rare skill. There was something fundamentally missing in Daragon, but also something so much more. Something never before expected. "I was just testing you."

This young man would never be able to hopscotch like the others, but his special inner vision would offset the lack. And certain people would be desperate to have access to what Daragon could do. Very desperate.

"We're through for today, child. Go out in the garden and help Hickory. I'm sure he can find more chores for you to do. I have to go talk with Chocolate."

Feeling as if she had failed in her lifelong training of her young ward, Soft Stone shuffled down the hall, head hung, to see the administrator of the Falling Leaves.

At the very least perhaps the Splinters could use this to save the monastery.

For several nights afterward, Teresa held Daragon in the dark. He clung to her even after they had tenderly made love, sharing each other. Though he couldn't explain it to her, Daragon needed her more now than he ever had before.

Something was wrong, something would happen to him soon, and it terrified him. Soft Stone had refused to explain anything to him, because she seemed just as frightened, but in a different way.

She could smell their musk, feel his soft skin against her. Shifting her arm, she pulled the blanket up to cover his shoulders. Daragon wasn't asleep, though he remained silent. She looked at him. His eyes flashed against hers in the shadows, straining, as if he was trying to exercise his mind, attempting to swap with her, just to show he could do it.

But Teresa felt nothing stir, no sense of joining with him. When she did this with Garth or Eduard, she could feel the linkage, the insubstantial bonds that told her if they just continued practicing, if they could just figure out the last little secret technique, they could hopscotch with each other.

But Daragon couldn't do it. Though he was a year older and should have been more skilled, more susceptible, he seemed crippled in some way, lacking in a perfectly normal ability.

Daragon finally squeezed his eyes shut, then buried his face in the hollow of Teresa's neck. She ran her fingers through his dark hair, squeezing him tighter.

"Chocolate says he wants to see me tomorrow," Daragon finally said. "Soft Stone will be with him. I think they're bringing in outsiders."

Teresa frowned. "You mean it's your testing? They're going to do it privately, not in the main gathering hall?"

"You know I'll never succeed in my testing. I can't! I don't have a clue how to hopscotch." He drew away from her. "This is something else. I think … I think I'm going to be taken away from here."

Teresa pulled him close again, comforting him because she cared for him. They had made love before, but this was more special for him, more desperate. Though he had been with them all their lives, Daragon remained something of a mystery to her. He tried and tried to be mentally intimate.

Still, Teresa could feel stirrings of maternal instinct inside her. In a sense, it was easier to give unconditional comfort to a relative stranger than to someone with whom she shared such an intimate understanding. She shushed him, told him everything would be all right, whispered meaningless but endearing phrases in his ear. Teresa held him, but Daragon did not sleep all night, and neither did she.

Anxious, Daragon waited in the administrator's office. Soft Stone stood there beside him, offering silent strength and comfort. Chocolate paced behind his carved desk, impatient.

Daragon didn't know what to expect, what they were waiting for. Not knowing made the experience worse. He tried to hold his head up, to be brave.

"Don't worry, child," Soft Stone said. "You'll do fine." The lie was plain in her voice.

Before Daragon could get up the nerve to inquire, he heard footsteps coming down the hall, the whicker of sandals and robes, the staccato drumbeat of boot heels. One of the lesser monks, intimidated and flushed, led two Beetles into Chocolate's office, an Inspector and a Sergeant. Both wore neat uniforms with different insignia; their demeanor denoted confidence and efficiency.

"Is this an attempted bribe?" the Inspector asked directly, wasting no time.

Chocolate blew air from between his lips, genuinely shocked at the suggestion. Soft Stone stepped up beside Daragon and met the Inspector's attention. She placed her hand on the young man's shoulder. "No, sirs. But we have something to show you, something you may find interesting. Something we believe the Bureau will value highly."

Daragon looked at the uniformed men. The BTL used a broad spectrum of abilities for locating and tracking people as they moved through a society where physical appearance and identity could be made meaningless. Some of the Beetles were slightly telepathic; some were gifted database surfers with a particular rapport with COM; some were just intuitive detectives. Daragon knew he had no such talent.

But as Soft Stone explained the problem to the two Bureau representatives, their interest picked up. They looked upon Daragon's failure as a different kind of potential.

"Test him if you like," Soft Stone said. "I'm confident he will prove himself in every way I have described."

"Yes." Chocolate bustled forward, joining Soft Stone and Daragon. "While this young man is physically incapable of swapping minds, his mental abilities have instead turned inward. He's not a throwback—he's … different."

"That remains to be seen," the Inspector said as the Sergeant withdrew several pieces of scanning equipment.

Daragon looked in alarm at Soft Stone, then at the scanners, the electrodes. He wished Eduard could be here. The monk squeezed his shoulder again. "Just relax." Her voice sounded like a cold wind. "You'll do fine."

Barely managing to restrain their excitement, the Beetles ushered Daragon away. They vowed to take care of him, to give him a respected position and important work in the Bureau. He had reached the age of adulthood, but remained young enough to be malleable, to be trained in their ways. The BTL had a rigorous curriculum already designed for talented people like him.

Soft Stone hugged Daragon, trying to crush away his fear and uncertainty. She mouthed the words, repeating that the Bureau did vital work in society, that with his special skill he could be a valuable asset. The BTL would treat him right. No other person from the Falling Leaves could hope for such a remarkable opportunity; no one else had ever passed the tests.

Beside him, the Beetles promised similar things. The main difference was that the uniformed men seemed to *believe* what they said.

As the others in the monastery gathered in shock, Daragon looked around himself, resigned. He feared to be separated from his friends. Garth, Teresa, and Eduard stood together in the hall, unable to believe what they were seeing. Teresa stared at the monks, at Soft Stone; her eyes sought an explanation, but no one would meet her gaze.…

As the young man was led away, taken out of the protective monastery, Soft Stone watched sadly. She had become accustomed to watching her children leave, one by one, out to a wider life as they grew old enough.

But the loss of Daragon was quite different. And she herself was responsible for it.

—VIII—

Under the pretext of searching for advice and guidance, Teresa went to see Soft Stone in her quarters. The woman had not emerged for days, hiding and withdrawn since the Beetles had taken Daragon away.

Teresa rapped a second time on the door frame, but after hearing no response she drew the heavy curtain aside and entered unbidden. Two candles lit the small room, shedding a little warm light. Teresa could smell the heated beeswax mingled with a stick of smoldering incense.

Soft Stone was deep in meditation, hunched over her cot. She didn't flinch. "I did not ask to be interrupted."

"I'll just meditate with you, then." She hunkered down in front of the old monk, waited for a few painfully long moments, then finally spoke up. "I miss Daragon."

Soft Stone reacted as if Teresa had thrust a dagger through her heart. "I surrendered one of my own children to the Bureau. What is he ever going to do with them?"

Teresa heard the horror in the woman's voice. "Probably the best he can, don't you think? Daragon always tried very hard."

"They'll make him one of their own." Soft Stone's entire body shuddered. Her once clear blue eyes now looked cloudy and old. "He was our ransom, to save the Falling Leaves. Selling him was the only thing we could do. I couldn't think of any other way."

In confusion, Teresa reached out to touch the female monk's wrist, below her ID patch. "What do you mean?"

"The BTL wanted to oust us from our monastery building so they could have a second headquarters here on the mainland. Chocolate tried everything, but we were going to be evicted. The other Bureaus sided with the BTL, and the Splinters had no way to challenge them." She looked Teresa directly in the eye. "Until I discovered what Daragon could do—and how much the BTL was likely to want it. Finally, they made a deal with us."

Teresa couldn't believe what she was hearing. One of the candles flickered, as if a ghost had just walked by. Two monks sauntered past the curtain, sandals scratching along the hallway, but she concentrated on Soft Stone. "You traded Daragon to insure the safety of the monastery?"

"We now have our title, free and clear. With no further claim by the Bureau of Tracing and Locations. Daragon was worth more to them than our entire building." Unable to control herself any longer, Soft Stone's body was wracked with sobs.

Teresa tried to comprehend the scenario. "But why would the Beetles want Daragon so badly?" She had loved the young man, felt a warmth when she thought of him, but why had the Bureau seen him as so special, so valuable?

"Because he can *see* people, child. Daragon can identify anyone he knows with just a glance, even without consulting an ID patch. He can't swap, but he can look where he cannot go."

Teresa frowned, shifting to a more comfortable position on the cold floor beside her mentor. Soft Stone continued, her voice forlorn, "The Beetles look at the world through frosted glass, much the way they see COM as a sweatshop of souls, rather than a congregation of lives, Heaven come down to Earth." She shook her head. Bristles of grayish hair had begun to poke out of her smooth scalp.

"And they see that as an advantage?" Teresa said. "I think it would be terrible never to swap with anyone, to experience only your own life and nobody else's. I'm so sorry for Daragon."

"Not just that, child," the monk said. "It implies to me that Daragon's soul is anchored, unable to separate from his body. What if that means he is unable to move on in the Wheel of Life? Did I fail him?"

Teresa went away from the old teacher, unsettled at having seen the tracks of tears on Soft Stone's rugged face.

Two days later Soft Stone emerged, pale and stoic, and went to see Chocolate again, this time determined. She had searched her mind and soul, and come to a decision. The Splinters would not like it, but they would accept it. They had no choice.

Shaken to her core by the loss of Daragon, Soft Stone decided she had reached the time for her own passage. The community of other presences inside COM beckoned to her.

"I can hear their whispers behind the glimmering phosphors on the interactive screens," she said, repeating her well-rehearsed words, which she had written down as a poem. "I can see snatches of nirvana hiding within the vast thinking sea. I want to be part of it, join those myriad others. I will drink the wine of knowledge, bathe in the milk of unending experience."

Behind his desk, Chocolate grew pale. He drummed his pudgy fingers on a desktop now clear of legal documents or demands of eminent domain from the Bureau of Tracing and Locations.

But the Falling Leaves was also without Daragon, because she had set him up as a sacrificial lamb. Soft Stone didn't deserve to remain here either.

"I cannot refuse your request," Chocolate said, "though it saddens me."

"We should view this as a time of celebration," she said, not believing it for a moment. "You of all people must treat it that way. Don't you believe in what COM offers to us all?"

"My question is, is your work here done?"

"It will never be done," she admitted. "But I am done with the doing."

Soft Stone had spent years isolated inside the monastery, hiding from wider responsibilities. Even as a young woman, back in the prime of her life, she'd always had second thoughts about closing herself away from the outside world. It seemed like shirking her responsibilities of what she could have accomplished out there. She could have been a strong cobblestone in society.

But instead she had retreated into the Falling Leaves, taken a new name. Soft Stone rationalized her cowardice by thinking of herself as a seed, helping special children to blossom, bright new souls who would grow and bear far better fruit than she could ever do herself.

Soft Stone had borne no children, nor fathered any in a male body. Seeing the discarded children like Teresa and Daragon, she couldn't understand how true biological parents could so easily abandon their children.

Instead, in the Falling Leaves, Soft Stone had adopted Garth and Eduard, Teresa and Kanshah and Daragon as her own. They, and their predecessors here, were her emissaries to the world, her great accomplishments in life.

Thus, the loss of Daragon was a tremendous blow to her.

Even before she had sequestered herself for days of reflection, meditation, and (she admitted it) wallowing in self-misery, Soft Stone had communed in the great Falling Leaves library. At times when she was alone, she liked to feel the computer/organic matrix around her, listening to all the data, all the stories, all the human spirits speaking to her. COM was a great unexplored world that called to her, but she had resisted the temptation, focusing on this world and her obligations.

Until now. Soft Stone was finished with all she could do … at least all she could do from here.

"I intend to upload myself tomorrow at noon," she said with finality, and turned to leave the administrator's office.

Chocolate didn't know what to say to her, and so he said nothing.

They gathered in the library and database room, Splinter monks as well as their charges of all ages. Some sniffled and looked sad, others whispered, others blinked with wonder and anticipation.

Garth didn't know what to feel. After the recent loss of Daragon, and the departure of Kanshah months before that, he had drawn even closer to Teresa and Eduard. Too many things were changing. Within a year, he and his two closest friends would have to leave the monastery themselves, becoming adults.

Soft Stone would not be there to ease them into their new life. She was going to vanish, willingly upload her soul into the vast computer matrix.

Since humans could hopscotch from body to body at will, and because COM was organic and multi-layered, it was possible through hardware and uplink cables to hopscotch into the network itself. Soft Stone would transfer her consciousness out of her body into the labyrinth of data, committing virtual suicide. The Splinters believed the soul remained there by choice, a part of a greater cosmic mind. No one ever returned from the matrix.

"We have already proven that our *selves* are detachable," Soft Stone had said during a teaching session, more than a year earlier. "Imagine swimming in the ocean of humanity's knowledge, watching every life, every transaction."

For the ceremony Chocolate wore his finest robes, welcoming everyone. Incense burned, smelling of pine needles and cloves—Soft Stone's favorite scent. Candles guttered next to the glowing data terminals, adding a warm light like starshine.

Teresa tugged at Garth's arm, pulling him and Eduard forward so they could stand closer to the front of the crowd. Tears brimmed in her eyes.

"It's not dying," Soft Stone had said. "It is living on a higher level. A much higher level."

She emerged from the rear entrance of the library, passing between some of her favorite paintings and sculptures. Garth remembered how Soft Stone had stood with him, looking over his shoulder as he studied the painters' techniques, the sculptors' details, teaching him from the masterpiece objects as easily as other students learned from COM databases.

Barefoot, the lean woman walked with grace and confidence, shoulders square, chin high. Her sky-blue robes were adorned with brass bangles that tinkled as she moved. Her skin was flushed, scrubbed clean; her newly shaved scalp glistened as if she had waxed it.

Soft Stone smiled, her blue eyes bright and clear again. As she glided forward, a hush fell on the gathered crowd. The beatific smile on Chocolate's chubby face flickered for just an instant of uncertainty.

She walked toward the main COM interlinks in the center of the library. Soft Stone reached out to brush the hands of her students, giving them a benediction, saying farewell. The younger children did not understand, some crying or giggling.

The old monk paused in front of Teresa, Garth, and Eduard, and suddenly her expression crumpled. Her shoulders sagged. She swallowed hard as the three friends reached out to touch her, then enfold her in a deep hug.

"Trust me always," Soft Stone said in a hoarse whisper. "I'll try to watch over you. Remember, COM has eyes everywhere, and I'll be part of it."

When she stepped up to the library terminals, she faced the others. Warmly, she kissed Chocolate on both cheeks. Then he backed away, leaving the female monk alone with the computer network.

The light tiles dimmed in the library chamber, and the candles flickered more brightly, burning like tiny attendant souls. She reached out with callused hands to touch the computer inputs.

All other monitors in the library chamber flared to life, glowing. Three-dimensional interactive portals painted an artificial sky with fluffy white clouds on the ceiling of the library.

Soft Stone closed her eyes and drew a deep breath.

Living lights swirled like comets along the walls, painting a forest, a river, birds and flowers. Chimes came unseen from the virtual distance, a resonant humming that tingled in Garth's bones. The spiritual ceremony was like an old VR multi-user experience room; he wondered how much was real, how much miraculous … and how much was staged.

Then the scenes changed, the images cracked, replaced by a different construct. Soft Stone's fingers tapped the edges of the milky interactive screens, trembling, but she added no direct input that Garth could see. This magnificent presentation flowed directly from COM, images broadcast as part of the computer experience.

Now the Falling Leaves library transformed into a great vault, an immense cathedral far larger than the monastery building, with stained-glass windows and a thousand different passages. A symbolic representation of the labyrinth of the computer/organic matrix. Soft Stone's mind could spend eternity in here, wandering among all knowledge, all recorded history, even other lives.

Garth stood with his mouth open, staring. The behind-the-mind music was like crystal, the light was like gemstones.

As Soft Stone's brow wrinkled with concentration, she mentally connected herself to COM and prepared to upload her soul. The others in the room, surrounded by the illusion, held their breath.

Glowing images appeared in the air around her, luminous beings that swirled like angels. Flashing entities from the network came to greet her. She raised her hands, then her eyes. The escort presences engulfed her like a safe cocoon, then they took her away into the sparkling labyrinth. The old monk left her body behind forever. A shadow of Soft Stone floated with them, younger and stronger, more vibrant. All the spirits vanished into the fascinating, unexplored stained-glass passageways.

Then the all images faded, and the library came into focus around them again. The old woman's body slumped to the library floor, an empty husk.

Garth stood cold and alone in the candle-lit room, surrounded by breathless people. Chocolate moved to kneel beside Soft Stone's body, cradling her bald head in his hands. Excited conversation erupted in the library.

Eduard leaned over to Garth. "Do you think those images were just computer constructs? Was that a show Soft Stone prepared for us?"

Teresa frowned at him. "Oh, Eduard, don't be so cynical."

Garth stood awed by the beauty of it. "I don't care what it was." He had found it more inspiring than anything he could remember. "I just hope that someday *I* can make something as beautiful, something as moving."

—IX—

Over the next few weeks, once the Beetles withdrew their interest in occupying the Falling Leaves monastery, the Bureau operatives plunged with greater enthusiasm into the search for anti-COM terrorists.

Squads raided another hideout, and most of the remaining technophobes were killed or captured. The ringleader and another deputy managed to escape again, but the chain of violence was effectively quashed.

Teresa wondered if perhaps the benevolent intercession of Soft Stone's new spirit in the computer/organic matrix had helped to make the peace. COM offered no further power outages or retaliatory weather disturbances. The city returned to normal.

But the monastery itself was forever changed. Teresa wandered the lonely halls, trying to distract herself with her studies, attempting to find other subjects that would interest her. Without

Soft Stone, without Daragon, even without gaunt young Kanshah, the big old building no longer seemed like home.

The dusty-smelling corridors, the brick walls, the window alcoves and meditation rooms felt empty now. Before, she'd been engrossed in what Soft Stone bemusedly called her Big Questions, wrestling with esoteric spiritual concepts. But now Teresa despaired of ever finding real answers. She had wandered into a deep philosophical jungle, and her only guide had gone away.

In the nights she clung to Eduard or Garth, or both. She held onto her greatest points of stability, loving them, trying to feel desperately close. The recent changes—Kanshah, Daragon, Soft Stone—were poignant reminders of how soon she, too, would have to go away from the Falling Leaves.

Since they were about the same age, at least she, Garth, and Eduard would be together, to face the world as a trio. They might be together … they *had to be* together. If only they could all three learn how to hopscotch at the same time.…

Teresa lay next to them now, sandwiched between Garth and Eduard on pushed-together sleeping pallets. Their naked skin was warm on hers, their scent muskier and much more masculine. What would it be like to inhabit their bodies, to move their muscles, experience physical and sexual responses as a man instead of a woman? She loved them both, and once they were able to swap themselves, male / female—it would make no difference.

They had all experienced sexual intimacy before, sharing each other in the way the Splinters taught. Bodily explorations had actually been encouraged by Soft Stone, so long as they used the proper precautions and maintained relative privacy to keep from confusing or frightening the younger children. As preparation for learning to hopscotch, Teresa needed to explore other bodies besides her own, by touching, sensing, feeling—trying to understand what other human beings enjoyed, and why.

She also worked hard to become totally familiar with her own biology, to know her nerves, her systems. Only with this awareness could she understand her individuality, and also the things she shared in common with all other people.

Lying awake, Teresa could sense the potential in herself, feel her thoughts floating free, her spirit soaring, ready to go. But so far she had not been able to exchange herself, to hand her soul to another person and take theirs into her home-body. She had tried and tried, but she had not succeeded.

Lately, each failure intimidated her, as well as Garth and Eduard. The three of them had seen Daragon's fate when he'd proven incapable of hopscotching. Teresa didn't dare let it happen to them; they needed each other.

In the night, she reached out and pulled them both close.

Without Soft Stone, the monks who took over the mental instruction of the three oldest teenagers were clumsy and unimaginative. Hickory was impatient and sharp-tongued, Chocolate was too busy, and the other monks had their own groups of younger children to attend.

The new teachers did not comprehend the best ways to communicate difficult concepts to Teresa. Soft Stone had been special.

Alone, Teresa found the most peace and concentration out in the garden. For months she tended the plants, plucking off dry leaves, removing weeds, adding mulch or loosening soil around the roots. She worked there in her free time even when she wasn't assigned the duties; Hickory seemed perfectly glad to let her have her way.

Teresa stared down at the sun-warmed vegetables, but her mind drifted far away … as if she could let it detach itself and travel elsewhere, hop into another body and exchange places. She could be someone else, share a different physique for a limited time.

If only she could teach herself how to hopscotch, then she could show Garth and Eduard. The three of them had a rapport already so close it seemed borderline telepathic. Never with anyone else had she achieved such a thorough sharing of thoughts and moods.

Of the three, Teresa was best at introspection, at working with the chains holding her mind to her body. She knew she could figure it out.

She had to.

Teresa bent over, felt the warm sun on her lower back, the sweat on her shoulder blades, and tried to imagine what it would be like if she could work in another, stronger body. Perhaps she would become an athlete in someone more lithe, or explore tiny confined spaces in underground maintenance conduits in a smaller, compact body. External appearances wouldn't matter—male or female, old or young, large or small, weak or strong—because it would still be *her* inside.

She parted velvety, pungent-smelling leaves of the tomato plants, searching for ripe, scarlet spheres. Teresa plucked one, large and slightly soft, and placed it in the basket at her side. She let her mind wander, her thoughts travel free—just the way Soft Stone had encouraged.

She picked another tomato, tugging, feeling the stem snap free, parting from the parent plant along an invisible but natural line. The ripe tomato came free—and she felt a similar *snap* in her own mind, as if something inside her head was also ready, prepared to separate.

Her vision reeled, and she blinked several times, trying to comprehend what had just happened.

She had dropped the tomato on the dirt and now picked it up again. The stem was broken on top, severed cleanly. Teresa let her mind open again, her thoughts flow, and wander … and *separate*.

No one else was with her in the garden, so she couldn't test her new idea, couldn't attempt to hopscotch. But she felt the change, the realization. She knew she could swap her mind, and she understood the implications.

And she knew how to communicate with Garth and Eduard. She understood know how to explain what she had done in a way that her two friends would comprehend, deep in their hearts. With them, she could speak a personal language that none of the monks could fathom.

Leaving the rest of the unpicked tomatoes behind, Teresa ran back inside the confines of the monastery.

"Follow me," she said urgently. "I've got to show you something. It might take a while, but I know you'll get it."

Practically dragging them by the arms, she took Eduard and Garth down into the lower levels of the Falling Leaves, heading for a place she knew they could be left alone, alone for as many hours as it might take.

They went into the small, forgotten storeroom where a long time ago Garth had painted his mural, now masked by a thick coat of tan paint.

Teresa hunkered down; Garth and Eduard gathered close to her. She had brought a portable light tile, so they wouldn't need to tend a candle. This exercise would require all of their concentration. The soft light shone on the old brick walls, illuminating ghosts of Garth's painstakingly drawn scene of imaginary nostalgia, barely visible behind the beige mask.

The floorboards creaked above, and Teresa knew the monks would be going about their rounds, checking on their trainees. With Soft Stone gone, no one watched Garth, Teresa, or Eduard very closely anymore, but someone would eventually notice their absence.

Teresa hoped they would have enough time together.

"Oh, if we can all learn this at the same time," she said, "then we can go out together, support each other in the city, help each other make the transition."

"We won't be all alone like Kanshah," Garth said.

"Or Daragon," Eduard said, though the BTL had taken Daragon so firmly under their wing that the young man wouldn't need to worry about anything ... except the freedom to do what he wanted to do.

"I think I understand how to hopscotch," Teresa said. "I was thinking, concentrating. Then something clicked."

"Soft Stone always said you were the deep one," Garth said.

"Yes, and now I have to show both of you." She closed her eyes and reached out with both hands, one touching square-shouldered, blond Garth, the other touching wiry, dark-haired Eduard.

"This is going to be strange, at first, I think." Her voice was husky with fear and uncertainty. "Here, let me teach you."

Garth stood naked in Eduard's body, staring at himself, at his two friends who appeared the same to him, but different behind their eyes. "Look at that."

The three of them had spent their lives leaning on each other, without parents and without last names. They had learned to depend on their mutual skills. Garth loved Teresa and Eduard wholeheartedly and equally.

And now this was so much more. Now they were thrust together in an entirely different way. They *were* each other.

Garth flexed Eduard's wiry arms, blinked his eyes. "This feels weird, familiar but … not. I'm stronger in some ways, smaller in others. I—"

Eduard interrupted him, standing inside Teresa's shape. He kept touching his skin, his arms, running his palms over his new breasts, tweaking his nipples. "Wait until you try this, Garth. She's got nerve clusters all over her body." He stroked the patch of hair between his legs, startling himself. "It feels tingly in places that never did anything for me. And empty in others."

Teresa wore Garth's home-body like a baggy uniform. "It's like I'm in a big suit of armor." She drew deep breaths, touched her rough face, fondled her new penis, which seemed to have a mind of its own and defied conscious muscle control. "And this—it's like an appendage, but I can't do anything with it."

"Yes you can," Eduard said. "You'll figure it out."

"But it doesn't move like any of my other body parts. I can't control the reactions—oh!"

Garth and Eduard both laughed.

Down in the small storeroom lit only by a portable light tile, they began to explore each other in new ways. The boundaries between friendship and sexual love and physical differences blurred, then vanished. Their shadows merged on the walls, becoming indistinguishable, three people, three different bodies.

"Oh, I never thought it'd be this strange," Teresa said, listening to the deeper voice in her head, touching the male muscles, the fine curly hair on her chest.

"So many things are the same, fundamentally equal, whether I'm in my own body, or Eduard's, or Teresa's," Garth said. "But every one is different, too."

"Not so different," Eduard said. "It's what you do with the body that matters." He looked over at Garth through Teresa's eyes, while Teresa looked down at her own hands, at Garth's hands.

"Then let's … *do* something," Teresa said, her voice small even in the large, blond body.

They'd made love before, but not like this. It was a strange and wondrous sacrament, the three of them *being* in their friends' bodies, looking at each other through new eyes.

Eduard made love to Garth, who was in Teresa's home-body, while Teresa herself stood by, wearing the blond-haired male form she had known as Garth all her life. Now, suddenly, they were inexperienced again, embarrassingly so. But they experimented without shame.

They swapped again. And again.

Teresa coached Garth and Eduard, instructing them both in techniques and responses she had learned through her own explorations of her own body. She helped, she touched, she participated.

Eduard had experienced sex with Teresa in previous years; this time the person inside was completely different, though the body remained the same. His reactions and responses in a female shape were different from what he had anticipated.

Garth was uncertain, but curious, trying to cope with a radically altered perspective. He was in a woman's body now, making love to a man, and he had to be aroused by a man, though he had never thought in such a way before. The mind had to adjust to a new reality, while the body's hormones and natural responses remained the same, assisting.

This was Eduard, his friend, his comrade … but when Teresa (in what had been his own body) helped him to touch the ultra-sensitive areas on his breasts, his skin, his clitoris—a vastly new sensation—he began to understand what he had to do. The sensations rapidly became overwhelming. The physical body knew what to do, and did it well….

Sweating and drained but tingling all over, Garth (in Teresa's body) came forward, touching what had once been his own buttocks, the backs of his thighs.

"Here, Teresa, let me show you something. I know you'll like this."

It turned out that the monks had no idea where to find them, and the three had hours to talk with each other, touch each other, swap again and again. They described the way their own bodies worked, demonstrating to their friends.

The lovemaking was satisfying, and exotic, and exhausting—but in the end they realized that for such deep friends, the very act of hopscotching into each other's bodies, was vastly more intimate than sex....

Epilogue

Far from the Falling Leaves monastery now, turned loose to explore the real world beyond the walls, Eduard, Garth, and Teresa drew strength from each other.

The three of them looked at Club Masquerade, intimidated and anxious. They had never been inside before, and now they tried to strengthen their resolve. "Look at that," Garth said.

"Isn't this place great? Let's go inside," Eduard said without taking a step forward. "I want to see it after all this time."

"We've got the freedom to do what we want now," Teresa said, somewhat downcast.

As children, then as teenagers, they had watched this place from the safety of the Falling Leaves. Club Masquerade was so exotic, so alien, a place unlike anything they had ever experienced. The monks always calmly encouraged them to discover new intellectual things, but very little true life experience. It was the Splinters' blind spot.

After having learned how to hopscotch and proving their skills to Chocolate and the other Splinters, the three had left the Falling Leaves together. With a few credits in their pockets and new opportunities before them, they made their way in the city. Garth, Teresa, and Eduard were on their own, yet together and strong.

The frenetic club atmosphere seemed so exciting that it had to be somehow forbidden. A swirl of eager customers flowed in and out, some furtive and nervous, others totally open. And the people who went in were not necessarily the same people who emerged again.

The monks had not talked about the Club, did not see fit to encourage wild stories or fascination over such businesses. Rumors among the other Splinter children portrayed Club Masquerade as a haze of body swapping, a confusing blur of shifting identities, a human exchange.

Teresa looked behind her, and the old brick brewery seemed far away. The "real world" also tugged on her now. Directly before them, the edifice of Club Masquerade fascinated and lured her.

Where did all those doors go? Why so many separate entrance arches? Each one passed into the main club, but different paths led through different experiences. She and Eduard and Garth could find out for themselves, as adults. As customers.

"Which door should we try?" Eduard asked. "I hear they're all different."

"I think Teresa should choose," Garth said.

She looked at both of them, tossed her auburn hair over her shoulder, and took a deep breath, steeling herself. She marched forward, across the numbered squares on the sidewalk, which illuminated under each footstep. Teresa passed under one of the many possible archways. "Come on."

With Eduard and Garth following her, Teresa entered Club Masquerade.

She stepped onto a floor strewn with dried redwood needles and tiny fir cones. The walls were made of massive knobbed trunks of sequoias with warty bark that oozed sweet-smelling pitch. The trees reached as high overhead as the tallest skyscrapers Teresa had ever seen—until she realized that the trunks vanished into a ceiling that was the holographic equivalent of a matte painting, projecting the illusion of vast height in a normal-sized room.

Teresa drew a deep breath, while Garth stood with his arms outstretched, his head craned upward, his mouth grinning. "Look at this!" he said. "Look at this!"

Rough wooden benches were scattered around the room, aromatic with a sour-spicy smell of fresh-hewn redwood. High above, in the imaginary upper levels of the conifers, rafts of cool mist clung to the branches.

"Oh, and smell the air," Teresa said, discarding her expectations of a hedonistic chamber of pleasure. She hadn't imagined this at all.

"I told you it would be amazing," Eduard said, already snooping around. He found a doorway in the side of one of the massive sequoia trunks. "Look in here—it's a medieval banquet hall!"

Other rooms offered equivalent wonders, but Eduard egged on

his two friends, wanting to get to the central room. Past the outer environment lounges, the three of them finally stepped into the huge main hall, the heart of Club Masquerade.

The sunken floor was surrounded by lights, girdled by a neon bar. Seats and floating tables appeared in convenient spots of light and shadow, depending on whether customers wanted privacy or spectacle. About half of them were occupied.

The lights and decor, sounds and smells bombarded them, perfumed steam, colored incense, spraying fountains, accompanied by music vibrations and the drone of conversation. The floor was packed with dancing bodies, swaying people who touched and swapped and flitted from form to form, male to female, young to old, average to beautiful, and back again.

"Hey, doesn't this sum up … everything you imagined the rest of the world would be?" Eduard said, breathless.

"Yes, but this isn't going to stop me from exploring, and experiencing, and learning," Garth said. "What an inspiration!"

They climbed to a mid-level table and sat down, already eager to find a new place where they could fit in. Since they had lost two friends and their mentor, the Falling Leaves had already stopped feeling like home. Garth, Teresa, and Eduard had been mentally weaned from the monastery long before they actually set foot outside the doors. The Splinters had arranged low-level outside jobs for each of them to use as a starting place, and also provided a small stipend for the first year. But now they were independent.

Club Masquerade was the first place they had gone, where they could sever their ties from the monastery, Soft Stone, and their past.

Teresa looked at the numerous patrons, overwhelmed and intimidated by the pressing responsibility of establishing herself from scratch. Here, even with the comfort of Eduard and Garth, she felt herself to be at the heart of a cyclone, a central calm, with vast energies ready to tear them apart.

People departing from the Falling Leaves went out on their own, losing contact with their fellow students, taking care of themselves. They sought to fulfill their destiny as special new souls out in the world. Daragon was already lost to them, swallowed up by the bureaucracy in the BTL. And no one had ever heard from Kanshah.

But the three of them were a team—they had all learned to

hopscotch at the same time, they had left the monastery together. Still, she was afraid of losing them.

So Teresa decided to do something to keep them together. "Let's make this our special place. Club Masquerade."

Both men looked at her, curious. They could see the concern on her face; Eduard and Garth knew Teresa well enough to sense her worries and the root causes.

"No matter what happens," she continued, "wherever we go or whatever we decide to do with ourselves, let's promise to meet here on a regular basis. We can do that, don't you think?"

"What's today?" Eduard asked. "The first Tuesday of the month? No problem."

"Sounds easy enough to me," Garth said, alarmed at the suggestion that they wouldn't be together. He had blithely ignored the possibility until that moment, but Teresa was right.

"I'll make a note on my calendar," Eduard said dryly. "But I think we'll be seeing enough of each other anyway."

"Oh, but things are different now," Teresa said. "No guarantees."

Still uncertain, Garth finally expressed himself by reaching out to clasp both of their hands, squeezing tightly.

The music continued to throb. They ordered drinks, sampled new concoctions, tasted flavored stim-sticks. Sometimes they engaged in vigorous conversations, but for long spaces they just looked at each other across the floating table.

Eduard, Garth, and Teresa remained together in the club for hours, relishing each other's company, until all three of them knew it was time to go.

Then, with the whole world awaiting them, they went out to embark on a great adventure—the rest of their lives.

In the first volume of my SF stories, I introduced readers to Alternitech, a group of prospectors who jump into parallel universes in search of subtle, and profitable, differences to bring back to our reality.

"Tidepools" is the second Alternitech story I wrote, after "Music Played on the Strings of Time." At the time, the concept of the multiverse was not well known among science fiction readers, and certainly not to the general public. But I loved the concept and wrote a whole series of stories.

In this one, I imagined the strands of medical research. What if scientific teams in one version of Earth stumbled upon a cure to a disease, a treatment that wasn't known in our timeline? I also learned about "orphan diseases," ailments so rare that no pharmaceutical company would find it financially feasible to produce the necessary drug, even if a cure were known. Fellow science fiction author George Alec Effinger suffered from one of these orphan diseases, which inspired the key idea to this story.

As a side note, this is yet another one of my stories inspired by the music of Rush, in this case, "Natural Science."

TIDE POOLS

The return portal formed in the air like razor blades slashing through clear ice. Andrea stepped across the threshold, her mixed elation and disappointment so overwhelming that she barely noticed the skin-fizzing sensation of hopping back home from an adjacent timeline.

"I got something!" she called, unslinging the backpack from her shoulder. "How about a miracle cure for multiple sclerosis, anybody?" It wasn't what she had hoped to find, but she had to make it look good.

In the receiving room of Alternitech, portals and complex control panels surrounded her. At her announcement, technicians and other cure hunters began to pay attention. "How much follow-up do we need?" asked the chubby man in the operating booth.

"Not necessary—I got all the right data." Andrea brushed a hand through her short, sweat-rimed dark hair, feeling her cheeks grow warm.

Cure hunters like herself dreamed of such unlikely chances. Peeping into parallel timelines, digging through other-universe medical libraries, Andrea searched for effective treatments that doctors in her own timeline had somehow missed.

Who would have thought that a drug used for skin disorders would be amazingly effective against MS? When injected into the spinal columns of those suffering from the disease, the drug dissolved the small white plaques covering nerve sheaths.

No one in her own timeline had thought of it, but in an adjacent universe, a doctor had stumbled upon the treatment and published it to high acclaim. Alternitech would profit greatly from the discovery, and so would mankind.

The man in the operating booth spoke into his intercom, summoning verification reps to paw through her data. Other cure hunters applauded Andrea as they waited for their own gates to open. She surrendered her backpack and its contents to the security guard.

It was phenomenally expensive to haul foreign mass from other timelines. Hunters like Andrea recorded pertinent data onto the diskettes or videotapes they carried with them. Apparently, there was no cost to transfer information between timelines, though Andrea supposed the entropy specialists would probably come up with something sooner or later.

After the announcement of her discovery, the reporters would come, the television interviewers, the applause from the public, the heartfelt thank-you letters from MS patients given sudden new hope for their conditions. She allowed herself to revel in the times she made a find like this.

Andrea also felt a disappointment inside, despite the rewarding rush of success. After all, she had not been looking for a cure for MS. She had failed in her primary mission.

The problem gnawing at her was whether or not she should tell Everett. He was the one who had everything at stake.

Home at last, Andrea entered through the front door, propping it open to let in the fresh breeze. Sunlight gushed through the bay windows, warming the sunken living room.

Everett straightened from his work by the laser generator. "Andrea? Is that you?" She stood in full view, and he was staring directly at her. His eyesight grew worse every day.

"Expecting someone else to barge in and blow you a kiss?" she asked.

"I expected you home hours ago. Wait, I have to start all this up again!" He held up his hands, then felt his way around the equipment, squinting at it, careful not to stumble. "I have a surprise. Where are you? Come into the foyer—I've set that up as prime focus."

Andrea smiled to see him looking so earnest, so bustling. This was much better than the phase of moping he had gone through a month earlier. She went where he directed her and looked around the walls. Tiny, faceted mirrors were mounted at strategic points around the room.

"Ta da!" Everett switched on his laser projector, and a 3-D holo sculpture congealed around her like a spider web of light, a kaleidoscope of rainbows. Each line was split, not quite resolved, so that it was really dozens of layered images overlapping each other, partially unfocused with chromatic aberration. His grids were out of phase, and she doubted Everett even knew it.

"My masterpiece," he said. "I wanted to leave something impressive behind. I call it *Timelines*. It's for you, Andrea."

Everett was looking at her with a childish expression of delight and anticipation on his face. His gaze was slightly off.

Timelines. She looked at the fuzzed edges of the light threads, the overlapping images that were almost but not exactly like each other. Perhaps it wasn't just some jittering lack of surety caused by Everett's fading eyesight and his trembling hands; timelines nearly overlapping but subtly different. He must have done it on purpose; she had to believe that, or else his failure would tear her heart apart. "I think it's beautiful, Everett. I don't know how you managed it."

He lowered his head to cover his smile. She almost expected him to say "Awww, shucks." Instead, he found a soft futon and sat down. "I was going to have it done by your birthday, but now everything takes me so damned long." He sighed. "Are you going to stay home with me tonight, or are you going back to Alternitech?"

Watching him made her wince her eyes shut. What good would a multiple sclerosis cure do for him? She had failed him at the time he needed her most. She had to keep searching.

Heidegger's Syndrome. The disease selectively attacked the myelin sheaths around the optic nerve, then chewed away at the medulla oblongata, deteriorating the nerves that controlled breathing and heartbeat. After a slow descent into blindness, Everett would one day just find himself without a heartbeat, then fall over and die. Andrea dreaded the morning she would wake up to find him cold in the bed beside her. She could not prevent it in any way.

Andrea stared at Everett in the living room. The solution was painful and obvious. But Alternitech had flatly denied her permission to hunt among the timelines for a cure.

She walked up behind Everett, threw her arms around his waist, then pressed her cheek against his shoulder blades. The tapestry of light glittered around them, defeating even the sunlight. Timelines.

"It's your best work, Everett," she said. "I love it."

Andrea fidgeted in the university office of a man she had never met. In the halls of the Neurological Wing of the Deudakis Medical Research Facility, she could hear annoying sounds of construction, hammers and saws and power drills. She had had to weave her way around scaffolding and construction barricades to reach Dr. Benjamin Stendahl's office. The hall lights flickered but remained on.

She looked at her watch again, sat down in the only uncluttered chair, then stood up once more. Stendahl's computer sat on a corner of his desk, glowing with a garish screen saver of multicolored lines. She ran her fingertips along the spines of the journals on his bookshelves, stacks of dusty manuscripts, technical papers held together with old rubber bands; one band near the bottom of the pile had snapped, splaying curled printouts.

A man stepped into the office breathing heavily and mumbling to himself. He came to a full stop as he saw her. His eyebrows were like fluffy gray feathers mounted on his forehead. "Oh! I forgot." He dropped a bulging briefcase atop the stacked books on his desk. "You're here to talk to me about Heidegger's Syndrome—your husband, right? Well, there's nothing I can do for him. You realize how rare the disease is? Only eight people a year are diagnosed with it in all of North America."

Andrea thrust her chin forward. "I've read all your papers. Looks like you were making good progress toward a cure. Why did you stop work on it?"

"Simple answer—no more money. That's the rotten part. Heidegger's isn't really an insidious bastard like cancer or AIDS.

Given some research data, I could do a lot. But our rhesus monkeys were rerouted and never arrived. I could afford only one grad student, but she got married and moved to Ohio. I couldn't get her replaced before the end of the fiscal year, when my funding went away."

Stendahl sat behind his desk, jiggling the mouse so that the screen saver dissolved to display a master menu. "I think 'orphan disease' is the colorful term they have for it. With research dollars so scarce, who wants to waste time coming up with a cure for something nobody cares about?"

"I care about it," she said. "Eight people a year care about it, and so do their families, and everybody they know."

Stendahl looked at her with sympathy in his big, dark eyes. "Look, millions of people get cancer, leukemia, cystic fibrosis. Heidegger's just doesn't cut it. The disease was a medical curiosity when it was first reported, little more."

Andrea stared at the journals on his shelves. Pounding hammers from the hallway punctuated her sentence. "And now?"

He shrugged again. "I'm working on other things."

Andrea wanted to spend her every waking hour hunting alternate timelines for a cure, but she needed to be with Everett. Each day was like Russian roulette with him, never knowing which heartbeat might be his last.

Seagulls wheeled overhead, tiny checkmarks that screamed against the booming rush of the Pacific. The ocean and the huge sky above made the universe seem oppressive in its grandeur. Headlands sprawled out in muted browns and grayish greens to the shore, where a string of tide pools dotted the wave-chewed rock like diamonds on a necklace. Barefoot and in cutoff shorts, Andrea and Everett picked their way among the rocks.

Andrea took sandwiches out of the pack, and they split a bottle of beer. Everett squatted beside one of the pools and dangled his fingers into the water, startling two crabs that ducked for cover beneath the rocks. He squinted to make out details. Eyeglasses would not help him; Heidegger's was not a problem of focus, but of the optic nerve itself.

The tide pools were colorful, filled with life, a microcosm of unfurled pale-green anemones, tiny fish, and shells. Snails worked their tedious way across the rock surface, finding rich patches of algae. Everett tossed a rock, watching the ripples spread to the boundaries of the tide pool, but constrained by the walls so that it could not affect the other tide pools.

"Each one is like its own universe," he said. "Full of life, nearly identical to the others, but different. I'm like an anemone in a tide pool, stuck to the bottom, waving my fronds in the hope that I'll catch something, but ultimately trapped right where I am. You, on the other hand, are more like one of those rock crabs. With Alternitech, you can scuttle over the wall and get to other tide pools, go see new places, look at what they've got, and maybe take something back with you."

Andrea didn't know what to say. She did indeed have the flashy, high-paying career. Who could imagine a world where a "research librarian" was considered a glamorous profession? Andrea was constantly being interviewed, receiving awards and applause. She had loved it—until the search had become personal, and desperate, and she had failed.

"I'm still looking for something to help you. I'll find it. Don't worry."

A wave curled against an outcropping partly out to sea, dashing spray into the air like tiny crystal droplets. Two gulls swooped down, then wheeled high overhead.

"Why help me when you can help thousands?" Everett said. His voice held a strong resignation that had emerged from his initial depression.

"As if one cure precludes another!" Andrea scowled. "Why do we pit the two types of research against each other, as if they were our only two choices? The government spends more money maintaining flower gardens around monuments than they do on Heidegger's research—why does one bit of science have to siphon money from other science, rather than something else? Everything isn't equal." She looked down, though she knew he couldn't see her face anyway. "Besides, if I find something, I'll just tell Alternitech that I found it by accident while doing other research. They can't prove otherwise."

Everett smiled, like a parent watching a child deliver promises with false bravado, then he reached for his sandwich. She watched him squint until he found it.

She swallowed a large bite. "We should get back. I can go out hunting at least two more times today."

Everett's face was a plain mask of disappointment, but he said nothing.

In her long search, most of the alternate universes appeared identical. Digging into the medical research libraries, sometimes she discovered even less progress on Heidegger's Syndrome, or none at all. Twice, she found minimal successes beyond her own timeline, but nothing worth bringing back. With a run of unlikely bad luck such as Stendahl's, it seemed obvious that in some other timeline he would have received his rhesus monkeys, his grad student would have stayed an extra six months.

Throughout her search, she also had to find enough other tidbits to keep Alternitech happy. They had told her not to waste time hunting a cure for an orphan disease, yet they were delighted when she found a way to artificially change eye color from blue to brown and back again. Plenty of cosmetic and commercial applications, they said. Their priorities made her sick.

She had lost count of the timelines by now. On each mission, Andrea went directly to a university's medical library and buried herself in Stendahl's publications, checking to see if he had anything new to offer. This time, according to the library, Stendahl had completed his experiments, but his crucial summary papers were "in press," which meant they were not yet published and would be available only in his office.

Andrea hurried along the dim corridor. So far, every timeline had the same chaotic construction in the west wing of the building. Perhaps chaos itself was the only constant among the timelines. Yellow barrier tape blocked off corridors, light fixtures lay on the floor, the sounds of hammers and power saws echoed in the halls. Andrea passed a pile of new-cut boards, ducked under a scaffold holding drip-splotched cans of paint. She hadn't yet been able to determine if they were building something up or tearing something down.

Stendahl's door was closed. Taped to the wall beside his office hung a handwritten note giving an address to send Get Well cards. Under that, she read a newspaper clipping that described how Benjamin Stendahl had broken his leg after stumbling in a construction area, and that he was not expected to return to teach classes for the remainder of the semester.

Stendahl's door would be locked, but all cure hunters kept lockpicking tools in their packs. If this timeline had some crucial information for Everett, she would take whatever measures were necessary. As she worked at fumbling the slim tools into the door's keyslot, construction noises drowned out the sounds of her hidden efforts. But she kept looking over her shoulder. She was not good at this.

Wrapping her sweaty palm around the knob, Andrea finally opened the door. She ducked inside and closed it behind her, flicking the light switch.

Stendahl's abandoned office smelled oppressive and long-empty, though he had been in the hospital for only a week. She switched on the computer, letting it boot up as she scanned the bookshelves. She did not have much time to find what she needed, and Stendahl's cluttered organization made the task more difficult.

She saw the title on the fresh manuscript lying on top of one pile, then found a folder filled with memos, his hand-jotted records of the experiments, raw data. She flipped through the pages. At the end of his summary Stendahl even suggested a few treatment methods. "Yes!" she said.

She glanced at her wristwatch, trying to determine how soon the Alternitech portal would come back for her. She could use her camera to photograph each page of the hard copy summary report, but this was raw data—files and files of it—experimental records, suggested follow-up tests. It would be laborious and time-consuming to copy all of it. More time than she had. But she could store everything onto one of her diskettes—if she could find the right files on Stendahl's computer.

Andrea went to the computer, glancing at the menu and searching for Heidegger files. As she feared, Stendahl had imposed little organization in his filing system. Some of the file names contained the word "Heidegger," but when she called them up, they were mere memos requesting supplies. Stendahl had named seven of the files REPORT1, REPORT2 … each taking up significant disk space. She checked the file-creation dates, then called up the most recent, but it had nothing to do with Heidegger research.

Out in the hallway, the construction workers used something that sounded like a jackhammer on the walls. Andrea tried to ignore the racket and concentrate on her work.

Finally, when she pulled up REPORT5, the words described all his tests, all his results, all his suggestions. Jackpot!

Excitement and anxiety growing within her, Andrea checked her watch again. She unzipped her pack and pulled out the various blank diskettes from her own universe. She pulled a disk out of its plastic sleeve and tried to slide it into the drive.

It was an eighth of an inch too wide. But she had other formats, other sizes to accommodate slight differences among the timelines. She tried another from her stack.

She finally found a diskette that fit. Stendahl's drive began formatting it. Alternitech experts had always been able to decode her diskettes, no matter how subtly different their computers might be. Of course, the techs might not help if she brought back something she had been instructed not to look for. She might have to call in all of the favors she had earned in her years working for Alternitech.

The disk finished formatting. It would take a few moments to copy the files. She didn't have much time; the portal would come back for her soon.

At the far end of the hall, one of the construction workers cursed as the jackhammer noise changed with an abrupt clank.

All the lights in the building went out.

Stendahl's office filled with blackness. The computer died. Andrea's hopes died with it.

By flashlight, she photographed as many pages of the draft manuscripts as she could. Working backward, Andrea snapped each image of conclusions, then the experimental method, and finally began plowing through all the raw data. She stared at her chronometer, watching the time tick down.

Alternitech's machinery cast her across the parallel universes at random like a fishhook in the water. Now that she had found a timeline that offered hope for a Heidegger's cure, chances were very slim that she would ever find herself back here. Frantic, she kept photographing the data, hoping that her flashlight provided enough illumination for the pictures to turn out.

Finally, when she could not wait a second longer, Andrea clicked one more photograph, then ran out of Stendahl's office, leaving the papers scattered all around. Glowing green EXIT signs shone in the darkness. She heard voices calling, complaining about the power outage. By the bobbing light in her hand, Andrea ran through the halls, dodging construction barricades. She had to get back to the portal.

A gruff voice yelled for her to bring the flashlight over so they could find the circuit panel, but she ignored it. She nearly tripped over a pile of pipes against one wall, but she caught her balance. Reaching the secluded stairwell, Andrea stumbled into the shadows just as the Alternitech portal slashed through the air.

Clutching her precious data, Andrea fell across the sea of timelines.

"Well," Stendahl said, raising his bushy eyebrows, "that's the good news." Andrea suddenly felt her stomach turn into ice.

He folded his hands on his desk and leaned toward her. Around him, she could see photocopies of the article and notes she had taken from the alternate universe. Stendahl had studied them, marked them with a red pen. She spotted several pieces of data circled, a few with exclamation points beside them. Andrea feared that she had not managed to include the one page that contained crucial measurements or descriptions of the one round of tests that would have allowed Stendahl to create a treatment for Heidegger's. It would all be lost.

Alternitech management had not been pleased with Andrea when she had returned with information on Heidegger's Syndrome, information she had been specifically told not to seek out. They had suspended her, until they received a phone call from an angry senator whose daughter was even now being treated for multiple sclerosis—using the prescription Andrea had brought back. The phone call seemed like a miracle cure to her situation.

Now, Everett was the only one who had something to lose.

Andrea met Dr. Stendahl's gaze. "What is it?" she said, her voice hoarse. "What's the bad news?"

"I've confirmed—er, I mean I agree with my own conclusions." He forced a wry smile. "This research does indeed suggest a treatment regimen that could offer hope for people diagnosed with Heidegger's Syndrome. But—"

Andrea flinched, but she didn't dare say anything else.

Stendahl looked away. "As with so many other ailments, beginning the treatment at the onset of the disease holds the key to the cure. If we could have started this right when your husband's eyesight was affected, when the disease was still confined to the optic nerve, we might have had a chance. He could have suffered a loss of eyesight, but the disease itself would be eradicated."

His feathery eyebrows rode up his forehead. "In your husband's case, the disease has already migrated to the medulla oblongata. The damage is already being done to the crucial nerves that govern involuntary functions such as heartbeat and respiration. This treatment itself purges the disease, but at the cost of destroying the nerves that are affected—somewhat like amputation."

Andrea took a long, shuddering breath. "Obviously, we can't do that in Everett's case. Not anymore." She felt a dry whispering sound in her ear, as of her own ragged hope draining away.

Stendahl was lousy at sounding optimistic. "From now on, anyone else diagnosed with Heidegger's will have a chance. You've saved those eight people a year you were so concerned about. No one else would have funded my research. You have that to show for your efforts, if nothing else."

Andrea found she couldn't listen anymore.

Mist generators sent a cool fog toward the ceiling of the room, making the bright green and red laser beams stand out. Everett had been furiously working on another sculpture, fine-tuning it and trying to finish while he could still function. He had cranked up the laser intensity to the maximum safe level, just so he could discern the beams with his failing eyesight.

With the rest of the house darkened and only a few stars visible out the window, Andrea lay next to him on the floor, looking up at the laser tracery.

Everett spoke in the darkness. "There was a poet during the Boer War who said to live every day as if it were your last, for one day you're sure to be right."

"When did you start reading poetry?" Andrea said, trying to change the subject.

"I've had a lot of time to do things while you were off at Alternitech." He sighed. "But I'm glad you found the cure anyway."

"You're still going to die!" Andrea snapped. Her failure seemed like fluttering wings around her head.

"We're all going to die," he countered. "But you've given a longer life to the other people who get the same stupid disease I did." He took a long breath. "I came to terms with this illness a long time ago. It's you who need to accept it."

"I had to try," she mumbled. But she began to wonder if her obsession to find a cure, her need not to fail at the task she had set for herself, was actually more for herself instead of Everett.

"I know you did," he said. "Thank you for trying, Andrea. But all those days you were gone hunting ... I would rather have gone to the mountains with you, done a few more bed and breakfasts up the coast." Everett's words stung.

"There are plenty of other versions of me in other universes who will have a long and happy life with you. In our timeline, I had an unlucky break. I got an incurable disease that nobody's ever heard of. It just doesn't happen in this timeline, with this Everett and this Andrea."

He sat up abruptly. "We've got money saved, so why don't we spend it? Besides ... you'll be getting a big life insurance check from me before long."

Andrea winced, but he gripped her hand. She thought of the hours she had lost in her desperate hunt. "I suppose I could take a leave of absence from Alternitech," she said haltingly, "especially now. It would give them time to cool off." She flashed him a smile that was at first forced, but gradually grew sincere as she thought of the things they could do together, now that all the restraints had been snipped away.

"All right," she said. "Let's go be alive as long as we can."

PREVIOUS PUBLICATION INFORMATION

"Change of Mind" © 2015 WordFire, Inc. First published in *Pulse Pounders,* ed. Kevin J. Anderson, WMG Publishing, 2015.

"Club Masquerade" copyright © 2001 by WordFire, Inc. First published in *Analog,* November 2001.

"Collaborators" with Rebecca Moesta © 1995 WordFire, Inc. First published in *VB Tech,* July 1995.

"Dogged Persistence," copyright © 1992 WordFire, Inc. First published in *The Magazine of Fantasy and Science Fiction,* September 1992.

"The Happy Hookermorph," copyright © 1994 by WordFire, Inc. First published in *Hotel Andromeda,* ed. Jack L. Chalker, Ace Books, 1994.

"The Hind," copyright © 2020, WordFire, Inc. and Rick Wilber, first published in *Asimov's Science Fiction,* November / December 2020.

"Hole in the Wall," copyright © 2022, WordFire, Inc., first published in *Onward LibertyCon,* ed. Christopher Woods, LibertyCon Press, 2022.

"Log Entry" © 2006 WordFire, Inc. First published in *Space Cadets,* ed. Mike Resnick, SCIFI, 2006.

"Not a Prisoner: Deacon's Story," copyright © 2018, WordFire, Inc. and Steven L. Sears, first published in *Stalag-X* by Kevin J. Anderson and Steven L. Sears, The Vault, 2018.

"Prevenge," copyright © 2006 by WordFire, Inc. and Kirinyaga, Inc. First published in *Analog,* November 2006.

"Prisons" copyright © 1992 WordFire, Inc. and Doug Beason, origi- nally published in *Amazing Stories,* Vol LXVII #1, 1992.

"Tide Pools," copyright © 1993 WordFire, Inc., first published in *Analog,* December 1993.

"Travailiant," copyright © 2017 by WordFire, Inc. and David Boop. First published in *MECHWarrior: Age of Steel,* Ragnarok, 2017.

"Trouble in Paradise," copyright © 2021, WordFire, Inc. and Kevin Ikenberry, first published in *Freehold Defiance,* ed. Michael Z. Williamson, Baen Books, 2021.

ABOUT THE AUTHOR

Kevin J. Anderson has published more than 180 books, 58 of which have been national or international bestsellers. He has 24 million copies in print in 34 languages.

He has written numerous novels in the Star Wars, X-Files, and Dune universes, as well as the unique Clockwork Angels steampunk trilogy with legendary Rush drummer Neil Peart. His original works include the Saga of Seven Suns series, the Wake the Dragon and Terra Incognita fantasy trilogies, the humorous Dan Shamble, Zombie P.I. series and The Dragon Business series.

He has edited numerous anthologies, written comics and games, and the lyrics to two rock CDs as companions to his Terra Incognita trilogy.

Anderson is the director of the graduate program in Publishing at Western Colorado University, and he and his wife Rebecca Moesta are the publishers of WordFire Press.

IF YOU LIKED ...

If you liked *Science Fiction Stories: Volume 2*, you might also enjoy other WordFire Press titles by Kevin J. Anderson.

Our list of other WordFire Press authors and titles is always growing. To find out more and shop our selection of titles, visit us at:
wordfirepress.com

www.ingramcontent.com/pod-product-compliance
Lightning Source LLC
Chambersburg PA
CBHW030525310726
48979CB00010B/1804/J

* 9 7 8 1 6 8 0 5 7 7 2 5 9 *